Praise for MY SOUL TO TAKE:

'Both frightening and funny – a terrific t̶r̶i̶c̶l ̶r̶
it off.'

'Distinguished by superb ϵ
scapes and . . . rivetingly gr

..ϲpendent

'The numerous twists and turns are worthy of Agatha
Christie and keep the reader guessing until the very end.'
Sunday Telegraph

'A welcome second outing for the good-natured lawyer-sleuth
Thóra Gudmundsdóttir . . . Yrsa Sigurdardóttir's lightness
of touch is refreshing'   *Daily Telegraph*

'Dark, rich and satisfying.'   *Woman & Home*

'Glacially chilling and dark as an arctic winter, this gripping
Icelandic page-turner will keep you guessing all the way.'
Choice

'An irresistible read. And very, very chilly indeed.' *City AM*

'Considering its population is only around 300,000, Iceland
seems to have more than its fair share of good crime writers.
Yrsa Sigurdardóttir keeps up the standard . . . untypically,
instead of the usual gloomy middle-aged man, her sleuth is
a young woman . . . a personable heroine.'
Sunday Telegraph

Also by Yrsa Sigurdardóttir

Last Rituals

About the author

Yrsa Sigurdardóttir works as a civil engineer in
Reykjavik. Her books for children have won prizes
and great acclaim. *My Soul to Take* is her second
adult novel.

About the translators

Bernard Scudder was a highly respected translator
whose works included Arnaldur Indridason's
award-winning *Silence of the Grave*. He passed
away in October 2007.

Anna Yates is a writer and translator, living and
working in Iceland.

My Soul to Take

Yrsa Sigurdardóttir

*Translated from the Icelandic
by Bernard Scudder and Anna Yates*

HODDER

First published in Iceland in 2006 by Veröld Publishing

First published in Great Britain in 2009 by Hodder & Stoughton
An Hachette UK company

First published in paperback in 2010

8

A CIP catalogue record for this title is available from the British Library

B format ISBN 978 0 340 92066 4
A format ISBN 978 0 340 99587 7

Typeset in Sabon MT by Palimpsest Book Production Limited,
Grangemouth, Stirlingshire

Printed and bound by Clays Ltd, St Ives plc

Hodder & Stoughton policy is to use papers that are natural, renewable
and recyclable products and made from wood grown in sustainable forests. The logging
and manufacturing processes are expected to conform to the environmental regulations of
the country of origin.

Hodder & Stoughton Ltd
338 Euston Road
London NW1 3BH

www.hodder.co.uk

This book is dedicated to my newborn grandson, Reginn Freyr Mánason. Special thanks to Páll Kjartansson, the Scourge of Postmen.

Yrsa

February 1945

Prologue

The child felt the cold creeping up her legs and back, and she tried to sit up straight in the front seat to get a better view. She peered into the white snow surrounding the car, but could not make out any farm animals. It's too cold for the animals outside, she thought, wishing she could leave the car and go back inside the house, but she didn't dare say a word. A tear crept down her cheek as the man beside her struggled to start the engine. Pursing her lips, she turned her face away from him so that he wouldn't notice. He'd be so angry. She looked at the house where the car was parked and looked for the other girl, but the only living creature in sight was the farm dog, Rover, sleeping on the front steps. Suddenly he lifted his head and stared at her. She sent him a weak smile, but he stretched out again and closed his eyes.

The car spluttered to life and the man straightened up in his seat. 'About time,' he said gruffly as they drove away. He glanced at the girl, who had turned back to look straight ahead. 'Well, let's take a little trip.' She bounced around in her seat as they drove along the rough, bumpy track leading away from the house. 'Try to hold on,' he said without looking at her.

At last the car reached the road and they cruised along in silence for a while. The girl looked out of the window in the hope of seeing some horses, but the landscape all around was deserted. Then her heart skipped a beat when she realised where they were.

'Are we going to my house?' she asked hopefully.

'You could say that.'

The girl sat up even straighter and observed the scenery more closely. In front of them was familiar countryside, and clearly visible in the distance the rock that her mother had said was a troll who had turned to stone at daybreak. Instinctively she craned forward to look at it. A car appeared at the crest of the low hill ahead, driving towards them. It looked like a military vehicle. As they slowed down, the man ordered her to keep her head out of sight. Not unaccustomed to hiding, she did so without hesitation. He clearly agreed with her grandfather that nothing good ever came from the army. Her mother had whispered to her that soldiers were perfectly normal men, just like Grandfather. But younger. And better-looking. 'Just like you.' The girl remembered how sweetly her mother had smiled at her when she said that.

The child heard the other vehicle approaching, getting louder until they passed each other and then fading away. She wriggled in her seat.

'You can sit up,' the driver said, and she did so. 'Do you know how old you are?' he asked.

'Four,' she replied, taking care to speak clearly as her grandfather had taught her.

The man snorted. 'You're really scrawny for a four-year-old.'

Although the girl didn't understand the word 'scrawny', she realised that it was not good to be like that. She said nothing. There was a silence.

'Do you want to see your mum again?'

Her eyes widened and she looked up at the man. Was she going to see Mummy? Just thinking about it made everything OK. She nodded eagerly.

The little girl's thighs no longer ached from the cold. Everything would be nice again. They turned down the road she knew so well. She saw her home and smiled for the first time in ages. The car drew up to the house slowly and stopped. Entranced, she stared out at the large, imposing house. It looked so sad and lonely. No lights, and no smoke from the chimney.

'Is Mummy here?' she said fretfully. Something strange was going on. The last time she had seen her, her mother had been lying in bed in a room in the man's house. She was sick, just like Grandfather had been, with no one except her daughter to help her. Perhaps Mummy went back home the night after she vanished from the bed? But then why had she left her with the man? Mummy wouldn't have done that.

'Your mum isn't exactly here, but you'll still see her. You can be together for ever.' He smirked, and the girl felt uncertainty creep into her happiness, but she dared not ask any questions.

The man threw open the car door and got out. He walked round and opened her door. 'Come on. You're going on a little journey before you meet your mum.'

Cautiously, the girl climbed out of the car. She looked all around, hoping to catch sight of someone or something to encourage her, but could see nothing.

The man bent down to take hold of her mittened hand. 'Come on, I'll show you something.' He pulled her along with him and she almost had to run to keep up with his long strides.

They went behind the house to the cattle shed. A stench rose to greet them, becoming more rancid the closer they got. The little girl wanted to hold her nose but didn't dare. The man's expression implied that he could smell it too. When they reached the shed, he looked through a window, too high for the girl to reach. He leaped back, his hand over his mouth. She hoped nothing awful had happened to the cows, but she noticed that there was no sound from inside. Maybe the cows were asleep. The man tugged her onwards again.

'Bloody disgusting,' he said. When they had walked a short distance from the cattle shed, he stopped and looked at the expanse of snow. He relaxed his grip on the girl's hand. 'Where the hell was it?' he muttered irritably. He scuffed at the snow with his shoe.

The child stood still while he searched in the snow. She wasn't happy any more. Mummy wasn't here. She couldn't be under the snow. She was ill. Swallowing her sobs, she half whispered, 'Where's my mummy?'

'She's with God,' he answered, still poking around with his foot.

'With God?' she echoed, baffled. 'What's she doing there?'

The man snorted. 'She's dead. That's when you go to God.'

The child didn't really know what that meant. She had never met anyone who was dead.

'God's good, isn't He?' She wasn't sure why she said this. She knew the answer, because her mother and grandfather had often told her. God was good. Very good. 'Will she come back from God's house?' she asked hopefully.

The man exclaimed triumphantly and stopped digging. 'Here it is! At last.' He bent down and dusted the snow from the ground with his gloved hands. 'No, no one comes back from God. You'll have to go to Him if you want to see your mum.'

The girl stiffened. What did he mean? She watched as he brushed the snow away to reveal a familiar steel hatch, the one in the field where her mother had forbidden her to play. Could God be down there?

The man stretched before bending down again to open the heavy trapdoor. Glancing at the girl, he smiled again. She wished he wouldn't. He beckoned her over. Hesitantly, she walked towards him and the yawning black space that had been revealed beneath the hatch.

'Is God down there with Mummy?' she asked tremulously.

The man was still grinning. 'No, He's not there, but He'll come and fetch you from there later. Come on.' He gripped her skinny shoulder and pulled her closer to the hole. 'It's a good thing you've been baptised. God doesn't let anyone in who hasn't been baptised. But let's hope God remembers you, because He can't check the church records.' The man's smile turned even colder. 'Maybe we should make doubly sure and go through the ceremony again. I don't want God to refuse to take you.' He laughed quietly.

The girl was not listening. She stared into the abyss as if hypnotised. Her mother would never go into a hole like that. She heard the man muttering something about 'a quick baptism' but only looked up when he spun her round to face him, placed his snow-filled palm on to her forehead and said, 'I baptise you in the name of the Father, the Son and the Holy Ghost. Amen.' He opened his eyes and stared at her.

Although her forehead stung terribly from the cold, the expression in his eyes chilled her more. She twisted her head away and put her hands in her anorak pockets. She was frozen, and her woollen mittens offered little protection from the sharp wind. She felt something in her right-hand pocket and remembered the envelope. A deep apprehension seized her, momentarily eclipsing her fear of the man. She had promised her mother that she'd deliver the envelope, and now it seemed that she would fail her. This was the last thing her mother had said to her, and the child remembered clearly how much it had seemed to matter. She felt a tear trickle down one cheek. She couldn't give the envelope to the man, because her mother had expressly told her not to. Biting her lower lip, the girl didn't know whether to speak or keep quiet. She squeezed her eyes shut and wished that instead of standing here she was lying by her mother's side and that nothing had changed. Then she opened her eyes and they were still standing there, she and the man. A sense of hopelessness overcame her and she wept silently, letting the tears run down her cheeks into her scarf.

The man took her by the shoulder again. 'God will give you a good welcome now. Do you know any prayers?' Nervously she nodded. 'Good.' He looked down into the hole. 'I'm going to put you down there now, and God will come and collect you later. It's best if you say your prayers until He comes. You'll be cold, but then you'll fall sound asleep and before you know it you'll be with your mother in heaven.'

At this, the child started crying harder, trying desperately to stifle her sobs. This wasn't right. Why couldn't God just come and get her now, if He was so good? Why did she have to go down into that dark pit? She was afraid of the dark, and this was a bad place – her mother had told her so. The girl looked at the man and knew she was going down there whether she wanted to or not. She was rooted to the spot. The man put his hands under her arms and lifted her up, then slowly lowered her down into the hole. She turned her head to see her home for the last time, and stared in astonishment at the gable window facing them. Someone was standing there, watching, but the window was too dirty and the house too far away for her to see who it was. When she was completely inside the hole, she couldn't see a thing, and she tried not to give in to the terror she felt. God was good. It wasn't a ghost at the window. God was good. And the low, mournful wailing she could hear down below was *not* the crying of the dead children. God was good. Mummy said so.

It was much colder inside the hole than outside. She tried to sit down, but the floor was even more icy than the seat of the car had been. She hugged herself. The hatch swung down and just before it closed she heard the man say, 'Good luck. Say hello to your mother, and to God. Don't stop praying.'

Everything turned black. The girl tried to catch her breath, but her sobbing made it difficult. What upset her most was that the envelope would never be delivered. She squeezed her eyes shut, because the thought of sunlight always calmed her. Maybe someone would come to get her. Surely the person at the window would save her. Please, please, please. She didn't want to stay here any more. She clasped her hands together and whispered:

> '*Now I lay me down to sleep*
> *I pray the Lord my soul to keep,*
> *And if I die before I wake,*
> *I pray the Lord my soul to take.*'

Tuesday, 6 June 2006

I

'Letter aperture,' Thóra corrected them with a polite smile. 'In the documentation it's called a letter aperture.' She pointed to a printout on the desk in front of her and turned it towards the couple sitting opposite her. Their scowls deepened and Thóra hurriedly continued before the man began yet another tirade. 'When Regulation No. 505/1997 on basic postal services was superseded by Regulation No. 805/2003 on comprehensive postal services and their implementation, Article 12 on letterboxes and letter apertures was revoked.'

'See!' shouted the man, turning triumphantly to his wife. 'That's what I said. So they can't just stop delivering our mail.' He turned back to Thóra, sat up straight and crossed his arms.

Thóra cleared her throat. 'Unfortunately it's not quite that simple. The new ruling refers to a building regulation concerning letter apertures and their location. This states that letter apertures should be positioned so that the distance from the ground to the lower edge of the letter aperture should be between a thousand millimetres and twelve hundred millimetres.' Thóra paused briefly for breath, but couldn't stop for too long in case the man interrupted. 'The Postal Services Act No. 12/2002 then states that postal-service providers may return mail to the sender if the letter aperture is not in compliance with regulations.'

She got no further, because the man had heard enough. 'Are you telling me that I won't have any more mail delivered to me and have no right to appeal against all this red tape?' he harrumphed theatrically, waving his arms around as if fighting off an attack by invisible bureaucrats.

Thóra shrugged. 'You could always move your letterbox higher.'

The man looked daggers at her. 'I was hoping you would be more use, especially after you promised to look into the matter before we came.'

Thóra wanted to take the regulation and throw it in the man's beetroot face, but she made do with gritting her teeth. 'But I did,' she said calmly, forcing a smile.

She had expected the couple to be astonished at her encyclopaedic knowledge of the matter and her prowess in reeling off the numbers of the regulations, but she should have realised that this case would be like banging her head against a brick wall. The agitation in the man's voice when he had telephoned the lawyers' office two days earlier should have rung warning bells. Talking nineteen to the dozen, he had requested legal advice for himself and his wife about their dispute with both the postman and the postal company. They had just moved into a prefabricated house that they had imported from America, which had arrived with all the trimmings – including a front door with an unlawful letterbox. One day his wife had come home to find a handwritten note on the door stating that no more mail would be delivered because their letterbox was too low. In future they would have to collect their post from the post office.

'All I can do is advise you about your next move,' Thóra continued. 'Commencing proceedings against the postal service, as you propose, will bring you nothing but extra costs. Nor do I recommend suing the building committee officer.'

'It also costs money to replace the front door. I can't move the slot any higher – I told you that.' The man and his wife exchanged triumphant looks.

'A front door would cost less than any court case, that's for certain.' Thóra handed over the last document from the pile she had made before the couple had arrived. 'Here's a letter I've written on your behalf.' Both of them reached for the letter, but the husband got there first. 'The post office, or the postman, made a procedural error. You, that is both of you, should have been sent a formal notification by registered mail that the height of your letterbox was unlawful, and you should have been given a grace period to rectify it. Postal deliveries should not have been stopped until after that deadline.'

'Registered mail?' the woman snapped. 'How could we have received that if they're not allowed to deliver it to us?' She turned to her husband, looking pleased with herself, but she didn't get the response she wanted and her scowl returned.

'Oh, come on, don't be so pedantic,' he snarled. 'Registered mail doesn't come through the letterbox – you have to sign for it.' He turned to Thóra. 'Go on.'

'This letter insists that the postal service follows the correct procedures, sends a registered letter requiring rectification and grants you a reasonable deadline. We'll ask for two months.' She indicated the letter, which the man had read and handed to his wife. 'After that time there's not much we can do, but I suggest that you move the letterbox to the right height. If that can't be changed and you choose to keep the front door, you can get a mailbox. The hole in it must be within the same height range as for doors. If you opt for that, I advise you to use a tape measure when you put it up, to prevent any further disputes.' She smiled thinly at them.

The man glowered at her as he thought it over. Suddenly he grinned nastily. 'OK, I get it. We send the letter, get the registered letter back and have two months when the postman has to deliver our letters irrespective of the height of the letterbox. Right?' Thóra nodded. The man stood up, victorious. 'He who laughs last laughs loudest. I'll go and post the letter now, and as soon as I'm given a deadline, I'll lower the letterbox right down to the threshold. When the deadline runs out, I'll get a mailbox. Come on, Gerda.'

Thóra accompanied them to the door, where they thanked her and took their leave, the man eager to send off the letter and start phase two of his little war with the postman. Walking back to her desk, Thóra shook her head, astonished at human nature. The things people worried about . . . She hoped postmen were well paid, but had serious doubts that they were.

No sooner had Thóra sat down than Bragi, her partner in the small legal practice, put his head round the door. He was an older man and specialised in divorce; Thóra couldn't face handling those cases. Her own divorce had been quite enough for her. Bragi, on the other hand, was in his element and was particularly adept at untangling the most convoluted disputes and getting warring couples to talk without killing each other.

'Well, how did the letterbox go? Do you see it as a test case before the Supreme Court?'

Thóra smiled. 'No, they're going to think things over, but we must remember to send them the bill by courier. I wouldn't bet on them getting much mail delivered in the future.'

'I hope they get divorced,' said Bragi, rubbing his hands. 'That would be a battle and a half.' He took out a Post-it note and handed it to Thóra. 'This man phoned while the letterboxers were with you. He asked you to call when you were free.'

Thóra looked at the note and sighed when she saw the name: Jónas Júlíusson. 'Oh, great,' she said, looking up at Bragi. 'What did he want?'

Just over a year before, Thóra had helped a wealthy middle-aged businessman draw up a contract for his investment in some land and a farmhouse on the Snaefellsnes peninsula. Jónas had made a quick fortune outside Iceland by acquiring half-bankrupt radio stations that he turned round and sold at a huge profit. Thóra was not sure whether he had always been odd or whether having money had turned him eccentric. Right now he was into New Age philosophy and planned to build an enormous holistic-centre-cum-spa-hotel where people would pay to have their physical and spiritual ills cured using alternative therapies. Thóra shook her head as she thought about him.

'Some hidden structural defect in the building, I understand,' Bragi replied. 'He's unhappy with the property.' He smiled. 'Give him a call; he wouldn't speak to me. He claims your Venus is ascendant in Cancer, which makes you a good lawyer.' Bragi shrugged. 'Maybe a strong astral chart is just as good a qualification as a law degree. What do I know?'

'What a fruitcake,' said Thóra, reaching for the telephone.

Jónas had kicked off their professional relationship by drawing up her astral chart, which turned out favourably. That was why he hired her. Thóra suspected that the larger practices had refused to provide Jónas with information about their lawyers' exact time of birth and he had been forced to approach a smaller one; there could scarcely be any other explanation for a man of his wealth choosing to deal with a company with only four employees. She dialled the number that Bragi had scribbled down and pulled a face while she waited for Jónas to answer.

'Hello,' said a soft male voice. 'Jónas speaking.'

'Hello, Jónas. This is Thóra Gudmundsdóttir at Central Lawyers. You left a message asking me to call.'

'Yes, that's right. Thank you for calling back.' He sighed heavily.

'My colleague Bragi mentioned a hidden structural defect in the property. What is it exactly?' she asked, glancing over at Bragi, who nodded.

'It's awful, I'm telling you. The building is flawed and I'm certain the sellers knew about it and didn't tell me. I think it will scupper all my plans out here.'

'What kind of flaw are we talking about?' Thóra asked, surprised. The property had been examined by approved surveyors and she had read through their report herself. Nothing unexpected had come up. The acreage of the property was as the sellers had stated, it carried all the rights named in the sale description, and the two farmhouses that were included with the land were so old that a complete renovation was the only option.

'It involves one of the old farmhouses where I had the hotel built, Kirkjustétt, you remember?'

'Yes, I remember it,' replied Thóra, adding, 'You know that in the case of real estate, a hidden defect must affect the value by at least ten per cent of the purchase price in order for the right to compensation to be established. I can't imagine anything on that scale in such an old building, even one so large. Also, a hidden defect must be precisely that – hidden. The assessors' report clearly stated that the buildings needed to be completely renovated.'

'This defect makes the farmhouse effectively useless for my purposes,' Jónas said firmly. 'And there's no doubt that it's "hidden" – the assessors could never have noticed it.'

'What is this defect, then?' Thóra asked, her curiosity piqued. She imagined perhaps a hot spring appearing in the middle of the floor, as was said to have happened in Hveragerdi some years before, but she couldn't recall there being any geothermal activity in that area.

'I know you're not particularly inclined towards spiritual matters,' said Jónas levelly. 'You're bound to be surprised when I tell you what's going on here, but I beg you to believe what I say.' He paused for a moment before coming out with it: 'The house is haunted.'

Thóra closed her eyes. Haunted. Right. 'Well, well,' she said, twirling her index finger against her temple to signal to Bragi that Jónas's 'defect' was just crazy talk. Bragi moved closer in the hope of eavesdropping.

'I knew you'd be sceptical,' Jónas grumbled. 'But it's

true, and common knowledge among the locals here. The sellers knew but kept quiet about it while the sale went through. I call that fraudulent, especially when they knew of my plans for the farmhouse and the land. I have exceptionally sensitive people here, customers and staff alike. They feel bad.'

Thóra interrupted him. 'Can you describe this "haunting" for me, please?'

'There's just a horrible atmosphere in the house. Also, things go missing, strange noises are heard in the middle of the night, and people have seen a child appear out of nowhere.'

'So?' Thóra asked. That was nothing special. In her household, things always went missing, particularly the car keys, there were noises day and night, and children appeared out of nowhere all the time.

'There's no child here, Thóra. Nowhere in the vicinity either.' He paused. 'The child is not of this world. I saw her behind me when I was looking in the mirror, and words can't describe how . . . *unalive* she is.'

A shiver ran down Thóra's spine. The tone of Jónas's voice left no doubt that he believed this himself and was convinced he'd seen something unnatural, however incredible it might seem to her. 'What do you want me to do?' she asked. 'Do you want to discuss it with the sellers and try to negotiate a discount? Isn't that the point? One thing I do know – I can't exorcise ghosts for you, or improve the atmosphere in the house.'

'Come up here for the weekend,' Jónas said suddenly. 'I want to show you some stuff that's been found here and see what you make of it. The best suite in the hotel is vacant, and you can give yourself a treat at the same time. Have a hot-stone massage, whatever you want. You can recharge your batteries, and of course I'll pay you handsomely for it.'

Thóra could do with recharging, though she felt he was contradicting himself by promising relaxation in one breath and claiming the place was haunted in the next. At that moment her life was moving in ever-decreasing circles, mostly centred round the expected grandchild her son had fathered before the age of sixteen and her strained relations with her ex-husband, who insisted that the child had been conceived because Thóra was an unfit mother. Their son's hormones were a minor factor, in his view; it was all her fault. This opinion was shared by the parents of the little mother-to-be, who was fifteen years old. Thóra sighed. It would take pretty powerful stones to massage away all the cares from her poor soul.

'What do you want me to look at? Can't you just send it to my office?'

Jónas laughed coldly. 'No, not really. It's boxes of old books, drawings, pictures and all kinds of junk.'

'So why do you think this old stuff is relevant to the so-called "hidden defect" in the property?' she asked sceptically. 'And why don't you just look at it yourself?'

'I can't. I tried, but it gives me the creeps. I can't go near it. You're much more down to earth; you could probably go through it all without feeling anything.'

Thóra couldn't argue with that. Ghosts, ghouls and fairies had not bothered her much until now. The real world gave her enough trouble without her needing to cross the borders into fantasy. 'Give me a little while to think about it, Jónas. All I can promise is to try and make arrangements to come and visit. I'll call you tomorrow afternoon. Is that OK?'

'Oh, yes. You can call. I'll be in all day.' Jónas hesitated before continuing. 'You asked why I thought this old stuff was relevant.'

'Yes?' said Thóra.

Again Jónas paused before speaking. 'I found a photograph in the box I started going through.'

'And?'

'It's a picture of the girl I saw in the mirror.'

Thursday, 8 June 2006

2

Thóra fetched the file containing the documents regarding the property on Snaefellsnes. She couldn't glean much from reading through them; in any case, she found nothing to suggest Jónas's peculiar 'hidden defect'. It had been a relatively straightforward transaction, apart from Jónas's many stipulations over dates, such as insisting on signing the deeds on a Saturday. Thóra had gone along with it, asking no questions in case she prompted a lecture on celestial configurations. On Saturday, luck comes your way, she remembered, from the old proverb. Nothing else about the sale was out of the ordinary. It involved the land and everything on it, including chattels and resources. The sellers were a brother and sister in their fifties, Börkur Thórdarson and Elín Thórdardóttir. They were acting under power of attorney for their mother, who had inherited the land from her own father long before. They had made a lot of money on the deal, and Thóra had been green with envy at the time.

She smiled to herself as she wondered how to assess the haunting in order to devalue the property by 10 per cent, but her smile vanished when she visualised herself trying to persuade the sellers to pay compensation for the damage and citing ghosts as the reason. The brother had mainly handled the transaction on his mother's behalf, and Thóra had only met his sister once, when the deeds were signed. She had never met their mother, who according to Börkur was extremely old and bedridden, but the son struck her as pushy and over-confident. His sister, Elín, on the other hand, had been silent and withdrawn. At the time, Thóra had the impression that she was not as keen as her brother to sell the property. Recalling all this, she doubted that he would take a claim for compensation lying down. She put the documents to one side and crossed her fingers, hoping Jónas would change his mind. If not, it would take every ounce of her persuasive powers to get him to back down.

She turned to her other pending cases, but the few that had come in were pretty uninspiring. Unfortunately business was slow. With a groan she cursed her own financial stupidity. At the end of the previous year, she had worked on a case for a wealthy German who had paid her handsomely, and if she had had an iota of common sense, she would have used the money to pay off some of her debts. Instead she had put it towards a caravan and an SUV. She didn't know what had come over her. Even worse, she had taken out a loan to help pay for them, plunging herself further into debt. She vaguely recalled having a vision of touring the countryside in the summer sun, a typical modern family on holiday – a divorced mother with her two children, in her case a daughter of six and a son of sixteen who was himself soon to become a father. The grandchild had not yet been written into this rose-tinted dream, because Thóra would probably only see it every other weekend. Hopefully that would not be the same weekend that her own children were spending with their father. It would make an interesting sociological study, she thought: a weekend father who was still so young that he spent every other weekend with his *own* weekend father.

When Thóra had finished going through work stuff, she went on the Internet and on a whim searched for information about the land on Snaefellsnes or the old farmsteads situated in the grounds. She Googled the names of the farms that occurred in the deeds of sale, Kirkjustétt and Kreppa, but found nothing. With a shrug, she gave up. She decided to check her email and noted, a little wearily, that there was a message from Matthew. She had got to know the German while investigating the case that ultimately earned her the caravan and the SUV, along with the accompanying debts. In fact, she had done more than get to know him – she had got to know him 'intimately', as her grandmother would say – and now he wanted to visit her to renew their 'intimate' acquaintance. Matthew was enquiring about the best time for him to take a short break in Iceland. Thóra was dying for him to come over, but was well aware that the best time would be around 2020, when her daughter turned twenty. She wasn't sure Matthew could wait that long. She closed the message, deciding to wait until the morning before replying.

She stood up, tidied her desk and sighed. She wondered if her main problem was the desire for a better life, free from debt and untimely grandchildren, but realised that it was much simpler than that. She was depressed purely because she now had to walk past Bella on her way out. Bella, the secretary from hell, whom she and Bragi had been tricked into taking on as part of the lease agreement when they opened their office. Thóra steeled herself and hurried away.

'I'm off, then,' she said as she walked past the reception

desk. She wondered fleetingly if it might be possible to raise the desk higher, to show less of the unattractive young woman behind it, then with a pang of guilt flashed the secretary an unconvincing smile. 'See you tomorrow!'

Bella raised a heavy eyebrow and squinted at Thóra. She added a scowl to complete her look of displeasure. 'Are you still here? Huh.'

'Huh? What do you mean, huh?' replied Thóra, confused. 'Where else am I supposed to be? You saw me come in after lunch and you haven't seen me leave. I don't make a habit of jumping out of the window.'

'Pity,' Thóra thought she heard Bella mutter, but she couldn't be sure. In a much louder voice the girl said, 'Your ex phoned about something, but I said you weren't in. He wouldn't leave a message.'

Thóra was pleased, because Hannes's telephone calls were seldom a source of joy. She certainly did not want to give Bella the chance to gloat about the negative aspects of her life. She decided to let it go, long resigned to the futility of arguing with this creature, so she smiled again at Bella and took her coat from the cloakroom. She was poised to escape, standing by the door with her hand on the handle, when the girl cleared her throat to indicate that there was something else.

'Oh, yes, and the leasing company phoned. You're behind on your instalments on the caravan.'

Thóra did not even turn back, just strolled calmly into the corridor and closed the door behind her. At that moment she would gladly have accepted the massage that Jónas had promised her, with or without hot stones.

* * *

Birna looked around her and took a deep breath. She peered through the thin fog hovering above the water and watched a pair of seagulls plunging to compete for food. Neither bird won and they rose back up with a great fluttering of wings. Then they vanished into the denser bank of fog that hung a little farther out. It was low tide and wet seaweed lay spread across the rocky expanse. This was an unusual beach: no sand, only boulders of all shapes and sizes, their surface smoothed by the passage of a million tides. The position of the beach was unique, as well: a small cove surrounded by high cliffs of columnar basalt, which could have been custom-designed by the Creator as a high-rise dwelling for seabirds. Every ledge was occupied, with a corresponding volume of noise. Birna walked over to where the cliffs formed another cove, leading on from the one she was in now. The tide flowed in through a stone arch, and the cove was completely enclosed by cliffs. It could only be seen through the narrow gap between the high walls of rock, but the squawking of the birds inside nonetheless resounded along the whole of the beach.

Birna stopped. The fog had suddenly thickened, reducing her visibility to just a few metres. She inhaled deeply again, this time through her nose, savouring the scent of the sea. If she could, she would sleep out here in the open, wreathed in fog. She had absolutely no desire to go back to the hotel. It should not have been that way. She had loved that building and swelled with childlike pride every time she saw it, even while it was still under construction, the barest bones of what it would become. She had even liked the hole that had been dug for the foundations. The site of the hotel had somehow captured her imagination the first time she visited. The land overlooked the open sea on the southern shore of Snaefellsnes. In this it was like most other farms in the district, although slightly more remote; the farmhouse only came into view when one had walked almost right up to it. It had been built on a grassy patch in a rough field of lava that reached almost to the water's edge. The dramatic scenery inspired her. So did the old house. She had been commissioned to design a gigantic annexe, which must not overwhelm or smother the main house. This had caused her a lot of worry – grandeur, that was a piece of cake, but modesty was often the greatest challenge.

The sensations that the project aroused were unfamiliar to her. Much as she loved architecture, the other buildings she had designed had not made her feel this way, but she knew exactly why. This hotel was far and away her most successful project. From the moment she began sketching the first draft at her studio in Reykjavík, she had realised that she was on the right track. The building was so much better than all her previous efforts. She realised that she would make a name for herself at last. She would become sought-after.

She had often wondered why this project had seized her imagination so immediately and why the outcome had been such a success. There was nothing remarkable about the old house or the land, although the house was unusually grand for its age. It had also been exceptionally well maintained, considering no one had lived in it for about half a century. She soon realised that someone had looked after the house over the years, perhaps intending to use it as a holiday home or to get away from the city, but those plans had never materialised. Inside the building, there was nothing to indicate that the twenty-first century had begun. A thick layer of dust had covered everything, but mouse-traps here and there showed that someone had made sure that the interior and furnishings escaped unnecessary damage. The first time Birna went there, she had found it difficult to look at the tiny skeletons in some of the traps, but otherwise the house had impressed her, inside and out.

Birna looked at her watch. What was wrong with the man? Had he been delayed at that stupid seance? The message had been clear enough. She took out her mobile and scrolled through the texts. Yes, perfectly straight-forward: 'Meet me @ cave @ 9 2nite.' What a load of shit. Before putting her mobile back in her pocket, she double-checked that the cove was out of range. It was. That was one of the most annoying things about this area, she thought, bad mobile reception.

She decided to walk back to the cave. Maybe he was there. Although the cave was high up on the shore, visi-bility was so poor that she could have missed him. Also, the screeching of the birds drowned out everything else, so she wouldn't have heard him arrive. She set off, taking care to look down because it was easy to lose one's footing on the stones. They crunched together beneath the weight of her feet. Hopefully he had finally come round to her way of thinking. She had expended enough energy on this whole business. She didn't really think he'd changed his mind, as he'd been so adamantly opposed. If by any chance he had, she knew she had herself to thank for his change of heart. She had given in and slept with him. Some good should come of it, because it hadn't given her any pleasure. It was important to have several projects on the go when the competition came around. Although she had the prize pretty much in the bag, she needed to be sure, so she had to take on that burden. What did one quick shag matter, compared with winning the competition? She would be the talk of the town and, more importantly, her peers. Birna smiled to herself at the thought.

An unusually loud squawking from the cliff pulled her out of her reverie. It was as if all the birds of the heavens were calling out in unison. Perhaps they wanted to remind the world beyond the fog that they existed. Birna sighed. It had turned cold and she wrapped her anorak more tightly around her. What sort of summer was this, anyway? She reached the cave but could see no one. On the off-chance that he was there she called out, but no one answered. Ten minutes. She would give him ten minutes and then leave. This was just plain rude. Anger flared inside her, warming her slightly. How dare he make her wait like this? It wasn't like being late for a meeting at a café in Reykjavík. There she could flick through magazines to kill the time, but here there was nothing to do. And beautiful as the area was, right now there was nothing to see but fog.

Five minutes. She would give him just five minutes. She wanted to get back and she was dying for a piss. An odd thought struck her, nothing to do with the beach or being made to wait alone in the freezing fog. She felt suddenly sad that she had not learned more about the geology of this area and other parts of Snaefellsnes. For example, how was Kirkjufell, the mountain that fascinated her, formed? It stood alone in the sea on the northern shore of the peninsula, and she knew enough geology to tell that it was not volcanic. She wished she had taken more interest in her studies when she was at school. When she got back home, she was going to look it up, just as she had planned to do the first time she had seen the mountain.

Birna jumped as the noise of the birds got louder again, raucous cries from farther up the cliff she was leaning against. She took two steps away from the wall of rock. She shuddered, gripped by a feeling of unease, not for the first time. There was something about this place. Not just the obvious, those weirdos who worked at the hotel and claimed to be spiritual assistants to the guests. The guests too. All fruitcakes, but not quite as bad as the staff. No, there was something else wrong here. Something that had slowly but surely intensified, making its presence known on her first inspection and beginning with goosebumps on her upper arms when she saw the mouse skeletons. It had now transformed into a persistent unease that Birna found difficult to identify. It wasn't the rubbish about ghosts that scared her – she was pretty sure the hotel staff made those stories up, although God knows why.

She shuddered again, deliberately, trying to shake some sense into herself. What bloody melodrama was she tangled up in? Birna, who was known to her friends for being down to earth to the point of tediousness? There was work to do here. Jónas wanted more. There was a large market in hotels for idiots, which hardly surprised Birna. What astonished her was how much money those idiots seemed to have. Jónas wasn't exactly giving the accommodation away, to say nothing of 'spiritual guidance' from his employees.

Birna tried to smile as she recalled the behaviour of Eiríkur, the resort's aura expert, when she had arrived a week before. He had grasped her upper arm and whispered that her aura was black. She should watch out. Death was after her. She frowned at the memory of his foul breath.

Five minutes had passed. He'd be getting a piece of her mind for this. She could have been working: there was a lot to do and her time was precious. If she had not received the text message, she would have spent this time working on the plans for the new building, and maybe she'd have reached a conclusion by now. It was supposed to stand by itself, a short way from the main building. For some reason she had still not been able to decide on the exact location. There was something about the place she had chosen that disturbed her. No, that wasn't quite it: there was something about the spot that struck her, something that did not quite fit, although she had no idea what it was. Perhaps it was just nonsense; she was exhausted after working non-stop for the past year and a half. Jónas wanted an architect who would be fully immersed in the project – as well as being the right star sign – and he had arranged for her to stay there without a word of complaint. She had asked several of the hotel employees whether they could see anything odd about that patch of land, but in vain. Most of them had answered the question with a more obvious one: 'Why don't you choose another place if this one disturbs you? There's plenty of land here.' But they didn't understand her. They understood the relative configurations of the constellations. Birna, on the other hand, understood the relative configurations of buildings. This was the place; any other was out of the question.

The birds' squawking intensified again, but Birna was too deep in thought to notice properly. She threaded her way carefully along the rocks towards the gravel path above the beach. Suddenly she stopped in her tracks and listened. She could hear crunching on the pebbles behind her. She began to turn, looking forward to venting the anger that had been building up inside her since she got there. About fucking time.

Birna did not manage to turn round completely. Even over the noise of the birds on the cliff she clearly heard the rock swishing through the still sea air towards her head, and caught a glimpse of it as it struck her forehead with terrible force. She did not see anything more in this life, but she felt many things. In a vague and dreamlike state, she felt herself being dragged along the rough terrain. She felt the goosebumps that the cold fog brought out on her bare flesh as her clothes were removed, and she felt nauseous as she tasted the ferrous tang of blood in her mouth. Her socks were pulled off and she felt a terrible pain on the soles of her feet. What was happening? It all seemed unreal. A voice she knew well was ringing in her ears, but given what was happening, that couldn't be right. Birna tried to speak, but couldn't produce the words. A strange groan came out of her throat, but she had not groaned. How very strange this was.

Before everything turned black, it occurred to her that she would never read about the origin of Mount Kirkjufell. Oddly enough, this hurt the worst of all.

The same pair of gulls that Birna had watched plunging into the sea for food were waiting farther along the beach, watching what was done to her through the mist. Patiently they waited for calm to return. The beach and the sea look after their own. No one here has to starve.

Friday, 9 June 2006

3

'I can't understand what's become of Birna,' muttered Jónas, reaching for a floral-patterned cup containing the elixir whose praises he had just been singing to Thóra. This was a special brew of tea from local herbs that, according to Jónas, cured all manner of ailments and ills. Thóra had accepted a cup and taken a sip, and judging from the taste, the tea must have been exceptionally wholesome.

'I would have liked the two of you to meet,' he added, after taking a mouthful and placing the cup down carefully on the saucer. There was something quite ridiculous about this, for the cup and saucer were so oddly delicate, bone china with a slender handle that looked even smaller in Jónas's big hands. He was far from delicately built – big-boned without being fat, weather-beaten and with an air of one who would rather swig strong coffee from a mug onboard a trawler than sip undrinkable herbal tea from a ladylike cup following a yoga class.

Thóra smiled and made herself comfortable in her chair. They were in Jónas's office at the hotel, and her back ached after driving up west. The Friday traffic had been heavy, and it didn't help that she had had to drive her children to their father's house in Gardabaer on her way out of town. The traffic had crawled along as if every single resident of the capital were on exactly the same route. Although this was not officially his weekend to have the children, Hannes had offered to swap because he would be abroad at a medical conference the following weekend. Consequently Thóra had decided to take Jónas up on his offer and spend the weekend at the New Age spa hotel on Snaefellsnes. She was going to use the opportunity to relax, have a massage and unwind, as Jónas had suggested, but the main purpose of her trip was of course to dissuade him from claiming compensation for the supposed haunting. Thóra wanted to end the conversation as quickly as possible and go to her room for a nap.

'She'll turn up,' Thóra said, just for the sake of saying something. She knew nothing about the architect; the woman could easily be a raving alcoholic who had fallen off the wagon and would not be seen for weeks.

Jónas huffed. 'It's not like her. We were meant to go over the draft plans for the new building this morning.' He flicked through some papers on his desk, clearly annoyed with the architect.

'Couldn't she just have popped back to Reykjavík to fetch something?' Thóra asked, hoping he would stop talking about this woman. The ache in her back was beginning to spread to her shoulders.

Jónas shook his head. 'Her car's outside.' He slammed down both hands on the edge of the desk. 'Anyway. You're here at least.' He smiled. 'I'm dying to tell you about the ghost, but that will have to wait until we have more time.' Glancing at his watch, he stood up. 'I have to do my rounds. I make it a rule to talk to my staff at the end of every day. I have a better sense of the operations and the situation if

I know about any problems from the very start. That makes it easier to intervene.'

Thóra stood up, delighted to be free. 'Yes, by all means. We'll talk about it tomorrow. Don't worry about me. I'll be here all weekend and there's plenty of time to discuss it.' As Thóra slung her bag over her shoulder, she noticed an awful smell and wrinkled her nose. 'What's that stink?' she asked Jónas. 'I smelled it out in the car park too. Is there a fish-oil factory near here?'

Jónas sniffed deeply. Then he looked at Thóra with a blank expression. 'I can't smell anything. I suppose I've got used to it,' he said. 'A whale has washed up just down the beach from here. When the wind's in a certain direction, the smell wafts over the grounds.'

'What?' Thóra said. 'Do you just have to wait for the carcass to rot away?' She pulled a face when another wave of the stench swept in. If only the problem in the building was just something like this, it would be a doddle.

'You get used to it,' Jónas said. He picked up the telephone and dialled a number. 'Hi. I'm sending Thóra over. Have someone show her to her room and fix a massage for her this evening.' He said goodbye and put the receiver down. 'If you go to reception, I've reserved you the best room, with a lovely view. You won't be disappointed.'

A young girl accompanied Thóra from the reception to the much-praised room. She was so small that she barely reached up to Thóra's shoulder. Thóra disliked letting such a slip of a girl carry her bag for her, but had no say in the matter. She was glad her luggage was not that heavy, even though, as always, she had brought far too much with her. Thóra was convinced that different laws applied on holiday from everyday life, that she would wear things she normally neglected in her wardrobe, but she always ended up in the same clothes as usual. She followed the girl down a long corridor that appeared wider than it was because of the skylight that ran its length. The evening sun shone on the girl's thin, fair hair.

'Is this a fun place to work?' Thóra asked, making small talk.

'No,' replied the girl without turning round. 'I'm looking for another job. There's just nothing going.'

'Oh,' said Thóra. She had not expected such a frank answer. 'Are the people you work with boring?'

The girl looked back over her shoulder without slowing her pace. 'Yes and no. Most of them are all right. Some are real tossers.' The girl stopped by one of the doors, fished a plastic card out of her pocket and opened it. 'But I'm probably not the best judge. I'm not too keen on the bullshit they try to feed the guests.'

For the hotel's sake, Thóra hoped that this girl did not have much contact with the customers. She wasn't exactly the world's best saleswoman. 'And is that why you want to quit?' she asked.

'No. Not exactly,' the girl answered, showing Thóra into the room. 'It's something else. I can't explain exactly. This is a bad place.'

Thóra had entered the room first and couldn't see the girl's face as she said this. She couldn't tell if she was serious, but the tone of her voice suggested that she was. Thóra looked around the beautiful room and walked over to a wall of glass overlooking the ocean. Outside was a small terrace.

'Bad in what way?' she asked, turning to look at the girl. The view implied quite the opposite; the waves glistened beyond an empty, peaceful beach.

The girl shrugged. 'Just bad. This has always been a bad place. Everyone knows that.'

Thóra raised her eyebrows. 'Does everyone know that? Who's "everyone"?' If the place had a bad reputation that the sellers knew about but had neglected to mention, it might provide some flimsy grounds for a compensation case.

The girl looked at her with the scorn only a teenager can muster. '*Everyone*, of course. Everyone here, anyway.'

Thóra smiled to herself. She didn't know the population of the southern coast of Snaefellsnes, but knew that the word 'everyone' could not cover many people. 'And what is it that everyone knows?'

Suddenly the girl became evasive. She thrust her hands into the pockets of her far-too-large jeans and looked down at her toes. 'I've got to go. I shouldn't be talking to you about this.' She spun round and walked out into the corridor. 'Maybe later.' In the doorway she stopped and looked imploringly at Thóra. 'Don't tell Jónas I've been gossiping about this. He doesn't like me talking to the guests too much.' She rubbed her left hand, between the thumb and index finger. 'If I want to be able to find work, I need a reference. I want to work at a hotel in Reykjavík.'

'Don't worry. I'm not an ordinary guest. I'll tell Jónas that you've been particularly helpful and ask his permission to talk to you properly when things are quieter. Jónas asked me to come here to investigate various matters. I think you can help me, and that would help him too.'

Thóra looked at the girl, who glared at her suspiciously. 'What's your name, anyway?'

'Sóldís,' the girl replied. She stood in the doorway for a moment, as if unsure what to do, then smiled weakly, said goodbye and left.

Bergur Ketilsson walked at a leisurely pace, even though he knew that his wife was waiting for him at home with his nightly coffee. He preferred to spend the evening alone in the great outdoors rather than sitting at home with her in oppressive silence and fake marital bliss. He groaned at the thought. They had been married for twenty years, on reasonably good terms, but there had never been much passion between them, not even during their short courtship. They weren't that way inclined, or at least she wasn't. He had only recently discovered that side to his character – a little late to realise it, at forty. Life would doubtless have treated him differently had he found out before he married Rósa, the albatross round his neck. Perhaps he would have gone to Reykjavík to study instead. As a young man, he had taken delight in the Icelandic language, although he had never hinted at it to anyone. There was little to test the intellect of a lonely farmer. He scanned the eider nests mournfully. The recent cold snap had taken its toll on the ducklings. There would be fewer nests next year.

He walked on. In the distance he saw the hotel roof above the rocks on the beach. Silently he focused on it and tried to picture what went on inside, but he couldn't imagine. He shrugged and continued on his way. As he was feeling depressed, he decided to take the longer route home, via the bay. This was not completely random, because he wanted to know how the hatching seabirds had fared during the cold spell. Quickening his pace, he trudged on, deep in thought. The hotel was behind the emotional crisis that had seized him. If it had not been built, he would have gone on with his life, reconciled to it, neither happy nor sad. He could never form a firm opinion about what went on there, as in its way it had brought him too much joy and too much confusion for him to be able to think logically about it. Spotting a nest, he approached it slowly. Two tiny ducklings were lying dead inside. The mother eider was nowhere to be seen, so perhaps the cold had killed her too.

In the bay, the story was the same. He saw a few chicks in the nests resting on each ledge. Perhaps that was some consolation. Next year the eider and the scavenging seabirds would still be evenly matched. Turning from the cliff, he headed towards the farm. He walked slowly, reluctant to arrive. Not even the stench from the beached whale upset him; it suited his mood. Bergur quickened his pace slightly. Perhaps he should rush home and tell Rósa that he had found another woman. More fun, cleverer, prettier and younger too. A better woman than her in every way. For an instant, it seemed the right thing to do. He would give Rósa everything – the farm, the cattle, the horses, the eider colony. He would not have any use for them in his new, happy life. Then this dreamlike vision faded. Rósa could not run the farm by herself and would hardly rejoice at the news. She had never been particularly impressed by the countryside or the farm, greeting everything with the same flat expression bordering on indifference. The only thing that got a reaction out of her was the cat. The same went for their married life: she was never furious, never ecstatic. The strange thing was that he used to be exactly the same, but now he was a completely different man.

At the beachhead he stumbled and looked down in surprise. As a rule he was sure-footed and confident, with a knack for negotiating the rounded boulders and slippery seaweed. Looking down, he noticed something that he had never seen on the beach before among all the oddities that had washed up over the years. For a start, it was a much larger bed of seaweed than he had ever seen in the bay. More importantly, a human arm could be seen through the seaweed. There was no doubt about that. The fingers were curled and twisted in a way that no doll or mannequin manufacturer would have wanted to reproduce. Bergur bent down and the acrid stench of blood filled his nose. He jumped back. The smell had probably escaped when he'd uncovered the soft, slimy seaweed with his foot, and the metallic odour was so powerful that the stench from the rotting whale paled in comparison. Bergur put his arm over his nose and mouth to avoid inhaling the foul air.

He straightened up, since there was little he could do for the person under the seaweed. He could see the outline of a body under the weed, and patches of white flesh were showing through. Once he had discerned the shape of it, it was so obvious that he was amazed he hadn't noticed it immediately. Since he never took his mobile with him, there wasn't much he could do but rush home and call the police. Perhaps the coastguard should be called out as well. They would enjoy being involved. He breathed through the sleeve of his coat to stave off the smell of blood, then stiffened. He recognised the ring on the swollen finger.

Bergur fell to his knees. Oblivious to the smell, he grabbed the ice-cold hand to be certain. Yes, that was her ring. He moaned and began to tear the seaweed away from where he imagined the head to be, but stopped when he realised there was no face. He could tell from the corpse's familiar hair that his dream of a happy new life was over.

Thóra was trying to unwind. Lying on her stomach, she made an effort to relax, or rather to concentrate on appearing relaxed, because she didn't want the masseuse to think otherwise. The latter was a stringy, muscular woman, slightly younger than Thóra. She was wearing white canvas trousers, a pale green T-shirt and orthopaedic sandals on her feet. She had painted her toenails with light blue varnish. Thóra did not make a habit of scrutinising that part of people's anatomy, but the toes kept appearing as she lay on the bench with her face positioned in a hole at one end.

The worst of it was over; the woman had stopped massaging and begun arranging hot stones in a row down her backbone. 'Now you should feel how the energy from the stones flows through your back. It travels along the nerves and out into every part of you.' This speech was accompanied by soothing music from a CD the masseuse had told Thóra was on sale in reception. Thóra decided to look in at reception and find out the name of the group, to make sure she never bought one of their CDs by accident.

'Will it be much longer?' Thóra asked hopefully. 'I think

the energy's penetrated every single cell. I'm beginning to feel great.'

'What?' The masseuse was incredulous. 'Are you sure? It's supposed to take a lot longer.'

Thóra suppressed a groan. 'Positive. It's brilliant. I can tell I'm done.'

The masseuse began to protest, but stopped when a telephone rang somewhere inside the salon. 'Just a minute,' she said to Thóra, and her toes disappeared.

'Hello,' Thóra heard her say. 'I've got a client.' A long silence ensued. Then, in a much more agitated tone of voice, 'What? Are you serious . . .? Jesus . . . I'm on my way.'

The masseuse hurried back in and began removing the stones from Thóra's back. Thóra tried to conceal her relief by taking an interest in the telephone call. 'Is anything wrong? Don't worry about me; I'm all done, like I said.'

The woman was working quickly. 'Something's happened. Something terrible. Really terrible.'

Thóra propped herself up. 'Really?' she asked, not needing to feign curiosity this time. 'Is it something to do with the ghosts?'

An expression of horror spread across the woman's face and she put her hand over her mouth. 'Oh, I hadn't thought of that. A body's been found on the beach. Vigdís from reception thinks it's someone from here, and the police have arrived to talk to Jónas.'

Thóra leaped naked from the bench and reached for a gown. She quickly pulled it on, never having been in the habit of going around nude in the company of strangers, although she was not ashamed of her body. 'You get going

– I'll take care of myself.' She tightened the flannel belt round her waist and tied a knot. 'Was it an accident?'

'I don't know,' the masseuse said, shifting impatiently from one foot to the other. Clearly she was itching to go and find out more.

'I'll get my things together and leave,' Thóra said, shooing the woman off. 'I promise not to steal any stones.'

The woman didn't need telling twice. She turned on her heel and rushed out into the corridor. Thóra went up to the screen she'd undressed behind and began putting her clothes back on. Her mobile rang in her bag and she fished it out. 'Hello,' she said, trying to put on a sock with one hand. The connection was appalling and the line crackled.

'Hello, Thóra.' It was Matthew. 'I'm still waiting for a reply to my email.'

'Oh, yes,' Thóra said in German, abandoning her struggle with the sock. 'I'm just about to answer.'

'Name the date. I'll do the rest,' said Matthew. He clearly intended to come no matter what. 'Give me the green light and I'll be there.'

'It's rather inconvenient at the moment,' Thóra answered reluctantly. 'I'm working and something's cropped up.'

'What has?' asked Matthew, clearly unconvinced. 'Tell me.'

'Yes, well, it's all rather peculiar,' Thóra said, racking her brain to remember the German word for 'ghost'. 'I'm working on a case connected with ghosts, but it seems as though it may be getting more complicated. The police have found a body and it may stir things up.'

'Where are you?' asked Matthew.

'Me?' Thóra replied foolishly. 'I'm in the countryside.'

'Don't go anywhere. I'll be there tomorrow night.' His voice was solemn.

'Wait, it's all right. Don't come here,' Thóra gabbled. 'There's no murder, only a body.' She hesitated. 'As far as I know, anyway.'

'I'll look forward to seeing you tomorrow,' said the voice from the handset.

'But you don't even know where I am, and I'm not going to tell you. Wait a few days and let me find a better time. I promise. I want to see you too. Just not right now.'

'You don't have to tell me where you are. I'll find you. *Auf Wiedersehen.*'

Thóra couldn't argue any more. Matthew had hung up.

4

When she was dressed, Thóra decided to go straight to reception in the hope of finding out more about the body. On her way out, she noticed a bunch of keys the masseuse had left behind in her haste. She decided to hand it in at reception, as an excuse for going there. She strode quickly down the corridor, feeling pleased with herself.

There was no sign of the masseuse in the lobby. A young woman was leaning over the reception desk, deep in a whispered conversation with her colleague behind the counter. She was disturbingly thin and the snow-white tunic she wore over her matching trousers did little to conceal it. Thóra stood beside her and smiled at the two women in the hope of being allowed to join in. She was far from welcome; both looked most displeased to see her, but they recovered themselves and gave her frosty smiles. For a short while she pretended to look at a poster behind the reception advertising a seance the previous evening with a well-known medium from Reykjavík. Then she turned back to the others, smiling pleasantly.

'Hi,' Thóra said, to break the ice. Her curiosity got the better of her and she forgot the charade with the keys. 'I heard about the body that was found on the beach.'

The women exchanged glances and seemed to come to a silent agreement. The thin one turned to her. 'It's just *awful*,' she said emphatically, her eyes wide. 'You know the cops are here?' Removing her elbow from the counter, she stretched out her hand for Thóra to shake. 'I'm Kata, the beautician.' Her teeth shone pearly white.

Thóra greeted her, surprised at the strength of her grip considering her size. 'I'm Thóra. I'm looking into a little matter for Jónas. I'm not really a guest.'

The receptionist nodded. 'Oh, yeah, he mentioned it to me. I'm Vigdís, the reception manager. You're one of those lawyers, right?'

Not knowing exactly what 'one of those' meant in this context, Thóra nodded. 'That's right.' Looking around, she saw through the glass entrance doors that a police car was still outside. 'Where did the police go?'

Vigdís pointed to the right and whispered, although no one else was nearby. 'They wanted to talk to Jónas.' She leaned back in her chair and raised her eyebrows conspiratorially. 'He wasn't even surprised when I told him.'

'What did the police say?' Thóra asked. 'He might not have realised what the matter involved.'

Vigdís blushed slightly. 'Well, no,' she said reluctantly. 'They didn't say anything to me really, just asked for Jónas.'

'So how do you know there's a body?' asked Kata, the beautician, who was clearly no fool.

Vigdís's cheeks grew redder. 'I heard them say it. I showed them to Jónas's office, and when they introduced themselves, they stated their business with him.'

Thóra was certain that the woman had put her ear up to the door. 'Did they say anything about how this person died?' she asked. 'Was the body washed ashore, or what?'

'And was it a man or a woman?' the beautician interjected. 'Did they say?'

'It was a woman, apparently,' replied Vigdís, the flush leaving her cheeks. She clearly enjoyed holding all the cards, and when she started speaking again, she drew out every word for maximum effect. 'They didn't mention the cause of death exactly, but I swear they were implying that it was unnatural.' She took a deep, dramatic breath. Kata put her hand to her mouth, her colleague's theatrics clearly producing the desired response.

'Why did they come here?' Thóra pressed. 'Was the body found on the beach?'

Vigdís nodded slowly and pointed to a window overlooking the open sea below. 'I don't know exactly where, but it was in this area. Down there somewhere.'

Thóra and Kata looked out of the window. The weather outside was relatively calm and it was still bright daylight despite it being late. The beach itself was hidden from view because the lawn outside the window was a little above sea level.

'How could it have been directly below here?' asked Thóra, turning away from the window. 'Surely you would have noticed if the police had been active in that area.'

Vigdís shrugged. 'A huge amount of land belongs to the old farm and you can't see the whole beach from here by any means. The headland over there is one reason.' She pointed to a hill through the window. 'The farthest point west is on the other side of that hill, and we can't see it from here. That part can be reached by road from elsewhere.'

Thóra and Kata stared at the hill as if hoping to see through it. Then Thóra nodded slowly. 'Weren't there

originally two farms here, on two separate plots of land?'
Vigdís shrugged. Thóra continued, 'As far as I recall, there
were two plots of farmland owned by two brothers, but
one of them died childless so the other one inherited it.
Then he merged them into one. That would explain the
question of access. Generally there's only one driveway
up to each farm, not two. Do you suppose the boundary
lay across that hill?' Looking back, she saw that neither
woman was remotely interested.

'Sure,' Kata said, turning back to her friend. 'But who
is the dead woman? Did they say anything about that?'

'I don't think they have the faintest idea. When they came,
they asked me how many guests were registered at the hotel
and if any were missing.' She grinned conspiratorially at
her audience. 'I just told them the truth – that I had no
idea. This is a hotel, not a prison.' Then addressing Thóra,
she added, 'The guests have keys that they can take out with
them. They don't drop off the keys with me, so it's pure
chance whether I notice their movements. They seldom talk
to me, unless they're going for a hike and want guidance
about routes.'

'It has to be the wife from that drunk couple in number
eighteen. I've not seen either of them for two days,' Kata
said disapprovingly.

Vigdís shook her head. 'No, the kitchen sent food up to
their room just a while back. And drinks.' She emphasised
the latter firmly. 'The woman just phoned down to ask for
room service. She said they'd been indisposed and had
slept the whole day.'

Kata snorted. 'Indisposed, my arse. They were either
hung-over or pissed.'

Thóra could tell that there was little more of any use to be gained from the two women. She was generally not interested in gossip, especially about people she didn't know from Adam, so she decided to take her leave and put her hand in her pocket. 'I have some keys here that my masseuse left behind.' Thóra handed over the bunch of keys, which were on a keyring with a small enamelled Icelandic flag.

'Sibba, you mean,' Vigdís said, stretching for the keys across the counter. 'She can be incredibly absent-minded.' She noticed a large plastic card dangling from the patriotic ring. 'Oh my God, she's even got the master here. She's a real—' Exactly what she was was to remain a mystery, because the telephone rang. Vigdís turned to answer it.

Glancing at Kata, Thóra took the keys back. 'I'll just return them to her myself. I forgot to book another session, so I have to talk to her anyway.' She smiled innocently at the young woman. 'Do you know where she might be?'

The beautician shrugged. 'Maybe in the cafeteria.' She pointed at a corridor to the right. 'It's next to the kitchen.'

Thóra thanked her, then added, 'Do you know what room Birna's in? The architect? I wanted to say hello to her.'

Kata shook her head, but reached over for a book behind the reception desk. Vigdís was still busy on the telephone and paid no attention to them. 'Birna, Birna . . .' Delicate fingers with long French-manicured nails ran down the page. 'Aha. Here it is.' She slammed the book shut. 'She's in room five. It's on the way. She's definitely here because her car's parked outside. It's really flash.'

'That's nice,' said Thóra, who was not particularly interested in cars. 'Thanks very much. I might drop in to your salon tomorrow. I could do with a bit of plucking.' The young woman nodded, rather too vehemently in Thóra's opinion.

On her way down the corridor, various thoughts ran through Thóra's mind. What the hell was she thinking? She couldn't assume the dead woman was Jónas's missing architect. In all probability it was a completely different woman. And who was this Birna anyway? There was no excuse for going into her room. Thóra thought it over on her way, but the closer she came to room 5, the more determined she became to look inside. If it turned out that Birna *was* the woman on the beach, this would presumably be Thóra's only chance to examine her room. If the circumstances of death were suspicious, the police would seal it off. She tried to persuade herself that she had to take advantage of this opportunity, as Jónas's lawyer. Perhaps he would be a suspect. Eventually she convinced herself that she was doing nothing wrong. She simply wanted to put her head round the door and take a look. Nothing else.

Thóra stopped outside the door and looked around her. The women at reception, deep in conversation, didn't notice her. She swiped the plastic key card, opened the door and darted inside.

Jónas tried to act like an innocent hotelier, but was finding the role increasingly difficult. He had an instinctive dislike of the police, which had always appeared to be mutual on the rare occasions when their paths crossed. Police officers also had a tendency to look deep into his eyes while they talked to him, and Jónas had the feeling they had been trained to evaluate the truthfulness of replies from the movement of the pupils. He knew he was blinking far too much, which wasn't making a good impression.

He cleared his throat. 'As I told you, the description could fit the architect Birna, but it's much too general to say for certain. Wasn't the woman carrying any ID, a bag or something?' He stretched towards the window behind him. 'Don't you find it hot in here? Should I open the window?' Jónas was afraid that sweat would start pouring from his brow to complete the picture of a guilty man.

The police officers exchanged a look. They seemed to be keeping their cool in spite of being clad in full regalia, black uniforms with gold braid. Ignoring the stifling heat in the room, they had not taken off their jackets. They were holding their caps, however. Disregarding Jónas's enquiries about the window and the ID, they went on questioning him. 'When was she last seen, this Birna?'

'I don't know exactly,' Jónas replied, searching through his memory. 'She was here yesterday, definitely.'

'So you saw her yesterday?' asked the younger officer. He looked like a tough guy, and Jónas preferred the older one, who appeared to be a softer type in all respects.

'What?' Jónas asked rather idiotically, then hurried to add, 'What, yes. I met up with her. Several times in fact. She was struggling to complete the plans for the annexe that's to be built here and came to me throughout the day to consult me on various points.'

The officers nodded in unison. After appearing to bite

the inside of his cheek for a few moments, the older one asked, 'What about today? Did she come and see you today?'

Jónas shook his head fervently. 'No. Definitely not. We were supposed to meet this morning only she didn't turn up. I've been keeping an eye out for her but haven't bumped into her or seen her. I kept calling her mobile, but it was switched off. I just got her voicemail.'

'What kind of mobile did she have? Can you describe it?' the younger man asked.

Jónas did not need to think about that question. Birna's mobile was very distinctive. He had seen her with it many times. 'It's bright red, a clamshell phone. Shiny. Quite small. I don't know the make, though. There was a big silver peace sign on the front, but I don't think it was a brand logo, just a decoration.' The police officers darted glances at each other, then stood up together. Jónas stayed seated. He was feeling more confident after finally being able to answer one of their questions. 'This woman who was found . . . did she die in an accident?'

Neither of the officers answered him. 'Would you please show us to Birna Halldórsdóttir's room?'

Thóra took a last look around the room. She had not found anything significant. Admittedly it looked different to other hotel rooms, because the architect had clearly moved in for longer than most people. She had fixed sketches of buildings – which Thóra presumed to be proposals for the annexe that Jónas had said he was planning to build – to the walls. Notes had been scrawled on several of the drawings, some of them comprehensible to a layman, others not. Calculations had been made in some of the margins, and the sums were underlined in red ink. The figures were large ones, and Thóra hoped for Jónas's sake that they were not cost estimates.

Thóra had opened the wardrobe mostly out of curiosity, as she'd never expected to find anything important there. She had stuck a pencil through the handle to open the door, so as not to leave fingerprints. She needn't have bothered, because all the contents told her was that Birna was an exceptionally tidy person. There weren't many items of clothing: blouses, smarter trousers and jackets were on clothes hangers, and the other garments were neatly arranged on the shelves. The woman must have worked in a boutique at some point, as they were all folded perfectly. Birna had good taste; her clothes were unpretentious but stylish and looked expensive. Thóra tried to peek at the label on a jumper at the top of the stack, but couldn't read it without disturbing the pile. Closing the wardrobe, she went over to the telephone on one of the bedside tables. She used her fingernail to press the recall button and see the last numbers Birna had dialled, then took a blank sheet of paper from the hotel notepad beside the telephone and wrote down the three numbers. She folded the sheet of paper and put it in her pocket.

Looking around, she saw nothing that merited closer examination except the desk drawer. She had already gingerly shuffled the papers on the desk, but was none the wiser for it. They all seemed to be connected with the design of the annexe, mainly brochures from manufacturers of construction materials. Thóra nudged the desk chair to one side with her foot to reach the drawer. Now she faced a problem, because there was no handle on it. Pulling her sleeve over her right hand, she opened the drawer by tugging it from underneath. It contained two books: the New Testament and a leather-bound diary with Birna's name on it. At last she had found something useful. Still using her sleeve, Thóra fished the book up out of the drawer. She flipped it open. Bingo. The pages were filled with neat handwriting. Thóra grinned, but then her smile vanished. She could hear noises in the corridor, just outside the door.

In desperation she looked around. She had to get out. She couldn't possibly explain what she was doing there – she didn't even know herself. She ran over to the floor-length curtains and prayed that all the rooms were the same. Fortunately for her, they were, and with trembling hands she unlocked the French window and stepped out on to the deck. Then she pushed the door closed as carefully as she could and hurried away.

As Thóra rounded the corner of the building, she took a deep breath. Her heart was pounding. What had she been thinking? She must be insane. It had been a close call; she was certain she had heard the room door open just as she had closed the balcony door behind her. She inhaled deeply again. Her heartbeat slowed down, then leaped once more. The desk drawer! She had left it open. She tried to calm herself. So what? Everyone would assume Birna had left it like that. She sagged in relief, then jumped again – in her hands she was still holding a diary marked, 'Birna Halldórsdóttir, Association of Icelandic Architects'.

5

As the police car pulled slowly out of the drive, Jónas felt that the officers had done all they could to prolong their visit. They must have known that the sooner they left, the fewer visitors would have noticed them. He heaved a sigh of relief when the car finally disappeared from sight, praying they would not need to come back. He knew his prayers wouldn't be answered. After a quick look inside to check she wasn't there, they had sealed off Birna's room and ordered Jónas to make sure that no one went in until it had been searched. Clearly Jónas had not seen the last of them.

His only hope was that the dead woman would turn out not to be Birna, but that was wishful thinking. Before leaving the scene, the police officers had asked Jónas to point out her car in the car park. It was a dark blue Audi Sport, which she had recently bought, and was parked at the very end of the car park. Birna always parked as far away from other cars as possible, to reduce the likelihood of careless drivers opening their doors and scratching her pride and joy. The policemen had walked up to the car, and one of them had produced a little plastic bag from his pocket. Without opening the bag, he had pointed it at the car and squeezed its contents. The sports car had beeped and flashed. The police officers exchanged meaningful looks.

Jónas sighed. It was a very uncomfortable situation. Should he allow himself to grieve? He had liked Birna despite her flaws, and if he was honest with himself, he had been rather more than fond of her, although his affection had not been reciprocated. Should he feel aggrieved? This was a major setback for his plans to expand the hotel. Should he tell the staff or act as though nothing had happened? The police hadn't advised him either way. He had to be careful, because many people would undoubtedly scrutinise his reaction and interpret it to fit whatever stories were circulating. It was a small place and his staff were not known for their discretion. He sighed again. Perhaps the police would rule it an accident, but nothing in their behaviour suggested that.

Jónas turned and went inside. He hurried past reception to avoid being stopped by anyone. His ploy worked, but it was obvious just looking at Kata, propped up against the reception desk, that she was burning to know what the police had said. The beautician opened her mouth as soon as Jónas entered the building, but when he looked down and quickened his pace, she closed it again. She and Vigdís, the reception manager, watched despondently as he rushed past without saying a word. It wouldn't last long – in the end curiosity would get the better of them, even if they had to chase him down the corridor – but so far so good, Jónas thought, as he hurried into his office and closed the door behind him. He sat down, brooding. Maybe some good would come of this. Was there a chance that this tragedy could be spun in favour of the hotel, and Jónas himself? He picked up the telephone and dialled a number.

* * *

Thóra sat sheepishly on the edge of her bed. Birna's diary rested in her lap. She had not decided what to do with it, whether to sneak it back into Birna's room or whether she could plant it somewhere without arousing suspicion. Should she get rid of the book immediately or wait until she had read it? Her cheeks burned when she thought that Birna might well still be alive. What had she been thinking? Was she so bored by her postbox-obsessed clients and all the other nitpickers that she was starting to make more exciting cases out of nothing? She had come here to dissuade a half-crazy hotel owner from pointless litigation, not to become embroiled in a police investigation that was none of her business. The telephone rang and she reached for it, welcoming the distraction.

'Could you pop in and see me?' Jónas said cryptically. 'Something unexpected has cropped up and it might be connected with the hauntings.'

'What is it?' asked Thóra, intrigued.

'I'll explain when you come, but I think Birna, the architect, is dead and—'

'I'll be there in ten minutes,' Thóra interrupted him, and hung up.

Well, well. She turned from the telephone to look back at the diary. In a way she was relieved: at least she had not stolen the diary from a living person. She opened the book with her sleeve and flicked through the pages using the edge of her thumb. It was certainly an unusual diary. Instead of containing a few notes, each page was densely packed with small, tight handwriting. There were a lot of sketches of houses, buildings and design details. Some of the sketches seemed to be rough doodles from Birna's imagination;

others looked more likely to be real-life projects. One page per day had clearly not been enough for Birna, because she had filled the pages well into September – three months ahead.

Thóra looked at the last entries, hoping to find something along the lines of 'Met X on the beach – must be careful', but no such luck. The final two-page spread said, 'Bergur's birthday – mustn't forget. Transfer money for April' and listed a welter of names of companies that Thóra didn't recognise. Beside each name was a telephone number with measurements in millimetres followed by prices in krónur. At the very end of each line was a string of different abbreviations that she couldn't fathom: 'B., W., R., G., S.,' etc. At the top of the page, Birna had written 'Cladding,' underlined. She had apparently been seeking information about different types of cladding and had marked a cross against the line showing one of the lowest prices. Since the cladding could not be connected with the woman's death, a rather frustrated Thóra flicked back to the preceding pages. There was a plan showing, as far as Thóra could tell, the area surrounding the hotel and the location of the new building. The main measurements and distances had been written in, and an ornate arrow pointed north. Around the drawing were comments by Birna, mainly concerning the slope of the land and light conditions, but one aroused Thóra's interest in particular: 'What's wrong with this spot??? Old plans???' Just beneath, written with another pen, it said, 'Keens', also followed by three question marks. Thóra was none the wiser.

Although she would have liked to read the diary from cover to cover, she had to go to see Jónas. He knew she had nothing better to do, so it would be hard to explain being late. All the same, she flicked back until she found another, similar drawing. This showed the floor plan of a house, two adjacent rectangles divided up into rooms. A staircase was shown in the same place on both, so it must be a two-storey house. The rooms were clearly marked: two living rooms, kitchen, study, bedroom, toilet and so on. Various comments filled the margins, such as 'Built in 1920? Rising damp in SW wall. Foundations?' Birna had also written down a question that must have been plaguing her, because she had drawn a cross-hatched box around it: 'Who was Kristín?' Thóra looked at the floor plan. One of the rooms on the upper floor was marked 'Bedroom' like the other two, but beneath it was written in smaller letters, 'Kristín?' Thóra scanned the two pages in search of any indication that the drawing showed one of the local houses, and saw that the top of the left-hand page was marked 'Kreppa', the name of one of the farms. She closed the diary and slid it inside her suitcase. The cleaners would hardly start rummaging around in there.

Jónas seemed worried, and not his usual expansive self. He offered Thóra one of the two uncomfortable seats in front of his desk, then threw himself down in an up-holstered leather chair behind it. No herbal tea was offered, much to Thóra's relief.

'What did the police want, Jónas?' Thóra asked, to break the ice.

Jónas groaned. 'Does everyone know they were here?'

'Well, I can't answer for everybody, but a lot of people

know besides me. Most people know a policeman when they see one,' replied Thóra. 'What did they want?'

Jónas groaned again, louder than before. From under his sleeve he pulled down a steel bracelet set with a large brown stone, which he rubbed absent-mindedly as he answered her question. 'They found a body on the beach, the body of a woman they believe to be Birna, the architect I told you about.' He closed his eyes, still slowly rubbing the bracelet.

'Ah,' said Thóra. 'Did they mention the cause of death? There can be many reasons for people being found dead on a beach. More often than not it's suicide.'

'I don't think she committed suicide,' Jónas said morosely. 'She wasn't the type.'

Thóra didn't like to point out that there was no particular type that took their own lives. 'What did the police say? That's the most important thing. Presumably they've visited the scene?'

Jónas tore his attention away from his bracelet and looked at Thóra. 'They said nothing specific. It was more the way they acted and what they didn't say.' He looked back at his wrist. 'If she'd drowned, for example, fallen on to a rock, something that suggested an accident, they would definitely have asked me about her behaviour. You know – did she do a lot of hiking? Kayaking? Swimming in the sea? But they asked me nothing. All they wanted to know was whether anything was missing from here and whether I recognised her from the very rough description they gave.' Jónas suddenly stared at Thóra. 'Now that I think of it, it was extremely strange that they made no mention of her facial features. Do you suppose the head was missing?' Before Thóra could answer, he corrected himself: 'No, hardly, they described the hair colour.' His eyes widened. 'Could it be that the killer cut the head off, scalped it and put the hair on top of the body?'

Thóra put an end to his conjecture. 'I think you're letting your imagination run away with you. But I do agree that it sounds as if they suspect it was something more than an accident.' Casually, she added, 'Did the police examine her room?'

'One of them took a look inside. The other waited outside in the corridor with me. He was only in there for a minute or two. Then when he came out again, he just shook his head.'

'So he didn't say that any unauthorised person had been in there or ask you who had a key?' Thóra's cheeks flushed slightly.

'No, nothing like that. They absolutely forbade anyone to enter until the CID had finished its work. Then they asked to see her car. They had the key in a little bag.'

Thóra nodded thoughtfully. There was really no question of the dead woman's identity. 'Well, I never.' Looking at Jónas, she suppressed the urge to ask him to stop fiddling with the damn bracelet. It probably had some connection with alternative medicine, energy fields or something. 'Did anyone want Birna dead? Was she in some kind of trouble?'

Jónas shook his head slowly. 'No, she was just normal.' Thóra couldn't imagine what he considered normal, but assumed that his criteria were different from hers. 'A great person and a brilliant architect.' Jónas smiled awkwardly. 'Actually, she was a true Capricorn, consistent and committed. But a lovely person. A genuinely lovely person.'

'Didn't anyone really dislike her?' Thóra asked. 'Can't you think of anyone who could have got into a dispute with her, something that could have got out of hand?'

Jónas pushed his bracelet back under his sleeve and gave Thóra his undivided attention. 'Listen, I was wondering if it might be connected with the ghost.'

Thóra managed not to smile. 'Are you implying that a ghost murdered her?'

Jónas shrugged, then waved his hands. 'What do I know? It seems like more than a coincidence. This place is haunted. Birna is found dead just outside. She was working on modifying the premises. Ghosts want to keep their surroundings the same as when they left them. They fight with all their powers against any kind of disruption. What are you supposed to believe?'

Not a paranormal enthusiast, Thóra had never heard much about the behaviour of spirits. 'Jónas, I think we can rule out involvement by a ghost.'

'Are you sure?' the hotelier asked. 'Birna was very curious about the history of this place. She felt that she had to find out about it, because without that knowledge it was hard for her to get a feel for the site. We can't rule out her stirring up the angry spirit of a deceased inhabitant, which cost her her life. Maybe not directly, but perhaps indirectly.' He went on, seeing that Thóra was lost for words. 'There might not be a direct connection, but the situation now is this: this place is haunted, and the sellers concealed that fact. A woman has met a tragic death – perhaps because of something connected with the ghost. That will be difficult to rule out, because it can always be claimed that the murderer was governed by forces from beyond. Are you with me?'

Thóra could only shake her head.

'Yes, don't you see? You tell the vendors that a woman has died here and there are stories that a ghost has played a major role. The whole business will be brought up in court. My feeling is that those people wouldn't care to be linked to a murder, if only indirectly. Would you like to be a witness in a murder case in which the defence implied that you had kept quiet about information that led to such an atrocity?' Jónas shook his head on Thóra's behalf. 'No, you wouldn't care for that. Nor would they. That might persuade them to negotiate compensation terms.'

Thóra interrupted him. 'What difference would it make if you won compensation? You're stuck with the hotel. Presumably you don't want to break the contract at this stage? If you're serious about this ghost, I doubt whether you can bribe it to leave.'

Jónas smiled. 'Of course I can't. But I imagine I'll have to raise my staff's wages so that they don't all quit. They are spiritual people, sensitive towards supernatural matters. Some of them have already dropped hints about leaving. My business plan would be ruined and the small profit I was hoping for might easily be wiped out. Guests at places like this are sensitive too. They don't seek the company of beings from beyond, especially not if it could cost them their lives.'

Thóra needed a while to digest this. She had no desire to force people to strike a deal by making absurd threats about linking their names to a murder, but Jónas's claims about his staff were a concrete contribution. 'Let me think it over.' She was about to stand up, then decided to stay put. 'Actually, you still have to tell me all about this ghost. How exactly does it manifest itself?'

Jónas sighed. 'Gosh, I don't know where to begin.'

'At the beginning, perhaps,' suggested Thóra, a little irritated.

'Yes, that's probably best,' agreed Jónas, brushing off Thóra's slight. 'As I told you, most of the staff here are more sensitive than ordinary people.'

Thóra nodded.

'They started sensing an uncomfortable presence. If I remember correctly, it was the aura reader – his name's Eiríkur – who first noticed it. Then others became aware of it gradually. I brought up the rear, really. At first I thought it was just their imaginations.' Jónas regarded Thóra gravely. 'It's almost impossible to describe it to anyone who can't sense these things, but I can tell you it's by no means a pleasant feeling. Probably the best analogy is when you feel you're being watched. As if someone's sitting watching you from a dark corner. That's the way I've felt, anyway.'

His story only strengthened Thóra's conviction that this was a case of mass hysteria. One person had started a vague story and others had joined in until what they imagined had become a fact. 'Jónas,' she said firmly, 'you have to do better than this. Your claim is absolutely no use to me – I can't face the sellers of this property and repeat what you've just said. We need something tangible. It's not enough to say you get the occasional shiver down your spine.'

Jónas looked shocked. 'It's so much more than that. You can ignore a shiver; this feeling lasts. Oppressive may be the best word for it. Almost all of us have heard crying in the middle of the night, an infant crying.' Suddenly he became boastful. 'And I've seen a fully fledged ghost. More than once, as it happens. Its presence has become more intense recently.'

'And where have you seen this ghost?' Thóra asked sceptically.

'Outdoors mainly. Outside here.' Jónas gestured towards the window behind him without looking round. 'I can't describe exactly where the ghost was; I've only seen it in the fog. Some ghosts appear in certain weather conditions and this one comes when it's foggy.'

'So presumably you can't describe it in detail?' Thóra asked.

'No, not really. Except that I know it's a girl or a woman. The being was far too slight to be a male.' Jónas leaned back in his seat. 'I also saw it appear in my mirror. There was no question that it was a girl. It happened quite quickly, but all the same . . .'

'You said you recognised the girl from a photograph you found. Surely it didn't happen so quickly that you couldn't manage to commit her features to memory?'

'Well, I don't know how to describe it. I was brushing my teeth and I heard a rustling noise. I stood upright and watched in the mirror as the being darted past the door. My subconscious obviously managed to capture the features although I can hardly describe them, but I recognised the face from one of the photos.' Jónas opened a drawer in his desk and started rummaging while he continued his account. 'I couldn't even hold the photo after that. I threw it back in the box and closed it. You wouldn't have any trouble examining it, but I simply can't.'

'I doubt it would have much effect on me,' Thóra said, smiling reassuringly. 'I'd like to discuss this with some of your staff. This aura reader, Eiríkur, for example.'

'No problem. He's not here at the moment, but he'll be back tomorrow, I think.' At last Jónas found what he was looking for in the drawer. He handed Thóra a heavy key on a large steel ring. 'This is the key to the old basement. The boxes I told you about are down there. Take a look – there are some interesting things that might explain the hauntings.'

Thóra took the key. 'If memory serves, the old farm was called Kreppa, wasn't it?' she asked innocently.

Jónas looked surprised. 'Yes, that's right. Originally there were two farms that were merged. One was called Kreppa, the other Kirkjustétt.' He shrugged nonchalantly. 'Birna spent a long time there on the planned development.'

'Really? Why?' Thóra asked, even more curious. 'Is the old farmhouse still intact?'

'Yes, it's still there. Originally we planned to renovate there the same as we did here, but Birna was against it. She thought the two buildings were too far apart and the farmhouse was too dilapidated. You can look at it tomorrow if you want. The keys are under a stone by the entrance. It's quite interesting inside, because it's still fully furnished in the old style.'

'How come?' asked Thóra. 'There were no tenants on the land when the sale was agreed.'

'I have no idea,' Jónas replied. 'Some of that old stuff might have been removed now, as it happens, because the sister . . . um . . .' Jónas racked his brains for the woman's name. He twirled one index finger in the air as he thought about it.

'You mean Elín Thórdardóttir? The one who sold you the land?' suggested Thóra.

'Yes, that's her,' Jónas said. His finger stopped mid-twirl. 'Elín, the sister! She phoned me a couple of months ago and told me they were finally going to do something about taking that stuff away. I was in the city, so I didn't talk to her myself; I just got a message through Vigdís at reception. Her daughter came a while later and was told where to find the key. It was probably a good thing that neither of them met me, because I would probably have fired off a comment or two about that ghost.'

Thóra was sick of talking about ghosts. 'When did it turn out that they wanted those boxes of junk?' she asked. 'I don't remember any mention of that when the sale was going through.'

'Oh, it was verbal,' Jónas said. 'They discussed it with me and I told them just to pick it up whenever they wanted.' Then he added self-importantly, 'I told them they ought to get a move on, in case I either wanted to use the house or demolish it.'

Thóra nodded. 'I might take a look over there while I'm here. Who knows, I meet even bump into Elín or her brother.' She glanced at her watch. 'I think I'll wait until morning before I go through the boxes. It's far too late now.'

Jónas agreed. 'It's not the sort of stuff you want to look at before bedtime, I can tell you.' He grinned mischievously. 'Whether you believe in ghosts or not.'

The bed was the comfiest Thóra had ever slept in. She yawned and stretched, determined to enjoy her sleep to the utmost.

The thick feather pillow supported her neck perfectly, and she made a mental note to ask Jónas where he bought his bedding. Reaching over for the remote on her bedside table, she switched off the television. She felt sleep descending upon her the moment she closed her eyes, and soon her breathing became regular as she drifted into a dream. She did not even stir when an infant's soft crying wafted in through the open window.

Saturday, 10 June 2006

6

There were few things Gauti disliked more than doing an autopsy early on a Saturday morning, especially if he had had to prepare it the evening before. There were thousands of better ways to spend a Friday evening than stinking of disinfectant in the company of the deceased in the National Hospital basement. You were supposed to be at a bar surrounded by loose women, cocooned in cigarette smoke. Gauti wondered whether he should just look for a new job, as he had been threatening to for ages. It seemed pretty much anyone could find well-paid work these days. He wasn't sure the banking sector would be impressed by his five years' experience as an autopsy assistant, but all his friends seemed to have found jobs there. He tried to imagine himself in a suit behind a desk, an account manager busily dissecting his clients' financial position and then offering advice that would ultimately plunge them even deeper into debt. Perhaps there was more variety in the company of the dead, after all.

He scanned the tray to make sure that all the instruments were in place, and glanced at the body, which lay shrouded in a white sheet. The only thing that was missing now was the pathologist. Gauti looked at the clock on the wall behind him. The doctor was late. Hrannar Pétursson. He groaned. As if things weren't bad enough already.

Pétursson was irritating and arrogant, and unprofessional to boot. His slapdash technique rarely mattered, but Gauti had sometimes had to point out oversights that must have been screamingly obvious for him to have noticed them. Hrannar hated it when Gauti pointed out his mistakes, but Gauti did not let that stop him, as he actively enjoyed winding up the doctor.

The door to the autopsy theatre opened and Hrannar strutted in. He was accompanied by a medical student whom Gauti recognised, but he couldn't remember his name. He had been hanging around the ward for the past few weeks, but had never been present at an autopsy as far as Gauti knew.

'Good morning,' Hrannar boomed, flapping his hand to indicate his companion. 'This is Sigurgeir, a fifth-year medical student I'm allowing to observe. It's not every day we get a body like this to look at.'

Gauti nodded to Sigurgeir, who smiled excitedly, and pulled back the sheet from the woman's body. He watched the student's reaction – the boy could barely contain his nausea.

Oblivious, Hrannar bent so close to the dead woman's head that his nose almost touched it. Then he straightened, took out a Dictaphone and began talking into it. 'On the table is an unidentified woman who was found dead on the beach on Snaefellsnes. The facial features are beyond recognition due to extensive injuries and what would appear to be post-mortem animal predation . . .'

'Dad's no fun. He's asleep. So's Gylfi. I want to be with you.'

Thóra rubbed the sleep from her eyes and propped herself

up in bed. She had grabbed her mobile from the bedside table and answered it before actually managing to wake up, then cleared her throat and spoke to her daughter. She had a vague recollection of a dream about ghosts and crying babies, but it slipped away before she could remember it fully. 'Hello, Sóley. Are you awake already?' Looking at the clock, she saw that it was a few minutes to eight. 'Oof, it's so early. It's Saturday today. Your dad and Gylfi just want to sleep a bit longer so they can be more fun later.'

'Huh.' Her little girl's high, clear voice was full of reproach. 'They won't be any fun. I only like being with you. *You're* fun.' The reception was terrible and Sóley sounded as though she was talking from the bottom of a barrel.

Enjoy it while it lasts, thought Thóra, who had learned from raising Gylfi that this unconditional adoration would not go on for ever. Sóley was only six, and although she would soon be seven, there were still a few years left in which Thóra would play the lead role in her life.

'I'll be back home tomorrow evening. Then we'll do something fun. I'll bring you some shells from the beach, if you want.'

'Beach! Is there a beach out there?' Sóley sighed. 'Why can't I be with you? I really want to go to the beach.'

Thóra kicked herself for mentioning the beach. Since they lived on the coast, it had simply not occurred to her that a beach would arouse the girl's interest. 'Oh, sweetie, you know you're supposed to spend the weekend with your dad. Maybe we can come back here later in the summer.'

'And take the caravan?' Sóley asked excitedly.

Thóra stifled a groan. 'Maybe. We'll see.' If there was one

thing she could not stand it was driving with that contraption behind her, and she had still not learned to reverse with it. The few trips they had made with the caravan had been carefully planned so that Thóra hadn't needed to reverse once. 'Go and turn on the television – the cartoons have started. Dad and Gylfi will be up soon. OK?'

'OK,' muttered Sóley crossly. 'Bye,' she added.

'Bye-bye. I miss you,' said Thóra, and hung up.

She stared at the telephone for a while, wondering how things had ended up like this. Her marriage had fallen apart pretty quickly, and she had never given herself the time to deal with it. For eleven years they had got on fine; then things went rapidly downhill. She and Hannes were divorced a year and a half later. Her conscience nagged her a little about shuttling the children back and forth between their two homes, but there was not much to be done about it now, as she wouldn't take Hannes back even if he was the world champion at caravan-reversing. She got up, shook off these depressing thoughts and took a shower. Then she put on a pair of jeans, running shoes and a hoodie, and felt ready to clamber around in the dusty basement. In the large mirror she saw that all she needed was a balaclava to make a convincing bank robber.

A lavish buffet awaited her in the dining room. Thóra was generally not one for big breakfasts, but the food was so tastefully arranged and looked so tempting that she gave in and took a large plate, which she filled with poached egg, bacon and toast. She threw some fruit on top, for appearances' sake, but soon after sitting down she abandoned the idea of health food. Half the tables in the dining room were occupied. Thóra was curious to know what kind of people stayed at such a hotel, which was exorbitantly expensive but based on a hippyish philosophy. She could not identify any common characteristics among the guests, who – although of all ages and various nationalities – seemed to be mainly Icelanders.

At three tables were single guests like Thóra: two men, one old and the other young, and a middle-aged woman. Thóra guessed that they were Icelandic. In some indefinable way, the older man seemed out of place. Thóra guessed his profession as lawyer or accountant. The woman appeared out of sorts too, sitting in melancholy silence with her eyes glued to her coffee cup. On her plate was a pile of food that looked untouched. The woman was such a picture of misery that Thóra instinctively felt sorry for her. The young man, on the other hand, fitted right in, and Thóra allowed her gaze to linger on him. It helped that he was extremely good-looking – dark-haired, tanned and well muscled, but not a steroid-popping bodybuilder. Thóra smiled wryly, but her face froze when the young man looked over and smiled back. Embarrassed, she drained her coffee and stood up. The young man did the same. One of his legs was bandaged, and he picked up a crutch from the chair beside him. He followed her, hobbling, towards the exit.

'Are you Icelandic?' Thóra heard him say from behind her.

Turning round, Thóra saw that he was no less handsome close up. 'Me? Yes, I am, actually,' she said, wishing that she was not dressed like a burglar. 'And you?' she asked.

He returned her smile and held out his hand. 'No, I'm a Chinese Icelandophile. My name's Teitur.'

'Thóra.' She shook his outstretched hand.

'You must have just arrived,' he said, looking her straight in the eye. 'I'd definitely have noticed you.'

Here we go, Thóra thought to herself, but played it cool. 'I arrived yesterday. What about you? Have you been here long?'

The young man showed his sparkling teeth again. 'A week.'

'And you like it?' Thóra asked stupidly. As a rule she was very awkward in her dealings with the opposite sex if there was the slightest hint of flirtation.

He looked amused. 'Oh, yes. It's fine. I'm here combining business and pleasure, and I've managed both pretty well. Apart from this.' Supporting himself on the crutch, he lifted his bandaged leg.

'Oh,' said Thóra. 'What happened?'

'I fell off a horse, like an idiot,' he said. 'I can recommend everything here except the horse rides. I didn't fall really: the horse got startled and threw me off. I sprained my ankle, but I thank my lucky stars that someone witnessed the incident and managed to pull me away before anything worse happened. So stay away from the horse rental.'

Thóra grinned. 'Don't worry. I'm highly unlikely to try it.' Thóra would sooner climb on a dog sleigh than go around on horseback. 'You said you're working here? What kind of work can that be?' she asked curiously. She considered it unlikely that there was much work one could do here, unless the man was a writer.

'I'm a stockbroker. A pretty stressful job, but it has the advantage that I can do it almost anywhere – all you need is a computer and an Internet connection. What about you? What do you do?'

'I'm a lawyer,' Thóra said, nodding eagerly as if he might not believe her. God, she was pathetic sometimes, she thought.

'Oh, right,' said Teitur. 'Hey, why don't I show you around the place? I know it like the back of my hand after a week here.'

Thóra smiled at him. She doubted whether he could have become a local expert in the space of a week. Especially on just one leg. 'Who knows? We'll see.'

'I'm free and easy.' Teitur grinned. 'Just give me a shout.'

Thóra thanked him and said goodbye. That would be something else, strolling around the locality with an attractive man instead of crouching in a dusty basement looking at old photographs. Even if he couldn't move very quickly . . . Oh, well.

Most of the internal organs from the deceased were lying in steel trays. The brain was in one, the lungs in a larger one, the liver in a third and so on. This gruesome buffet had long since ceased to bother Gauti, but he did have to think back several years to recall a body in worse condition. He hoped the woman had either died quickly or lost consciousness before the end.

Hrannar walked over to the sink, slipping off his gloves. 'So. The woman was brutally raped, but the cause of death was repeated blows to the front of the head. The facial features are unrecognisable as a result of this and of post-mortem mutilation by animals, presumably scavengers. It cannot be determined whether the woman was conscious for the duration of the rape, but there are no visible injuries on the body to suggest that she resisted. Thus it seems likely that she had already sustained some cranial injury before the rape began, but was dead when it finished. The deceased may even be assumed to have been beaten during the act.

'Semen, presumably from the assailant, was present in the vagina, and an analysis of that together with the hairs collected by combing her pubic area may identify the assailant. This seems the only likely method of identification. In fact, the exceptional volume of semen gives grounds for investigating the possibility of more than one assailant.' He addressed his words to the medical student, who was standing beside Gauti looking pale and weak. 'And the pins must be carefully described in the autopsy report. It's not every day that a body is found with such objects in the soles of the feet. I have a suspicion that the murderer attached some significance to that act. The most immediate inference is that he is seriously deranged or sadistic. At least, I can think of no logical explanation for this.' He pointed to ten bloodstained pins that he had extracted from the soles of the woman's feet and placed in a transparent plastic jar.

He took off his gore-spattered surgical gown and ran his fingers through his hair. 'Be sure to label everything carefully and send it off for immediate analysis. The police need the findings quickly.' He turned on his heel and left.

'You get used to it, don't worry,' said Gauti to the student, patting him on the shoulder. He left a bloody handprint on the boy's white plastic overall. 'You did very well.'

'Repulsive,' the student muttered softly to himself. 'What

possessed me to pick this over a summer job at the health-care centre?'

Thóra stared at the stack of boxes in the poorly lit basement. Light shone feebly from a bare bulb in the middle of the room and through a tiny window so dirty that it glowed almost brown. The smell of damp crept into her nostrils. Ugh. She should have asked Jónas to have the boxes moved up to her room. To make matters worse, all the timber struts supporting the ceiling above her looked pretty rotten. Thóra grimaced at the thought of the insects that undoubtedly thrived there, but braced herself and went over to the lowest stack. As far as she could tell, there were about twelve large, ancient crates, but the way that they were arranged made it difficult to determine their exact number. Carefully she lifted the lid from the top box, leaning back in case something jumped out. When nothing happened, she peered cautiously inside.

Her eyes widened. She had been expecting almost anything. But not this.

7

On the top of the box lay a folded Nazi flag. The white field around the black swastika had turned slightly yellow, and the material was rough to the touch. Thóra frowned as she carefully removed it and put it to one side. Beneath the flag was a pile of magazines, the uppermost one even more faded than the flag. The magazine was called *Iceland*, and a Nazi emblem was centred under the title. Jónas had not mentioned this in his cryptic account of ghosts and the house's murky history. Thóra picked up the magazine and saw that the others in the pile were the same. They were published by the Icelandic Nationalist Party. Thóra shook her head. She knew there had been a small Nazi movement in Iceland before the war, but couldn't remember much about it. It had clearly been involved in publishing, although the magazines were thin and not big on content, judging from the headlines.

Leafing through the pile, she also noticed several issues of a student newspaper called *Mjölnir*, whose publisher, according to the masthead, was the Nationalist Students' Association. Thóra removed the pile of magazines from the box to see what was concealed underneath and found a folded shirt, a swastika armband and what appeared to be a military belt with a shoulder strap attached. How could anybody be into this?

By now Thóra was close to the bottom of the box and she noticed a brass object, which when she picked it up turned out to be yet another swastika. Its base was a kind of socket, whose purpose, if any, was unclear. There were also various scraps of paper advertising dances, camping trips and meetings that the nationalists had apparently organised, along with items of no political significance, such as an old wallet, shoes and photographs of people who did not seem to be wearing swastikas. There were no children in the photographs, but they shared a common theme: smartly dressed people in the prime of life, either sitting on blankets as if picnicking, or posing against the wall of a house. Although the same wall featured in more than one of the photographs, not enough of it was visible for Thóra to make out whether it belonged to the old farmhouse upstairs. Judging from the outfits, the photographs had been taken during the war and just afterwards.

Thóra tried to replace the objects in the box in the right order, although the box looked like it hadn't been opened for ages, so there was little chance of the person who had packed it noticing the difference. It just seemed better to leave it as she had found it. There was little to pique her curiosity in the next box that Thóra looked at. It mostly contained finely crocheted tablecloths, quite old, and an old-fashioned floral-patterned vase with a gold trim. The third box contained an aged photograph album. Thóra's grandmother had owned a similar album, and she suddenly felt sad as it struck her how short life was and how quickly we were forgotten. It would be difficult, now, to find someone who recognised the people in the album. Soon it would be impossible. She sat down on one of the boxes to browse through the photographs.

She lifted the thick cover. On the first page, under a flysheet that looked like carbon paper, were some snaps taken by the old farmhouse. The building, which looked almost new, was virtually unchanged, and a carved wooden sign above the entrance read, 'Kirkjustétt'. Thóra carefully unhooked the photograph from the corner mounts. On the back was a stamp showing that the photograph had been taken, or developed, in 1919. In delicate handwriting, which must have been female, was the inscription 'Bjarni Thórólfsson and Adalheidur Jónsdóttir'. Examining the photograph more closely, Thóra deduced that the photographer must have had his back to the sun, because the couple were trying their best not to squint to keep the sun out of their eyes. They were a handsome couple; he was tall with thick bushy hair falling in a quiff over his forehead, and she young and wearing a calf-length skirt, smart flat shoes and an old-fashioned hat that fitted tightly to her head. Blonde hair gleamed beneath it. He was dressed in light, baggy trousers with a pronounced crease, and a shirt and braces. They were standing beside each other by the front wall, their hands by their sides. Old-style proud homeowners.

On the same page was another photograph with the same subject, featuring these two with another couple. Thóra carefully remounted the first photo and took out the second. In the same handwriting, it said that the second couple were called Grímur Thórólfsson and Kristrún Valgeirsdóttir. Even without the shared surname, it was obvious that Bjarni and Grímur were brothers. Their clothing was very similar, but in different colours. Thóra scrutinised the picture but could read nothing from their expressions as they grimaced into the sun. She could see that the woman who must be Grímur's wife was very different from the fair-haired Adalheidur. She was older and more buxom, stouter and less smartly dressed, in a plain skirt, thick sweater and heavy flat shoes. Her dark hair was tied back in no particular style. Thóra wondered how these two very different women would have got on together. She turned the page.

On the next pages were three photographs of the young Bjarni and Adalheidur, all taken outdoors. They had not changed much from the previous shots, except that the young woman was no longer wearing a hat. Thóra kept going and examined two more pictures in which the elder brother and his wife again joined the younger couple, along with a little dark-haired girl, a chubby, bonny baby dressed in the fashion of that time. Looking at the back of the photograph, Thóra saw that the girl was named as Edda Grímsdóttir, so she must be the daughter of the elder brother, Grímur. It was taken in 1922, and the girl looked about a year old. The following pictures were taken at intervals of several years. In one of them, dated 1923, Thóra thought Adalheidur, the younger woman, looked pregnant, but there was no sign of another baby in the photographs that followed – not until she chanced upon one from 1924, taken at a studio and showing the young couple holding a baby, several months old. The child was swaddled in a mass of frills, and on the back of the photograph she was identified as a girl by the name of Gudný.

Another picture of the first girl followed, but an extremely peculiar one. She seemed to be sleeping, wearing a crocheted frilly cap that barely covered her head, and a white frilly dress, but her body was in a very strange position. Neither of Thóra's children had ever slept like that, with their arms crossed across the chest and legs stretched out straight. Thóra removed the photograph to read the back. The girl's name, Edda Grímsdóttir, was written there, then two dates with a cross drawn in front of the latter one. She had died the same year that Bjarni and Adalheidur had been blessed with their little girl. Thóra put it back in the album and sighed heavily. She knew that it had been a custom at that time to take pictures of the dead, but she had never seen such a photograph, let alone held one. She wondered if this was the photograph Jónas meant when he said he had seen one showing the ghost.

Thóra felt she was just beginning to get to know the people from the farm as she flicked through the remaining pages. This imaginary familiarity left her saddened, as she saw how time had taken its toll on the family. There were no photographs of the elder brother after 1925, for example. It was as if he and his wife had moved away or otherwise disappeared from the young couple's lives. Perhaps the loss of their daughter, Edda, made them abandon their farm. Adalheidur also vanished from the photographs after 1927. The last shot of her, in which she was obviously pregnant, was dated 1926. The penmanship also changed that year, becoming rougher, and it did not take a handwriting expert to see that it was male. Thóra felt she could see grief on Bjarni's face from then on. Yet he still smiled sincerely at little Gudný, who judging from the photographs grew and blossomed, beautiful like her mother but also uncannily like her father's side of the family.

The album was not full. The last two snaps of Gudný showed her standing up against the wall of the farmhouse, which was apparently the family's favourite spot for posing for photographs. She was well into her teens, a shapely girl with fair wavy hair. Thóra could well imagine that she would have been considered beautiful; she was easily as attractive as the handful of film stars Thóra could remember from that era. Both photographs were from 1941 and would have been sweet if they had showed Gudný alone, but they didn't; on either side of her was a young man, each standing bolt upright with a sombre expression. It was not the boys' stiff posture that made the photographs look odd, however, but their clothing. They were both wearing plain dark trousers and white shirts with swastika armbands. They wore strange belts with straps at the side, and each rested one hand on a large flagpole beside them. The flag drooped lifelessly down against the pole, but it was obviously a Nazi flag; the pole was topped with the swastika that Thóra had found in the first box. The socket was clearly designed to fit on the top of a flagpole. The young men's names had not been written on the back of the photographs, only Gudný's and the year.

There were no more photographs, only three empty double pages. A photograph had undoubtedly been removed from the first one: the dark space where it had been mounted stood out on the faded page, and the little corner mounts were still stuck in place. Thóra shook the album, hoping the photograph had been slipped in between the pages, but nothing fell out. She put the book down.

Thóra stood up. The light in the basement was dim, and she would be able to examine the photos better in her room. Also, she wanted to ask Jónas which of the two little girls in the album was the 'ghost'. Every step of the wooden staircase creaked as she made her way up and Thóra was glad she wasn't any heavier. On her way back up to the hotel, she took a deep breath, relieved to be free from the smell of rising damp. After savouring the fresh air for a moment, she headed for the lobby.

Through one of the corridor windows she noticed Sóldís, the petite girl who had shown her to her room when she arrived the previous day. She was outside, smoking. Thóra decided to make a detour to discuss in a little more detail the stories that Sóldís had hinted were connected with the farmland or the farmhouse.

'Hi, Sóldís.'

The girl turned round. From her blank expression, Thóra could not tell whether she was pleased or annoyed to see her again. At least she didn't run away. 'What?'

Thóra walked over to the girl. 'Hello again. Do you remember me?'

'Yes, of course. You're a guest here. One of Jónas's friends.'

'Right,' Thóra said, smiling warmly. 'Listen, yesterday you mentioned some old stories about this place that you said you'd tell me later. It would help me a lot if you could fill me in now.'

The girl frowned, avoiding Thóra's eye. 'I've got to get back to work.'

'It would help Jónas out. I'm trying to assist him with something and, strange as it may seem, the local stories about this place might make it easier for me to help him.' Thóra waited.

The girl thought it over, then shrugged nonchalantly. 'OK. I don't mind.'

'Great,' said Thóra. 'Maybe we should go inside?' The weather was still overcast, although the fog had lifted. In fact, it only seemed to have lifted a few metres, because all that could be seen of the nearby mountains was the lower slopes.

The girl gave another shrug. 'OK. Like I said, I don't mind.'

Thóra followed her through the staff entrance to a large kitchen, which presumably served the dining hall. Sóldís sat down at a little table reserved for the staff and gestured to Thóra to take a seat too. Then she reached over for a huge Thermos flask and took two cups from a mismatched collection at the end of the table.

'I was brought up here, see, and my granny told me all sorts of stories from the countryside around here. Trolls and stuff, you know. Most of it was crap, of course, but she said some of it was real,' Sóldís began as she handed Thóra a cup of piping-hot coffee.

Thóra nodded. 'Like what?' She took a little carton of long-life milk and added a dash to her cup.

'Well, like the land here. Granny said there was a curse on it.'

'A curse?' Thóra could barely stop her eyebrows from shooting up.

'In the old days, this lava field was famous for abandoned babies. Local women who couldn't provide for their children used to leave them to die of exposure, here in the lava.' She shuddered. 'Disgusting. You can still hear them, you know? I've even heard them myself.'

Thóra almost choked on her coffee. She leaned closer. 'Are you telling me that you've heard crying babies who were left out here to die hundreds of years ago?' she asked.

Sóldís gave Thóra a scornful look. 'I'm not the only one who's heard it, if that's what you think. Most people here have heard the crying. It's been getting worse recently, actually. No one ever heard it when I first started working here.'

'Why would that be?' wondered Thóra aloud.

'I don't know. Granny told me it comes and goes. She remembers stories about awful crying that was heard here around 1945. One of the farmers came looking for it because he thought it was a real child, and he heard a weak voice crying right beside him but couldn't find a child anywhere. He rushed off home and never came near the farm again. Granny said that the war came to an end soon after and the abandoned children might have sensed that and were letting people know they were happy. Or annoyed. Maybe there's something bad in the offing now. Or something good.'

Talk about covering all bases, thought Thóra. Things were always happening, so obviously there was always *something* in the offing. Regardless of whether the news was good or bad, it could always be used to explain why the dead babies started crying again. It was hardly surprising that the story about the ghost had spread among the staff like wildfire, if it could be used to explain pretty much anything that happened.

'Have you seen one of these abandoned children?' Thóra asked. 'Or has anyone else at the hotel?'

'Christ, no,' Sóldís said. 'Thank God. They're horrible, apparently. I reckon it would drive me nuts, you know?'

'I doubt it,' Thóra said reassuringly. 'This story about babies being left to die in the lava field – does everyone know it?'

'Totally,' Sóldís replied. 'They say no one can raise a child to adulthood here. Everyone around here knows that.' She could see that Thóra was sceptical. 'Look in the cemetery. Read the gravestones. You'll see it's not bullshit.'

Thóra's thoughts turned to the photograph of the little dead girl, Edda Grímsdóttir. 'Let's say the hotel's haunted by the dead children,' she said. 'How do you explain the ghost that Jónas has seen, and apparently other people too? That ghost wasn't a baby.'

'That ghost isn't an abandoned child,' Sóldís said. 'It might be the mother of one of the children, condemned to look for it for ever. Or the ghost of the beggarwoman.'

'The ghost of the beggarwoman?' echoed Thóra, baffled. 'So there are other ghosts apart from the babies?'

'Yes,' said Sóldís. 'Loads of them. But the abandoned children and the ghost of the beggarwoman are the only ones I know about on this particular plot of land. That story happened here too. Before the two farms were built, there was a camp.'

'A camp?' Thóra said.

'Oh, you know, a sort of fishing camp, that kind of thing,' Sóldís replied. 'Lots of migrant workers, you see. Fishermen, mostly.'

'What does that have to do with the curse?'

'Loads,' Sóldís said haughtily. 'Granny told me the

fishermen at the camp here killed a beggarwoman and used her flesh as bait.'

'Bait?' Thóra pulled a face.

'Yeah, bait,' the girl said, delighted at her reaction. 'They fished really well with her and decided to stay out fishing all night instead of going back ashore. When it was dark, the boat capsized. Only one man survived, and apparently he was against the whole plan. He said the boat was overturned from underneath, you know. There was something in the sea that rolled it over, and he claimed it was the ghost of the beggarwoman.'

'OK,' Thóra said curiously. 'So the ghost around here is the woman who was used for bait?'

Sóldís shook her head. 'Not necessarily – it could also be the ghost of one of the fishermen she killed, because their bodies were washed ashore and they haunt this place.' She leaned in towards Thóra conspiratorially. 'And you know what?'

'No. What?' Thóra asked.

'The bodies were washed ashore where the cops have been investigating, where the body was found the other day.' Sóldís sat back up straight.

'How do you know the police have been there?' said Thóra.

Sóldís looked at her, affronted. 'I know everyone around here. My aunt phoned me and told me. Don't you think people notice the cops?'

'Yes, of course they do,' Thóra said. She pondered for a moment. 'But presumably the fishermen were all men. Is there no story about a local ghost that was a child? A young girl?'

Sóldís considered the question, her brow furrowed. 'You mean the ghost that the hotel staff are talking about?'

'That's the one,' Thóra said hopefully. 'What do you reckon about that ghost? Has your grandmother told you anything about it?'

'Well, I asked her and she didn't know anything about it, but I heard from another woman that it might be the daughter of the farmer who lived here before. His name was Bjarni, I think.' Sóldís paused before continuing, 'That woman said it was common knowledge that Bjarni abused his daughter. Incest.'

'Ugh,' said Thóra. She conjured up mental images of the people from the photograph album, in particular Gudný and her father, Bjarni. Nothing like that had crossed her mind.

The girl shrugged. 'They both died, apparently. TB.'

Thóra nodded slowly. 'Well, I never. But what do you think? Do you believe this ghost is the girl from the farm?'

Sóldís stared into Thóra's eyes. 'I've seen the ghost, but I've never seen *her*, so how would I know?'

'You've seen the ghost?' Thóra asked, astonished.

'Sure I have,' came the scornful reply. There was a provocative look in Sóldís's eyes, as if she were daring Thóra to doubt her.

'I see,' Thóra said carefully. 'Where did you see the ghost, may I ask?'

'Outside here. In the fog. I didn't see it in any detail, but it was definitely a girl.'

Thóra nodded. 'It wasn't just one of the kids from around here?' she ventured.

Sóldís laughed sarcastically. 'Around here? Where around

here? It's five kilometres to the nearest kid and he's a boy, see. Why would he drag himself all the way over here to roam around in the fog?'

Thóra had to admit it seemed unlikely. She was wondering what to ask next when her mobile rang.

'Hello, Thóra,' said Matthew's familiar voice. 'Have you decided to tell me where you are, or should I send out a search party? I'm at Keflavík Airport. I've just landed.'

8

'I'm telling you, my stockroom's been broken into,' Stefanía said, piqued, her hands on her hips. She tried not to be annoyed by Vigdís's malicious sniggering from the reception desk. She had enough on her plate. Someone had forced the lock on the little stockroom where she kept her merchandise, and the fact that nothing seemed to be missing didn't make it any less serious.

Stefanía was long accustomed to being shown limited understanding by women. She wasn't sure if it was her good looks or her field of work, sex counselling. More often than not she had the feeling that other women thought she had chosen that particular discipline simply to seduce married men, which was absurd. It wasn't her fault if they made the occasional pass at her.

She scowled. 'It's not funny. The lock's buggered. Take a look if you don't believe me.'

Vigdís raised an eyebrow. 'There's no need to get worked up about it. Why make a song and dance about a burglary in which nothing's been stolen?' She went back to her computer. She hated Stefanía with her 'sex-counselling' nonsense. That woman thought the world revolved round her, and this burglary business was probably just a ploy to get attention. She wasn't likely to succeed this time, given that she had to compete with the discovery of a dead body. Vigdís looked up from the computer screen and glared at Stefanía. 'I don't know what you expect me to do about it, anyway.'

What Stefanía most wanted that bitch Vigdís to do was throw herself into the tank at a piranha farm, but she decided to keep that to herself. 'Do? I don't know. Shouldn't we at least let Jónas know that someone's broken into a locked stockroom? What if it was a junkie looking for dope? He might come back.'

'Dope?' laughed Vigdís. 'Who'd go looking for dope in your little cubbyhole? This happens to be a hotel that specialises in homeopathy and spiritual welfare. You'd have to look a long way to find a less likely place on Snaefellsnes for keeping drugs.'

Stefanía took a deep breath. 'I'm sorry, but hardened drug users might not be too well informed about hotel specialisation. Besides which, it could have been one of the guests. Or one of the staff,' she added with a mean smile.

Vigdís glared at her. 'One of the staff? Are you crazy?'

'I just mentioned it. If it wasn't a junkie, it was presumably an ordinary person. Maybe someone really wanted what I'm selling but was too shy to approach it through the regular channels. Who knows?' Stefanía widened her eyes in affected innocence.

Vigdís was determined not to get drawn into a discussion of stimulatory ointments and sex aids. Stefanía knew that she found the topic uncomfortable and Vigdís did not want to give her the pleasure of seeing her blush. 'So why was nothing stolen?'

Stefanía hesitated. 'Well, I don't know. Of course, I haven't checked every box and every item. They *might* have taken something.' She got no further with her speculations.

'There's too much going on around here to worry about a burglary in which something "might" have been stolen.' Vigdís made sarcastic quotation marks with her fingers.

'Oh?' said Stefanía, curious. 'What's happened?' She was irritated – something always happened when she was away. She went home to the nearby village of Hellnar in the evenings and rarely worked weekends. That may have been one reason why she didn't get on with the other employees, most of whom stayed in small chalets that Jónas had had built next to the hotel.

'A body was found on the beach. Down in the bay, right by the cave.' Vigdís paused dramatically before continuing. 'They think it was Birna, the architect.' Again she paused. 'She was probably murdered.' She glowed smugly as Stefanía turned pale and clutched her chest.

'Are you making this up?' gasped Stefanía.

'Nope, I swear. Dead, probably murdered.' Vigdís turned back to her computer and changed the subject just to annoy her colleague. 'Do you have an empty box to give to the lawyer? She needs a large one to put some stuff in.'

'What? Oh, sure,' Stefanía said distractedly. What on earth had happened? She thought about the counselling she had recently given the poor woman. Had her advice led to the woman's death? Dazed, Stefanía mumbled a farewell and started to hurry away, but she needed to know one more thing. She turned back. 'Was sex anything to do with it? Do you know if she was raped by any chance?'

'Yes, I think she was,' Vigdís replied, although she hadn't

the faintest idea. Something told her this answer would get a reaction.

Stefanía turned and walked off towards her office, blushing furiously. This was all she needed.

Thóra put the heavy cardboard box on the newly made bed in her hotel room. She grimaced at the labelling on its side. When she had collected the box, she had initially thought it was a joke, some kind of candid-camera stunt. The box was labelled in English on all sides with large black letters, 'Vibrating Dildo. Genuine Rubber. New Aloe Vera Action!' For customers with limited English, a drawing of the contents had helpfully been provided. Thóra had blushed to the roots of her hair when she took the box from Vigdís at reception, who said, 'I didn't think this was as bad as the artificial-vagina box.' She smiled sweetly and added, 'The only person with any spare boxes was the sex therapist. Sorry.'

It had taken Thóra most of the morning to go through the remaining items in the basement and gather together the ones that interested her. She was only concerned with old documents, letters and photographs, and left the rest behind: cups, clocks, candlesticks and other ornaments. She put papers that were clearly irrelevant back into the old boxes, but took all the photographs regardless of what they showed, since she couldn't tell what she might find when she took a look at them in a better light.

There weren't many, but one in particular aroused her interest – it was in a beautiful old frame and showed a teenage girl whom Thóra was fairly certain was Gudný Bjarnadóttir from the old farm. The girl was sitting on a hillside with her legs folded under her, smiling prettily into the camera. She was wearing a low-cut white blouse with a large bow at the front. The blouse somehow emphasised that this was a young girl and not a woman, but Thóra was fairly sure the girl had intended it to have the opposite effect. She put the photograph on her bedside table. It was hard to make it balance, because the stand had been damaged in storage. Taking a long look at the picture, Thóra prayed that Sóldís's story about incest on the farm was pure fiction. If not, she was almost certainly looking at the victim.

Thóra's stomach rumbled. A glance at the clock told her that it was well past twelve. She phoned reception and found out that the kitchen was open until half past one. She'd have to be quick. She hastily washed her hands and combed her tangled hair. Being in the basement hadn't made her look her best, but she wasn't about to let dirty clothes stop her from reaching the dining room before it closed. She could always turn up dressed to the nines that evening to make up for being scruffy now.

There was only one other guest in the dining room when Thóra entered. It was the elderly man whom she had taken for an accountant or lawyer at breakfast. He didn't look up or make any attempt to greet her, just stared sadly out through the window, oblivious to the fact that the number of diners had doubled. Where had she seen him before? Thóra chose a table a good distance from him.

She was barely seated when a young man with a professional smile came over and handed her the menu. After thanking him, Thóra ordered a glass of sparkling water to begin with. While the waiter fetched it, she read the lunch menu and chose an omelette with salad. According to the description, the salad was supposed to contain dandelion and sorrel, and she selected it more from curiosity than any other motive. The waiter appeared with her drink at the very moment she put the menu down and he praised her for her choice when she ordered. Thóra suspected he would have done just the same had she ordered raw pork, if it had been available. He did not give an impression of great sincerity.

'Is there any news about the body that was found?' she asked as he filled her glass with water.

Startled by her question, he splashed a little water on the cloth. 'Oh, sorry. I'm so clumsy,' he said as he took a linen napkin from the next table.

'That's OK.' Thóra smiled. 'It's only water.' She waited for him to finish mopping it up. 'So is there any news?'

The waiter wrung the damp napkin between his hands and prevaricated. 'Um, it's all a bit embarrassing. I really don't know what I'm allowed to say. The owner's holding a meeting with us afterwards to outline what we should tell the guests. We don't want to start rumours that could cause you unnecessary stress. People come here to rest.'

'I'm not a regular guest. You can tell me anything. I'm working for Jónas. I'm his lawyer, so I'm not just being nosy.'

The waiter looked dubious. 'Oh. I understand.' He clearly didn't, because he said nothing else.

'So you don't know any more about it? Has the victim been formally identified?'

'No, not officially. Everyone agrees that it's Birna, the architect.' He shrugged. 'But it may turn out to be someone completely different.'

'Did you know her?' asked Thóra.

'Slightly,' replied the waiter. Thóra found his face hard to read. 'She was here a lot, so I couldn't help having dealings with her.'

'You don't sound as though you thought much of her.' Thóra sipped her fizzy drink and felt the dust from the basement washing away down her throat.

The waiter had clearly had enough of this conversation. 'I'd better take your order to the kitchen. The chef sulks if he has to stay later than half past one.' Then he smiled. 'To tell you the truth, I couldn't stand her. She was a total bitch and her being dead doesn't alter that. She's still a bitch.' He walked away.

Thóra watched him until he disappeared inside the kitchen with her order. So not everyone agreed with Jónas that Birna had been a lovely person. If the corpse even *was* Birna.

After lunch, Thóra went back to her room. She had not managed to wheedle any more information out of the waiter, apart from the fact that his name was Jökull. In the end she had been alone in the dining room, because soon after the waiter had taken her order to the kitchen, the elderly man had stood up and left without so much as a glance at her. Thóra had watched him walk past and again had the feeling that there was something familiar about his face, but she couldn't place him. It could have been anyone, a bus driver from her childhood, perhaps, but she still thought that she ought to recognise him.

Thóra looked at the dreaded box and sighed. She was well aware that the most sensible thing to do would be to get started going through its contents, or sneak a look at Birna's diary, but the thought of a quick shower was far too tempting. She could get rid of the dust from the basement and have a lie-down. Siestas were a luxury she could rarely allow herself; there were always chores to do at home, and her own bed was nowhere near as appealing, soft, clean or elegant. She treated herself to both.

Thóra woke with a start. She had set the alarm clock to wake her up after an hour, but it hadn't gone off. She looked around the room, perplexed, until a knock on the door made her realise where she was. She reached for the dressing gown she had put on after her shower and called out hoarsely, 'Who is it?' There was no reply, just another knock. She put on the gown, ran over to the door and opened it enough just to put her head outside. 'Hello?'

'Hello, yourself,' said Matthew. 'Aren't you going to let me in?'

Thóra cursed herself for her lack of make-up and for her damp hair, which she had been sleeping on. She ran her hand over it in a vain attempt to tame the wild mop. 'Well, hello. So you found it.'

Matthew came in, grinning. 'Of course. It wasn't complicated.' He looked all around. 'Nice room.' His eyes came to rest on the box from the sex therapist.

Thóra hadn't thought to push it out of sight. She smiled awkwardly.

'Looks like I came just in the nick of time,' he said.

9

Thóra had never tried anything like the box's former contents, but she was quite convinced that such devices paled in comparison with the real thing, just like all other surrogates. Smiling to herself, she sat up in bed. Her dressing gown lay crumpled on the floor and she stretched out lazily to pick it up. She should do this sort of thing more often, she thought as she wrapped it round herself and looked for her clothes. Although she had been completely uninhibited before, she wanted to be wearing something when Matthew came back. He had popped out to his hired car to fetch his luggage and throw it into the room he had booked. Thóra couldn't see what use he had for a room of his own, but she appreciated the courtesy he had shown her by not assuming that he could jump straight into bed with her – even though he had. She smiled again at how terribly pleased she was to see him, glad that he had come in spite of her objections. The problem was, their relationship was already doomed. He was a foreigner and unlikely to thrive in Iceland. When he arrived, she had awkwardly tried to find a topic of conversation and asked him what he thought of the Eurovision Song Contest winner. He had given her a blank look and asked if she was joking. Anyone who was not interested in Eurovision would hardly last a week in Iceland. She dressed hurriedly.

Matthew reappeared just as she was putting on her second sock. 'Damn,' he said, disappointed. 'I'd forgotten that you're the world champion in speed-dressing.' He smirked at her. 'Of course, the upside is that you're pretty quick at undressing too.'

'Very funny,' said Thóra. 'What do you think of the hotel?'

Matthew took a look around and shrugged. 'Great. A bit off the beaten track. But what on earth are you doing here?' He added quickly, 'Not that I'm complaining, not at all.'

'I'm working for the owner. He's thinking of suing the people who sold him the property.'

'Ah. Was he ripped off?' Matthew asked. He walked over to the window and pulled open the curtain to admire the view. 'Lovely,' he said, and turned back to Thóra.

'Oh, it's all quite silly, really. He claims this place is haunted and the previous owners must have known.'

'Haunted, yes.' Matthew's expression was the one she expected to see on the judge's face, if the case ever went that far. 'You don't say.'

'The business here is vulnerable to that kind of thing, so it's not quite as absurd as you might think.' Thóra smiled at him. 'It's a New Age hotel. They focus on things such as healing, clairvoyance, organic food, crystals, magnetic fields, aura readings and all that. Most of the staff are clairvoyant, or worse, so they're not very fond of ghosts.'

'Indeed,' said Matthew, pulling a face. 'So, all perfectly normal.'

'God, no,' Thóra hurried to say. 'But in fact it's not that unusual in a place like this, which has long been considered a centre for belief in the supernatural, so to speak. Legend has it that the glacier is inhabited by a man named Bárdur who went inside it in a bout of depression after his daughter drifted away to Greenland on an iceberg. He's considered to be the guardian spirit of the area, and the glacier's supposed to have supernatural powers. I don't know whether the powers belong to this Bárdur or the glacier itself.'

'Supernatural powers from a glacier?' Matthew's disbelief was written all over his face. 'It's just a mountain with snow on it that never melts, correct me if I'm wrong.'

'Ha, ha,' Thóra said. 'I'm just telling you the background, not my opinion. Faith in the power of the glacier goes way beyond Iceland – people flocked here from all over the world to welcome aliens from outer space just before the turn of the century.'

'And of course that wasn't a wild goose chase, was it?'

Thóra shrugged. 'Opinions differ. The spokesman for the group said they had come, but just in spirit. No spaceship or anything. Some kind of mental transportation.'

'Mental being the operative word, I suppose?' grinned Matthew.

Thóra returned his smile. 'Could well be. But it is an incredibly powerful mountain.'

'And where does the body fit into the picture?'

'Oh, that. The body's nothing to do with this spiritual stuff, actually. I don't think so, anyway. The owner doesn't agree entirely. He thinks the ghost's involved somehow. He's quite an unusual character.'

'You don't say,' replied Matthew, frowning. 'Was the body found here at the hotel?'

Thóra gave Matthew a brief account of where the body had been found, telling him that it was a woman who had been working for Jónas and she was thought to have been murdered.

'And is there a suspect?'

'Not to my knowledge,' Thóra replied. 'I doubt whether the police have even formed an opinion yet. The case is still at the most preliminary stage.'

'I hope for your sake that it's not this Jónas,' said Matthew.

'No, it's definitely not him,' Thóra said airily, then added cautiously, 'As it happens, I do have something that might shed light on the matter.'

'You've got something? What kind of something?' asked Matthew. His eyes were bright with curiosity.

'Well, I have the diary of the woman who is very likely the murder victim. A sort of notebook, really,' Thóra replied, blushing but affecting nonchalance.

'What?' Matthew exclaimed. 'Did you know this woman?'

'Never met her.'

'But you have her diary? How did that come about?'

'I came across it,' she said, then added more truthfully, 'I stole it, really. Accidentally.'

Matthew shook his head. 'Accidentally, right.' He clasped his hands in prayer and looked up to heaven. 'Dear God, don't let her have killed the architect for the diary. Even accidentally.'

Jónas stood in the lobby watching three plain-clothes detectives prepare to examine Birna's car. They had driven up in a customised van and parked it to one side. There, they had jumped out and, without announcing themselves to anyone at the hotel, begun photographing the little sports car and the ground around it. Vigdís had phoned Jónas from reception to let him know as soon as she noticed the van, and he had run down to the lobby.

'What are they doing, anyway?' Vigdís asked.

Jónas jumped. He had been so preoccupied with watching the detectives at work that he hadn't noticed Vigdís. Clutching his heart, he looked at her. 'Christ, you scared me.' Then he went back to watching what was going on outside. 'They're examining Birna's car, as far as I can see. God knows why.'

Vigdís squinted for a better look. 'Do they think she was murdered in the car, or what?'

Jónas shook his head. 'Hardly. The car hasn't been moved for days. I'm sure I told them that.'

'What difference does that make?' Vigdís asked. 'I mean, she could still have been killed in the car, right there in the car park.'

Jónas spun round to face her. 'That's fucking nonsense. For a start, we don't know whether it *was* murder yet, let alone where it might have happened.'

Vigdís shrugged. 'Who do you think would drown on the beach here? It's this deep.' She held her thumb and index finger a centimetre apart. 'She must have been murdered.'

Jónas was about to tell Vigdís not to exaggerate when he saw one of the detectives take his mobile out of his pocket. The distant ringing could be heard from where they were standing. The detective answered the call and they watched him talking. Suddenly he looked up in the direction of the lobby. His gaze fixed on Jónas, who felt his stomach sink. The officer ended the call without taking his eyes off the hotelier, and walked over towards the entrance.

'Wow,' Vigdís whispered to Jónas. 'Did you see that? He's definitely coming to talk to you.'

Thóra rushed to Jónas's office. He had phoned and asked her to come, without any explanation except that the police were making allegations against him that he knew nothing about. She had a weird feeling that Matthew's remarks about Jónas had been a premonition, and for an instant the thought crossed her mind that the glacier might have strange powers after all.

'Excuse me,' she said after knocking on Jónas's office door and opening it. Jónas was sitting behind his desk, facing someone, his face bright red. The other man had his back to her. He looked round when she said brightly, 'Everything all right in here?'

'No, it's certainly not all right,' the hotel owner snapped, standing up to pull up a third chair.

The police officer was middle-aged and very tall. He lifted himself five centimetres out of his seat and extended his hand to Thóra. That was enough for her to realise that he was also extremely wide and well muscled. 'Hello. I'm Thórólfur Kjartansson, detective.'

'Hello. Thóra Gudmundsdóttir, lawyer.' They shook hands. 'What's the problem?' she asked, directing her words at Jónas.

'They seem to think that I'm somehow involved in that woman's death,' Jónas snarled. He gestured at the man facing him and added, 'He gets to take away my computer and printer, and he says he has a warrant to take my mobile phone.' In his fury, Jónas was suddenly lost for words and made do with looking daggers at Thórólfur.

'I see,' Thóra said calmly. 'May I see the warrant? I'm Jónas's lawyer and he's asked for my legal counsel.'

Thórólfur silently handed her a printout. Skimming it, Thóra saw that it was a warrant issued by the West Iceland District Court to seize Jónas Júlíusson's mobile telephone, citing as grounds that it was in the interest of the investigation into the murder of Birna Halldórsdóttir. Thóra's heart skipped a beat. Here it was in black and white.

'May I enquire why the telephone is needed?' she asked levelly.

'We think the phone may contain information that could be of use to us,' Thórólfur answered, equally impassive.

'Various kinds of information are stored on mobile phones,' Thóra said, stalling as she tried to recall the model that Jónas owned. Some information could be obtained from the telephone company, so they were hardly trying to establish whom Jónas had called. They must have been after his calendar or photographs, if such features were included. What made the warrant unusual was that the police were interested only in the telephone. They were not insisting on a regular search of premises, unless such a request had been turned down. 'Actually, it says here that you may take the phone, but there's no mention of the SIM card. Can he keep that?' Thóra asked, vainly hoping that whatever they wanted was stored on the card and not in the phone itself.

Thórólfur snatched the warrant out of Thóra's hands. 'It says mobile telephone number –' he scanned the page and when he had found it he turned it round proudly for Thóra to see, stabbing at the number with his finger '– 667 6767. See, that's Jónas's number. It even states that he is the registered user. If you give me the phone without the card, you're not handing over what the warrant requires.' Smugly, he leaned back in his seat and addressed Jónas. 'You have to hand the phone over to me.'

Thóra looked at Jónas. 'Are you opposed to giving them the phone?'

Jónas bristled indignantly. 'Of course I am! What am I supposed to do without a phone? Admittedly, the reception out here isn't up to much, but I don't care. It's my phone.'

'I advise you to advise your client to hand over what the warrant demands. Doing otherwise would be extremely unwise.' Thórólfur could not conceal his irritation at the delay.

'I didn't kill Birna!' Jónas slammed his fist down on the desk. 'How could you think I did?'

'No one's claiming that. Least of all me,' Thórólfur replied, more calmly than before. 'However, your behaviour does raise certain questions.'

'What are you insinuating?' Jónas bellowed. He hit the desk again, this time so hard that a pen-stand and other loose objects juddered on its surface. 'I had nothing to do with this murder, and I insist on taking a lie-detector test to prove it, but you shan't have my phone.'

Thóra leaned over to Jónas and gently gripped his hand. 'Jónas, lie detectors aren't used in Iceland. They're inadmissible as evidence in this country. I advise you to hand over the telephone. Especially if you haven't done anything wrong.'

'That's out of the question,' said Jónas firmly. He crossed his arms over his chest and leaned back in his chair as if to emphasise his determination. Then he inclined forward and whispered into Thóra's ear, 'They mustn't take the phone under any circumstances. Believe me, that would be a seriously bad idea.' He leaned back away from her and smiled at the police officer.

'OK, I understand. Give me your phone.' She stared him in the eye. 'Trust me.'

Jónas looked at her suspiciously. 'No. You'll give it to the police.'

'Jónas. Trust me, I said.' Thóra held out her open hand.

Jónas just stared dubiously at her. After a moment's thought he took his mobile out of the pocket of the jacket hung over his chair. He handed the phone to Thóra, but did not let go. 'I mean it; you mustn't let him have the phone.'

Thóra nodded. 'I know. You can let go.' She heaved a sigh when he finally released his grip. She was relieved to see that it was not a camera phone.

'Please hand the phone over to me,' Thórólfur said, holding out the sheet of paper to affirm his right.

'One moment,' Thóra said, and put her own mobile on the table. She opened the back and removed the SIM card. Then she did the same to Jónas's mobile and swapped the cards. 'Here you are. One mobile phone, number 667 6767, registered user Jónas Júlíusson.' She handed her mobile to the police officer. 'Completely in accordance with the warrant, if I have not misunderstood the wording.' She smiled at Thórólfur.

* * *

'Brilliant, brilliant,' Jónas was enthusing as they burst into Thóra's room. They had gone straight there with the mobile phone, after Thórólfur had made a call to confirm that Jónas was considered to have fulfilled the conditions of the warrant. However, a new and more precisely worded warrant was pending, so Thóra didn't have long to find out what it was that Jónas didn't want the police to see.

'Matthew – Jónas. Jónas – Matthew.' A brief introduction would have to do, since Jónas was short of time. Matthew simply nodded. Although clearly startled by the intrusion, he asked no questions. She turned to Jónas. 'Why on earth didn't you just let the man have the phone?'

'There are numbers in it that I definitely don't want him to see. And texts too.' Jónas lowered his voice. 'I smoke the odd joint. There are two guys I score from and their numbers are on my phone. There are probably texts that I've sent when they don't answer their phones. If you read them, the exact nature of our business is pretty obvious.'

Thóra nodded, astonished at Jónas's stupidity, although actually she thought this was an excellent indication of his innocence in Birna's murder. Judging from the way he bought drugs, he would have left a note on the body with his name on.

She handed him the phone. 'I can't advise you to do anything illegal, but here's the phone. I should remind you that time is running out. My PIN number is 4036.'

Jónas switched on the mobile and entered the PIN. He went straight into his address book and erased two names, which Thóra studiously avoided seeing. Then he went to the message menu and erased several that he had received. As he scrolled through the sent messages, he suddenly said,

'What?' and held the mobile away to focus better on the screen. 'What the fuck is this?'

Thóra leaned over and grabbed for the phone. 'What? What have you found?'

Jónas let her take it. 'That's not right.' Something had clearly shocked him deeply.

Thóra read the header of the top message, which was presumably the most recent. 'Meet me @ cave . . .' This filled the screen line, so she opened the message. She groaned when she read it in its entirety. 'Meet me @ cave @ 9 2nite need 2 discuss ur idea Jónas.' The message had been sent the previous Thursday at twenty-five past seven, the evening before the body was found.

'Please tell me that's not Birna's number,' Thóra said anxiously, handing the phone back to Jónas.

He looked at the mobile, then up at Thóra, and slowly nodded his head.

10

'Everything all right?' Matthew asked in English, looking from Thóra to Jónas, who was still gawping at the mobile phone.

Thóra and Jónas had taken a while to regain their powers of speech. Although Matthew had understood almost nothing of what passed between them, he could tell something was amiss.

Jónas, still standing open-mouthed and speechless, turned to him. 'Who is this, anyway?' he asked, clearly relieved to have something else to think about.

'This is Matthew, my friend from Germany,' Thóra replied. 'He was a detective, but now he handles security for a bank. I met him on another case. You can trust him – this won't go any further.'

'If you say so,' Jónas retorted, looking unconvinced. 'I can't understand this at all. I didn't send that text message, I swear.'

Thóra turned the phone over in her hands thoughtfully. 'Someone did, Jónas, and you're undeniably the most likely candidate.' She turned to Matthew and quickly translated. Jónas waited in fretful silence. When Thóra had finished, he chipped in.

'How many times do I have to tell you? I did not send

that message. End of story.' He'd switched to English, clearly hoping to enlist Matthew's support.

'Did you let the phone out of your sight that evening?' Matthew asked. 'If you didn't send the message, someone presumably used your mobile, either to cast suspicion on you or to trick this Birna woman down to the beach. It might be someone she wouldn't have wanted to meet otherwise.'

'In either case we're dealing with a very cold-blooded murderer, someone who intended to murder Birna and had a plan,' Thóra said. 'I must say that's unusual for Iceland. Murders here are generally committed in the kitchen, when two drunks start fighting and one of them grabs a carving knife. I can't imagine what Birna must have got herself into for this to happen.'

Thóra and Matthew both turned to Jónas. 'It's vital that you remember where you were when the text message was sent,' she said. 'Are you in the habit of leaving your mobile lying around?'

'That's the point,' said Jónas. 'The mobile connection here is very erratic, so there's no point in lugging it around with me.'

'But where were you? Do you remember?' Matthew asked.

Jónas scratched his head. 'I don't recall right now. If I had some peace and quiet, I might remember. I can't force myself; my mind is a total blank. I'm not used to having to come up with alibis – it doesn't usually matter where I was.'

'Hash screws up your short-term memory, Jónas,' Thóra

said. 'You ought to be able to remember where you were: it's only two days ago. Wasn't that the evening of the seance? I saw it advertised in reception.'

Jónas tapped his forehead. 'Yes, yes. Of course. Thursday night.' He still looked blank. 'But I can't quite remember what I was doing. I wasn't at the seance, that's for certain.'

'Great,' Thóra said. 'But keep trying to remember. It's important.' She took the mobile out of his hands and browsed through the messages once more. 'One thing strikes me as odd,' she mused after reading them all again. 'Why should Birna obey the message? If I received a message from you telling me to meet you by a cave, I'd call you back to ask why.'

'She wouldn't have wondered about that. She'd suggested I build a little restaurant on the beach by that cave, but I wasn't terribly excited at the prospect. She would have rushed straight there if she thought I'd changed my mind,' said Jónas.

'And was this common knowledge?' Matthew asked.

'More or less,' Jónas replied. 'She talked a lot, Birna did. Discretion wasn't exactly her middle name.'

Thóra stared at Jónas, deep in thought. 'Tell me one thing. Since you didn't kill her, who could have done it? You described her as a wonderful person, someone nobody disliked. I can't imagine many people would have a motive for killing a fairly run-of-the-mill architect.'

Jónas looked from her to Matthew. 'Ahem. Maybe I didn't quite tell the whole truth. She was actually a total cow. None of my staff could stand her. She talked down to them, took the piss out of them for the hotel's philosophy . . . So there's a long list of people who hated her. But

I don't know how many would have gone so far as to kill her. Who would? It's crazy.'

'I hope for your sake that you're overlooking a very obvious lead,' said Matthew, 'otherwise the police will make you prime suspect.'

'Go off and try to remember where you were on Thursday evening,' Thóra said. 'In the meantime Matthew and I will try to find out some more about Birna. Be prepared to have to hand over your mobile. Don't resist. They've probably seen the message on Birna's mobile and just want yours to confirm it. Under no circumstances delete it. That would just look even more suspicious.'

'Oh. Would it?' said Jónas glumly.

'And give me back my SIM card. There's no need for the police to get hold of that.'

'Somehow I'm convinced the murder is connected with this house or the area,' said Thóra, plucking a blade of grass absent-mindedly.

'What makes you think that?' Matthew asked, sipping his coffee. They were sitting in loungers on the lawn behind the hotel, enjoying the view across Faxaflói Bay. 'The motive is much more likely to be in the present than the past: love, money, madness. The murderer could even have been a complete stranger; maybe he saw a woman on her own and lost control of himself.'

Thóra chewed on the stalk. 'The text message suggests otherwise.' Twirling the piece of grass between her teeth, she added, 'I just have a feeling that it's connected with the hotel in some way. There's something about this building. And her diary too. It doesn't contain a word about love or money. It gives the impression Birna was a workaholic.'

'Couldn't it be just her work diary? Maybe she kept another one about her private life.' Matthew watched the blade of grass flicking up and down in the corner of Thóra's mouth. 'I didn't know Icelandic women chewed the cud.' He grimaced. 'Does that taste good?'

'Try it. It focuses the mind,' Thóra said, plucking another piece. She handed it to him and smiled when he pulled a face but forced himself to try. 'There's bound to be something in that diary to help us discover the murderer.' She watched Matthew chewing the grass. 'Don't you like it? You just need a pair of rubber boots and you'll make the perfect Icelandic farmer.'

'Rubber belongs in tyres, elastic bands and tennis balls, not footwear.' Matthew removed the blade of grass from his mouth. 'Shouldn't we take a look at the diary?'

Thóra sat up in her sunlounger. 'Maybe we should do one thing. The diary contained a plan of the other farm on this land. It included all kinds of remarks that we might be able to puzzle out if we go there.'

Matthew sat up as well. 'It's up to you. I'll follow and play bodyguard.' He winked at her. 'I have the feeling that this investigation will lead you into all kinds of dubious territory. You've already burgled a dead woman, stolen her belongings and hindered the course of justice by allowing Jónas to erase suspicious information from his mobile. I can't wait to see where this ends.'

'The name Kristín is written here, followed by a question mark. Maybe we should start there.' Thóra pointed at the pages showing the plan of the farmhouse. They were standing in a room leading from the hallway of the old farmhouse and faced the choice of going upstairs or inspecting the ground floor, which according to the drawing ought to consist of two living rooms, a kitchen, storeroom, toilet and study.

'Isn't that upstairs? Shouldn't we check down here first?' Matthew said, peering through a doorway to his left.

'Sure,' Thóra said, slamming the diary shut. She had given up trying not to leave her fingerprints on it, as she didn't intend to return it unless she was forced to. 'Ugh, what a stink.' A strange smell that Thóra couldn't place permeated the house. It was a mixture of rising damp, dry dust and mothballs. One thing was certain – the place had not been aired properly for decades. 'Yuck,' she said, putting her hand over her nose and mouth.

Matthew took a deep breath. 'You should try and get used to it as quickly as possible. You stop noticing it after a while.' Bold words, but he pulled a face as soon as he had spoken them. 'Oof, can't we open a window in here?'

They entered the room on the left, which according to Birna's plan was a study. The door handle was antique, made of thick wood, but so short that it needed a good tug to open. The door seemed to be warped, and Thóra was struck by how much thicker modern doors were. She went in behind Matthew and they looked around in silence.

'Not much to see here,' he muttered after they had scanned the empty bookshelves along the walls and opened the drawers of a large desk beneath the dirty window. The drawers turned out to be as empty as the shelves, apart from one ancient pencil. It had been sharpened with a knife, and there was no rubber on the end.

'Look at this, though,' said Thóra. 'It looks like there were books on these shelves not that long ago.' She pointed to the dust. It was thick at the edges but thinner towards the back of the shelves, the difference barely perceptible.

Matthew went over to examine them. 'I agree. Do you suppose Birna took the books? Maybe they were valuable.'

Thóra shrugged. 'I doubt it. She didn't mention any books in her notes, although I guess she wouldn't have if she planned to steal them. The previous owners must have taken them. Jónas said they told him they'd remove all the contents.'

They went farther inside the house, where they found two adjoining living rooms with old-fashioned furniture: a tatty three-piece suite that would have been stylish in its day, an imposing sideboard and a mahogany dining set with a faded embroidered cloth on the table. There were small side tables with no ornaments. Two paintings hung on the walls, one of a ship and the other showing Snaefellsnes glacier. Both were too filthy to read the artist's name. The sideboard was empty, as was the cabinet.

'I dare you to throw yourself on to the sofa,' said Matthew, pointing at the dusty upholstery. The vague outline of a flower pattern was visible through the dirt. 'I really want to see the cloud it would send up.'

'No, thanks,' Thóra said. 'You do it. I'll give you a hundred krónur.'

Matthew stroked her arm. 'I could think of a better reward than hard cash.'

Thóra smiled. 'We could come to some arrangement.' Then she looked back at the sofa and wrinkled her nose.

'But I think you should give it a miss; I'm not sure the dust would settle before evening and we might not find our way back out. Come on, let's check the kitchen.'

The kitchen was not as spartan as the other rooms, but it was just as antiquated, with modest oiled-wood cupboards and a small, shallow sink. Compared with a modern kitchen, the work surface was not large, but there was much more floor space than Thóra was accustomed to. Wooden spoons and a steel fish slice hung from hooks on the wall, and a tin coffeepot stood on the stove.

'Weird that they left so much personal stuff,' Thóra said, looking around.

Matthew opened one of the kitchen cupboards and found an assortment of cups and glasses. 'Isn't it one of those boring chores, though? Always getting put off until later, and then it never gets done. Maybe the householders died and didn't have any use for it, and the heirs must have already had enough coffeepots and furniture, so couldn't be bothered to—' He stopped short and pointed at a cardboard box on one of the kitchen chairs. 'Look, what's that?'

The box was full of items wrapped in newspaper. Beside it lay a pile of magazines. Thóra picked one up to see the date. 'It's from this May. The previous owners have been here packing up quite recently. And what's this?' she continued, pointing at a Thermos flask that had been obscured by the box. 'This isn't old.' She lifted the flask and shook it. Liquid splashed around inside and Thóra unscrewed the lid. She took a cautious sniff. 'Coffee,' she said. 'This must have been left by Elín and Börkur, or by whoever they sent to remove all this stuff.' She put the flask down again.

'Who are these former owners, Elín and Börkur? Did they live here?' asked Matthew.

'They're the brother and sister who inherited the land. Middle-aged. Whether they lived here I don't know, but I doubt it, considering how old all this stuff is.' Thóra looked around the kitchen. 'They were fifty at most. This stuff is much older, so they couldn't have been brought up here.'

'But why suddenly clear the place now?' wondered Matthew. 'The property must have been sold several years ago. Surely the new part of the hotel wasn't built in a couple of months.'

'No, you're right. I suppose they were spurred on by Jónas's plan to build an annexe to this farmhouse, although it fell through later.' Thóra opened the kitchen drawers one after another and peered inside. Nothing in them caught her eye.

They finished inspecting the lower floor without finding anything else. The storeroom contained items that had obviously spent decades on the shelves, along with a few new cardboard boxes. They opened a couple of the boxes and assumed that the others also contained ornaments that had been cleared from the living rooms and the dusty old books from the shelves. Thóra left Matthew to check the downstairs toilet, and his expression when he returned suggested that she hadn't missed much.

'Let's go up,' he said, his face pale as he headed for the stairs.

First they peeked through a door leading down to the basement, but because there was no light inside, Thóra decided it was not imperative for them to go down there and they went up instead. On the landing they found five doors, all closed. The first one Matthew tried turned out to be locked. Gripping the handle of the next, he suddenly stopped. 'Take a quick look at the drawing and tell me which one is the bathroom.'

After checking Birna's diary, Thóra proposed they examine the room marked, 'Kristín?' 'I think that interested Birna most,' Thóra said, pointing out the door.

'I'll never forgive you if you're playing a trick on me and this is another bathroom,' he said before he opened it.

'You'll see,' Thóra said, and pushed open the door the moment he turned the handle.

They walked into a child's bedroom, presumably a little girl's. At the head of a white-painted bed sat a scruffy teddy bear with one eye missing. It was covered in light brown fur, apart from the chest, which was made from grey material. Its limbs were attached by black steel buttons at the shoulders and hips, and Thóra was moved to see how the faded red ribbon round its neck had yielded to gravity and now dangled down to the middle of its chest. A tatty doll sat beside the teddy bear, its painted eyes staring at the wall opposite the bed.

'There's something really weird about this,' said Thóra, disturbed.

'Yes,' answered Matthew. 'Someone clearly left in a hurry. Look.' He went up to a shelf where a few dusty books were arranged. Beneath the shelf was a white-painted desk and a sheet of paper with a half-finished drawing on it. Crayons were spread across the desk. He picked up the drawing to examine it more closely. The corners were curled, and a layer of grey dust covered the surface. He blew on it, sending up a cloud that he batted away. Then he handed the drawing to Thóra. 'The child didn't even have time to finish her drawing.'

Thóra scrutinised the picture. It would have been by a child only slightly older than her daughter, Sóley, who was six. It showed a burning house, with thick flames climbing skywards through the roof. Roughly half the picture had been coloured in.

'An odd subject,' Thóra said, putting it down. 'Do you suppose it's a drawing of this house?'

Matthew shook his head. 'No, I don't think so. Although it's a child's drawing, it clearly only has one floor.' He frowned. 'The door's unusually large as well.'

Thóra pointed to the window. 'Are those eyes?' She stooped for a better view. 'I'll be damned. The kid's drawn someone inside the house. Look, there's an open mouth but no nose.'

Matthew bent down. 'Charming subject for a picture. Maybe the child was a bit strange.'

'Or had seen something disturbing,' Thóra said, turning away from the desk. 'I think we should find out about the family who lived here and why they moved away. I know the man who lived here was called Grímur, and I think he had only one daughter, who was so young when she died that she couldn't have drawn this picture. Another family may have lived here after them.' She went over to a small door set into the wall. Opening it carefully, she saw that it was a wardrobe. There were several hangers on the rail. Two still had clothes hanging from them, a small sweater and a thin cotton shift dress. Both were too large to belong to Edda, who had died in her fourth year, according to the album in the hotel basement.

'What's behind there?' Matthew asked, pointing inside the wardrobe.

Thóra stuck her head inside and noticed that at the back of the wardrobe there was a frame around a rectangular board, not quite flush with the wall surrounding it. She pressed the board and it fell inwards. 'Oh, look!' she exclaimed. 'It's a little door on hinges and there are some stairs leading up.'

They took turns peering into the dark hole and Matthew took out his car key. There was a tiny light on it that he could use as a torch. He illuminated the stairs. 'Look,' he said, gesturing towards one of the steps that he had lit up, 'a footprint in the dust. Someone's been up here.'

'Birna. It's bound to have been Birna,' Thóra said firmly. 'She recorded the condition of the beams in her diary and wanted to see the state of the rafters. This must lead up to an attic. Shall we go up?'

Matthew looked amused. 'Sure, just wait here while I go and fetch a knife. I just need to chop off my arm, and maybe the shoulder for good measure.' He pointed to the hole. 'There's no way I could get through there.'

'Give me your key, then,' Thóra said. She put it in her mouth while she clambered into the wardrobe and squeezed from there through the narrow hole. Before heading up the steps, she turned to Matthew, grinning. 'See you. I'll kill you if I trip over a rat.' She went up the first step. Then a thought occurred to her and she leaned back through the hole. 'Or a mouse. I'll also kill you if there's a mouse.'

The attic was completely empty. When Thóra aimed the weak beam of the torch along the floor, she could see Birna had been walking around up there. She was apprehensive about stepping on to the floor in case it wouldn't take her weight; Birna was much smaller than her, judging by the clothes Thóra had seen in her room. Thóra would have preferred to examine the attic from the steps where she was standing, but when the light caught something glittering by one of the wooden posts supporting the beams, she couldn't resist temptation. She inched her way cautiously out on to the floor. It creaked and groaned with each step she took, and she half expected to plunge through on to Matthew in the room below. Or, far worse, into the bathroom. She aimed the tiny torch farther across the attic and saw that Birna – or whoever's footprints they were – had also been there. When she finally reached the post, she breathed a sigh of relief. She bent down and brought the light closer to the object she'd seen.

Gold. Or gold-plated, anyway. With a smile, Thóra picked up a winged brooch. Thóra squinted at it in the dim light – it looked like it might be a pilot's badge. She put it back and picked up a cracked china cup. Inside were a silver spoon that had turned black, two white milk teeth and a crucifix necklace. A few curling photos of film stars lay in a neat pile nearby. Thóra began to straighten up but stopped dead halfway. She shone the light on to the vertical beam and leaned right into it. An inscription had been scratched into the wood. She twisted round to read it.

'Matthew!' she called out. 'Kristín's name is here!'

'What?' she heard him reply.

She bent down again to reread the inscription and memorise it for Matthew, since he obviously couldn't hear her properly. It said, 'dad killed kristín. i hate dad.'

11

'Yes, they finally decided to remove that stuff, like I said,' said Jónas, leaning back in his chair. They were relaxing by the fire in an alcove beside the bar, where old pictures adorned the walls. Out of courtesy to Matthew they were speaking in English, and the hotelier's almost accent-free pronunciation reminded Thóra that he had made his money abroad. 'I asked Birna to inform them that work on the annexe was pending, so they should take anything they wanted before construction began. In the end the plans for the annexe fell through, but they started clearing it all the same. I have no idea what progress they've made. At least, no one has notified us that they've finished.'

Matthew took a sip of his beer. 'Have they ever stayed here?'

'No, they've never asked for a room, but they've been here several times and dined in the restaurant.'

'Have they both been here to clear the farmhouse, or just Elín?'

'I have no idea,' Jónas replied. 'I remember quite a few of them coming once, the brother and his wife, the sister and two kids, his son and her daughter. I don't know whether they were just visiting for the day or if they stayed somewhere in the area. Vigdís told me the young girl had come to reception once or twice to ask us for cardboard boxes. They still own some land out here on the peninsula, I seem to recall, so they might have stayed there. I think they also own a house in Stykkishólmur or Ólafsvík, which they use as a summer house. Neither place is far away.'

'Could any of them have had anything against Birna?' Thóra asked.

'Not as far as I know,' Jónas said. 'I know that she talked to the brother, but I believe it was all on very friendly terms. She was looking for local information from back when the farms were inhabited. I think she was hoping he had old maps or something.'

'And did she find any?' asked Thóra.

'No, I don't think so,' Jónas replied. 'I seem to recall that he didn't have anything like that, or possibly he gave her something that turned out to be of no use. I know he let her look through the old stuff in the basement at Kirkjustétt, and on the other side at Kreppa.'

'Do you remember Birna ever mentioning the name Kristín?' Thóra asked. 'Did she ask them about her?'

Jónas shook his head. 'I don't think so. Who's this Kristín?'

'No idea,' Thóra replied. 'I'm sure she has nothing to do with this. We found her name in—' Thóra just managed to stop herself before she mentioned Birna's diary '– carved on a beam at the farmhouse. Maybe it's just the name of a pet – a cat, a lamb even. We think it was written by a child.'

'Kristín's quite a strange name for a cat,' Jónas said. 'But I don't remember Birna ever mentioning any Kristín, human or animal.'

They fell silent for a while. Thóra sipped the white wine Jónas had ordered for her, and contemplated their surroundings. The snug was cosy, with old-fashioned décor despite being in the modern annexe.

'Are they local?' Thóra asked, pointing to the old photographs on the walls.

'No, I bought them at an antique shop. I have no idea who those people are. It was Birna's idea.' Jónas looked around. 'Quite a good one, I think.'

Matthew and Thóra nodded in agreement. 'Maybe you should ask the family for permission to use some of the photos in the boxes down in the basement?' suggested Thóra. 'There are several albums and a few in frames, and I think they show the former inhabitants. They might look quite charming here. I took most of them up to my room to take a better look at them, so I can show you if you like.'

Jónas shuddered. 'No, thank you, but thanks for the offer. The less I know about them, the better.'

'Which photograph was it, exactly, the one you recognised the ghost from?' Thóra asked. 'I've been through them and there are a number of candidates.'

'It was a framed photo of a young girl,' replied Jónas. 'Blonde. The spitting image of the creature that appeared in my room.'

'So it wasn't a child?' asked Thóra. 'I was under the impression it was a child.' The only framed picture that Thóra had come across was of Gudný, the one she had put on her bedside table. Gudný was not a child in the photo, but well into her teens.

'Child or not,' Jónas said, 'a young girl, much younger than me – a child in my eyes.'

'And you're positive that this happened?' interrupted Matthew. His expression spoke volumes. 'You didn't dream it?'

'No,' snapped Jónas. 'That's out of the question. I was tired, which explains a lot. When you're in that state, the mind's defences are down and you're more receptive to otherworldly phenomena. It happened, I promise you.'

'OK, then,' Thóra said briskly. 'Let's leave that for the time being. How are you getting on with remembering where you were on Thursday evening?'

'Oh, that,' said Jónas. 'Not so badly. I remember I was here when the seance was about to begin, then decided not to go to it. I was afraid of what might come out of it.'

'Afraid?' exclaimed Matthew. 'Afraid of what?'

'Of what might be revealed. This place is turning out to be full of evil, and I don't feel the need to have that confirmed by departed souls,' Jónas explained, as if it were a normal thing to say. 'So I decided to go for a walk and regenerate my energy centres. There was a low fog, which is always conducive to that.'

Thóra spoke quickly, before Matthew had time to ask him about energy centres. 'Did you meet anyone on your walk?'

'No,' replied Jónas. 'No one. The weather was foul and it's low season, so there wasn't a soul about apart from me.'

'You're forgetting Birna,' said Thóra. 'And the murderer. They must have been out at the same time.' She looked imploringly at Jónas. 'Please tell me you didn't go down to the bay where Birna's body was found.'

'No, I didn't go there,' he said. 'I only walked part of the way. I was pretty wound up; I was just roaming around, really. I'd called in a local guy to mend the drain under the drive, and that very day he'd dug up the road, then just gone home without finishing the job. The guests at the seance had to leave their cars by the main road and walk the rest. Two kilometres. I'm sure a lot of people turned back, and you can only imagine how irritated the other hotel guests were at discovering their cars were blocked in.'

'When was it mended?' asked Matthew.

'First thing the next morning,' Jónas said, still grumpy at the memory of the road-digger. 'He didn't dare do otherwise after I gave him a piece of my mind.'

'So no cars would have been able to go between the hotel and the bay, where Birna was probably murdered that evening?' Thóra asked.

'No, that would have been impossible,' Jónas said. 'There was a huge hole in the road.'

'Did you have your mobile phone when you went for the walk?' asked Matthew.

Jónas didn't hesitate. 'Definitely not. It emits waves that disturb me when I'm regenerating my energy centres.'

Matthew's brow furrowed. He seemed about to ask Jónas to explain when Vigdís came over carrying some printouts.

'These are the lists you asked for,' she said, handing Jónas two sheets of paper. 'These are the names of the guests staying at the hotel on Thursday and Friday night, and these are the people with reservations who either didn't turn up or cancelled.' She flashed Thóra and Matthew a fake smile. 'I must get back to reception to man the phones.' She strode off and Jónas called his thanks after her.

After scanning the lists, he handed them to Thóra. 'This is

a printout from the reservations system, although it's probably not much help. I can't imagine that one of the hotel guests would have murdered Birna. That seems quite unbelievable to me.'

'You never know,' Thóra admonished him. She began reading. It was not a long list. 'Are these bookings quite low? There aren't many names here.'

'No, not at all,' Jónas replied, looking wounded. 'You can't expect the hotel to be fully booked except right in the middle of summer. The tourist season is so short it can hardly be called a *season*. I've been thinking of arranging events here this winter to attract people. Otherwise it will be rather bleak.'

Thóra nodded without taking her eyes off the list. 'According to this, eight rooms were occupied on Thursday night and ten on Friday.'

'That fits,' said Jónas. 'Of course, I don't memorise the figures, but that's probably about right.' He reached for his beer and took a sip. 'This is organic beer,' he said as he put the glass back down and wiped the froth from his upper lip.

Thóra noticed Matthew's eyebrows twitching. He sniffed suspiciously at his glass. Before he could grill Jónas about brewing methods, she showed Jónas the list and said, 'Do you know any of the guests? Are there any regulars here, for example?'

'We opened so recently that we haven't established a regular clientele unfortunately, but I must be able to remember them.' Jónas put his finger against the name at the top and began there. 'Let's see, Mr and Mrs Brietnes – no, they were an elderly couple from Norway and are very unlikely to be involved in the fatality.' He moved his finger down. 'Karl Hermannsson – I don't remember him; he seems to have stayed just the one night. But I remember this couple, Arnar Fridriksson and Ásdís Henrýsdóttir – they've been here before. They're interested in what we're doing and take lots of treatments. They can't be involved in any way. Hang on. Who's this? Thröstur Laufeyjarson?' Jónas thought to himself. 'Oh, yes, the canoeist. He's been paddling around here, training for a race. He's booked until Wednesday. Very quiet, very moody. Could well be a murderer.'

'Not necessarily,' said Thóra, who didn't believe murderers were any more reserved or secretive than the rest of us. 'What about these foreigners?' She pointed at the next names.

'Mr Takahashi and his son.' Jónas looked up at Thóra and smiled. 'Far, far too polite to kill anyone. Both very quiet, and the father's recovering from cancer treatment to boot. His son never leaves his side. You can rule them out.' He looked at the next line. 'I don't know who these two are, Björn Einarsson and Gudný Sveinbjörnsdóttir – I can't place them. But you ought to recognise this one, Thóra: Magnús Baldvinsson, an old left-wing politician.'

When Thóra heard the name, it clicked with the face of the man she had seen in the dining room at lunchtime. 'Yes, of course. I saw him at lunch. I read an article about him in the paper the other day. He's the grandfather of that city councillor Baldvin Baldvinsson, quite a rising star in politics. What's he doing here?'

'Just relaxing, I think. He's not exactly chatty, but he did tell me he was brought up in the countryside around here. I suppose the heart and mind return to childhood haunts when people grow older,' Jónas said. He carried on down the list. 'I don't recall this Thórdís Róbertsdóttir, no idea who she is. I remember this one, though, Robin Kohman – he's a photographer shooting for an article in a travel magazine about western Iceland and the West Fjords. There was a journalist with him for a while, but he's just left. On Tuesday or Wednesday, I think. This Teitur is a stockbroker who's been here for a few days; he seems pleasant enough in a slightly snooty way. He was injured in a riding accident after he arrived and I was certain he'd leave, but he's still here. The rest of the names, I don't recognise. No one arrived on Friday, and no one cancelled.' He put the papers down on the table, and Thóra picked them up.

'Is it OK if I try talking to these people?' Thóra asked.

'Of course,' Jónas said. 'But try to treat the guests with consideration. Don't offend them.' With a sideways glance at Matthew, he whispered in Icelandic, 'Don't let him interrogate anyone. Just make it look like a chat.' He straightened up and slapped his thigh. 'I'll go and check on the cops. They're examining Birna's room now; I don't know what they think is hidden there.'

Matthew winked and grinned at Thóra. 'Nope, they definitely won't find anything there,' he said, deadpan.

'And they've got my mobile-phone handset now,' Jónas said, 'so at least they can keep themselves busy writing down everything on it.'

Steini sat and brooded, staring out at the driveway through the window. For all the traffic that passed, he could have been alone in the world. No cars, no people. He had already watched enough TV to last a lifetime, and he was only twenty-three. If his life had unfolded properly, things would have been different. It wasn't supposed to turn out like this; in fact, he was still waiting for someone to come and tell him that it was all a misunderstanding, that it hadn't happened to him, but to someone else. Anyone, he didn't care who, as long as it was someone else. 'Sorry we put you through all this unnecessarily, mate, but these things happen sometimes. You can stand up. Go on. It was all a misunderstanding. Your car isn't in the scrapyard; someone else's is. And you weren't in it.' A harsh, bitter laugh escaped him. Fat chance.

As he shifted in his seat, the reflection of his face appeared in the window. He flinched and pulled his hood further over his head, leaving as little of his face visible as possible. He would never get used to this. Never. With practised hands, Steini grasped the wheels of his wheelchair and rolled away from the window.

Where was Berta? She had promised to come, and she always kept her word. Dear, wonderful Berta. Without her, he did not know how he'd manage. Therapists, doctors, psychiatrists, whoever, they never stopped nagging him to go to Reykjavík, enrol at the university and do something with his life. It wasn't over just because he was in bad shape. With proper therapy he might be able to get along OK without the wheelchair most of the time, although it would be a slow and painful process. Those people didn't understand him. He had to stay here. He belonged here; this area was his home. There weren't too many people, and most of them knew him. No one recoiled in shock at the terrible mask where his face should have been. In Reykjavík that would happen to him a hundred times a day. He would wither and die in no time. He was infinitely grateful to Berta. She was largely responsible for enabling him to stay here in such a helpless condition.

Had Berta abandoned him? Had she had enough? Helped him for the last time? Steini wheeled himself over to the television and picked up the remote. He would rather watch trash than follow that thought through to its logical conclusion. He turned up the sound and focused his attention on the screen. Don't think about it. Don't think about it.

Thóra and Matthew clinked their glasses. 'I do hope this isn't organically cultivated,' he said before tasting it.

Thóra laughed. 'No, hopefully it's grown using gallons of insecticide and preferably mercury fertiliser.' She took a sip. 'Whatever the vintner used, the end result is delicious.' She put her glass down and picked up a canapé to nibble. 'I'm starving, absolutely *starving*.'

'Uh-huh,' Matthew said. 'I'm glad that hasn't changed. And you haven't changed.' He winked at her. 'Even your taste in clothes is still so . . . what's the word . . .?'

Thóra looked down at her plain sweater and then stuck her tongue out at him. 'What was I meant to do – bring an evening gown and stilettos in the hope that someone would invite me out to dinner?'

'I doubt whether you'd have turned up in an evening gown even if you *had* been invited out.' He adjusted his tie theatrically.

'Ha, ha,' said Thóra. 'I'm too hungry to defend myself against your hilarious jokes. Where's the food?' She looked at the clock. 'Damn. I have to phone home before Sóley goes to sleep.' She picked up her bag, then remembered that her mobile was in police custody. 'Sorry, can I borrow your phone?'

'Sure,' said Matthew, handing her his mobile. 'Are your kids all right? I hardly dare ask – are you a grandmother yet?'

Thóra took the phone. 'You can relax – you're still dining with a young woman.' It was a clamshell phone and she flicked it open. On the display was a photograph of a little black girl with cornrows. 'Who's this?' she asked, turning the mobile to face Matthew. Was he a father? Did he live with someone? He'd never mentioned it.

He smiled. 'That's my daughter.'

'Really?' replied Thóra. 'She doesn't exactly take after you.' She looked at the picture again. 'Apart from the hair, perhaps.' She wasn't sure what else to say.

Matthew laughed and ran his hand over his short hair. 'No, we're not related. I'm her foster parent through a charity.'

'Oh, how sweet.' Thóra took a sip of wine to conceal her relief. 'I thought for a moment that you had a wife or girlfriend. I don't go in much for married men. On a scale of attractiveness from one to ten, they rank minus two.'

'Women are strange,' Matthew said. 'I find you attractive, and still would if you were married.'

'Then you're lucky that I'm divorced,' she replied, looking back at the photograph. 'She doesn't live with you, does she?' She absolutely couldn't imagine Matthew washing children's clothes, let alone producing such neat plaits on that little head.

'No, no,' said Matthew. 'She lives in Rwanda. I know a woman in her village who works on a relief programme for the Red Cross. She talked me into it.'

'What's her name?' Thóra asked.

'Who, the woman or the girl?' he teased.

'The girl, of course,' she replied.

'Laya,' he said.

'That's a pretty name,' Thóra said, placing both her hands over one of his where it lay on the table. 'I'll be quick, because when the food arrives, I'll quite happily hang up on my own children.' She dialled her son's number. 'Hi, Gylfi, how's it going?'

'Are you abroad?' said her son's startled voice.

'No,' said Thóra, hastily adding, 'I borrowed a phone from some foreigner at this hotel because mine isn't working. How are things?'

'Rubbish. This is dead boring. I want to go home,' Gylfi replied crossly.

'Now, now,' Thóra said soothingly. 'I bet it's fun. Is Sóley having a good time?'

'She always does; I don't know why you bother to ask,' Gylfi grumbled. 'But I'm going nuts here. Dad's been clowning around with Sóley's *SingStar '80s*. If I hear him do "Eye of the Tiger" once more, I'll walk out of the door. I mean it.'

'Well, sweetie,' Thóra said, 'it'll be over soon. Can I have a word with Sóley?' She didn't feel inclined to defend his father's karaoke skills.

'Don't stay on for too long. I have to phone Sigga. She put her mobile on her stomach just now and let the baby kick a text message to me.'

'Did she?' said Thóra, who had long since ceased to be surprised by anything. 'And what did it say?'

'"jxgt",' Gylfi answered proudly. He handed the mobile to her daughter without any further explanation and a sweet little voice shouted, 'Mum, Mum. Hi, Mum!'

'Hello, sweetie,' said Thóra. 'Having fun?'

'Yes. It's OK, but I want you to come home. Dad and Gylfi are always arguing.'

'It won't be long, baby. I'll be really glad to get you back too. Say hello to your dad from me, and I'll see you tomorrow.' Thóra said goodbye, closed the mobile and handed it back to Matthew.

'I didn't understand a single word of that,' he said, putting the phone back in his jacket pocket. 'Will you speak Icelandic to me later? In bed?'

'Of course I will, you idiot,' said Thóra in the language of the Vikings, as she moved her foot from the floor to a much warmer place. The wine was starting to have an effect. 'Aren't you relieved that I'm not wearing stilettos now?'

Rósa stood by the cooker, making coffee in an old-fashioned pot. The process required no concentration and she let her mind roam, but any positive or joyful thoughts refused to linger, invariably yielding to more depressing ones. She forced herself to remember how eagerly her favourite lamb, Stubbur, had drunk from the bottle that morning, but the image dissolved at once. It was forced out by the memory of Bergur coming home the night before last and telling her about the body he had found on the beach. She tried to banish the memory by thinking about her brother's impending visit. That would surely cheer them up; he was always really boisterous. And it was about time. These days the house was so quiet that a visiting stranger might have taken the couple for deaf and dumb. She smiled sadly. As if any strangers visited. Even their acquaintances never called. No one except their closest relatives ever dropped in. It was hardly surprising. Who wanted to come to a house where even the potted plants were infected with unhappiness?

Rósa sighed. She had no close friend she could ask for advice, but doubted they'd be able to tell her anything she didn't know. Bergur was unhappy because he lived with her and didn't love her. She was unhappy because she lived with him and loved him and her love was not reciprocated. Although she didn't know exactly when he had stopped loving her – if he had ever started – she clearly remembered when she had fallen in love with him: the day they met. She still recalled how handsome he was, so different from the other young men she had known. He had come from the west to help with the spring chores on the farm, and had swept her off her feet immediately. They worked together side by side, up to their elbows in blood from the lambing, and her attraction for him grew as it gradually dawned on her from their conversations how well read and knowledgeable he was. Also, he had been much better spoken than most people, and still was. That gave him a certain cosmopolitan air, although he had never been outside the country. Back then, and even now, she felt like a yokel beside him. She had always known she wasn't good enough for him. Eventually he would leave, and that knowledge filled her with a sadness that was smothering their marriage. Which came first, the chicken or the egg?

For God's sake. She shook herself. You sap, stop feeling sorry for yourself. The aroma of coffee filled her nostrils and cheered her up slightly. Better times might lie ahead after all. She fetched a freshly baked sponge cake and a knife to slice it. Bergur would be back any second and she wanted to have everything ready for him when he returned, weary after his evening's work. He was mending the leaky roof of the barn, and she knew it was both boring and difficult for him. He could hardly be called a handyman, that was for sure. She didn't care, though. It wasn't his carpentry skills that had attracted her.

For dinner, she had boiled the last frozen black pudding from the previous autumn, with potatoes. Realising that it wasn't the most exciting of meals, she planned to jazz it up by serving her husband sponge cake with his coffee after dinner. She peeped inside the pot and saw that the water was about to boil. A tear suddenly ran down her cheek. That fucking bitch. She wiped away the tear, sniffled and lifted the knife. Fucking little bitch. He was spoken for, couldn't she see that? The lid on the pot rattled suddenly and Rósa jumped. Then she smiled to herself as she lifted it and turned down the heat on the stove. Fucking dead bitch. Dead, dead, dead bitch. Rósa's spirits lifted as she stood with the knife poised above the cake. Dead, and soon to be buried. She had never heard of anyone leaving their wife for a dead bitch.

Matthew raised his head from the pillow. He was thirsty and wondered whether that was what had woken him up or a noise from outside. He smiled at his own foolishness when he realised there was nothing but silence outside the open window. With a yawn he got up, taking care not to wake Thóra. That was easier said than done, because she had managed to sprawl in such a way that he had great trouble not disturbing her as he climbed out of bed. He went to the bathroom and let the water run while he fetched a glass. The glass was under the tap when a strange sound reached his ears. He turned off the water at once and listened; it sounded like a crying child. Ears pricked, Matthew left the bathroom and tried to work out where the sound was coming from. Suddenly, to his surprise, it stopped. Perhaps there were guests at the hotel with a baby that couldn't sleep. That must be it. Chiding himself for overreacting, he went over to the window to close it properly. Unlike him, Thóra liked it wide open and the room was quite cold.

While he was locking the window, the child began crying again. Now there was no doubt that it came from outside. Matthew opened the curtain and peered out into the bright night. He saw nothing and the noise stopped again, just as suddenly as before. He stood by the window for a while, waiting to hear it once more, then got back under the duvet, certain that he had heard a child crying but equally sure that the child was not a ghost.

Sunday, 11 June 2006

12

The Japanese father and son were so overwhelmingly polite that Thóra felt like a drunken oaf in their presence. She tried her best to talk calmly, move slowly and avoid all unnecessary facial expressions, but to no avail. Matthew was faring much better. Thóra, suspecting that he'd learned from his experience working for a German bank, kept her head down and let him do the talking. They had waited in the lobby for the Japanese to return from the short walk that, according to Vigdís from reception, they always took in the mornings. Now they were all sitting in wooden chairs at the front of the hotel, enjoying the rare sunshine.

'So you didn't know her?' Matthew asked in a low, clear voice. He was still a little annoyed at Thóra, who had teased him about the crying child he'd heard in the night. She thought he'd dreamed it.

The son translated Matthew's words into Japanese for his father. Then he turned back to them. 'No, sorry. We don't know who you are referring to.'

'She was an architect, working for the owner of this hotel. A young woman, dark-haired,' Matthew explained.

The old man put a skinny hand on his son's shoulder and said something. The son listened intently, then nodded. He addressed Matthew. 'It is possible that my father saw that woman. She was out in the front here, talking to a man in a wheelchair and a young girl. He says she was holding some drawings and writing on them. Could that be her?'

Matthew looked quizzically at Thóra. 'Was she connected with anyone in a wheelchair?'

She shook her head. 'Not that I know of.'

Matthew asked if the elder man knew who these people were.

Again the two men exchanged words that the son translated into English for Matthew and Thóra. 'No, my father didn't know them, but he had seen them before – the woman at the hotel, and the young people nearby.' He bowed his head slightly before continuing. 'My father says he noticed the young couple because of how especially caring the girl seemed to be towards the crippled boy, but he doesn't know anything else about them, or about the architect. I don't remember the woman myself, so I am of no help.'

Matthew and Thóra exchanged a glance. It was pointless to disturb the men any further, so they stood. 'Mr Takahashi, thank you very much,' Matthew said with a bow. Thóra followed suit. 'We hope you have a nice stay.'

'Thank you,' the son said, also rising. He helped his frail father to stand. 'This is a good place to stay. My father has been ill, but the fresh air makes him feel better.'

'I hope he gets well soon,' said Thóra, smiling warmly at the old man. He smiled back and they exchanged farewells.

When they were inside the lobby, she turned to Matthew. 'Not much joy there, I'm afraid.'

He shrugged. 'You can't have expected them to know

who the murderer is.' Then he frowned. 'But I do think it's odd that the son had no idea who Birna was, although his father had almost certainly seen her. You remember what Vigdís said about those two? The son follows his father everywhere, like a shadow. So where was the son when the father saw Birna with the young couple?'

'Maybe the father saw them through the window,' suggested Thóra. 'The son would have told us if he remembered. Why wouldn't he?'

'I don't know,' Matthew said pensively. 'But it's strange how long they talked to each other when you think how short the answers were when the son translated them. It's also weird that they didn't ask why we were enquiring about Birna.'

'Isn't it something to do with Japanese politeness? Curiosity might be considered as bad as theft in their country.' Thóra was hungry. She stole a glance at the clock above their heads. 'Come on, let's get something to eat before they clear breakfast away.'

Matthew looked at her in surprise, then consulted his own watch. 'They don't close the dining room at eight, do they?'

'Come on,' she said again, hopping impatiently from foot to foot. 'I'll die if I don't have some coffee. There should be other guests in there who we can talk to as well.'

'Well, I don't want you dying on me,' Matthew said, following her. 'Even if you didn't believe me about that crying I heard.'

'Whooo,' Thóra chanted. 'We're the ghoooost children – whooo.' She chuckled at Matthew's petulant expression. 'Don't be so silly,' she said. 'Some coffee will perk us up.'

Only three tables were occupied in the dining room. An elderly couple Thóra had not seen before were sitting at one, at another sat Magnús Baldvinsson, the old politician, and at the third a gloomy-looking young man. He was sunburned and looked as if he was in good shape, although his physique was hard to see under his trendy clothes. Thóra decided to concentrate on him. She nudged Matthew and murmured, 'That must be the canoeist, Thröstur Laufeyjarson, who Jónas said might be connected with Birna's death. Looks pretty moody, doesn't he? Let's take the table next to him.'

They went up to the buffet and Thóra quickly threw a few pieces of food on to her plate. To her chagrin, Matthew seemed to be taking his time to explore the selection, strolling round the table. She nudged him again. 'Quick. He mustn't leave before we sit down.' Matthew looked disappointed, but grabbed a yoghurt. They walked over to the table next to the canoeist's. Thóra smiled at him as she sat down. 'Hello. Lovely weather, isn't it?'

The man didn't look up, and seemed unaware that she was addressing him. He yawned and took a sip of orange juice. Thóra tried again. 'Excuse me,' she said, loudly enough that there could be no doubt she was talking to him. 'Do you know if there's a boat rental around here? We were thinking of renting a boat. Or a kayak.'

The man swallowed, startled. 'Sorry, were you talking to me?' he said in English. 'I'm afraid I don't speak Icelandic.'

'Oh.' Thóra was caught a little off balance. Clearly this was not Thröstur Laufeyjarson. She smiled apologetically. 'Sorry,' she said, also in English. 'I thought you were someone else.' She changed the subject to keep him talking. 'Have you just arrived?'

He shook his head. 'No, I've been here a while on and off, because I've been travelling.'

Thóra nonchalantly feigned interest in his travels. 'Where have you been? There's so much to see.'

The young man didn't seem to mind having company. He swung round in his seat to face Thóra and Matthew. 'Mainly in the West Fjords. I work for a travel magazine and we feature unusual destinations.'

'That sounds like an interesting job,' said Thóra, taking her first sip of coffee. She couldn't remember the man's name, but he must be the photographer Jónas recognised on the guest list.

The young man laughed. 'Well, it can be tiring, like any other job. I'm a photographer, which can sometimes mean working long, gruelling hours.'

Thóra stuck out her hand. 'How rude of me not to introduce myself. My name's Thóra.' She nodded at Matthew. 'And this is Matthew, from Germany.'

The young man stood and stretched over the table to shake their hands. 'Hi. I'm Robin, Robin Kohman, from the States.'

Thóra tried to look as if a thought had just occurred to her. 'Wait a minute . . . didn't I see you with Birna?'

Robin looked blank. 'Birna?'

'Yes, Birna, the architect who was here . . .' She trailed off expectantly.

'Ah, yes, the architect, Birna,' exclaimed Robin cheerfully. He pronounced the name completely differently from Thóra. 'Yes, I know her; I just didn't recognise her name thc way you said it. I haven't quite mastered the pronunciation. All your words sound the same.' He finished his juice and wiped his mouth with a serviette. 'Yes, I got to know her a little. I took a few shots for her and she told me about places around here where I could find interesting subjects to photograph.'

'Do you remember when you last saw her?' asked Matthew. He had not bothered to open his tub of yoghurt.

Robin thought for a moment. 'No, I think it's been a few days. Is anything wrong?'

'No, I don't think so,' fibbed Thóra. 'We just wanted to meet her.' Out of the corner of her eye, she saw Magnús Baldvinsson stand up and leave.

'If you bump into her, perhaps you could let her know I still have her photographs.' Robin stood up.

'In the unlikely event that we see her, we certainly will,' said Matthew, smiling cryptically. When Robin had left, he picked up the tub of yoghurt and waved it in Thóra's face. 'Can I get something decent to eat now?'

Magnús Baldvinsson walked around the hotel site, trying to find a signal for his mobile. His room had no reception and he didn't want to talk surrounded by people in the corridor or in the dining room, where he knew all he could get was a weak signal. Twice he stumbled on loose rocks. It was difficult to keep an eye on the display on his mobile and watch where he was going. Breathing a sigh of relief as a few bars of signal appeared on the screen, he hurriedly dialled his home number. He was in the car park, and people would probably start coming outside soon. He waited impatiently as it rang. Eventually it was answered.

'Frída, darling, did I wake you?'

'Magnús? What time is it?' His wife yawned noisily.

'Just gone eight,' he snapped.

'Is something wrong?' Frída asked anxiously, the sleepiness gone from her voice.

'No, nothing's wrong. I just wanted to tell you I'll be staying a bit longer.' Magnús watched the hotel door open. A young man in a tracksuit came out. He was relieved when the man headed for the beach, not the car park. 'There are some people here asking questions about Birna.'

'Questions? What kind of questions? Have they spoken to you?' Frída would have continued firing questions at him had he not interrupted her. The terror in her voice was audible.

'Frída, stay calm.' He took a deep breath and tried to control his temper. Frída's nerves grew worse each year, and it didn't take a murder to unbalance her. When he thought about it, she was actually holding up OK, now that the pressure was really on. 'I don't know why these people are nosing around. And no, they haven't approached me yet. I just called to say I'll be a few days longer. It would look suspicious if I rushed off. The police have already been to the hotel twice, and I'm hoping they'll talk to me while I'm still here.' He sighed. 'Surely they'll want to talk to everyone who was at the scene.'

Frída said nothing for a short while, then murmured, 'Baldvin phoned.'

'What did he say?' asked Magnús warily, although he couldn't help swelling with pride at the mention of his grandson in spite of Baldvin's recent tribulations. The lad was an up-and-coming politician, just as his grandfather had been at that age. They even looked strikingly similar, and one newspaper had included a photograph of the young Magnús alongside an interview with Baldvin to show the resemblance. Magnús smiled to himself; surely no one would mix them up in real life, him so old and Baldvin so young and handsome.

'He was asking after you. When you'd be home,' Frída replied. 'I think he plans to come up there.'

'No!' barked Magnús. 'Under no circumstances is he to come here. That would make things even worse. Imagine if he'd stayed at home the other day instead of trying to help me.'

'He means well,' said his wife. 'Maybe it won't make any difference. If that Birna had spoken to anyone, you'd know by now. Perhaps it all died with her.' She sighed. 'Shouldn't we just hope so and call it a day?'

Magnús groaned. 'We can't be sure, Frída. I've risked too much to give up at the last hurdle. Not to mention Baldvin. I'll stay here and see how it all unfolds. Things will become clearer in the next couple of days, I'm sure of it.'

'Should I come? Are you taking your medication?' Frída sounded on the verge of hysteria.

'No. Don't come. And for God's sake, stop Baldvin from doing anything stupid like heading up here again.' Magnús took a deep breath. 'Frída, the signal's so weak here that you probably won't get through to my mobile, but don't call the hotel either. You never know who's on the line. I'll keep phoning you.'

He hung up, stood for a moment surveying the beautiful coastline, then turned to admire the mountains to the north. He waited to be filled with peace and well-being, but nothing happened. He suddenly felt furious. With her devious plotting, Birna had ruined what was most dear to him: his childhood haunts. Now the only feeling they aroused in him was apprehension, and he was too old to deal with fear. He had no self-confidence left. This would end badly, for him and for Baldvin. His rage had died down a little, but it was replaced by melancholy. Perhaps Birna had been the root of the problem, and her murder would put an end to it. But when all was said and done, it was his fault.

He had read somewhere that past sins haunted you for ever, and no one could hide from them. He should have thought of that at the time.

13

Sitting behind the reception desk, Vigdís watched Thóra and Matthew heading for Jónas's office. She wondered whether to tell them Jónas was out, but decided not to. They'd find out soon enough. She turned back to the online news site she was reading. You couldn't really describe the articles she liked to read as 'news', but Vigdís had long ago lost interest in the Middle East, politics, the economy and all the other stuff journalists were constantly banging on about. That kind of news went round in never-ending circles, but the stories Vigdís read were easy to follow and had a beginning, a middle and an ending. It was always obvious who were the good guys and the bad guys, and they were always illustrated with glamorous photographs. This was celebrity gossip – stories of the rich and famous. She scrolled down excitedly – she now had irrefutable proof that both Nicole Richie and Keira Knightley were anorexic. She scrutinised a close-up of the latter's ribs, protruding through a slash in the side of her dress. Vigdís shook her head sadly.

'Excuse me,' a voice said, momentarily distracting her from her concern for the young actress's well-being. Vigdís looked up. 'Do you know where Jónas is?' asked Thóra.

Vigdís closed the window on her computer so that the reservations screen showed. 'Jónas popped down to

Reykjavík. He'll be back this afternoon.' She smiled professionally. 'Can I help?'

Thóra looked at Matthew, then back at Vigdís. 'We were just wondering which guests were in. We'd like to meet anyone who may have known Birna. The canoeist, for example.'

'Thröstur Laufeyjarson?' said Vigdís, who was good with names – a talent that had proved useful in her job; in fact, it was one of the main reasons Jónas had employed her. Vigdís also had such a command of the computer system that he completely ignored any other shortcomings she might have.

'Yes, that's him,' Thóra replied. 'Is he in?'

'No, he's always out training at the crack of dawn. Actually, I saw his canoe on the beach yesterday evening. Maybe he's out in it. If it isn't at the little jetty down below, then he'll be at sea. He always leaves it there.'

Thóra interpreted this into German for Matthew and they decided to go down to the shore in the hope of seeing Thröstur. Before they left, Thóra turned back to Vigdís. 'What about Magnús Baldvinsson? Is he in?'

Vigdís shrugged. 'I don't know. He was wandering around outside just now. Generally he doesn't go far, just short local walks, never for more than an hour. He's pretty old.'

'Is he a widower?' asked Thóra. 'Jónas said he was here on his own.'

'No, I don't think so,' Vigdís replied. 'His wife has phoned him here several times.'

'Strange that she isn't with him.'

'Maybe she's ill,' suggested Vigdís. 'Housebound or something.'

'Perhaps we'll have a look for him later,' said Thóra.
Vigdís nodded emphatically. 'Yes, you really should.'

'Should we?' said Thóra. 'Why?'

'Well, because he knew Birna,' Vigdís answered. She
paused, then added, 'At least, I think he did. He made a
point of asking after her when he checked in.'

'Really?' Thóra was surprised. Jónas had not mentioned
any connection between Magnús and Birna. 'Do you know
how they knew each other?'

Vigdís shook her head. 'No idea. I don't really know
any more than that. He asked after her and I answered his
question. I never saw them together. He didn't ask where
he could find her, and she never mentioned him.'

Thröstur Laufeyjarson laid the paddle across his canoe
and looked at the stopwatch on his wrist. In spite of all
his training, he seemed to be doing worse than before. The
canoe rocked gently in the sea as he pondered how to
improve his training schedule, which seemed to be making
no difference. He took a deep breath and exhaled with a
groan. The problem was obvious, really: it must be because
he wasn't working out enough. The small gym at the hotel
was not well equipped, making it difficult to maintain a
reasonable muscle mass, let alone increase it. Thröstur
rotated his shoulders three times to release the tension and
felt a drop of sweat drip down his spine inside his dry-
suit. The prospect of a hot shower, perhaps followed by a
massage, incited him to turn the canoe slowly landwards.
That was enough for the time being. He would go out
again after lunch, and paddle harder.

When the prow of the boat was pointing towards the hotel,

he hesitated, eased his tight grip on the paddle and squinted at the shoreline. Who were those people on the beach? It looked like they were waving at him. He groaned. Was there anything more boring than tourists and their stupid questions? 'Do you hunt whales in that thing?' 'Have you ever paddled to Greenland?' He considered his options. Should he resign himself to meeting these idiots or paddle away and go ashore elsewhere? That way, he would be left in peace, but he'd end up much farther from the hotel. Licking his dry lips, he tasted the tang of salt. The people were waving even harder now, and Thröstur thought he recognised the woman as a recent arrival at the hotel. It looked like that woman who was asking about the architect when he walked through reception the day before. He had no intention of talking to her. Who knew what she might ask? Calmly, he turned the canoe back round. Before setting off, he looked instinctively at the paddle, half expecting still to see blood on it. Of course it was gone. He had washed it off himself, and whatever he did, he was always thorough. He paddled away.

'What's going on?' shouted Thóra when the canoe started moving away from them. She had been waving madly to attract the canoeist's attention, but now lowered her arms. 'He definitely saw us. What's wrong with him?'

Matthew put one hand to his forehead as he watched the man paddle determinedly westwards, away from the beach. 'Yes, he definitely saw us. Either he's busy or he's avoiding us.' The boat moved out of sight behind some rocks. 'I think he didn't want to talk to us. Maybe he's shy.'

'Shouldn't we wait here a while?' asked Thóra, who was eager to meet the unfriendly canoeist as soon as possible. Whatever might be said of Jónas, he was pretty canny, and he'd been suspicious of Thröstur. 'I think it's obvious that he's hiding something, otherwise he'd talk to us.'

'Not necessarily,' argued Matthew. 'Perhaps he's just tired and can't be bothered to talk. He doesn't know what we want to ask him. Why don't we just go back inside? We're bound to run into him later. Come on, we can talk to that old Magnús guy instead.'

Thóra had to admit that this was a much more sensible plan than standing on the beach on the off-chance Thröstur might return, so they went back inside, where Vigdís told them that she still hadn't seen Magnús that morning, but he might be in his room. They went to the top floor.

'Leave the talking to me,' Thóra whispered as she knocked firmly on the door. They heard movement inside. 'He's so old that I'm not sure he speaks any language except Icelandic, and possibly Danish.' A crack appeared in the door and Baldvinsson peered out. 'Hello, Magnús Baldvinsson? My name's Thóra. This is Matthew. Could we have a few words with you?'

'Why?' he growled. 'Who are you?'

'Oh, I'm sorry. I'm a lawyer working for Jónas, the owner of this hotel, and this is my assistant.' Thóra suppressed the urge to stick her foot in the door and force it open. 'This won't take a moment. I'm hoping you can help us.'

The gap in the door narrowed slightly. Then Magnús opened it all the way. 'Please, come in.'

'Thank you,' said Thóra as she took a seat. 'We promise not to keep you for long.'

Magnús glared at her. 'I'm not busy, so you needn't worry about that. I've learned from experience that time is only precious when you're young. You'll find that out one day.'

'I'm not sure I agree,' said Thóra politely. 'But we'd like to talk to you about Birna, the architect who was found dead on the beach.' She observed Magnús's reactions closely.

'Yes, I heard about that. Terrible business,' he said, displaying little emotion. 'I heard they think it was murder, which makes it sadder still.'

'That's what they're saying,' she agreed, smiling at him. 'We're trying to find out who might conceivably have wanted her dead.'

'And you include me in that category?' Magnús asked dryly.

'No, not at all,' Thóra replied hastily. 'We understand that you knew her and we were hoping you might know something useful.'

'Knew her?' he snapped, startled and unable to conceal his irritation. 'Who said I knew her? That's simply not true.'

'"Knew" may be an overstatement,' she said. 'I heard you were asking after her at reception, so I just assumed you must have been acquainted with her.'

The old man hesitated. 'I don't remember that, but my memory's not so good these days. If I did enquire about her, I must have seen her name somewhere, maybe on a list on the desk. My wife and I are looking for an architect, and her name may well have rung a bell. I seem to recall something of the sort, but I can't be sure. Are you sure that the receptionist meant me?'

Thóra could tell he was lying. She wondered how old he actually was – he didn't look a day younger than eighty. Why would a couple in their eighties need an architect? Her parents had just turned sixty and they baulked at the idea of buying a new car, let alone major construction work. 'Are you having a house built?' she asked.

'What? Oh, no,' Magnús said slowly. 'We have an old summer chalet by Lake Thingvallavatn that we want to convert for year-round habitation. We need to consult an architect about the plans.' His face was blank and guile-less. 'It's been impossible to find one. The economy's booming at the moment.'

'Surely you didn't come here in the hope of finding an architect?' she asked, determined not to let the old man off the hook so easily.

Magnús glowered at her. 'No, of course I didn't. The reason I came here is none of your business, and I would prefer to end this conversation here and now.' He stopped, waiting for them to react. They both sat in silence, Matthew because he couldn't understand a word and Thóra because she didn't want to anger him further. When it became obvious that they didn't intend to say anything, the old man resumed talking. He seemed less angry now. 'I suppose I can tell you why I'm here. Maybe then you'll leave me in peace. You seem to think I have something to hide, but nothing could be further from the truth.'

'No, we don't,' Thóra assured him. 'We're simply trying to get to the bottom of what happened. Nothing else.' She smiled. 'Please excuse us if we sounded aggressive or accus-atory; that wasn't our intention.'

'If you say so,' Magnús answered warily. 'The fact is,

I've been ill and I wanted a little rest. Experience has taught me that solitude is the best nourishment for the body, to say nothing of the soul. It's just not that easy to find these days in all the hustle and bustle of modern life.'

'So why did you choose this hotel? It specialises in homeopathy and spiritualism, and I hope you don't take it as an insult if I say that neither are likely to appeal to your generation.'

He smiled for the first time since he'd opened the door. 'You're quite right: I don't believe in that nonsense. I came here because I grew up in this part of the country. I was raised on a farm not far from here. "Strong is the bond that draws men back to the soil their fathers ploughed," as the poem says.'

Thóra's eyes widened. 'Really? You knew the people from the farm?'

Magnús was baffled. 'Yes, actually, I did. Does that matter?'

'Probably not. I just know that Birna was very interested in the history of the farm, and I have a hunch that it's somehow connected with her death, but I have nothing to back it up.'

Magnús's face had gone pale. 'Isn't that a bit of a long shot?' His voice quavered slightly.

Studiedly casual, Thóra said, 'Yes, I'm sure it is. But it's great that you're familiar with this place. Maybe you could tell us a little about the local history, or any ghost stories you might know?'

Magnús seemed lost for words. He cleared his throat and appeared to recover his composure. 'I don't believe in ghosts, and haven't listened to that kind of talk since I was a child. Those stories have been going round here for a long time, but you'll have to ask someone else.' Magnús had slumped a little in his chair, but he straightened up before continuing. 'I'm no historian, and at the time I didn't have enough interest in my family tree to bother digging up details of what went on here in the old days, so I won't be much use to you.'

'But you knew the farmers who lived here, didn't you? That man . . . what was his name again . . .?' Thóra tried to remember what had been written on the backs of the photographs. 'Björn something?'

Magnús sat frozen, as if rooted to his seat. 'Bjarni, Bjarni Thórólfsson, from Kirkjustétt.'

'That's right!' exclaimed Thóra. 'Didn't his brother live on the farm next door?'

'Yes, Grímur from Kreppa was Bjarni's brother.' Magnús grimaced. 'Grímur qualified as a doctor. He was older than Bjarni. A terribly tragedy, the whole business with those two. But fate and fortune do not always go hand in hand, as the sagas say.'

'Really?' Thóra was curious. She'd had a bad feeling about the photographs at the time, but she'd assumed that was because everyone in them had died and been forgotten. It had made her uncomfortable to have evidence in black and white of how quickly lives pass into oblivion, but perhaps something else lay behind her uneasy feeling. 'How come?'

Magnús groaned. 'Their father was one of the main operators of fishing schooners out here on the penin-sula. He also ran two fishing stations with rowing boats and became very wealthy. Maybe nothing like fishing entrepreneurs or bankers these days, but by the standards of the time he was very well-off. I can't remember how many schooners he owned, but it was quite a few. He was based in Stykkishólmur.'

'Did the brothers run the business with him?' asked Thóra.

'No,' replied the old man. 'Before they came of age, he'd got rid of the fishing operation and invested the money in land. He bought a large proportion of the farming land on the southern side of the peninsula. It was a very smart move, because the fisheries took a dive soon afterwards. The trawlers took over and most, if not all, of the old schooner companies went bankrupt.'

'So did he know that was about to happen?'

'No, he wasn't psychic, if that's what you mean. He just didn't want his sons to go to sea. He'd seen too many young men drowned or injured to want his sons to go the same way. He sent them to Reykjavík to be educated when they were still young. Grímur was a brilliant scholar and became a doctor, as I said, but Bjarni was less bookish. He was always good fun, sociable, a bit of a practical joker. Nowhere near as serious as his elder brother. It would be hard to find two more different brothers. You should bear in mind that this isn't a first-hand account; I heard it from my father, but he was a truthful man and not given to embellishing his stories.'

'So was Grímur the local doctor here?' Thóra asked.

'Yes, he moved back and had the farm called Kreppa built. He did some farming alongside his medical duties, because he couldn't earn a living as a doctor here. He tried to make farming his main occupation, but he wasn't very successful. When Bjarni devoted himself to farming, on the other hand, he flourished. Later he made a lot of money from investments.'

'So where's the tragedy?' pressed Thóra. It all sounded pretty positive so far.

'Tragedy, ah, yes,' Magnús said gravely. 'Love was to blame, as is often the case. Bjarni was married very young, to an exceptionally fine woman. Her name was Adalheidur.' The old man's expression was almost wistful. 'I was just a lad, but I'll never forget her. She stood out from everyone around her. She was the most beautiful woman in the area, and friendly too. She worked hard. Bjarni met her in Reykjavík, and when they moved here, she knew absolutely nothing about farming. She always dressed as if she was on her way to a party, you know the type. Understandably, the locals didn't have much faith in her as a farmer's wife, but she proved them wrong. Made an effort to learn how it all worked. It took a lot of grit and hard work, but she soon silenced her detractors, I can tell you.

'Kristrún, Grímur's wife, was completely different. She was from these parts, hard-working like Adalheidur but not in the same way. She slogged away very reliably, but Adalheidur always had a smile on her face and laughed if anything went wrong. They were good matches for their husbands, that's for sure. Bjarni was very jolly, but Grímur always had a face like thunder.'

'Did Adalheidur die young?' asked Thóra suddenly, remembering the woman's disappearance from the photographs.

'Yes,' sighed Magnús. 'They had a child, a little girl called Gudný. A beautiful girl, the spitting image of her mother.

Not long before, Grímur and his wife had had a daughter too. Her name was Edda, but she died around the time Gudný was born and that caused friction between the two women. Grímur's wife accused Adalheidur of poisoning her daughter, which was preposterous, but the woman was beside herself with grief and probably not in her right mind when she said it. The brothers' friendship cooled, so much so that they weren't on speaking terms any longer by the time disaster struck.'

'Disaster?' echoed Thóra.

'Yes, Adalheidur died of blood poisoning and they say Grímur's wife went crazy. Nobody saw her for years, so the two brothers were left behind: one a young widower with a baby daughter, and the other with a mentally ill wife but no children. Their pride prevented them from rebuilding their friendship, so each of them battled his private demons alone. Then Grímur and Kristrún had another daughter much later. Her name was Málfrídur; she was born just before the war. The wife supposedly died in childbirth, although there was a rumour that she committed suicide and Grímur fiddled the death certificate. He wrote it himself. But I don't think there are any grounds for believing that: by that time Kristrún was getting on a bit, and childbirth is more difficult for a woman as she gets older, as you know.'

'Oh, yes,' agreed Thóra. 'And were the brothers never reconciled?'

'No, but there was a little contact between the two households when Bjarni fell ill.'

'Wasn't it tuberculosis?' Thóra asked, remembering what young Sóldís had told her.

'Yes,' replied Magnús. 'He shut himself away and refused to go to a sanatorium in Reykjavík. He died a few years later.' He took a deep breath. 'But not before he'd infected Gudný, his daughter, who was taking care of him. It wasn't long before she went too. His brother kept the farm going while they were ill, but it would have turned out differently if Bjarni had just gone to Reykjavík to be looked after.' Magnús shook his grey head sorrowfully. 'Shortly after that, Grímur moved to Reykjavík with his daughter, Málfrídur. He inherited his brother's whole estate, so he didn't need to sell the farms or other property here on the peninsula. He didn't live long either, though – in fact, he died just a few years after they moved away. He had serious mental problems, a bit like his wife.'

'And what about Kristín?' asked Thóra. 'Who was she?' Magnús stiffened. He opened his mouth as if to speak, then shut it again. 'Was there anyone by the name of Kristín at either of the farms?'

Magnús's face was stony. 'No. There was no Kristín here.' He coughed. 'I think that will do.'

'One last thing – do you know anyone who could have been connected with a Nazi organisation in this area?' she asked quickly, before he could show them the door.

'I have nothing more to say,' said Magnús, standing up. He swayed a little and Thóra feared for a moment that he might faint, but he regained his balance and gestured at the door. 'Goodbye.'

Thóra saw that it was futile to grill the man any further. But what did Nazis have to do with the fate of the farm? Or Kristín? And who was she, anyway?

14

'I advise you to clear your schedule for the next few days,' said Thórólfur, the detective, solemnly. He was phoning from Reykjavík. 'That is, if you intend to act as your client's counsel.'

Thóra sighed. 'I don't know if I can. I need to get back to Reykjavík today.'

'Well, you do what you must,' he replied. 'I just wanted to let you know that we'll be there over the next few days taking statements, mainly from tourists whom we can't be sure of getting hold of later. We fully expect to spend some time talking to Jónas. You've declared yourself as his lawyer, so we just wanted to keep you informed. Of course, you are free to do as you see fit.'

'Oh, am I?' she said bitterly. Thóra hated to be patronised, but she had to stay on good terms with the police for Jónas's sake, so she softened her voice. 'Thank you for notifying me. I'll see if I can sort something out.'

They rang off and Thóra dialled Jónas, who was borrowing Vigdís's phone while the police still had his. He had found Thóra an antiquated mobile the size of a brick, into which she'd put her own SIM card. After what had happened before, Thóra doubted the police were in any hurry to return her phone.

Jónas picked up after a few rings. From the sound of it,

he was in a car. She told him the police would want to talk to him the following week while taking statements from the hotel guests.

'They want to talk to *me*?' Jónas sounded genuinely surprised.

'Yes, of course,' replied Thóra. 'Have you forgotten that text message? Naturally you're a suspect.'

'But I didn't send it. I told you that.' Jónas sounded almost hurt.

'I know what you told me. That doesn't alter the fact that it makes you look suspicious, to put it mildly.' Thóra heard a car beep in the background at his end. 'Do you want me to be present when you give your statement, or can you manage it by yourself?'

'I can't do it alone,' said Jónas fearfully. 'I don't know how to handle it. You have to help me.' Then he seemed to perk up slightly, adding, 'It would be best for me if you could find the murderer so they stop suspecting me. I'll pay you.'

Thóra couldn't help laughing. 'The police will find the murderer, Jónas. Don't worry. If you're innocent, you'll go free.'

'I'm not so sure,' Jónas said dubiously. 'I want you there when I'm questioned.'

'Fine,' said Thóra. 'So I'll have to make arrangements for prolonging my stay. Is there a room free at the hotel?'

'There are bound to be. It's not fully booked until July.'

'Then I'll stay on here, as long as I can find someone to look after the kids,' said Thóra. 'It was their father's weekend to have them, but it's Sunday now and they're supposed to come home afterwards.'

'No problem – just have them sent up here!' suggested Jónas cheerily. 'Children love nature and they'll find plenty to occupy themselves down on the beach.'

Thóra smiled to herself. Gylfi would be happy pottering around on the beach as long as it had a computer and an Internet connection. 'Hopefully that won't be necessary,' she said. 'I'll let you know.' They exchanged farewells and Thóra groaned as she turned to Matthew.

'What?' he asked, curious. 'That's not a very happy noise.'

'No, it isn't,' frowned Thóra, fidgeting with her heavy telephone. 'Jónas has asked me to be present for his police interrogation.'

Matthew grinned broadly. 'That's great, isn't it? I'm in no hurry to leave.'

Thóra smiled wanly in response. 'Sure. It would be great if it weren't for the children. They're with their father now and I was meant to pick them up later.'

'Ah,' he said understandingly, although he clearly couldn't identify with her situation. 'Can't you phone and ask for them to stay there a bit longer?'

'Yes, I have no choice,' Thóra said grumpily. She hated having to ask Hannes for favours because she knew how he enjoyed making her jump through hoops before agreeing – only because she behaved exactly the same towards him whenever possible.

After a lot of wrangling by telephone, Thóra and Hannes reached an agreement that the children would stay an extra night with him, but no longer. Hannes had to go to the gym and run various errands he had been forced to postpone because of the time he had spent with his children.

Thóra sweetly told him that she understood, and that she'd been wondering if he'd put on weight recently. Then she hung up, praying he'd rupture something on the treadmill. She even gave in to the urge to poke out her tongue at the phone before putting it down.

'Nice to see how mature you are about your divorce,' Matthew said. 'Not all men have such understanding ex-wives.'

Thóra pulled a face at him too. 'Are you speaking from experience?' she said, then added, 'The children can only stay there one extra night, so I'll have to make other arrangements or go home.'

'I'm not divorced. I've just had trouble finding the right woman,' Matthew said. 'Although things have been looking up a little lately.' Seeing Thóra's disapproving look, he clapped his hands and changed the subject. 'Well, since there isn't much time, we ought to use it wisely. I think we've done enough walking. What do you fancy doing?'

'One thing I'm sure about is the more I know, the better equipped I'll be to help Jónas at the interrogation,' Thóra said, then thought for a moment. 'We ought to try to meet more guests or locate Eiríkur, the aura reader, who's the originator of the ghost stories. Jónas said he was expected back yesterday.'

Matthew looked crestfallen. 'That wasn't exactly what I meant, and I wasn't planning on involving the other guests, or an aura reader.'

Thóra blushed, but pretended not to understand. 'Come on, let's get a move on. As you said, I have to make the most of the time I've got.'

* * *

174

Eiríkur stared at the Tarot cards he'd laid out. King of Pentacles – good. Death – bad. He ran his index finger along the edge of the card showing Death and let his mind wander. Exactly the same cards had turned up twice, and although he was no expert in the Tarot, he knew that the probability of this was extremely slight. What were the cards telling him? He wondered whether to find someone who knew more about the Tarot, but decided that was too much trouble. He would have to go into the hotel and leave the cosy staff chalet, and he simply couldn't be bothered. There was no landline, and he knew what the mobile reception here was like. Besides, Eiríkur never used a mobile. As an aura reader, he knew that the waves they emitted could have a bad effect, to put it mildly. He would rather walk to the nearest landline than babble into a mobile, knowing that his aura grew dimmer with every word. No, he must surely be able to interpret this himself. He lowered his forehead on to his palm and stared at the cards, concentrating. King of Pentacles. Death.

Eiríkur sat up. Might Death not represent his own death at all, or even that of someone close to him, but simply the death of the architect? He nodded to himself. Of course. It foretold that her death would have a great impact on his life. That was why the card appeared repeatedly. But what about the King of Pentacles? Eiríkur had a little knowledge of the Tarot and seemed to recall that the King of Pentacles signified money. How was that connected? Could he be about to grow wealthy by her death? He had warned her. Her aura had been black as a thundercloud, which never boded well. Might he be able to somehow use this prophecy to advertise his service? Damn shame he hadn't told anyone but her about it beforehand. Now he was the only one left to tell the tale and people would think he was making it up.

Eiríkur groaned as he tried to suppress the urge for a cigarette. Jónas frowned upon smoking among his staff and Eiríkur couldn't stand having to sneak around like a teenager. He was too old for that. Huddling up behind a wall, hoping no one would see. It was pathetic. Perhaps it made sense to ban the nutritionist and personal trainer from smoking, but what guest in their right mind would complain about an aura reader lighting up a cigarette? None, of course. Eiríkur gave a start – his reflections on smoking had stirred something in the back of his mind. What was it that Vigdís had said? The body had been found on the Friday, and no one had seen Birna since the Thursday evening – the evening he'd slipped out of the seance to have a sneaky cigarette. Suddenly he understood what he hadn't realised at the time – what that person had been up to. Of course – he had seen the murderer. And they say no good can come of smoking, he thought smugly to himself.

Eiríkur gathered up the cards and smiled. Now he realised how the King of Pentacles was connected with the murder, as represented by Death. The money was for him, because where there was muck, there was brass, as the proverb went. The amount would need to be negotiated – surely confidentiality was priceless? But he was a fair man, and was not overly concerned about the small print. He just needed to nip over to the hotel to use the telephone, and he also had a few choice words to say to his employer, Jónas. It would be fun to talk to him without having to make nice to keep his job. Long-awaited financial independence was in sight, and there was no need to suck up to the boss any more.

He put the cards back in the pack, stood up and went outside. There was no time to lose; he needed to begin negotiations. He was in such a hurry that for once he didn't stop to admire himself in the little mirror hanging beside the coat rack by the door. If he had, he would have seen that his aura was heavy and dark. Almost black.

Thóra sighed. 'So everyone's out?'

Vigdís regarded her dispassionately. 'Well, I wouldn't say that, but most people do some sightseeing or other activity while they're here. We have very few guests who check in and then just hang around in their rooms waiting to meet *you*.'

Matthew flashed a sweet smile at Vigdís, having not understood a word she'd said. 'Lovely day,' he interjected in English.

'Very nice,' agreed Vigdís. 'That may be why there are so few people inside.' She turned back to Thóra. 'I'm not being rude, but I just can't help you. People start getting back around dinnertime. New guests come earlier to check in, of course, but I don't think anyone has arrived yet today.'

'Damn,' said Thóra. 'And there are no free staff who wouldn't mind a quick chat?'

Vigdís shook her head. 'There aren't many staff in, and they're all very busy. It calms down for them after dinner.' She eyed them suspiciously. 'What are you after, anyway?'

'Nothing special,' Thóra said. 'We just wanted to find out a bit more about Birna – what she did, who she hung out with. Someone may have information that explains her death.'

'Her murder, you mean,' Vigdís corrected her. 'If you're completely stuck, you could always go up to the church. I know Birna went there sometimes, because I lent her the key.'

'Church?' asked Thóra. 'What church?'

'The little church near here. It isn't part of this estate, actually, but we keep the keys. Coaches go there sight-seeing sometimes. Foreigners think it's cute.' Vigdís reached under the reception desk and handed over an old key. 'You have to shove the door a bit when you turn the key.'

Matthew took the key and Vigdís gave them directions. 'Although the church dates from 1864, it still serves the local farms, so don't make a mess.' Vigdís yawned. 'I remember Birna was terribly excited about the cemetery. I think she was looking for a gravestone.'

He'd turned the room upside down. He'd torn everything apart but found nothing. What had the stupid woman done with it? He sighed, frustrated, but made sure to keep very quiet. If he could just find it, this whole sorry story would finally end. He put an ear to the door and listened. All seemed to be quiet out in the corridor. He turned back to the room. Should he go on searching, or accept that it wasn't here? Further investigation seemed futile. He went to the door leading into the garden and peeked cautiously through the curtains. No one about. He carefully opened the door and crept outside into the fresh air. Then he pushed the door to and left, slipping off his gloves and putting them in his pocket. So where was it?

15

The church was on an area of grass not far from the beach. It stood at the top of a little hill; tiny, built from jet-black timber, it reminded Thóra of the churches she had drawn at primary school – little buildings with a small tower and a cross on the top. Hers had been much more cheerfully coloured, in fact, but she had to admit that black suited this church. The white-painted windows and door set it off nicely, and overall it looked as though the local people had built as impressive a church as their finances allowed. Thóra couldn't recall ever having seen a church this colour before, and wondered whether it was an attempt to replicate the building's original appearance. Scant though her knowledge of architectural history was, she thought the walls had been tarred, which was presumably done instead of painting in the old days. After deciding to herself that this was the explanation, she fed it to Matthew as cold, hard fact. He swallowed it.

The broad stone wall enclosing the churchyard was almost entirely covered with grass and moss, revealing only the occasional flash of grey. Directly in front of the church door was a high iron gate leading into the churchyard. They opened the gate, which gave a mighty creak, and walked through.

'Look,' Thóra said, 'there's the cemetery.' A few graves could be seen at the far end.

'Fewer people must have died here than they were expecting,' Matthew said, surveying the expanse of ground between the church and the gravestones.

'Yes,' Thóra said. 'That's odd. Vigdís said the church still served the local community, so it might fill up over time.'

'Seems unlikely,' said Matthew. He went up to the church door and examined the lock. 'What am I supposed to do again? Push or pull?'

'Push, I think. Or pull. One of the two,' Thóra said vaguely. Instead of watching Matthew, she scanned the cemetery and gravestones. 'Do you think we'll find Kristín's grave?' she said, turning back to Matthew. He was struggling furiously with the door. 'Birna must have been looking for it when she was here.'

'I don't know,' he snapped. 'I'm more concerned with opening this bloody door.' He pressed one shoulder against the wood and turned the key. A soft click was heard. '*Na endlich!*' he said proudly, and pushed the door open. '*Bitte, Frau.*'

The vestibule would have held four people at the most. It led to the nave with an altar, pews and pulpit. Most of the interior was timber, painted in soft colours and embellished with flower patterns around the edges of the ceiling and along the pews. The overall effect was neat and cosy, with the exception of the altarpiece showing Christ's crucifixion on Calvary.

'Why are these pews so small?' asked Matthew, trying to sit down. His backside hardly fit on to the bench, and the one in front left no leg room.

'I bet it's to make sure you don't fall asleep,' Thóra

replied. 'Or to save space. Actually, that's a more likely explanation.'

'Unless the Icelanders used to be a nation of dwarves,' said Matthew, standing up. He walked over to where Thóra stood, by the stairs up to the balcony. 'Should we have a look up there?' he asked. 'I reckon we've seen everything down here in the fifteen seconds we've been here.'

They went up the narrow stairs and on to the balcony. Everything was painted in the same subdued colours. There was a good view over the nave from the handrail and for the first time Thóra noticed a brass chandelier in the middle of the ceiling. They looked all around, but there wasn't much to see: just an impressive organ with an open book of sheet music on it and a wooden chest that turned out to contain hymn books and other choral paraphernalia. There was nothing else on the platform.

'That was a waste of time,' she said, disappointed. 'I expected something much more exciting.'

'Like what?' Matthew asked. 'There won't be anything connected with the murder here. Birna was just excited about the building. She was an architect, after all.'

Thóra frowned, unconvinced. 'Shouldn't there be some kind of storage room here? Surely the ministers don't have to lug everything to the church and back when they come here for the service.'

Matthew shrugged. 'There's a Bible on the altar. Maybe that's enough for them. And a couple of candlesticks.'

'What about church records? Aren't all churches obliged to keep records?' Thóra went back to the handrail for a better view of the church. Maybe there was a cupboard or box cleverly hidden away somewhere, though she couldn't see anything to suggest that. 'They have to record everything that takes place here.'

Matthew regarded her quizzically. 'What do you mean?'

'Weddings, christenings, confirmations – it's all written down in the church records.' Crossing to the wall at the far end of the balcony by the stairs, Thóra walked along it hoping to find a hatch. 'I knew it!' she shouted excitedly, spotting a rectangular hatch on the ceiling above. 'There's something up there.'

Joining her, Matthew looked up. The ceiling was low, so he had no trouble opening the hatch. They both looked up into the dark hole. 'I think I can see steps,' he said. 'We need more light.'

Thóra flicked an old-fashioned switch by the stairs and a few wall lights came on. 'Is that better?'

'Yes and no,' he said. 'It's better in that I can *see*, but worse in that I can see there's nothing there.'

'Nothing? No books?' asked Thóra disconsolately, craning to see inside.

'No,' replied Matthew. 'It's just for access to the steeple, as far as I can tell. I doubt any books are kept there.' He grabbed the edge of the opening with both hands and heaved himself up. 'No, there's definitely nothing here.' He lowered himself to the floor and clapped his hands to brush the dust off them. 'Maybe Vigdís knows where the church records are kept. She has the keys, so who knows, maybe she's been put in charge of stuff like that.'

'I'm just going to have a closer look at the altar,' Thóra said. 'They must be here somewhere.' They descended from the balcony, and she walked ahead of Matthew towards the suffering Jesus. A cursory glance revealed only the Bible and two large candlesticks. They sat on a table covered in a beautifully embroidered purple cloth, against the far wall beneath the altarpiece. Lifting the cloth, she saw that the table was in fact a small cupboard. 'Matthew, look,' she called. She bent down and took hold of the recessed handles. Fortunately the cupboard was unlocked and the doors opened with a soft creak. Thóra beamed triumphantly over her shoulder at Matthew and took out three large leather-bound books.

The top one looked quite new, and when Thóra opened it, she knew she needn't waste any time examining it: the date on the first page was 1996. She opened the next book and flicked through it until she found a date around 1940. 'I think Kristín was here during the war,' she said to Matthew. 'The film-star photos I found under the rafters were from then.' She flipped through the whole section, but found nothing. There were several births, christenings, marriages and deaths, but no Kristín was to be found anywhere.

There was something strange about the entry for 1941, where the left-hand page ended with the name of a bride but the page facing it appeared to refer to a funeral. 'That's odd,' she mused, opening the book wider and examining the join in the centre. She handed it to Matthew. 'Look,' she said, 'a page has been removed. Maybe two.'

Matthew examined the book and nodded. 'You're right,' he replied, passing the register back to Thóra. 'Bizarre. Who would do such a thing? Someone who wanted to erase a wedding?'

'Or someone who wanted to erase a child's christening,' Thóra said. 'If you erase the birth records of a child born in that era, you've pretty much succeeded in wiping out every trace of it. I don't know whether the national registry had been established by then, and even if it was, we can't know whether it was used properly in rural areas. It can't have been too difficult to keep yourself, or someone else, outside the system.'

They replaced the books after Thóra had searched through them all with no sign of Kristín.

Outside in the cemetery, they didn't need to walk past many graves to appreciate how much times had changed. Most of the graves in the tiny cemetery bore inscriptions like 'Boy – stillborn' or 'Girl – unchristened'. More often than not, several children of the same parents lay side by side, or one gravestone served a group of siblings. Thóra carefully examined every inscription in the hope of finding names she recognised. She found two graves whose headstones bore the name Kristín, but both occupants had died in old age. She thought it unlikely that these women were connected with the inscription under the rafters.

Eventually they came to two neighbouring plots separated by a low fence. Both had particularly large and impressive headstones, at least five feet high and carved from pale stone. Orange moss or lichen had spread across them. The carving on one showed a snake curling round to bite its tail, along with an oil lamp. Thóra recognised neither symbol, but she remembered that there was a lamp on the cover of the Gideon Bible. She asked Matthew whether the images meant anything to him, but they didn't. She read the inscription, which bore the names of the family from Kirkjustétt, the farm that was now part of Jónas's hotel. At the top was the head of the household: 'Bjarni

Thórólfsson, farmer from Kirkjustétt, b. 1896 d. 1944'.
Beneath it stood 'His wife, Adalheidur Jónsdóttir, b. 1900
d. 1928'. Two more names were inscribed below: 'Bjarni b.
1923 d. 1923' and 'Gudný b. 1924 d. 1945'.

'These are the people from the photograph I told you
about, the ones Magnús Baldvinsson knew.' Matthew
didn't need to speak Icelandic to understand the head-
stone, so he stooped to read it. Thóra continued,
'According to Magnús, the farmer and his daughter died
of TB, and his wife of blood poisoning years earlier.' She
pointed to the dates on Adalheidur's inscription. 'A girl
who works for Jónas claims that incest was committed at
the farm. Presumably it involved Bjarni and his daughter,
Gudný.'

'We can't assume that's true,' Matthew pointed out.
'How would a girl her age know about incest that took
place seventy years ago?'

'Her grandmother told her,' said Thóra. 'As a rule I don't
think grandmothers tell lies.'

'Not all grandmothers are the same,' grinned Matthew.
'I'd take a story like that with a pinch of salt, even if it
was a sweet little old lady telling it.'

'I suppose so,' Thóra conceded. 'And I hope for Gudný's
sake that it *was* nonsense.' Then she pointed out the name
of the son who had died in his first year. 'I noticed in the
photographs that Adalheidur appeared to be pregnant, but
there were no pictures of a baby. He must have only lived
a few days.'

'Like most children around here,' Matthew said, indicating the other graves. 'More than half of these seem to
be children who didn't survive infancy.'

'It does seem that people here had trouble raising their children to adulthood,' she said, looking around. 'Unless infant mortality was this common all over Iceland.' She shuddered. 'Thank God that's all in the past,' she said, moving on to the next gravestone, which was more modest. 'That's strange.' It looked half empty. 'Just two inscriptions: "His wife, Kristrún Valgeirsdóttir, b. 1894 d. 1940" and below it "Edda Grímsdóttir b. 1921 d. 1924".' Thóra looked at Matthew. 'The husband's name is missing, but it must be Grímur Thórólfsson, the elder brother. The woman has the same name as his wife, and the child as his daughter.'

'Is he likely to be the "dad" who killed Kristín? Maybe a murderer would not have been buried with his loved ones,' he said. 'Or could he still be alive? Either way, he's not buried here.'

Thóra shook her head. 'No, that can't be right. Magnús said Grímur died a few years after moving to Reykjavík.'

'Where is he, then?' asked Matthew. 'He's supposed to be here. There's plenty of room for his name. It feels weird, seeing it blank.'

Thóra turned and looked around the cemetery. 'He can't be buried here, since he's not mentioned on this stone.' They strolled around the rest of the churchyard but found neither Grímur's nor Kristín's grave. 'Maybe Kristín was just a cat after all,' Thóra said glumly, as they left through the squeaking gate.

'Then what about the missing page in the church records? I think our next move should be talking to the brother and sister who sold Jónas the land,' said Matthew. 'You could use that ghost nonsense as a pretext to grill them about the history of the farm, and about Grímur and Kristín.'

Thóra nodded thoughtfully. That wasn't a bad idea . . .

Elín Thórdardóttir kept her hand on the telephone after hanging up. She heaved a deep sigh, lifted it again and put it to her ear. She quickly dialled a number and waited impatiently for an answer. 'Börkur,' she blurted, 'guess what?'

'What is it, Elín? Now's not a good time.' Börkur was always moody when his sister phoned him. 'There's a situation here.'

'What's going on?' Elín asked, although she knew it must involve Svava, Börkur's wife, who was a bag of nerves, always on the brink of a nervous breakdown over something minor.

'None of your business,' growled Börkur. 'What do you want?'

Accustomed to his unfriendliness, Elín ignored it. In fact, she enjoyed winding him up. She had always been against selling the land but had given in to his constant nagging in the end. It was a pity their mother had not opposed the idea, because the place had still belonged to her even though the proceeds would go to her children. Börkur had managed to talk her into selling. Now Elín had the chance to take revenge on her brother for his bossiness. 'A woman called Thóra phoned. She's a lawyer for Jónas, who bought Kirkjustétt and Kreppa.' She paused deliberately, determined to force him to ask.

'And?' asked her brother, irritated but intrigued. 'What did she want?'

'Turns out there's a problem, dear brother,' Elín said smugly. 'She wants to see us about a hidden defect she says Jónas has found in the property.'

'What bollocks! A hidden defect? On a plot of land? They need their heads read. What the hell could it be? Is it soil contamination?'

Elín let him run on for a while before interrupting. 'We didn't go into details. She just wanted to arrange a meeting. On-site if possible.'

'On-site? Does she think I've got nothing better to do than trek over to Snaefellsnes?' Börkur was almost shouting now. 'I'm up to my eyes in work! Drowning!'

'Oh, poor you,' said Elín, feigning sympathy. 'Maybe I should just go by myself.'

Börkur thought for a moment. 'No. I'll come too. When do we have to meet her?'

'Tomorrow,' she replied. 'Wouldn't it be easier to pop over to Stykkishólmur tonight, so we don't need to drive there early in the morning?'

'We'll see. Call me later. I might do, if I can sort some business out before this evening.'

'Börkur,' said Elín, 'one more thing. I think "hidden defect" might be something weird. The lawyer acted very strangely on the phone.'

'How do you mean, "strangely"?' asked Börkur.

'Just strangely,' she told him. 'There's something odd going on, that's for sure, but I don't know what.'

'Do you think it might be to do with the body that was on the news?' he asked, his voice suddenly shrill with panic.

'Oh. No, that hadn't crossed my mind,' Elín said, surprised. Her brother didn't sound like himself.

They hung up and Elín sat by the telephone, deep in thought. She tried to remember what she had heard about the body, and had an idea it had been found just before the weekend. She frowned. That was when Börkur had been out to Snaefellsnes on some fool's errand. How odd.

16

16

'This must be the place.' Thóra scanned the beach. 'We won't learn much from coming out here, really.' The stones at her feet glistened. The tide was out, but the smooth rocks were still damp. Nothing in this dramatic landscape suggested that a body had been found here not long ago, and Thóra wondered what she'd expected to see. Yellow police tape, perhaps?

Matthew looked at his watch. 'Except that it took us exactly thirty-five minutes to walk here from the hotel.'

'But we weren't hurrying,' she said. 'What's the quickest we could have got here?'

Matthew shrugged. 'I don't know. You might be able to get here in twenty-five minutes, not much less, unless you were running.'

'So somebody could have come down here from the hotel, murdered Birna and got back within the hour,' mused Thóra.

Matthew smiled. 'Well, that doesn't give the murderer much leeway. He would have had to come here explicitly to murder the woman, as there wasn't time for them to meet up and argue.'

'What an awful noise those birds make,' Thóra said, facing the cliffs. 'Their poor chicks.' She watched the chaotic mass for a moment, before turning back to

Matthew. 'No one would have heard her scream. Not through this din.'

Matthew waved his arms. 'Who was there to hear, anyway? There's never anybody out here.'

Thóra looked around, and was about to agree when she noticed two people at the top of the incline leading down to the beach. 'You may have spoken too soon,' she said, nodding in their direction.

They watched the pair slowly descend the pebbled slope – a young woman pushing someone in a wheelchair. They could not discern the sex of the occupant, whose head and face were concealed by the hood of their coat. The girl seemed to be struggling to move the wheelchair through the loose shale on the track.

'They must be the young people the Japanese mentioned,' Thóra said. 'The ones they saw talking to Birna. Should we have a word with them?' She looked at Matthew.

'Why not?' agreed Matthew. 'It wouldn't be the silliest thing you've done for this weird investigation.' He added hastily, 'Not that I'm complaining. I'm enjoying it, even though I don't have the faintest idea where it's all leading.'

Thóra elbowed him in the ribs. 'Have you suddenly turned anarchist in your old age? Come on.'

They set off slowly up the slope towards the pair. At first, when they drew nearer, Thóra thought she must have something in her eye – no matter how she tried, she couldn't focus properly on the face visible beneath the hood – but soon she realised there was nothing wrong with her eyes. Her stomach knotted, and she fought the urge to turn back and run. What was wrong with the wheelchair occupant's features? Although she tried to concentrate on the girl, who was rosy-cheeked and smiling, her eyes kept involuntarily returning to the face under the hood and the stretched, shiny pink skin that covered its entire left half. Thóra couldn't look directly at the man's disfigured eye sockets, the tragic remnants of his nose and the scarred, plasticky skin that went from his chin to his forehead, as far as she could see under his deep hood. Thóra prayed that the poor man – who looked young – was unaware of the effect he had, but deep down inside she knew he couldn't be. She hoped Matthew was coping better than her, but didn't dare glance over at him in case her expression revealed her horror.

She squeezed out a smile. 'Hello,' she said, addressing the girl.

'Hello,' the girl answered, smiling warmly. She had a thick blonde ponytail that swung when she spoke. She looked vaguely familiar, but Thóra couldn't place her. 'I'm not sure we'll make it down there,' the girl said. 'And if we do, it'll be even harder getting back up.'

'There's not much to see,' replied Thóra. 'If you want, Matthew here can help you down.' She pointed at Matthew without looking at him. 'And back up, of course.'

'Well, maybe,' the girl said, bending her head over the wheelchair. 'What do you reckon?' she asked the man. 'Should we accept their help or just turn back? Apparently there's nothing to see.' The young man mumbled something that Thóra couldn't hear, but the girl seemed to understand. 'OK, if that's what you want.' She looked up at Thóra. 'I think we'll just head back. Could he lend me a hand, perhaps?'

Matthew took control of the wheelchair and they all set off up the slope.

'I could have done with your help last Thursday,' grinned the blonde girl.

'Thursday?' Thóra said, startled. 'Were you here in the evening?' Might the girl and the young man have witnessed something without realising its significance, or could they be implicated in Birna's murder? Thóra waited eagerly for the reply, but was disappointed when it came.

'No, we weren't here,' the girl said, still panting after the ordeal. 'We were both planning to go to the seance at the hotel but in the end I went by myself because I couldn't get the wheelchair over a huge hole that had been dug across the driveway. That was quite a drag because there's not much going on around here and Steini was looking forward to it.' She rolled her eyes at Thóra. 'Actually, he didn't miss much. It was pretty ridiculous, and I think the medium was a fraud.'

Thóra decided not to ask whether the girl thought any mediums were genuine. She looked back down at the bay. 'Were you going beachcombing?' she asked.

'We were just going to see where the body was found,' replied the girl, as if nothing could have been more natural. 'We knew the woman who died.'

Deep down, Thóra was relieved. Now she didn't need to tiptoe around the topic of the murder. 'How funny,' she said, as casually as she could. 'We were here for exactly the same reason. We wanted to see the scene.'

The girl looked astonished. 'Really? Did you know her too?'

Thóra shook her head. 'No, not properly. We were connected with her, indirectly. My name's Thóra.'

The girl held out her hand. 'Berta.' She turned away and

scanned the beach. 'It was awful,' she said sadly. 'I heard on the news that she'd been murdered.' She looked back at Thóra. 'Why would anyone want to kill her?'

'I have no idea,' Thóra said truthfully. 'Perhaps it was nothing to do with her personally. She might just have been in the wrong place at the wrong time and met some lunatic.'

'Do you think so?' Berta asked, a hint of fear on her face. 'Here?'

'No,' Thóra said. 'I doubt it. But it's still more likely than a ghost being involved.'

'A ghost!' exclaimed Berta, the colour draining from her face. 'The fishermen, maybe? This is the same beach where they were washed up.' She shuddered. 'I've always had a funny feeling about this place.'

Thóra stared at the girl, taken aback. She had expected her to laugh when she'd mentioned ghosts. Clearly the undead were no joking matter in these parts. 'Do you believe in ghosts?' she asked carefully.

'Oh, yes,' Berta replied fervently. 'It's haunted around here for sure. I get really scared after dark.'

Not knowing how to answer, Thóra made a mental note that Berta was a potential witness if the compensation claim for the 'haunting' ever went through. They made good progress up the slope and Thóra decided to skip ghosts for the moment and get straight to the point. 'How did you know Birna?'

'She was the hotel architect. My mother used to own the land, and I helped her out.' She glanced up ahead to where Matthew, with some difficulty, was still pushing the wheelchair up the slope. 'She was really decent.'

Thóra did not push it, but took the glance to mean that

Birna had been kind to the boy in the wheelchair. Then it dawned on her why the girl looked familiar: she closely resembled Elín, her mother, whom Thóra had met when the deeds of sale were drawn up. Perhaps it would be unfair to make her testify against her own family in court, and Thóra hoped it wouldn't come to that, though it was definitely good to know about her. 'What did you do to help Birna out?' she asked.

'She was interested in local history, but neither my mother nor my Uncle Börkur could be bothered to discuss it with her. I told her what I knew and looked for old plans and drawings for her. Actually, I couldn't find any, but I did dig out a few photographs. She was really pleased.'

'Do you remember what they showed?' Thóra asked. She was puzzled. There were plenty of photographs in the basement, more than enough for Birna. Maybe they were all too similar – always the same wall, although with different people.

'Yes, they were mostly of the old farm, my great-grandfather and great-grandmother. There were other people as well, but I didn't know who they were.' The girl fell silent, then shot an anxious look at Thóra. 'Do you reckon I'll get the photos back? Mum and Uncle Börkur don't know I lent them to her.'

'I'm sure you will,' said Thóra. 'Just ask the police. They should be here tomorrow. Do you live locally?'

'No, not really. We have a house in Stykkishólmur where I can stay. I try to come as often as I can.' Staring intently at Thóra, she whispered, 'Because of Steini. He doesn't want to live in Reykjavík.'

Thóra nodded. 'Are you related?' she asked. She and the

girl had dropped back, but they weren't far enough away for Thóra to risk asking what had happened to the young man. She didn't want him to hear her asking about his appearance.

'Yes, he's my cousin on my father's side.'

In front of them, Matthew stopped and turned, clearly out of breath. They had reached the top of the slope. Thóra hurriedly changed the subject back to the murder. 'Do you have any idea who could have killed Birna? Was she in a relationship with anyone, or had she made enemies?'

The girl shook her head. 'She didn't have any enemies I don't think. At least, she never mentioned it. We met quite a few times – I'm clearing up some family stuff in the old farm at Kreppa and she often used to go there. It was great, chatting to her. I don't know if it's relevant, but she said she had a boyfriend.'

'A boyfriend?' Thóra asked eagerly. 'Do you know anything about him?'

Berta thought hard before replying. 'Well, I don't know whether I ought to tell you. He's married, so they kept it a secret. She confided in me, so she obviously wanted to talk to someone about it. I don't want to break Birna's trust, even if she is dead.'

Thóra thought Birna must have been very lonely to confide her secrets to such a young girl. Berta couldn't be older than twenty. 'I think you'll have to tell us. Silly as it may seem, it's usually love affairs that lead to situations like this. You don't want the person who did it to get away with it, do you?'

Berta shook her head vehemently. 'God, no.' She dithered, standing with Thóra beside Matthew and Steini.

'Can we go now?' said a hoarse voice from beneath the hood. 'I want to leave.'

Berta took hold of the handles of the wheelchair. 'OK, Steini,' she said, and thanked Matthew for his help. Then she turned to Thóra. 'See you around, maybe. Do you have a chalet here?'

'No, we're at the hotel,' Thóra said, annoyed that she hadn't learned the boyfriend's name. She watched as the girl waved goodbye and set off slowly, pushing the wheelchair.

Berta had only gone a few steps when she suddenly turned. 'His name's Bergur. He's the farmer from Tunga.' Then she continued on her way without another word.

Thóra and Matthew stood and watched the young girl plodding away over the bumpy track. When they were out of earshot, Matthew turned to Thóra. 'What on earth happened to that poor boy?'

Vigdís stuck her head over the reception desk and peered around. No one. Looking at the clock, she decided that no guests would be back just yet. In spite of their diverse nationalities and interests, most seemed to fall into a fixed pattern after checking in – getting up between eight and nine, and going out for a stroll after breakfast. As a rule they didn't come back until the afternoon. She knew this worried Jónas, because his original plan was for people to spend more time – and money – within the walls of the hotel. The masseuses, healers, sex therapist, aura reader and all those other experts were equally annoyed, because they were paid for performing actual treatments. They were busier in the evenings and at weekends, and most of them had been forced to dream up special offers in order to make a living. Jónas expected they would have more to do when the Icelanders began to turn up as winter approached. Then he could offer weekend specials. But the summer was only just beginning, and it seemed obvious that some staff would fall by the wayside if demand for their services did not pick up.

Vigdís didn't care about those charlatans' employment prospects; the current situation suited her just fine. She was dying of curiosity. After the police made her and Jónas promise that Birna's room was off-limits to everyone, she was seized by an overwhelming urge to disobey. Jónas had taken a quick peek inside when he opened the room for the detectives, but said there was nothing much to see. Even so, Vigdís had to see it for herself. Maybe there was blood – or worse – that Jónas had missed from where he was standing, or perhaps he'd seen something that he couldn't or wouldn't talk about.

Vigdís stood up, taking the master key with her. After checking there was no one down the corridor, she marched to the door of Birna's room and stuck the key in without a moment's hesitation. Swiftly she pushed the door open, slid inside and closed it behind her. The instant she heard the lock click shut she realised she'd made a terrible mistake. It was a total mess. There was no blood, but clothes were spread everywhere, torn papers mixed in with them. Vigdís realised that she would have to tell the police that someone had broken into the room, but what was she supposed to say she had been doing inside? Dusting? Perhaps she could lie and say she had heard a noise inside, but that would confuse the investigation – they might think

it had just happened. With a groan, Vigdís fumbled behind
her for the door handle. As she slipped back out, she desperately tried to think up a credible excuse for having sneaked
inside.

'Is this meant to be a joke? Who was in charge of the crime
scene?' Thórólfur glared at his subordinate. He gestured
at a heap of steel trays containing the objects retrieved from
the area around the body on Snaefellsnes. 'Shells and dead
crabs!' He closed his eyes for a moment and rubbed his
temple. A major headache was on its way.

'Um, it was Gudmundur. He's new,' Lárus mumbled.

'It looks like a ten-year-old's been on a school beachcombing trip. What did this Gudmundur think he was
supposed to do? Hoover the bloody beach? Maybe I should
be glad I haven't got an in-tray full of sand.' He walked
around the desk and examined the trays.

'Pebbles,' Lárus muttered, regretting it immediately when
Thórólfur spun round and glared at him. 'The . . . the
beach is pebbly, not sandy.'

'Pebbles, sand, what's the difference?' Thórólfur snarled.
'This Gudmundur of yours appears to have had no idea
what he was doing. Firstly, he seems to have combed an
enormous area, and secondly, it looks like he took everything that wasn't nailed down.' Thórólfur stuck a pencil
in an old, dented beer can and lifted it up. 'Like this,' he
said, wielding the can. 'Anyone with an ounce of sense
can see this has been outside for months. And this . . .' He
moved to the next tray and threw his hands up in the air.
'A dead catfish!' He turned to Lárus. 'Have you seen the
photos of the body? How could a dead catfish be connected

with this woman's death? Does this Gudmundur think she slipped on a dead fish, perhaps, and hit her head on a rock? In your opinion, is that what happened?'

Lárus said nothing, just shook his head. Thórólfur had started shouting, never a good sign. He shifted his weight from one foot to the other and opened his mouth to speak, but before anything intelligent occurred to him, his boss remarked, in a much calmer tone of voice, 'What's that? Some kind of sex toy?' Lárus walked over to get a better look. He was right. Poking out from under the catfish's gaping mouth was a battered plastic object that looked very much like a dildo.

17

Thóra nudged Matthew and nodded in the direction of the young man walking past. 'That's Jökull, the waiter who was so unpleasant about Birna,' she whispered as she stood up. 'Something must have happened to make him hate her that much. I'd love to know what it was.' They'd been drinking coffee in an alcove off the hotel lobby and debating their next move – inconclusively, although they agreed that they would have to find Birna's lover, Bergur from Tunga. They couldn't work out how to approach him and Thóra was bored stiff with discussing it, so the waiter was a welcome distraction.

She strode after him. He was heading for the dining room, but Thóra managed to tap him on the shoulder before he escaped inside. 'Hello.' She smiled. 'Remember me?'

Jökull turned, caught off-guard. 'Huh? Oh, yes. Aren't you the lawyer?'

'That's right. My name's Thóra. Have you got five minutes? I'd really like to talk a bit more about Birna.'

The waiter looked at his watch. 'Sure, why not. But I can't tell you much. You know what I thought of her. There's really not much more to say.'

'You never know,' replied Thóra. 'Can we sit down here?' She pointed to a sofa that had been positioned in the corridor and was clearly intended to be merely decorative. This was probably the first time it had been used, she thought as she sat down. She patted the seat beside her, sending up puffs of dust. 'How do you know her? Just from the dining room?'

Jökull perched on the edge of the sofa. 'I didn't know her really, but this isn't a big place so I couldn't help seeing her sometimes. I haven't been working here long and I avoided her, so we never became particularly well acquainted. I'm the last person who can tell you anything about her.'

Thóra frowned. 'I don't understand – you say you hardly knew Birna, but you seem to have formed a very strong opinion about her. Very strong, and very negative. There must be a reason.'

A flash of anger passed across his face. 'I'm just a good judge of character,' he said, without further explanation.

Thóra decided to head into safer waters so as not to scare him off. 'Your name's Jökull, isn't it?'

'Yes,' he answered, still on the defensive. 'Jökull Gudmundsson.'

'Are you a local?' she asked.

'Yes, actually, I am,' Jökull said. 'I was brought up on a farm near here. Then I went to Reykjavík to train as a waiter and stayed on there, but I jumped at the chance to come back when Jónas advertised for staff.'

'That's understandable,' Thóra said. 'It's quite beautiful. I can well believe that you'd want to come back.'

'Yes, it's very different from Reykjavík,' replied Jökull, and smiled for the first time.

'Do you know much about local history?' she asked. 'For

instance, do you know anything about the farm allegedly being haunted?'

Jökull clammed up again. 'There's no point talking about ghosts to people from the city,' he said. 'You don't get it. If something's not made of tarmac or concrete, you can't take it seriously.'

Thóra raised her eyebrows. 'I'm not putting down your belief in the supernatural – I'm actually preparing litigation for Jónas, which involves ghosts. That's all there is to it. Any knowledge you might have about local ghost stories would be very useful to me.'

'I'm sure it would,' Jökull said mutinously. 'But you'll have to get it from someone else. I'm no expert on ghost stories, although I do know a few. I think the world's a complex place, and people from Reykjavík don't know everything there is to know.'

'In that case, forgetting about the ghosts, do you know anything else about the place? For example, would you know anything about the people who used to live on the farm?'

Jökull shook his head. 'No, nothing. I'm not old enough to be interested in history.'

That was a good point, thought Thóra, making a mental note to look for older people who knew the area. 'Do you still have any relatives here?'

'One sister.'

'Did your parents move to the city?'

'No, they died,' Jökull answered tersely.

'Oh, I'm sorry,' said Thóra. She didn't want to pry. 'Forgive my obsession with local history, but do you know anything about a Nazi movement that operated around here?'

Jökull's eyes widened, and she believed him when he responded instantly, 'No, I've never heard of it. Although I don't chase around after the past, I'd definitely have remembered that. That can't be true.'

'You're probably right,' Thóra replied. 'But since you come from around here, there's one thing you can definitely tell me. It's nothing to do with the past.'

'What?' asked Jökull suspiciously.

'I met a young man today and I think he's from around here. I can't work out how old he is, but he could be your age. He was in a wheelchair and in a terrible state, probably from burns. Do you know what happened to him?'

Jökull didn't answer. He stood up. 'I've got to go and work. Your five minutes were up ages ago.' He pressed his lips tightly together, as if afraid to speak.

'So you don't know him?' Thóra asked, standing up as well.

'I'm late. Bye,' said Jökull.

Thóra watched him walking away. She had clearly struck a nerve.

'He was very odd,' said Thóra, taking a sip of her coffee. It had long gone cold. She swallowed and pulled a face.

'Do you think he's connected with the murder,' Matthew asked, 'or is he just a bit weird?'

'To tell the truth, I don't know whether he's involved. He clearly hated Birna, but he wouldn't explain why. He just said he was "a good judge of character". Might he be an ex-lover? Perhaps she dumped him for the farmer.'

'Or maybe he really is just a great judge of character,' shrugged Matthew. 'I'm starving. What time is it?'

Thóra ignored him. 'No, there's something weird going on. And he turned on me when I asked about the young man in the wheelchair.'

Matthew was shocked. 'You asked about him? What on earth did you do that for?'

'I just did. They are both from around here and about the same age. I thought he might know what happened,' she said. 'I know I can be a bit too nosy, but I didn't expect a response like that – what reason would Jökull have to be touchy about it? At least now I know I have to find out what happened.'

'I just think that's really inappropriate,' said Matthew said, still scandalised. 'Asking personal questions about a complete stranger. *And* he's disabled.'

'So? Is it illegal to ask about disabled people?' replied Thóra. 'You're just grumpy because you're hungry. Let's go and have something to eat.' She stood up.

Matthew perked up. 'Why don't we go somewhere else to eat?' he asked. 'Is there anywhere nearby?'

'Sure,' she said. 'There's Hellnar, for example. Who knows, we might meet someone who'll tell us about the ghosts, or about Bergur the farmer.'

Matthew groaned. 'God, I hope not.'

With a mighty effort, Eiríkur opened his eyes. The aura reader was suffering from his worst headache for years. He tried to move, but was immediately seized by such overwhelming nausea that he had to squeeze his eyes shut. When the worst had passed, he tried to get his bearings.

What had happened? Had he been drinking? He didn't think so, and there was no taste of alcohol in his mouth. He vaguely recalled laying out Tarot cards in the staff chalet – had he been telling his own fortune or someone else's? He had a feeling he'd had words with Jónas, but couldn't remember what it was about. Would it have been something to do with his job, or the Tarot reading? He couldn't remember.

Suddenly his thoughts were sent spinning in all directions by a terrible surge of pain in his legs. At first it was so intense that Eiríkur had trouble locating it precisely. Were both his ankles broken, or had some other part of his legs been injured? Then the pain eased slightly and he realised that it was a burning pain on the soles of his feet. What had happened? Was he at the hotel?

Eiríkur was lying on something warm but hard. He felt around himself on both sides and decided it felt like grass or hay, though that disgusting smell suggested that he wasn't outside. He could hear a strange sound, but couldn't place it. Was it breathing? Was someone else there? Cautiously, he opened one eye and saw that he was indeed indoors. It was quite dark, but there was a dim glow somewhere behind him. He didn't have the strength to turn round and see where the light came from – even breathing was hard work. He inhaled and exhaled cautiously – in, out, in, out – and fought the nausea that was worsening by the minute. It seemed stupid, but he didn't want to vomit before he found out where he was and what had happened. Then he realised.

The cards. The King of Pentacles, or money, and Death. His heart pounded in his chest and he turned his head as slowly as he could, hoping his memory was deceiving him, but it wasn't. He was in the stables. There was no money in sight, but he had a feeling death was close at hand. He lost control of his breathing and vomited copiously, unable for a while to focus on anything else. The sickness soon passed, and when it did he was gripped by terror again. He heard a loud neighing, followed by the heavy clatter of hooves. Which direction had the sounds come from? Where was the horse? Eiríkur made a huge effort to prop himself up and open his eyes. That made him retch again, but the first bout of vomiting had been so powerful that almost nothing came up. When the spasms receded, he managed to get up on his elbows and take a cautious look around. He looked down at himself and, in spite of his confused state, realised where the unbearable stench was coming from. He fought to suppress the scream that rose in his throat. Then he forced himself to look away from what was tied to his chest – the bloodied fur, the gaping mouth, the dangling head – and focus instead on what stood over him. He was desperate to untie the rough cord binding the horrible thing to him, but the urge to live was stronger. He raised his head slowly.

Legs. Four slender but powerful legs. What had he been told? That everyone would think it had been an accident. A bizarre case of death through misadventure. That couldn't happen. People had to know that this was murder, not a stupid accident. Over the years, Eiríkur had had to put up with enough jokes about his work. He was suddenly determined to ensure that mockery would not follow him beyond the grave. He felt an urge to communicate this, almost as strong as the desire to stay alive. Now that he knew what was happening to him, he had to find a way to make it known.

Eiríkur tried to concentrate. He was in a confined space, so he didn't have many options. He could hardly spell it out with pieces of straw, because they wouldn't still be in place when someone finally turned up. No, he had to write it. He had to find a surface that would be safe from the animal's hooves. His eyes darted around the stall and his gaze fell on the nearest wall. With a determination he never knew he possessed, he managed to keep sickness at bay long enough to drag himself closer to it. On the way, he prayed to God that he would manage to scratch a few letters on the wall with his ring before it was all over. The animal's breathing quickened and Eiríkur froze. He had been told that the moment the stallion noticed him on the floor, it would be driven mad with fear and trample him to death. When its breathing had slowed, he waited a while and inched his way towards the wall again. He was absolutely incapable of standing up; the pain in his feet was so intense it felt as though the skin had been burned off.

Eiríkur's shoulder bumped against the wall. He stretched out his hand and began scratching his ring against the panelling, but the stallion snorted as soon as it heard the ring scrape against the wall. To his horror, Eiríkur saw its mad brown eyes roll towards him. It whinnied. He tried to scratch letters into the wall as fast as he could, but dared not take his eyes off the beast. The horse pawed at the ground, then turned and kicked at him with its back hooves. All he could think about was whether his scrawlings would be enough to expose his murderer. If only he had a little more time – no one would understand it. A fearsome sound came from the horse and Eiríkur instinctively covered his head, as if that could save him.

But that was as futile as believing that the creature could read what was written on the wall: R E R.

18

'The stallion belongs to my wife. I'm not fond of horses,' said Bergur, staring at the floor.

Thórólfur leaned across the old kitchen table, taking care to keep his sleeves out of the coffee Bergur had spilled when he'd filled his cup with shaking hands. 'So what were you doing in there, since you claim you're not much of an equestrian?'

'The horses have to be fed every night. That's my job,' Bergur replied without looking up. 'You don't have to be a horsey person for that.'

In his many years in the police force, one thing Thórólfur had learned was that he could trust his intuition in interrogations. He had a very strong feeling that the man hunched in front of him had something to hide. God alone knew what it was, but Thórólfur was determined to find out. 'No, I suppose you don't,' he agreed, then continued, 'How come you still have your horses stabled? I understand from my people that they're normally put out to pasture in June.'

'We hire out horses,' replied the farmer. 'Well, my wife does, actually, but I help out when needed. I handle the feeding and so on.' He gnawed at a cuticle on his left hand. 'We're going to put the stallion out in the paddock; we just haven't got round to it yet.'

Thórólfur scribbled in a notepad, then looked up. 'When did you realise something was wrong?'

Bergur shrugged. 'I don't know the exact time, if that's what you mean. I don't wear a watch or carry one of those around –' he pointed to Thórólfur's mobile, which lay on the table between them '– but obviously it was very soon after I went into the stable block.' Bergur stopped talking and swallowed audibly.

'Yes, of course,' said Thórólfur impatiently. 'But how come you noticed it immediately? The stall is at the far end of the stables. Was there any particular reason you went straight there?'

Bergur swallowed again. 'I always feed the stallion first. He's not broken in yet and he gets agitated. He's hard work – he's incredibly wary of people, so he becomes really worked up when I'm in the stables. If he's fed first, he leaves me in peace to feed the other horses.'

'I see,' said Thórólfur. 'He's in the biggest stall with the highest partitions, is that right?' Bergur nodded silently. 'Why is that? Is it because of his temperament?'

'No, not just that. Stallions are always fenced off more securely. It stops them getting in with the other horses, which could end in disaster.'

'So this stallion wasn't particularly bad, perhaps?' asked the detective. 'I mean, are they all like that? Do they pose a special threat to other horses?'

'Well, stallions are more aggressive than geldings and mares,' answered Bergur quietly, 'but this stallion is exceptionally wild. I'm no expert, but I'm pretty sure of that.'

'Fine,' said Thórólfur, although it wasn't clear to the

farmer what he meant. 'So you say you went straight over
to that pen—'

'Stall,' the farmer corrected him.

'Stall, then,' he said crossly. 'And you immediately saw
a man lying there?'

'Yes, pretty much,' Bergur replied. 'It was all so surreal
I have trouble describing it in detail.'

'Why don't you give it a go?' suggested Thórólfur.

'I think I noticed the fox first, then the man. I remember
seeing blood in the sawdust and thinking the horse had
injured himself. Then I saw the fox and thought the blood
must have come from that, and then . . .' Bergur was
breathing heavily now, trying to stay calm. 'It was awful.
He was just lying there. I wondered at first if he was still
alive, but when I leaned over for a better look I could tell
he was dead.' He inhaled deeply and repeated, 'It was
awful. And his feet. God help me—'

'So you haven't got used to it?' interrupted Thórólfur,
drumming his fingers on the table.

Bergur looked up, surprised and anxious. 'What do you
mean?'

'This is the second body you've chanced upon in a couple
of days. I thought it might not be so bad the second time,'
said the detective. 'Come to think of it, it's a hell of a
coincidence, wouldn't you say?'

'I don't know what I'm supposed to say,' Bergur whispered. 'I couldn't bear to go through that again, and I wish
it had never happened to me. Neither time.' He sat up and
looked Thórólfur in the eye. 'I had no part in this, if that's
what you think.'

'No, no, I'm sure you didn't, but it's interesting all the

same,' said the other man, meeting Bergur's glare with a quizzical look.

'It was an accident,' said the farmer mulishly. 'Surely no one doubts that?'

'How would you explain such an accident?' asked Thórólfur.

'Well, I don't know,' replied Bergur, then paused. 'A hunter who followed a fox into the stable? Or something . . . weirder.'

'What do you mean, "weirder"?' enquired Thórólfur.

'There are cases of men who go into livestock enclosures to . . . satisfy their needs. Maybe he was one of them,' said the farmer, flushing slightly.

'Then he would have taken a stool or box to stand on, wouldn't he? And how does the fox come into it? And what about the pins?' snapped Thórólfur, stony-faced. 'Both your explanations are pretty implausible.'

Bergur sat back in his chair. 'I'm not investigating this; you are. I have no idea how the man ended up in there. You asked me and I answered. All I know is, I wasn't involved.'

'Fine, but it's still your shed, and—'

'It's a *stable*. Sheds are for cattle,' said Bergur peevishly. His anger subsided immediately and he added in a much calmer voice, 'I'm not sure I feel up to discussing this any more. I still haven't recovered from the shock.' He bowed his head and returned his gaze to the table.

'It's almost over,' replied Thórólfur, who had little sympathy for the man opposite him. 'I noticed a rifle on the wall inside. Is it yours?'

'Yes,' Bergur said. 'It's mine. I very much doubt that

you'll find a farmer in these parts who doesn't own a rifle.'
He looked up, annoyed. 'The man wasn't shot. What's
wrong with you?'

The detective smiled coldly. 'No, but the fox was, if I'm
not mistaken. Did you shoot that fox?'

Bergur picked awkwardly at the faded oilcloth on the
table. 'No. Maybe. I don't know.'

'Oh, really?' said Thórólfur with an exaggerated air of
bafflement. 'Could you explain that a little better? I'm not
sure I understood. You don't know whether you shot that
fox?'

Bergur stopped fiddling with the cloth and looked up.
'I shoot foxes if and when I notice them. There's an eider
colony here, and we can't have a predator loose around
them, but I haven't shot a fox for months, apart from one
the other day that got away. I know I hit it because I found
blood and some scraps of fur, but I never saw its corpse.
I thought it had escaped, but who knows? It might be the
same fox.'

'Indeed, who knows?' echoed Thórólfur. 'Maybe you can
describe to us exactly where this was, and of course there
are plenty of other things we need to go over more closely.'

'Not right now,' moaned Bergur, who was clearly
exhausted. 'I simply can't.'

'No problem,' said Thórólfur jovially. 'Just two final
points and we'll discuss it later. Firstly, are the stables
normally open or locked? And secondly, did you know or
recognise the deceased?'

Bergur did not look up. 'The stables are never locked.
Until now it hasn't been considered necessary.' Then he
raised his head and looked wearily at Thórólfur. 'I have

no idea whether I knew the man. It could be anyone – you saw the state he was in.'

'Fair enough,' said the detective, getting to his feet. 'Oh, sorry, one final question.'

Bergur looked resigned. 'What?'

'We found some writing on one wall of the stall, or rather scratchings. It was just a few letters, but we were wondering whether they were there before.'

'Letters?' repeated Bergur, surprised. 'I don't remember any letters there. What did they say?'

'It looked to me like "RER". Does that mean anything to you?'

Bergur shook his head. 'Nothing. I've never seen that and don't know what it means.' Nothing in his face suggested dishonesty, but Thórólfur couldn't shake the feeling that Bergur had something to hide. The question was, what?

'If I weren't so hungry, I'd suggest we look somewhere else,' Matthew said as he opened the door for Thóra. The restaurant specialised in vegetarian dishes and in spite of Thóra's rough translation of an assortment of framed press clippings in the window singing its praises, Matthew was far from excited.

'Beer's a vegetable,' grinned Thóra. 'Or made from vegetables, anyway.'

Matthew shook his head ruefully. 'I don't know what information you have about beer, but believe me, that's not right.' He followed her inside. 'At most, beer is a grain product.'

'Grain, vegetable,' said Thóra as she looked around for

a waiter. 'There's no difference.' She noticed a woman she recognised sitting at the bar and gave Matthew a nudge. 'That woman works at the hotel. Maybe we should go over and talk to her.'

'I'm not going over there unless we can get a menu and order from there,' Matthew said. 'And only if they have salted peanuts.'

'It's a deal,' said Thóra, and smiled at the waiter who came over. 'We'd like to start at the bar, if that's OK,' she said. 'But we're pretty hungry, so it would be great if we could see the menu now.'

They went over to the bar area, which was small compared with the dining room, and Thóra sat on a bar stool beside the woman. There were only four stools, so Matthew sat down on the other side of Thóra, directly in front of a bowl of peanuts.

'Hello,' Thóra said, leaning forward so the woman could see her face. 'Don't I know you from the hotel? Jónas's place?'

The woman had clearly had a little too much to drink. In front of her was a gaudy glass with a bright green mixture in it, and beside it were several tiny red plastic swords, each speared through a cocktail cherry. It took her a while to register that she'd been asked a question and she used the time to refocus her eyes, which seemed to be half full of tears behind heavy make-up. When she started speaking, though, she didn't sound anywhere near as drunk as she looked. 'Do I know you?' she asked, fairly coherently.

'No, we've never met, but I've seen you around. My name's Thóra, and I'm doing a little project for Jónas.' Thóra held out her hand.

The woman's handshake was feeble. 'Oh, yes, that's right. Now I remember you. I'm Stefanía, the hotel's sex therapist.'

Thóra managed to stop her eyebrows shooting up, as she was certain the woman would not appreciate it. 'I see. Is it a busy job?'

The woman shrugged and sipped her cocktail. 'Sometimes. Sometimes not so much.' She put down her glass and licked her red lips. 'Jónas claims business will pick up. To tell the truth, it's got off to a very slow start.'

'Oh, dear,' Thóra said sympathetically. 'But isn't it a nice place to work apart from that? It's a lovely hotel.'

The woman snorted and scowled. 'No, it isn't!' She turned to look at Thóra, but was still having trouble focusing.

'Are you talking about the ghost?' asked Thóra. 'Does it disturb you?'

Stefanía shook her head firmly. 'No. Fortunately I'm never there in the evenings. I haven't seen any ghosts, but I guess they only work nights. I've never heard of a ghost scaring people during the day.' She pushed back a lock of hair that had fallen over one eye. 'No, my problem is the women who work there.' She sighed. 'It's always the women. It would be great if it was all men.' She hiccupped. 'And me, of course.'

'Well, yes, of course,' agreed Thóra. 'But which women do you mean? I haven't met many, though I did speak to Vigdís on reception.'

'Vigdís, Pigdís,' Stefanía mumbled. 'She's a real bitch.'

'Oh,' said Thóra, startled. 'Obviously I don't know her well, but she seems all right. Maybe I've got that wrong.'

'You bet you have,' Stefanía hissed. 'She can't stand me, even though I've never done anything to her.' Suddenly serious, she added, 'Actually, I've analysed it and know what her problem is.' She paused dramatically. 'I'm a threat to her – a sexual threat.' She looked at Thóra triumphantly.

'What do you mean?' said Thóra, perplexed. 'Is she frightened you'll rape her?'

Stefanía chuckled. Her laugh was unexpectedly light and natural. 'No, silly. As a woman, she feels a primal threat from other women who are more attractive.' She smiled smugly. 'You don't need X-ray vision to see that I'm sexier than her.' She took a sip of her drink. 'It's always happening to me. I ought to know the signs by now.'

Matthew tugged at Thóra's sleeve. 'Can we order? I know what I want, and I'm starving.'

Thóra looked at the empty bowl of peanuts. 'No problem. Just call the waiter and order.' She went to turn back to Stefanía, but Matthew stopped her.

'What about you? What do you want?' Matthew pointed at the menu. Thóra hadn't even glanced at it.

'Anything,' she replied. 'Just order me anything.' She went back to Stefanía while Matthew called the waiter over. 'Speaking of women,' she said, 'did you know Birna, the architect?'

Stefanía's expression changed instantly. Her face fell and for a fraction of a second it seemed to be melting. 'Oh, God,' she said with a lump in her throat. 'It's so awful.'

'Yes, it is,' agreed Thóra. 'So she wasn't one of those annoying women?'

'No, not at all. She was lovely,' said Stefanía. She emptied her glass in one gulp. Then she removed the tiny sword with the cocktail cherry, which she put in her mouth and sucked before ceremoniously placing it on the bar beside the others. 'I'm devastated by all this, and I don't really know how I feel.' She looked up at Thóra. 'I'm not in the habit of coming here on Sunday evenings, even though I live locally.'

'I understand,' said Thóra, although she didn't, not at all. 'You seem to have known Birna well – do you have any idea who could possibly have wanted to harm her?'

Stefanía lifted her empty glass and spun it. The last few drops swirled round in the bottom. 'Yes, I do,' she said calmly.

'Really?' Thóra could not conceal her eagerness. 'Who is it?'

Stefanía regarded her beadily. 'I'm sworn to confidentiality. Sex therapists are like doctors in that respect. And lawyers.'

Thóra was careful not to burst out laughing at the analogy. Perhaps it was not so far-fetched – some of the divorce cases handled by her colleague Bragi could verge on sex counselling. 'Well, I'm a lawyer and there are exceptions to the rule. The greater good, for instance.'

After thinking for a while, Stefanía conceded, 'If you're a lawyer, it's safe to tell you, right? It's only a couple of names, and you won't tell anyone, will you? It's certainly not a question of that *greater good* of yours.'

Thóra could hardly believe how well this was going. She had envisaged a long session at the bar, waiting for Stefanía to drink enough to forget her oath of confidentiality. 'Absolutely not, I can't tell anyone, I promise.'

'Great,' Stefanía said. 'I've felt sick ever since I heard

the news, because I can't tell anyone. Maybe this'll make me feel better.' She looked Thóra in the eye. 'Promise?'

'I promise,' Thóra repeated. She crossed her fingers behind her back – she'd have to tell Matthew. 'Who wanted to harm Birna?'

Stefanía clearly hadn't exaggerated about needing to get this secret off her chest. When she spoke, it was at triple speed. 'She was having an affair with a married farmer from around here. His name's Bergur and he lives at Tunga. The sex was kind of extreme, and she came to me for counselling. She thought it had gone too far.'

'And could you help her?' asked Thóra. 'Did you advise her to stop seeing him?' A break-up might be sufficient grounds for a man to commit murder, if he was unbalanced.

Stefanía put down her glass. 'No.' She put one of her red fingernails in her mouth and bit it, hard. When she removed the finger, there was a white mark on the nail where the varnish had cracked. 'No, I didn't.' She stared at her empty glass as if in a trance. 'I told her just to go for it. That rough sex wasn't necessarily dangerous.'

'Oh, dear,' said Thóra. 'I can see why you feel bad.'

The sex therapist nodded slowly. When she looked up at Thóra, she spotted Matthew behind her. Until now she had been so absorbed in her own misery that she hadn't really noticed him. She smiled, a little unpleasantly. 'Who's that? A friend of yours?' she asked coquettishly.

Thóra decided to use the language barrier to her advantage. 'He's a foreigner. He's here to relax.' She leaned over to Stefanía and lowered her voice. 'AIDS.' Then she nodded conspiratorially and sat up straight again.

Stefanía's eyes widened. 'What a shame,' she said, crestfallen. 'If you want, I know a few techniques that could help you. You can have a lot of fun without actual penetration.'

'No, thank you.' Thóra smiled politely. 'But thanks for the offer.' She turned to Matthew. 'Come on,' she said in German, 'the food should be on its way.'

Stefanía smiled at Matthew. 'It's very important that you eat well and don't miss any meals,' she said sympathetically.

'OK, thanks,' said Matthew, bemused.

Thóra put her hand on Stefanía's shoulder. 'Thank you very much. I'll definitely see you soon, because I'll still be working on this project for Jónas.'

Stefanía looked at her in astonishment. 'Don't you want to know who the other one is?'

'Which other one?' she asked, confused.

'The other man who wanted to harm Birna,' replied Stefanía with a hint of irritation.

Thóra nodded quickly. 'Oh, yes, definitely.'

Stefanía leaned over to whisper in her ear. When she was so close that Thóra was certain her ear had been smeared with lipstick, Stefanía said in a low voice, 'Jónas.'

Thóra watched the police cars pull up. Three cars – clearly something was going on. They drove slowly on to the gravelled space outside the hotel and parked side by side in one corner. The slamming of car doors broke the silence as six officers got out, including one woman.

'What now?' Thóra wondered aloud. 'They said they weren't coming back until tomorrow.'

They watched the group stride towards the lobby, where she and Matthew were sitting in the evening sun with a glass of wine each. She was still hungry, because Matthew had repaid her indifference to the menu by ordering her just a green salad. He had hardly fared better with his vegetable lasagne, which was barely a mouthful. As a result, they had twice had to order extra bread, and even that had not sufficed.

She knew two of the officers by sight; the pair who had questioned Jónas and confiscated his mobile. The elder one was named Thórólfur, she thought.

'Good evening,' she said, addressing him.

'Hello,' he said dryly.

'You weren't expected until tomorrow,' Thóra said. 'Is something wrong?'

Without stopping or looking at them, Thórólfur answered as he passed their table, 'Things change.' Then the group of officers vanished through the door.

19

Thóra cleared her throat. 'There's one thing I don't understand.' She looked at Jónas, who was sitting beside her, his face ashen. 'Why do you want to talk to my client? He doesn't own the stables, and I can't imagine that anything has emerged in your initial investigation to suggest that he was involved in this.' She regarded Thórólfur steadily. 'Has it?'

Now it was Thórólfur's turn to clear his throat. 'I would have thought it was obvious. The last time a body was found here in the neighbourhood, it turned out to be a woman who worked for your client, and since that was only a few days ago, our first question must be whether anyone is missing from here. We have reason to believe that the same person was responsible.'

Jónas leaned forward in his chair. 'Would you please use my name? I don't exactly feel comfortable at being called "a client".'

Thóra suppressed a groan but looked at Jónas and nodded. Then she turned back to Thórólfur. 'In other words, you're only here to ask Jónas whether the deceased could be a guest or employee of the hotel? Not because you consider him connected in any other way?'

Thórólfur clenched his fists. 'I didn't say that. The investigation is only in its early stages, as I indicated. However, it should be clear that at this point in time we are only trying to discover the identity of the deceased. What happens after that is completely undecided.'

'These stables,' said Thóra, 'am I allowed to ask who owns them?'

'Ask what you like,' Thórólfur answered moodily. 'I may answer.' He cracked his knuckles. 'But it's no secret that the stables in question belong to the farm at Tunga.'

Thóra gave a start, and hoped that Thórólfur hadn't noticed. 'Is it close to here?' she asked casually.

'It's the next farm along, just west of here,' Jónas chipped in, relieved to be able to contribute.

'I see,' Thóra said. 'Then it must be very close to the beach where Birna's body was found, right?' She addressed the question to Thórólfur. Since he didn't seem about to answer, she added, 'Oughtn't you to be talking to the people who live there, rather than those at the hotel?' She had decided not to tell the police about the farmer's relationship with Birna until she had met him herself. She resolved to contact Bergur first thing in the morning, since the truth was bound to come out. Once that happened, she might not get the opportunity to speak to him.

'Let's get back to the subject,' Thórólfur said tetchily, turning to Jónas. 'I presume you know the stables in question?'

'Yes, sort of,' Jónas answered. 'I know where they are and I've been inside.'

'Do you ride?' asked Thórólfur.

'No, not at all,' Jónas answered. 'Just interested. I hope to go into that line of business in the future. At the moment the hotel operation is keeping me busy.'

'So what were you doing in the stables, that time you went inside?' said the detective.

'Rósa was kind enough to show me the horses,' Jónas said, adding hurriedly, 'Rósa is the lady of the house, Bergur's wife. We've discussed horses on the few occasions that we've met, and she wanted to show me a young stallion they had just bought. That was quite a while ago, at least six months.'

'Do you remember the name of this stallion?' Thórólfur asked.

'Yes,' Jónas said. 'I think it was called Snowy.' He smiled. 'It ought to have been called Fire, really – I've never seen a horse with such a temper.'

Thórólfur took his time formulating his next question, scribbling something on a notepad. Thóra was ill at ease. There was something about these questions about the horse that suggested that this was more than a fact-finding mission. She decided to wait and see what happened.

Eventually Thórólfur looked up from his notepad and glared at Jónas. 'In other words, for six months you have known that in these particular stables is a horse that is rather bad-tempered – indeed, uncontrollable? Is that correct?'

'Yes,' said Jónas, looking surprised. 'Why do you ask?'

'No particular reason,' the detective said, jotting something down. 'And what about foxes?' he asked. 'Can you tell me anything about foxes around here?'

Astonished, Jónas looked from Thórólfur to Thóra. 'Am I meant to answer that?' he asked, perplexed. Thóra nodded. She was dying to know where all this was heading. Jónas turned back to Thórólfur. 'I don't quite understand the question. Do you want to know about foxes in general, or whether I have any?'

'Well,' said Thórólfur, 'I would like to know whether there are many foxes in the vicinity. But if you keep foxes, it would also be good to know that.'

Jónas leaned back in his chair and frowned. 'I don't keep any foxes. Why would I keep foxes? This isn't a fur farm.' He was addressing his words to Thóra, who shrugged but motioned him to continue. Jónas did, although he clearly found it uncomfortable. 'But there are wild foxes around here. I know because they attack the eider ducks and the farmers complain about it. To tell the truth, that's all I know about foxes.' He fell silent for a while before adding, 'Well, except that they are the only mammal that was native to Iceland at the time of the settlement.'

Thórólfur smiled, but it didn't reach his eyes. 'I wasn't asking for a lecture on the natural sciences.' He ran his fingers through his hair. 'Tell me another thing. Do the letters "RER" mean anything to you?'

The hotelier shook his head. 'No. I can't say they do.' He looked at Thóra. 'How about you?'

'I haven't the faintest,' she answered, and turned to Thórólfur. 'What does it mean?'

'It's not important,' he said firmly, then changed the subject. 'Do you have a sewing room in the hotel here?'

'No,' replied Jónas. 'Do you have a loose button or a hem that needs mending?' he asked, in apparent sincerity.

Thórólfur did not answer Jónas, but continued, 'Do you offer acupuncture?'

'I don't personally, but we have discussed calling in an acupuncturist temporarily,' Jónas answered, startled. 'It's an ancient practice, but you can achieve incredible results with all sorts of ailments. I know of a man who smoked a pack a day of unfiltered Camels for thirty years—' He got no further.

'In case you hadn't noticed, we're not making small talk here,' Thórólfur growled. 'I ask; you answer. Preferably yes or no, as appropriate.' He had been rubbing one of his shoulders as he talked, and Thóra prayed that Jónas would not offer him a hot-stone massage.

'What I want to know is this: is there a sewing room here? Is acupuncture practised? If not, do you offer any kind of service that requires pins or needles?'

Jónas thought for a moment, then answered in accordance with Thórólfur's instructions. 'Yes,' he said.

The policeman sighed. 'Yes, and . . .? What kind of service?'

Thóra indicated that Jónas should answer. 'In each room is a little sewing kit, the size of a matchbox. It's for guests who need to make minor repairs to their clothes. I can fetch one of those sets if you want. There are several colours of yarn, one needle, two or three buttons and a safety pin, if memory serves. There's nothing else in it.'

'No other pins?' Thórólfur asked.

'No,' said Jónas, shaking his head. 'I'm fairly sure of it.'

'I'd like to see one of those sets before I leave,' Thórólfur said. 'And take a look at where you keep the stock.' He paused, glowering at Jónas. 'One last question. I've been notified that Birna's room was broken into.'

'What?' exclaimed Jónas. 'I didn't know that. Who told you that?'

'That's none of your business, unless you know who

did it and when it happened.' Thórólfur's glare didn't waver.

'I don't know anything about it. I haven't been in there since you had the room cordoned off on Friday evening and banned everybody from entering. I swear it wasn't me.' Jónas was gabbling now. 'I have no reason to go in there.'

'That's what you say,' Thórólfur said, finally looking down at his notebook. 'Somebody felt they had a reason. If not you, then who?' He looked back up at Jónas.

'Well, I don't know. The murderer, I suppose,' said Jónas, flustered.

'Is that everything?' interrupted Thóra. 'You said, "One last question," and Jónas has answered it now. Can we go?'

Thórólfur flapped his hand dismissively. 'Please do. But I definitely need to talk to you again tomorrow,' he said to Jónas. 'Don't go anywhere.'

Jónas's eyes widened, and Thóra spoke before he could. 'No, of course. We won't. I should remind you that I wish to be present any time Jónas is questioned. I assume that won't be a problem.'

'No, no,' replied Thórólfur. 'Why would it be?'

Thóra and Jónas left the office that he had lent to the police officers – if you could call it an office. It was used as a store for cleaning supplies, but happened to also contain a desk that wouldn't fit anywhere else. Chairs had been fetched and arranged as comfortably as the limited floor space allowed, but the result was a little unconventional. As soon as they had entered the room, Thóra had been struck by how unthreatening it was. She wondered if that would put the police at a disadvantage during their preliminary interviews. After being inside for a while, however, she had realised that the smell of disinfectant was so overpowering that it more than made up for the unimpressive atmosphere. She was indescribably relieved to walk out of there, and her mind was buzzing. Foxes? Pins? RER?

Jónas was knocking back brandy. He had invited Thóra and Matthew into his flat, as she needed to talk to him after the interrogation. Small but cosy, the flat was part of the hotel building. Thóra was sitting beside Matthew on a soft leather sofa, a glass of water in her hand, with a magnificent view of the glacier to the west. Jónas sat in a chair beside them.

'They think I killed Birna and that man,' he complained, taking another gulp of his cognac. 'Are you sure you don't want any of this? It really calms you down.'

'Do you know more than you told the police just now?' asked Thóra. 'What was that about foxes and needles? And the letters?'

'I don't have a clue, I swear,' he replied. 'I know nothing about that man and even less about foxes, needles and letters. I was freaking out. I thought it was a trap.'

'That's highly unlikely,' Thóra reassured him. 'But it was certainly very odd.' She waited as Jónas finished his drink and reached over to refresh it. 'Tell me one thing, Jónas.' He looked round. 'Did you know that Birna was involved with a farmer from around here? A married man?'

Jónas blushed. 'Well, I suspected she was, yes,' he said, a strange look on his face.

'And you are presumably aware that the very same farmer owns those stables?' she persisted.

'Yes, I realised that,' he said, 'but I didn't want to say anything.'

'Why not?' she asked.

'I just didn't,' Jónas replied, taking another swig.

'Could it be because you were having a relationship with her yourself, and didn't want to risk being implicated further?' she said.

'Maybe,' answered Jónas sulkily.

'Why didn't you tell me that you were together?' shouted Thóra, frustrated.

'It was nothing, nothing,' he replied. 'I had no reason to hurt her.'

'So you split up amicably?' she asked. She looked sideways at Matthew, who was smothering a yawn. She was conducting the conversation in Icelandic so that Jónas's responses would be as natural as possible. Poor Matthew had to sit there like a gooseberry, looking out of the window at the glacier. She admired his composure; her ex-husband would already have nudged her several times to ask if they could leave.

'Yes, pretty much,' Jónas replied. His eyes were a little glassy, but Thóra couldn't tell whether through tiredness – it was past midnight – or alcohol. 'I wouldn't have minded it going on a bit longer, but she wanted to move on. Said I was too old.'

'It sounds as though you weren't too pleased about it,' Thóra said. 'Did she go straight from you to Bergur?'

'Yes,' scowled Jónas. 'I suppose she did.'

'You seem quite angry,' Thóra said. 'Maybe I'm missing something, but I find it strange that you wanted her to continue working here under the circumstances, even if the split was amicable.'

'It was. I'm not lying,' he said. 'What could I do? She didn't want me any more. Life's like that sometimes. She was a good architect, and she understood my plans for developing the area. I'm man enough to be able to keep business and pleasure separate.'

'Good for you,' said Thóra. 'Let's just hope that the other witnesses back you up when they're questioned.' She looked at him sternly. 'If not, it won't look good.'

'Why not?' Jónas asked, affronted. 'Aren't I allowed to have girlfriends?'

'Of course you are,' said Thóra, slightly annoyed. 'But you know what I mean. And another thing – who's the man in the stables? Maybe it's Bergur. What then?'

He turned pale. 'I . . . I don't know.'

Thóra started to get up. 'I shouldn't be painting too dark a picture. We don't even know yet if it was an accident or something worse.'

Jónas looked at her. 'Do you think the police would ask me about foxes and cryptic letters if a farmhand had fallen out of the hayloft? No, there's some connection with what happened here.'

Matthew's arm rested lightly on Thóra's shoulders as they stood on the beach watching the surf. She had asked him to take a short walk with her before they went to sleep, because the smell of disinfectant was still in her nostrils and would give her a migraine if she wasn't careful. She closed her eyes and was about to say something romantic when her mobile rang.

'Anyone would think the hotel was the only place around here where there's no mobile reception,' sighed Matthew.

Thóra answered it quickly.

'Hi, Thóra. Sorry to call you so late,' said a female voice. 'It's Dísa from next door.'

'Oh, hello,' Thóra said, surprised. Had her house caught fire?

'I did try to call earlier, but your phone must have been switched off,' said Dísa apologetically.

'No, I'm on Snaefellsnes and the signal's patchy,' Thóra said, hoping her neighbour would get to the point. 'It comes and goes.'

'Yes, I knew you were out of town. That's why I called you. I saw somebody driving away in your SUV with the caravan, at about eleven. I thought it was rather strange. Did you lend it to anyone?'

'No,' said Thóra, perplexed. 'Thanks, Dísa. I'll check whether anyone borrowed it, and if not, I'll call the police. Thanks again.'

She hung up and saw that six text messages were waiting for her. She opened the most recent one. It said, 'call me asap – gylfi left and took sóley with him.'

Thóra let out a laugh that turned into a groan. She looked at Matthew and said wearily, 'Never have children. Stick with that little girl in Africa.'

Monday, 12 June 2006

20

Thóra was pacing in circles round the car park, trying to get a mobile signal. Matthew watched her in bemusement. 'Why don't you use the phone in your room?' he asked, hopping up and down to keep warm. The weather was horrible – Thóra couldn't tell if they were in the middle of a bank of fog or if it was just low cloud.

She had made a fruitless attempt to contact her son the previous evening, and wanted to start the day by locating both him and her caravan. The boy did not have a valid driver's licence, but he was taking lessons. Thóra was petrified that something bad had happened. The sequence of texts on her mobile had painted a clear picture of the scenario as it unfolded. The first three were from Gylfi. In the first he expressed displeasure at not being able to go home as planned, in the second he said his dad was driving him mad, and the third merely stated, 'eye of the tiger – im out of here.' Several texts from her ex followed, declaring Gylfi impossible to live with and blaming her for that. Thóra erased those messages. Gylfi was generally fairly soft-spoken, a keen student and far from the yob his father described. He was only young, though, and sometimes had trouble holding his tongue, especially on the subject of his father's dreadful attempts at karaoke. 'Eye of the Tiger' had clearly been the straw that broke the camel's back. Thóra could not recall Gylfi ever being excited about going to stay with his father, even without his sister's PlayStation *SingStar*. After their divorce, Hannes had met a woman who was a passionate horse lover and had been bitten by the same bug. Neither Gylfi nor Sóley shared his interest – in fact, Gylfi was frightened of horses, a fear he had picked up from his mother. He always felt uncomfortable at his father's house, with the threat of a horse ride hanging over his head. In spite of all Thóra's efforts to explain, Hannes refused to understand. He always said their son 'just hadn't got the hang of it yet'.

Thóra sighed deeply, waiting for Gylfi to pick up. She wondered whether she should call his girlfriend's parents, but quailed at the thought. Gylfi had obviously taken her with him on his impromptu caravan journey, because Thóra had received a text from the girl's mother and didn't care to recollect the language she had used. As a mother, Thóra could well understand the woman's fury; she would not be best pleased if it were her daughter, Sóley, on the verge of giving birth in her sixteenth year, absconding with a boy hardly any older in an SUV pulling a caravan. She thanked her lucky stars that Sigga's parents had not realised that Gylfi was driving without a licence.

Eventually her call was answered and Gylfi's sleepy voice came over the line. 'Hello.'

'Where are you?' shouted Thóra, who had intended to remain calm.

'What? Me?' Gylfi asked foolishly.

'Yes, you, of course. Where are you?'

Gylfi yawned. 'Somewhere near Hveragerdi, I think. We drove past it yesterday.'

Thóra cursed herself for not having made more effort to travel around the country with the kids. From previous experience she knew that the whole of southern Iceland was 'near Hveragerdi' to Gylfi's mind, just as the whole of north Iceland was 'near Akureyri'.

'Are you in the caravan?' she asked, adding in the next breath, 'And who's this *we*?'

'*We* are me and Sigga,' Gylfi said, then muttered, 'Oh, and Sóley too.'

'Sóley's still with you?' yelled Thóra. 'Why haven't you dropped her off at your grandmother's? You don't even have a driving licence yet, and even if you did, you wouldn't be allowed to tow a caravan. To say nothing of your pregnant girlfriend and six-year-old sister.'

'Driving's a cinch,' Gylfi said with masculine self-confidence. 'And just so you know, Sóley's here because she refused to tell me where you hid the keys to the SUV unless I took her along. Even she'd had enough of Dad's caterwauling. She couldn't use her PlayStation since he wouldn't get off bloody *SingStar*.'

Thóra groaned. 'Gylfi,' she said, as calmly as she could manage, 'don't move the caravan another inch. I'll come and collect you tonight. Are you at a campsite?'

'Uh, no,' Gylfi replied. 'I don't think so. We're just somewhere I stopped.'

'I see,' Thóra said. She closed her eyes and shook her head to ward off a scream. 'Find out exactly where you are and let me know. Send me a text; the connection's dismal here. Don't go any further. You don't want to end up injuring yourself or someone else in the traffic.'

After Gylfi had agreed, she ended the call. Thóra could

only hope that he would do as he was told. As a rule he was obedient, but if they had parked at the roadside or somewhere equally random, they would surely get hungry and need to move soon. She put her mobile in her pocket and turned to Matthew. 'I said it last night and I'll say it again. Never have children.'

Thóra drummed against the edge of the desk with the pen she was holding between finger and thumb.

'Does that help you to think?' asked Matthew. 'I hope so, because I can't keep a thought in my head with that racket.'

She put down the pen and turned glumly to Matthew. 'This is important. I'm trying to keep my mind on this, but I can't stop thinking about my children in that caravan.' She closed her eyes and inhaled deeply. 'Why on earth did I buy that contraption?'

'Because you're rubbish with money?' He smiled.

They were sitting in the hotel room, Thóra at the desk and Matthew on the bed. He was reclining comfortably against the headboard. She was sitting on a modern-looking chair that valued appearance over practicality or comfort.

'Start by writing down what you know for certain,' he said, making himself even more comfortable. 'The rest will follow.'

Thóra picked up her pen and thought for a while. At her suggestion, she and Matthew were going through the details of the case in preparation for meeting Börkur and Elín, the brother and sister who had sold Jónas the land. She had a feeling this would be her only chance to ask them detailed questions, so she wanted to have everything straight. 'OK,' she said, and started writing.

When she looked up, she had filled three pages of A4 paper. Admittedly they were widely spaced, so there was not that much text – she wanted to keep the details she remembered clear. She looked over to the bed, feeling pleased with herself. 'Wake up,' she said, seeing that Matthew had dozed off.

Matthew woke with a grunt. 'I wasn't asleep,' he responded. 'Have you finished?'

'Yes,' Thóra said, picking up the sheets of paper. 'At least, this is all I can remember right now.'

'Tell me,' Matthew said, propping himself back up. His body had slid down from the head of the bed when he fell asleep.

'Firstly, there's the ghost. I've talked to quite a few people and they all agree this place is haunted. Although most of the locals are fairly gullible, I'm inclined to believe something happened here—'

Matthew interrupted her. 'Are you kidding?' he asked. 'You think there's some truth in the ghost story?'

'No, of course not,' Thóra said tetchily. 'You didn't let me finish. I was going to say that presumably there's a natural explanation. Most people here believe in the supernatural and might interpret strange goings-on in those terms – incidents for which there might be other, more normal explanations. I think we ought to try to find out what they are. Ghosts on the lawn, the sound of children crying in the middle of the night, apparitions in the bedrooms.'

'The ghost only appeared in *Jónas's* room,' Matthew

said, pedantic as ever. 'But that might not matter. How can you explain all that? Maybe it's aliens?'

'Ha, ha,' said Thóra humourlessly. 'The thought struck me that it might just have been Birna and Bergur having sex outside. The counsellor said they went in for rough sex. Who knows, the wailing sound might have come from them and the "ghosts" could have been them, looking for somewhere to go?'

'I heard the crying, and it had nothing to do with sex,' said Matthew, blushing slightly because he knew Thóra thought he'd imagined it. 'Besides, Birna was dead by the time I heard it.'

Thóra regarded him thoughtfully. 'I don't know how to say this, but I don't think you heard anything. I think you dreamed the whole thing.' Seeing that Matthew was about to protest, she quickly went on, 'Anyway, I'm sure there's an explanation and I've resolved to find it, because it could be linked to the murders.'

'Wouldn't doing that ruin Jónas's case about the concealed defects in the property?' he asked. 'If you can explain the ghosts, you have nothing to base the compensation claim on.'

'No, of course, that would be a major setback – if the case had any legal merit to begin with,' she replied. 'I do think Jónas is telling the truth about what prompted him to bring the action, though: these "ghosts" have a negative effect on his employees and therefore on his business. If I can explain the hauntings and prove that they were not supernatural, I've achieved his ultimate goal. The employees will be happy, and Jónas can stop worrying about resignations and demands for pay rises.'

'That's if they believe you,' said Matthew. 'Even if people listen, they don't necessarily hear.'

Thóra put down one sheet of paper and picked up another. 'Whatever. Either way, I think there's a logical explanation.' She skimmed the page and looked up. 'Then there's Birna's murder. There are several things about it that need closer examination.'

'Such as your weird client?' smirked Matthew.

Thóra resisted a momentary urge to throw the ashtray at him. Instead she said, 'Yes, actually. Among others. He may well be more involved in this than he admits. For example, he didn't tell me the truth about his connection with Birna. It would be good to hear an unbiased account of their relationship and how it ended.'

'What do you think about the message sent to Birna from his mobile?' Matthew asked. 'Do you believe it was sent without his knowledge?'

Thóra shrugged. 'Damned if I know. Actually, I find it hard to believe Jónas killed Birna, whether he sent that message or not. He's the type who wouldn't admit to sending it, because of what happened afterwards. He mightn't have met her there, even if he sent the text. Maybe something came up, or he simply changed his mind.' After a pause she added, 'If so, Jónas might have told the murderer where they were going to meet and he saw his chance.'

'Who, though?' asked Matthew.

'I don't know, but Jónas might be able to tell us something.' Then she shook her head. 'No, he won't, actually. He can't say anything without admitting that he sent the message. We'll never get him to do that.'

'The other possibility, of course, is that the murderer stole his mobile and sent the message in Jónas's name. He said he never has his phone on him,' Matthew reminded her. 'There are plenty of people who'd have had the opportunity. Guests at the hotel, staff and of course the audience at the seance. The problem with this theory is that no one at the hotel, or at least no one attending the seance, could have made it down to the beach to kill Birna – not if the murder was committed around nine, as the text message suggests.'

'Agreed,' said Thóra, looking back at her notes. 'Then there's this farmer, Bergur. I put him at the bottom of the page because he's doubly involved through the man who was found dead at his stables. I think that's a hell of a coincidence. Two bodies in three days, one his mistress, the other on his property. I'd really like to know the identity of that man.'

Matthew's eyes narrowed. 'Have you considered Bergur's wife? She would seem to have ample reason for getting rid of Birna, if their marriage meant more to her than to her husband.'

Thóra nodded slowly. 'You're right, of course. Maybe we ought to pay her a call. What pretext should we use?'

'We could offer to muck out the stables,' suggested Matthew, laughing. 'She's bound to need that done.'

Thóra smiled. 'Yes, that might work – if she's blind and stupid. No one would believe you're a shit-shoveller. You might as well offer her Icelandic lessons.' She inspected his neatly pressed trousers and crisp white shirt. 'Perhaps you could say you're a Mormon missionary. You wouldn't even need to change your clothes.'

Matthew ignored her. 'Why don't we tell them the truth?' he suggested. 'We could meet them both separately.'

'And what's the "truth"? That we suspect her of murder?' Thóra shook her head. 'That won't work.'

'The truth has many sides,' Matthew said. 'You just say you're investigating the hauntings. That's no lie.'

Thóra pondered. 'Actually, that's true. Also, they might know something about the history of the farm and the area. That's not such a bad idea.'

'What else have you got?' asked Matthew. 'Surely you don't have only three candidates?'

Thóra read quickly down the page. 'No, of course not. I find that canoeist, Thröstur Laufeyjarson, very suspicious. We need to talk to him.'

Matthew shrugged, unconvinced. 'What, just because he paddled away when he saw us on the beach?'

'Among other things, yes,' she replied. 'And I thought the Japanese father and son were quite odd, although that's probably just my imagination.' She looked back at the page. 'That waiter, Jökull, was very negative about Birna as well. Then there's the old politician, Magnús. He was definitely hiding something. Why wouldn't he admit asking after Birna when he checked in, for example?'

'You're kidding, right?' said Matthew. 'He's so ancient he couldn't kill a pot plant. He may well have something to hide, but I can't quite envisage him sending a text and then scrambling down on to the beach to kill someone. And why are you just focusing on men? The murderer could just as easily be female.'

'Like who?' Thóra asked. 'Vigdís the receptionist? Or that drunken sex therapist, Stefanía?'

'Why not?' retorted Matthew. 'Or Bergur's wife, as I said earlier? I'm just pointing out that you know far too little to rule anyone out.'

Thóra sighed. 'I know. Unfortunately.' She picked up the last page. 'Then there are things that I want to look into even though they may have nothing to do with Birna's murder.'

'Fire away,' said Matthew. 'This is fun.'

'I'd like to know who Kristín was,' Thóra said. 'Her name's in Birna's diary, so it's possible that she's linked with the murder.'

Matthew snorted with laughter, but stopped when Thóra glared at him. 'Go on.'

'Also, I'd like to take a look at Birna's studio. I've been in her room and although I'm not an architect, it's obvious that she did only a limited amount of work there. There was no computer, for example.'

'Have you asked Jónas?'

'No, I haven't. It only occurred to me just now when I was making notes. But I will. Since someone went to the trouble of tearing her room apart, there must be something worth having in it.'

'I agree,' said Matthew. 'But if her studio's in Reykjavík, the police are practically certain to have sealed it.'

'I'm almost positive she did some work out here. Jónas seemed to think so,' said Thóra, turning the page over. 'And there's more,' she continued, reading through her last few notes. 'I'd like to know where Grímur is buried.' She looked up from the sheet. 'Plus I'm dying to find out what happened to that young man in the wheelchair.'

'My God,' Matthew said. 'Don't start that again.'

'I have to know,' insisted Thóra. 'If only because the waiter acted so strangely when I mentioned him. It was very odd.' Looking back at the page, she added, 'We also need to find out why the police asked Jónas about foxes and pins, and of course what "RER" stands for. And, as I said, I'd like to know more about the second victim.'

'It's good to know exactly what you want,' teased Matthew. 'That on its own is enough for some people.'

Thóra wasn't listening. 'I also need to know a bit more about Nazi activity in Iceland,' she said as she gathered up the papers.

Matthew gave such a mighty groan that Thóra thought for a moment he was in pain. 'God, the bloody Nazis,' he grumbled. 'They always turn up sooner or later.'

21

Thóra felt as though she had been transported back in time at least half a century. She was sitting in a living room crammed with highly polished furniture.

'Jónas is very unhappy that this didn't come up when the deeds were signed,' she said, the springs of the old sofa creaking as she leaned back. It was an imposing piece of furniture with exceptionally deep seat cushions, so when she finally touched the back of the sofa, she realised what a stupid position she had ended up in and hurriedly sat up again. She was only just tall enough to sit against the back of the sofa without her feet dangling in the air.

Börkur and his sister, Elín, had called her earlier that morning and invited her to their house in Stykkishólmur. Thóra decided to take them up on it instead of having them come to the hotel. She welcomed the chance to get away, hoping a change of scenery might clear her mind.

The house was one of the most elegant in town. It had clearly been built by a man of means, and was very well maintained. Probably their great-grandfather's house, Thóra thought. He had made money from schooner fishing and had the sense to sell out before the trawlers took over. When they arrived, Matthew had admired the house. It was beautifully decorated, with white-painted gables, window frames and guttering. Because the conversation would be held in Icelandic, he had opted instead to look around the town, so Thóra was sitting by herself beneath the watchful eyes of Börkur and Elín, who sat facing her with their hands resting authoritatively on the arms of their ornate chairs.

'Those are old wives' tales. I would never have thought them relevant in a modern business deal. Ghosts of abandoned children! I don't know what to say,' said Börkur dismissively. 'And I can't help wondering if it would have made a difference if he *had* known. All that man was worried about was clinching the deal. He wasn't interested in the salmon run in the river or anything.'

'Actually, given the nature of his business, I'm certain this would have mattered a great deal to him,' she corrected him politely. 'Salmon would be a secondary consideration in this context, but the supernatural definitely wouldn't.'

Börkur snorted derisively. 'And what's he asking for, exactly, based on this nonsense? A discount on the sale price?'

'Yes, for example,' replied Thóra. 'That would be one option.'

'I've never heard anything like it,' he bellowed. 'Do we need to hire a lawyer?' He turned to his sister, his face thunderous.

Elín, sitting impassively at his side, replied, 'Shouldn't we discuss this further? I'm sure we can resolve it.' She addressed Thóra. 'Can't we? Or is Börkur right?'

'If I thought the only solution was a discount or damages, I'd have sent you a letter to that effect,' Thóra answered. 'I've come here to discuss the matter and see if we can't find another way round it.'

'Damages,' muttered Börkur. 'I'm the one who ought to be claiming damages. I should be at work instead of sitting here having this ridiculous conversation.'

'Oh, come on,' his sister said irritably. 'I bet your staff were glad to get rid of you. They'll probably have a whip-round and pay you to stay away.'

Börkur flushed beetroot-red, but chose not to answer. Instead he turned to Thóra again. 'Here's your answer,' he snarled. 'You can tell Jónas that we don't give a shit about this gobbledygook, and neither will anyone else. I can't believe any court would award damages because of a *ghost*.' Breathing heavily, he added, 'You must have been pretty hard to find – a lawyer who's prepared to take on rubbish like this.'

Thóra did not care for the implication that she was a third-rate lawyer, but decided to hold her tongue. She knew that losing one's temper was the best way to lose an argument. 'Naturally, it's up to you what you do,' she said calmly, 'but I would like to remind you that judges get annoyed when people don't try their utmost to resolve disputes before litigating. Courts are a last resort, not the first step.'

Elín placed her hand over her brother's, which was gripping the carved arm of his chair. 'I understand,' she said to Thóra. 'But how else can we resolve this? What do you propose?' She turned to her brother, smiling encouragingly. 'We're open to suggestions.'

'Call in an exorcist, maybe?' grunted Börkur. 'How about that?'

Ignoring him, Thóra focused on Elín. 'Shouldn't we start by discussing whether you two have ever been aware of any supernatural activity there?'

'Yes, why not,' Elín replied, her grip on her brother's fingers tightening. 'That's easy. I've never been aware of anything strange going on, because I've hardly spent any time there. Our mother was brought up at Kreppa with our grandfather, Grímur. His brother, Bjarni, owned the land at Kirkjustétt where the hotel was built, but he died young. If there were any stories about that farm, we wouldn't necessarily have heard them.'

'How about you?' Thóra asked Börkur. 'Have you ever noticed anything, or heard any accounts of either farm being haunted?'

He shook his head impatiently. 'Of course not. There's nothing to notice or hear. I don't go in for that bullshit. And I've spent even less time there than Elín.'

Thóra turned her attention back to the sister. 'So how come the farms are in such good condition? I didn't see Kirkjustétt before the hotel was built, but we took a look at Kreppa and I assume that Kirkjustétt was in a similar state.'

'Yes, it would have been,' Elín answered, her voice level. 'We looked after the farmhouses well.' She gestured around the room they were sitting in. 'This house has been in the family ever since my great-grandfather built it. We've always used it as a retreat when we come to this part of the country. It's much more homely, and not as remote as those two old farms. My brother and I don't come here often, but we could easily have shared it.'

'But why maintain the farmhouses? What was the point?' asked Thóra.

'Well,' Elín said. 'It meant a lot to Mother when she was still in good health. She didn't want to disturb anything because she planned to move back to the countryside in her old age and wanted to keep everything the way it was. That never happened, though, because care provision for the elderly is very basic here, compared with Reykjavík.' She lifted her chin. 'Nonetheless, we kept the houses after Mother fell ill, because we had the idea that Börkur's children and mine could eventually inherit one farmhouse each. Although the two of us don't mind sharing this house, we knew that someday our children might want to come here with their own families.'

'So why did you sell them?' Thóra asked. 'You kept the farms in good shape for decades because of your children, then sold them once they'd grown up.' By way of explanation she added, 'I've met your daughter, Elín – Berta – and I expect your other children are of a similar age.'

Elín smiled coolly. 'That's just the way it turned out. I only have the one daughter, actually, but Börkur has two sons. Neither of them has shown any interest in Snaefellsnes, so there's no need to hold on to the farms.'

'What about Berta?' Thóra asked. 'I met her here and it sounded like she comes out here quite a lot.'

Elín gave the same cold smile. 'Berta spends a lot of time here, that's true. But Börkur and I have agreed that I'm going to buy his share of this place, so it's unnecessary for my daughter and me to own two houses in western Iceland. It's enough of an investment for the family to own all those farm properties. In fact, we're getting rid of them one by one.'

'Do you own other farms around here?' Thóra asked.

'Yes,' Börkur chipped in, his chest swelling with pride. 'Quite a few.'

Thóra wrinkled her brow. 'So why didn't you just sell Jónas one of those?' she asked, puzzled. She thought that for most people the last thing they sold would be the property with sentimental value.

'Jónas was looking for farmland with an old house on it,' Börkur replied morosely. 'He really wanted to buy the site once he heard there was not just one farmhouse on it but two.'

'He made us a very good offer, as you know,' Elín added. 'It was simply time to make a decision.'

Thóra wondered whether to probe further into their reasons for selling the farms. She wasn't convinced, particularly given Elín's chilly demeanour. Not wanting to provoke the woman with more questions, she changed the subject. 'Did you know anything about the history of the farms?'

'Did we know anything about it?' repeated Elín. 'Of course we did, but unfortunately I'm not much good with things like history and genealogy.' She released Börkur's hand. 'The same goes for my brother, I'm afraid.'

Börkur sat up a little and cleared his throat. 'I've always meant to look into it in more detail, but I can never find the time.'

'But you must have heard stories from your mother over the years?' persisted Thóra. 'Don't you remember any about the farms?'

'Our mother didn't really discuss her life here,' Elín replied. 'She was so young when she moved to Reykjavík with Grandfather.' Elín looked down at her lap. 'It's no secret that her life wasn't a bed of roses. Kristrún, our grandmother, died when Mum was still a baby, and we understand that Grandfather was far from being a model father. He had a few issues, shall we say, and never recovered properly after Grandmother died.' Elín looked up again, into Thóra's eyes. 'Unfortunately I don't remember him, so I can't judge for myself, but I'm sure he wasn't a bad man.'

Thóra frowned. 'Why do you phrase it like that? Did he mistreat your mother?' Could this be the incest story Sóldís had mentioned?

'In a way, yes,' replied Elín. 'He committed suicide. Mother was only nineteen, and I know I would never let my own child find me dead, so to my mind he wasn't a good father, whatever else can be said for him.'

'Oh, come on,' objected Börkur suddenly. 'You know he was ill. You can't expect someone who's clinically depressed to behave in a way society would deem normal – that's discrimination.'

Elín glared angrily at him for a moment without answering. Then she relented slightly. 'Of course, my brother has a point. I love Mother so much that I can't help feeling bitter about how he failed her.' She looked around the room. 'I'm pretty sure the reason Mother kept the farm going was that everything was wonderful when she lived here. It wasn't until they moved to the city that Grandfather's illness developed. She wanted to hold on to her memories of a happy childhood.'

'I understand. It must have been difficult,' said Thóra sympathetically. 'I noticed your grandmother's gravestone in the cemetery by the farm, but your grandfather Grímur doesn't seem to buried with her. If you don't mind me asking, why is that?'

Elín pursed her lips. 'Mother said she'd decided that after he died. He left no instructions as to his preferred place of rest, and she didn't want to have him buried here on Snaefellsnes. I think perhaps she wanted to have him close to her, because she was living in Reykjavík.'

This seemed a strange kind of logic to Thóra. She made herself more comfortable on the sofa. 'Tell me, do you know anything about your Great-Uncle Bjarni, who originally lived at Kirkjustétt?'

'He died young from TB,' said Börkur quickly, clearly pleased at getting his answer in first. 'He lost his wife young too, so the brothers' lives followed a similar pattern. They were both young widowers, each with a daughter.'

'She died too,' Thóra said. 'I mean his daughter, Gudný. TB, wasn't it?'

'Yes,' said Elín firmly. Judging from her expression, she didn't like losing control of the conversation to her brother. 'They both fell ill and refused to go to Reykjavík and stay in a sanatorium, as they used to call TB clinics in those days. I don't know if it would have changed anything. I know precious little about tuberculosis – nothing, really – but I know that Grandfather looked after them as best he could; he was a doctor. That wasn't enough, unfortunately.'

Thóra leaned forward. 'I have to ask you something now, and I'm aware you might find it uncomfortable.' She paused. The brother and sister sat and waited, as if paralysed. 'I've heard stories about incest on the farm. They say Bjarni abused his daughter. Could that be right?'

'No!' snapped Elín. 'That's rubbish. It just goes to show that back then people had nothing better to do than invent filthy stories about respectable folk who had died and couldn't defend themselves against gossip.' She fell silent, her face bright red. It clearly wasn't the first time she'd heard this.

'How can you be sure?' Thóra asked cautiously. 'Your mother might not have known about it because she was so young, and – as you said yourself – you didn't know your grandfather, so you can't have heard his side of the story.'

Elín glared wrathfully at Thóra. 'I've heard my mother deny it so passionately that for me there's not a shred of doubt. It's pure fabrication.' She frowned. 'To tell the truth, I don't see any point continuing this conversation. If you don't have any more intelligent questions, I think we ought to call it a day.'

'I'm sorry,' Thóra said humbly. 'Consider the subject closed.' In desperation she tried to broach another subject to avoid being thrown out. 'Do you happen to know why your grandfather and his brother quarrelled?' she asked hurriedly. 'I understand they didn't speak for years.'

Elín was still too angry to answer, so Börkur replied. 'It was more to do with their wives. The women fell out, and their husbands followed suit. I don't think anyone knows exactly what the dispute was between Grandmother and her sister-in-law, but it was serious enough that the brothers were never the same with each other, even when both women were dead. Stubbornness and grudges run in the family—'

Elín interrupted. 'Mother told me that our grandmother Kristrún lost a baby, and in her confusion she blamed her sister-in-law for killing it. The accusation was completely unfounded; the child had been ill, but Grandmother's mental state was starting to deteriorate at the time. Bjarni was insulted by her accusations against his wife and he and Grandfather had a furious argument, but they had made up by the time Bjarni died – I understand Grandfather treated Bjarni well, looked after him in his illness when no one else would go near him for fear of infection.'

Thóra nodded. 'Do you know if there was ever a fire at either of the farms?' she asked, visualising the drawing of the burning house she'd seen on the child's desk at Kreppa.

'A fire?' they said in unison.

Elín shook her head. 'No, I've never heard that. Both farmhouses are in their original state.'

Thóra nodded again. 'And do you recognise the name Kristín in connection with the farms?'

'Not that I can recall,' said Börkur, seeming unfazed by her change of topic. 'There must have been a few Kristíns in the area, but I don't remember having heard of any.' Elín shook her head. Both seemed sincere.

Thóra carefully formulated her next question, which she expected to be her last. 'Do you know whether either or both of the brothers were sympathetic to the nationalists during the war?'

'Nationalists?' Börkur echoed, reddening. 'You mean *Nazis*?'

'Yes,' said Thóra.

'This is quite enough,' Elín said, slamming her hands on the arms of her chair and standing up. 'I refuse to waste any more time on this nonsense.'

Thóra also stood up. 'One final question, on a different subject. You have presumably heard about the woman who was murdered last week. Now another murder has been committed, in all probability last night. Did you happen to be around here on the evenings in question?'

In anger, the brother and sister looked uncannily alike. The expression of fury that appeared almost simultaneously on their faces made them suddenly almost identical. 'The only polite answer I can think of to your unpleasant insinuation is no – neither of us is in any way connected with these murders. You should leave now,' spat Elín. 'Ghosts, incest, Nazis and now murder. I won't put up with this crap any longer.'

Matthew was leaning casually against a lamppost outside, but stood up straight when Thóra appeared. The door slammed loudly behind her as soon as she stepped on to the porch, and he smiled mischievously. 'Did you ask about the young man with the burns?' he said.

'No,' said Thóra grumpily. 'I didn't get that far.'

Matthew smiled even more broadly. 'Doesn't matter,' he said. 'Come on, I need to show you something.'

22

'What's the big deal?' asked Thóra, turning away from the little shop window. She didn't understand Matthew's glee as he'd shown her the bric-a-brac crowding the dusty white shelves in the window. 'It's just a bunch of old crockery, so what?'

'Look,' he said, rather disappointed, and pointed at a small object sitting between a ceramic falcon and a vase with a faded rose on it.

Peering through the glass, Thóra saw a silver shield engraved with a helmet and two swords. Because it lay flat on the shelf, she had to stand on tiptoe to see it properly. 'What is it?' she asked.

'It's a German medal from the Second World War,' said Matthew smugly.

'So?' she replied. 'Do you want to buy it?'

He laughed. 'No, of course not,' he said as he led her towards the entrance. 'But I caught a glimpse of the owner and he looked even older than the stuff he's selling. I thought we might go inside and ask him about Nazis on Snaefellsnes. He's bound to know a thing or two. That medal will make a good ice-breaker.'

'Ah,' said Thóra. 'Now I get it.'

As they entered the shop, the bell on the door chimed loudly. Thóra couldn't see a need for it, because the shop was so tiny that the shopkeeper couldn't fail to notice if anyone wandered in. Every square inch was loaded with knick-knacks, making the space look even smaller than it was. The crammed shelves on all four walls reached almost to the ceiling. A ladder was propped up against one wall. Everything was lightly coated in dust, which suggested trade was not brisk. At the back of the room, a white-haired old man stood behind an old-fashioned cash register, which Thóra doubted would meet the tax authorities' exacting standards. After browsing for a while, they squeezed their way towards the counter, navigating the various small items of furniture that littered the tiny floor space.

'Good afternoon.' Thóra smiled at the man when they eventually reached the counter without breaking anything.

'Afternoon,' the man said calmly, not smiling back. 'What can I do for you?'

'My friend here is from Germany, and he saw a brooch in the window that aroused his curiosity,' Thóra replied. 'Could we take a look at it?'

Nodding assent, the old man inched past the bric-a-brac towards the window. 'Ah, yes, this has been with me a long time, I can tell you,' he said as he reached for it. 'Actually it's a medal, not a brooch.' He turned and put it down on the counter. 'A decoration for those wounded in battle.'

'Oh,' said Thóra, picking it up. As she had thought, it was carved with a helmet and two swords, but now she noticed a little swastika on the helmet. A laurel wreath ran around the edge of the medal. 'So it was awarded to soldiers who were wounded in the war? Aren't there a lot of these in circulation?'

The old man frowned reproachfully, and Thóra regretted

her comment. Presumably he now thought she was about to start haggling. He took the medal out of her hands. 'A lot of them were awarded, yes. At the height of wartime, it was also given to civilians who were injured in air raids. What makes this one remarkable is that it's made of silver. There were three different ranks, awarded in accordance with the seriousness of the soldier's injuries. Regular, silver and gold. The regular rank was often granted for being wounded in combat. It was by far the most common.'

'How badly did you have to be injured to get the silver one?' asked Thóra.

'There were various grounds for winning the silver, including losing a limb or minor brain damage.' He lifted up the medal and allowed the weak sunlight to play across it. 'It wasn't a medal people particularly coveted, I can tell you that.'

'Not to mention the gold,' offered Thóra. 'I don't think I want to know what you had to sustain to deserve one of those.' She smiled at him. 'My friend's sure to be interested in buying it. Do you know anything about its background?'

The old man smiled back. 'No, unfortunately. I got it from the estate of someone who died several decades ago, along with some other personal effects. There was no information about how it ended up there.'

'I thought it might have belonged to an Icelander,' Thóra said. 'That would be interesting.'

'Not as far as I know,' the old man said. 'It's possible, but I doubt it. I think it was awarded exclusively to Germans, especially when it came to civilians.'

'But didn't some Icelanders fight on the German side?

Could one of them have earned the medal?' suggested Thóra, who was trying to steer the conversation towards Nazis on Snaefellsnes.

'Very few, I think. A couple of nutcases joined the Germans in Norway and Denmark, but I don't think any of them ever set foot on a battlefield.' The man placed the medal on the counter. 'The Icelanders who went for that sort of stuff at the time were no heroes. Bunch of idiots. I think they were mainly attracted by the uniforms.'

'Really?' said Thóra. 'I must admit I know absolutely nothing about the situation in Iceland. So there was a Nazi movement here?'

'Oh, yes,' said the shopkeeper. 'They were nationalists, mainly teenage boys who enjoyed marching with flags and fighting the socialists. I think they were driven more by youthful energy than any political leanings.'

'Was the movement widespread here on Snaefellsnes?' Thóra asked innocently.

He scratched his head. Thóra noticed that his hair was unusually thick for such an old man, even though it had turned white. 'Happily, it never got a foothold here,' he said, looking at Thóra with pale, watery eyes. 'There was one man on the south coast near here who tried to spread the word and recruit, but he fell ill before he made any progress. The local boys he managed to convert to nation- alism soon lost interest after he dropped out of the picture, so nothing ever came of it.'

Thóra could have cheered, but she kept her voice light and disinterested. 'Yes, of course. Wasn't it Grímur Thórólfsson, the farmer from Kreppa?' she said, crossing her fingers and praying she was right. If it had been Börkur and Elín's grandfather, that would explain the Nazi paraphernalia she had found in the box.

The old man squinted at Thóra suspiciously. 'I thought you said you didn't know anything about it,' he said. 'You're not far off, considering.'

'I only know the family,' Thóra mumbled evasively. 'I don't know anything about the nationalist movement.' She turned to Matthew and shot him a conspiratorial wink the old man couldn't see. 'Well, aren't you going to buy the brooch?'

'Medal,' he corrected her as he pulled out his wallet. 'How much does it cost?'

The shopkeeper named his price, and judging from Matthew's expression, it was no bargain. He paid in silence, then turned to Thóra while the man was wrapping it up and asked, 'When's your birthday? I've got the present.'

Thóra poked out her tongue, then turned to the old man to take the wrapped medal. 'Thank you,' she said, and they threaded their way towards the door. There, she turned round, determined to ask who the nationalist farmer was, but she didn't need to say a word.

The old man was still standing in his place behind the counter, resting his hands on it. He stared long and hard at Thóra, then spoke before she could get the question out. 'It was Bjarni,' he said, slowly and deliberately. 'Grímur's brother. Bjarni Thórólfsson, from Kirkjustétt.'

'Bjarni sounds like a pleasant chap,' Matthew said, putting the medal on the table between them. 'Abuses his daughter and spreads Nazi propaganda.' He turned the medal so that the helmet and swords pointed away from Thóra. 'I think this'll look great on you.'

Thóra pushed it away. 'What's wrong with you?' she said. 'I'd never wear that. It's bound to bring bad luck, and it might make people think I'm mentally impaired.' She gestured at the plate in front of Matthew. 'Eat up – it's not often I take a man out to lunch.' They were sitting in a little restaurant, where Thóra was treating Matthew as compensation for what he'd had to buy. 'It goes towards the medal, remember?'

She loaded her fork with pasta and put it in her mouth. After swallowing, she said, 'But I still don't have a clue whether this has anything to do with Birna. I'm really in the same position as before.'

'I'd have to say that a swastika sketched on a notepad isn't very much to go on.'

'No, maybe not,' Thóra replied. 'I just have a hunch that it's all connected.'

'Sometimes hunches are worth paying attention to,' said Matthew, 'but unfortunately not always.' He sipped his water. 'It would be best if you could support this hunch of yours with actual arguments. Preferably logical ones.'

Thóra poked at her pasta with her fork. She looked up, pleased. 'Do you know what I should do?'

'Um, I don't know, forget all about this and leave the investigation to the police?' said Matthew hopefully.

'No,' Thóra retorted. 'I just need to get on the Internet, and also study Birna's diary a little more closely. I didn't read it properly because I felt guilty. I may well have overlooked something.' She clinked her glass of lemonade against Matthew's water. 'Let's drink to that.'

* * *

Thóra sat in reception at the computer that provided Internet access for guests. She had a laptop in her room, where there was supposed to be a wireless connection, but after ten fruitless attempts to connect she had given up and dragged Matthew out with her. 'This must be him: "Grímur Thórólfsson, born in Stykkishólmur in 1890, died in Reykjavík in 1957."' She was browsing Reykjavík cemetery records and had found Grímur's name. Clicking it, she read from the screen: '"Fossvogur Cemetery. Plot H-36-0077."' She looked triumphantly at Matthew.

'I don't want to spoil your fun, but what good is that to us?' he asked.

'I'm curious to know what his gravestone says. Who knows, Kristín might be lying by his side. Unfortunately you can't search by the plot references, so I'll have to send someone in person.'

'Who?' asked Matthew. 'Hopefully not your fugitives in the caravan.'

'No,' Thóra answered. 'Our very own Wonderwoman – Bella.'

'Yes, Bella, I'm asking you to go down to Fossvogur Cemetery to find a grave for me.' Thóra mimed a groan and rolled her eyes at Matthew, who grinned.

'Then I need you to tell me what the gravestone says, and whether anyone named Kristín is buried either there or close by.' She paused to listen to her secretary's protestations, then interrupted her. 'Of course I realise that you can't be at the office at the same time as you're in the cemetery. It won't take long. You can forward the switchboard calls to your mobile, and before you know it you'll be back at your desk.' Thóra clutched her forehead as she listened. 'Great. And let me know what you find out.' She hung up. 'Bah. Why can't I have a normal secretary who jumps at the opportunity of getting out into the fresh air? Even if it is in a churchyard.'

Matthew smiled. 'She's OK. You just need to give her a chance.' He was lying in bed, pleased with everything and everyone, including Bella. It was thanks to her that he and Thóra had had some time to kill, and he'd made full use of it. Bella hadn't answered when Thóra first tried to telephone her, or the second time, or the third. Thóra had then decided to give Bella half an hour before making the fourth attempt.

Wearing a dressing gown, Thóra sat sipping the coffee that she had made in the tiny machine in the hotel room. In front of her on a small side table lay Birna's diary. She tapped one page. 'This is strange.' She looked over at Matthew, who was half dozing under the duvet in the large bed.

'Are you trying to make absolutely certain that your fingerprints will be on every square inch of that book if it ever ends up in the hands of the police?' he asked drowsily.

'No, listen,' Thóra said excitedly. 'On the pages before the swastika, she'd been going through the boxes that I looked at in the basement. I recognise the description of some of the things in them.' She held up the page to show Matthew. 'Look, she's listed some of the contents. Maybe she made some notes. She must have come across the same objects I did, including the Nazi flag. I opened that box first, but she didn't necessarily open them in the same order.'

'So?' asked Matthew. 'What does this brilliant discovery of yours mean?'

Thóra put down the diary. 'I'm not quite sure,' she said, turning to the page with the swastika on. 'It's obvious that it meant something important to her, considering how carefully she drew the symbol and coloured it in. Look.' She held up the diary again for Matthew to inspect.

'Just wait until you're forty,' he said, propping himself up for a better look. He squinted at it, then put his head back down on the pillow. 'It's a very carefully produced drawing, you're quite right. What has she written around it?'

'This and that,' Thóra said. 'Parts of it are illegible because she's scrawled over it, but I can make out "Swastika??" and "So where was he?" Then come a couple of phone numbers that I can't read properly because she's crossed them out.'

'Maybe she crossed them off after calling them?'

'Five, eight, something . . .' said Thóra, her nose almost touching the page. She straightened up and slapped her thigh. 'Hang on, I wrote down the numbers that Birna dialled from her hotel room. I could try calling them.'

She fished a piece of paper out of her pocket, went to the phone and dialled the first number. Eventually it was answered. 'KB Bank. May I help you?' said a voice on the other end.

Thóra put the receiver down. 'No luck there,' she said to Matthew and dialled the next. She put a finger to her lips to indicate to Matthew to keep silent when it answered.

'Reykjalundur Rehabilitation Clinic. Can I help you?' said a cheerful female voice.

Thóra, who had hoped it would be the private number

of someone who would remember Birna, was caught unawares. She decided to get straight to the point. 'Hello. My name's Thóra.'

'Hello, how can I help you?'

'I'm looking for information about Birna Halldórsdóttir, an architect. She jotted down this number and I was wondering if you knew her, or could check who she knew at your establishment.' Thóra could have kicked herself – there was no way this approach would work.

The woman on the other end of the telephone took the enquiry in her stride. 'Unfortunately we don't keep records of visits or calls. There are so many patients here that it's impossible.'

'It might not be a patient,' said Thóra, hoping Birna had been trying to contact an employee.

'We don't monitor that either,' the woman said. 'I'm afraid I can't help you. Excuse me, but I have another call. Goodbye.'

'Reykjalundur,' she told Matthew, groaning. 'A clinic. No way to find out who she called there.' She picked up the piece of paper again. 'This is the last number. Pity I scribbled it down so badly. Is that a five or a six?' She picked up the telephone and dialled once more. On the tenth ring she was about to give up when a mechanical voice informed her that the call was being transferred. This time, the phone was answered after a single ring.

'City Hall. Can I help you?'

'Hello,' Thóra said. 'Excuse me, I didn't quite catch that. Did you say, "City Hall"?'

'Yes,' said the girl at the other end. 'Were you trying to reach Baldvin?' When Thóra hesitated, she added, 'I saw you dialled his direct extension. He has a telephone clinic

between four and six on Wednesdays. Try again then.'
Cheerfully, she said goodbye.

Thóra turned to Matthew. 'It was the number of Baldvin
Baldvinsson's office at City Hall. He's a councillor, so he
must have an office there.'

'And who is this Baldvin, again?' Matthew asked indif-
ferently.

'The grandson of old Magnús,' she replied, reaching for
the diary. She peered at the numbers that had been crossed
out. 'He's considered one of the most promising politi-
cians around, but I doubt whether Birna called him to
discuss converting his grandfather's summer house for year-
round use. And I'm certain this is one of the numbers
Birna wrote down in the diary.' She flicked back through
it. 'I think I also saw an email address before, but I didn't
read it properly. That might be his.' She leafed quickly
through the book until she found a page where 'baldvin.
baldvinsson@reykjavik.is' was written in the margin. 'Here
it is. It can't be anyone else.'

'What do you think she wanted with him?' Matthew
asked.

'I don't know, but I do know we have to take another
shot at the old man,' Thóra replied. Then she picked up
the diary again and flicked through it. 'There's bound to
be loads of useful information here if I only knew how to
sort the wheat from the chaff.'

'Can you imagine how delighted the police would be if
they had that diary?' asked Matthew. 'They might have
the murderer behind bars by now.'

'What do you mean?' said Thóra. 'Are you saying the
police are cleverer than me?'

'No, no,' Matthew replied, 'but you don't have the resources to investigate a matter like this.'

Thóra picked up the diary and started reading. At a loss for an answer to his remark, she pretended to absorb herself in a page she opened at random. It turned out to be the plan for the building site and Birna's comments. 'What's wrong with this spot??? Old plans???' She scrutinised the two pages, then moved on when she noticed nothing new. On the next page was written, 'Maybe the rock?' After it was, 'There must be plans – talk to Jónas.'

Thóra stood up and walked over to the window. It offered a view of the area that had interested Birna so much, and Thóra wanted to see if anything about it caught her eye. She pulled back the curtain and looked over the grass. The land was fairly level and seemed to Thóra like an ideal plot for construction. She consulted the previous pages in an attempt to work out the location of the annexe. It was on the east side of the hotel area, far enough away not to obstruct the view from the rooms that had already been built.

'There's nothing wrong with that land,' she said, more to herself than to Matthew. 'It's just an ordinary lawn. The grass needs cutting, though.' She squinted. Sticking up from the green grass as it rippled in the wind was a large grey rock. 'Come on,' she said to Matthew, tugging at the corner of the duvet. 'Get dressed. We have to go and look at a rock.'

23

'And you dragged me out of bed for this?' complained Matthew, looking around. They were standing in the tall grass in the meadow behind the hotel. 'It's just grass,' he said.

'I'm not interested in the grass,' said Thóra as she bent over the rock protruding from the green expanse. 'I want to look at this.'

'Oh, well, in that case, I understand completely,' he said as he walked over to where she was. He shook his head. 'It's a grey stone, Thóra,' he said. 'You don't need to touch it to confirm that.'

'Yes, but it doesn't belong here,' Thóra told him, pushing the grass away from it. It was triangular, like a huge piece of Toblerone. 'Look around you,' she said, 'do you see other rocks in the meadow?'

'No,' conceded Matthew after glancing around. 'The plot thickens,' he added sarcastically.

'Seriously, though,' Thóra said, looking up from where she knelt. 'People went to great lengths to clear the stones out of meadows in the old days. Why would they leave behind a huge rock in the middle of it?'

'Because it was too heavy?' he suggested, squatting down beside her. 'Or could it be an enchanted elvish rock?'

Thóra shook her head. 'No, they were much larger;

boulders, really.' She stood up and went round to the other side of the rock. 'I'm no expert, but I think this side has been smoothed down. Look.' Matthew followed her round the rock and saw that she was right. On the other side the surface was rough and uneven, but here the stone appeared to have been sawn or cut, and then polished. Thóra ran her palm over it. 'Look at that,' she said, excited. 'There's something carved on it.' She pushed the long grass away and they saw a worn inscription in the middle of the rock.

'What does it say?' Matthew asked.

Thóra bent down closer and peered at the inscription. Her first thought was that it was a gravestone, but she soon saw that a verse had been carved into it, not a name and dates. She read out:

> *'Kerns I should have cast,*
> *A farm was meant for me,*
> *I should have been wed,*
> *Just like thee.'*

'What does it mean?' Matthew asked eagerly. 'Is it something significant?'

Thóra leaned back from the rock. 'I don't know really,' she said. 'It looks like a verse, but I don't understand it entirely. There's a word here whose meaning I'm not sure of.' Thóra bent back down to the stone to make sure that she had definitely read the word 'kerns' correctly. She stood back up. 'I wonder if this is what bothered Birna about the meadow?'

'This rock?' He laughed. 'I doubt it. It'd be easy to remove, so I can't see that it would have prevented the land being developed.' He looked back across the meadow. 'This is a perfectly ordinary patch of grass with a rock in it. Perhaps the verse is by a farmer who had a high opinion of his own poetry. There may have been a flower bed or a pet's grave here. Is the verse anything to do with animals?'

'No,' Thóra said, standing up. '"Kerns,"' she said thoughtfully. 'Could it be that the word I thought was "keens" in Birna's diary was this word?'

'Search me,' said Matthew. 'Why do you think it hasn't been mown here?' he asked suddenly, looking down. The grass was so thick that he couldn't see his shoes.

'What?' Thóra said. 'Why should it be? It's great like this. Natural.'

'In the meadow at the other end of the hotel, the grass has been mown,' Matthew pointed out.

'Actually, you're right.' She pointed at a little brown mound of dirt close to them. 'What's this?' she asked, going to look at it.

'Is there no end to your powers of detection?' said Matthew as they peered down at the low pile. 'Look, you found some dirt.'

'I know it's dirt,' Thóra said. 'The question is, what's it doing on top of the grass?'

Matthew looked around. 'It looks as if someone has been digging in the meadow,' he said. 'There are more heaps of dirt here and there.'

'What's the explanation? Could it be connected with the hotel annexe?' She started walking away. 'Maybe Vigdís at reception knows, and she might also know why this patch hasn't been mown.'

'You can ask her at the same time if she knows whether

Birna had somewhere to work other than her room,' Matthew said as he followed her.

She turned round, grinning. 'Are you beginning to think I'm on the right track?'

Matthew smiled enigmatically back. 'You're as far off the track as a cross-eyed racehorse.'

Vigdís was sitting at her place at reception, but her cheeks were flushed and feverish, her eyes glassy and her hands trembling. She was so distracted that she didn't notice them until they resorted to clearing their throats loudly. She jumped and finally looked up, open-mouthed. Then she slammed down the telephone receiver she had been staring at. 'Jesus Christ!' she said, and shuddered.

'Is everything OK?' asked Thóra.

Vigdís looked up at her, wide-eyed. 'No, it most certainly is not,' she answered, her voice quavering. 'Everything is so far from being OK that I really don't know what to say.'

'What happened?' Thóra asked anxiously. 'There wasn't another body found, was there?'

'No, there wasn't,' Vigdís answered. 'I just heard who it was who died in the stables.' Her cheeks grew redder. 'It was Eiríkur,' she said, shaking her head sadly.

'Eiríkur?' repeated Thóra. 'Who's he?'

'Who *was* he,' Vigdís corrected her. 'We have to get used to talking about him in the past tense. God, this is weird. First Birna, and now Eiríkur.'

'And he is . . .?' Thóra repeated, then hastened to correct herself. 'Was, I mean.'

'He was the aura reader at the hotel here,' Vigdís replied.

'A tall guy, thin, going bald.' She moaned. 'This is unbelievable.'

Thóra relayed the news to Matthew. Not knowing the German word for 'aura', she tried to mime it, which Matthew in turn mistakenly interpreted as a halo. Impatiently, Thóra said she would explain his field of work later. She turned her attention back to Vigdís. 'How do you know this?' she asked. 'Did someone call you?'

'Yes,' whimpered Vigdís. 'His sister. They found a credit-card receipt in his pocket and traced the name. They phoned her and asked her to come and identify the body. She was his next of kin. The body's in Reykjavík now.' She sighed as if that was the worst thing about the whole matter. 'His sister was completely devastated. She said he'd been trampled to death.'

'By a horse?' asked Thóra. The cause of death hadn't been given when the police spoke to Jónas.

'She didn't say. I was so shocked that it didn't even occur to me to ask.' Vigdís looked suddenly terrified. 'Do you think it's safe to stay here? What's going on?'

'That's up to everyone to decide for themselves,' Thóra said, adding reassuringly, 'I don't think there's a serial killer on the loose, if that's what you mean. We don't even know yet that this man didn't die accidentally. It may just be a coincidence.' Thóra thought for a moment. 'Did his sister mention whether the police were treating it as suspicious?'

'No, she didn't.' Vigdís hesitated. 'But there was something odd about her,' she said. 'When she said goodbye, she told me to be careful. It was as if she was suggesting that there was something wrong.' Vigdís's eyes narrowed inquisitively. 'But who would have wanted to kill Eiríkur?

He wasn't exactly a barrel of laughs, but he wasn't a bad person. Oh, the poor man.' She blinked and Thóra had the feeling that she was trying to squeeze out tears. 'Maybe I should've treated him more decently. He was so weird, though, and he had a habit of coming over for a chat just when I was busiest.'

Thóra didn't want to witness any histrionics, or waste time consoling Vigdís. 'Was he a horse lover, do you know?' she asked.

'God, no, I don't think so,' Vigdís replied. 'He was so pale that I doubt he ever went outdoors except for a smoke.' Then she added firmly, 'He was definitely not horsey.'

'Was he . . . interested in foxes?' Thóra asked, trying not to think about how stupid she sounded.

'Foxes?' said Vigdís, astonished. 'What do you mean?'

'Oh, nothing,' Thóra replied. She threw in another fox question, since she had already made herself sound like an idiot. 'His sister didn't mention foxes, did she?'

'No,' Vigdís said, and looked at Thóra with the cautious expression of someone who doubts the mental health of the person they are talking to. 'I've told you everything she told me.'

'Do you think Eiríkur had any business going to the stables?' Thóra asked, determined not to discuss foxes any further. 'Were he and Bergur, the farmer there, friends?'

Vigdís lifted one eyebrow. 'He wasn't Bergur's friend,' she said, adding in a seductively gossipy tone, 'But Birna . . . Birna and Bergur were *intimate* friends.'

'Yes, I gathered that,' Thóra said, and watched Vigdís's relish at delivering gossip evaporate. 'Did Eiríkur talk to Birna much, or mention her? Were they friends at all?'

'Definitely not,' Vigdís said confidently. 'There couldn't be two more different types than those two. He was a bit, well, I mean . . .' She faltered.

'You may as well tell the truth,' said Thóra. 'There's no need to pretend he was a saint just because he's dead.'

This appeared to cheer Vigdís up. 'You're right,' she said. 'The truth is, Eiríkur was a slob. He was dirty. He hardly ever shaved. He dressed like a tramp. He was bolshie, frankly, and a bit of a miser.' Vigdís clearly didn't need to be told twice to take off her rose-tinted glasses. 'Birna, she looked after herself, always nicely turned out. Deep down, though, she was completely different. Sweet enough if she needed something, but if she didn't, forget it. She had Jónas wrapped right round her finger.' She finally stopped to draw breath. 'Actually, there is one thing she and Eiríkur had in common: they were both obsessed with money. Apart from that, they were chalk and cheese.'

Thóra nodded gravely, taking care not to show her alarm at this flood of vitriol. 'So they never spent any time together?' she asked. 'Eiríkur wouldn't have known what she was up to any more than anyone else?'

'No, absolutely not,' said Vigdís with authority. 'Birna wouldn't have talked to Eiríkur if they were the last two people on earth.'

'I see,' said Thóra. 'Tell me, did Eiríkur or Birna behave at all differently just before they died? Do you remember either of them doing or saying anything unusual?'

Vigdís thought it over, then shook her head. 'No, I don't recall that. I don't actually remember the last time I saw Birna, but if she'd been acting strangely, I'm sure I'd remember. The last time I spoke to Eiríkur was when he came by looking for Jónas.' She put her hand over her mouth. 'Oh, that was probably just before he died.'

Thóra took a deep breath. 'And did he find Jónas?' she asked calmly.

'Well, I don't know,' the girl replied. 'I told him to try his office, but I didn't see if they met up.'

Thóra didn't know what else to ask about Eiríkur, so she returned to her original question. 'Why is it,' she said, 'that the west side of the lawn seems to have been mown, but not the east side?'

Vigdís looked startled by Thóra's change of direction. 'I have no idea.' She narrowed her eyes. 'Why do you ask?'

'I just wondered,' Thóra answered. 'I thought it was a bit odd.' She added quickly, 'Do you know whether Jónas had any little holes dug to test that patch of land? Or Birna perhaps?'

Vigdís gave her a blank look. 'Holes to test the land? Do you mean just ordinary holes, dug in the ground?'

Thóra nodded. 'Just little holes, more like scratches in the earth, really. They don't appear to have been made by earth-moving equipment, certainly.'

Vigdís shook her head emphatically. 'Definitely not. If anyone had been asked to go out there to dig it up, I would have known. I keep an eye on everything. Jónas is so absent-minded sometimes that I have to be the eyes and ears around here.'

'Did Birna have an office or studio nearby?' Matthew interrupted. 'Apart from her hotel room?'

'I don't know, but it wouldn't surprise me,' replied Vigdís. 'She was often away from the hotel, both mornings and afternoons. She didn't hang around outside, so she must have had somewhere to go.' She glanced slyly at Thóra. 'Maybe she went to see Bergur.'

'Who knows?' Thóra said, smiling conspiratorially at her. She looked at her watch. 'One final question and we'll stop bothering you: who mows the lawn?'

Vigdís looked uncertainly at her, then shrugged and answered, 'Jökull. He's a waiter here too.'

'Are you joking?' Jökull asked, looking around as if he expected to see a hidden camera. 'You want to know why that lawn hasn't been mown?'

'Yes,' smiled Thóra. 'I'm told it's your job.'

Jökull pulled a sulky face, which clashed with his smart black-and-white waiter's uniform. 'Yes, I'm doing it to earn some extra money. There's nothing to do except at meal-times, so I have time to do both.'

'Smart thinking,' Thóra said. 'But why isn't that area's grass cut? Is it that big rock?'

'No, that doesn't get in the way,' muttered Jökull. 'There's some other thing under the grass that plays hell with the mower. Something lumpy. The mower's always cutting out and I have trouble moving it around, so I just decided not to mow it. No one's complained. Did Jónas say something?'

'No, not at all,' Thóra reassured him. She went to leave, then turned back. 'Could you lend us a spade?'

'Honestly,' Matthew said, emptying a shovelful of dirt behind him. 'I have to admit you are unique among women. I wouldn't pick up a spade for anyone else.'

'Shh,' said Thóra. 'Less chat. More digging.' They were

back out in the meadow where Thóra had fumbled her way until she found a hillock that she ordered Matthew to dig up. 'This is bound to be something.'

He groaned. 'It had better be.' He thrust the shovel into the ground and put his hands on his hips. 'There you go.'

Thóra came up beside him and peered into the shallow hole. 'It looks like some kind of foundations.'

Matthew scratched his forehead. 'For a building? Do you think a house stood here?' He picked up the spade and scraped more earth away on either side. 'I'll be damned.'

'Can you see what I can see?' Thóra said as she bent down. She stood up again and showed him the palm of her hand. 'Ash.' She looked at Matthew. 'This building burned down.'

'Like in the child's drawing?' Matthew asked. He fell silent, then said, 'Wasn't there someone inside the burning house in the picture?'

24

'She hung up,' grimaced Thóra. She looked at the screen of the mobile Jónas had lent her. 'Unless I lost reception.' She shook her head. 'No, she hung up.'

'Are you surprised?' Matthew asked. 'She and her brother practically threw you out of their house this morning – she'd hardly be dying to speak to you.'

'No, perhaps not,' Thóra said grumpily, putting the mobile back in her pocket. 'It would just have been really helpful to know what building used to stand here.' She and Matthew were now at the edge of the lawn, as there was no mobile connection by the rock. 'Maybe her daughter, Berta, knows something,' Thóra mused. 'Hopefully I haven't offended her too.'

'I doubt it,' Matthew said. 'But she'll turn her back on you pretty quickly if you start asking questions about that friend of hers with the wheelchair.'

'No,' said Thóra. 'I'll steer clear of that for the time being. Right now I just want to find out more about this building.' They set off towards the hotel. When they passed the patch where Matthew had dug down to the foundations, Thóra came to a halt. 'How come Birna didn't know about this? She seems to have spent a lot of time thinking about this patch of land, if her diary is anything to go by.'

'Isn't it obvious?' replied Matthew. 'Jökull mows the

279

lawns, so he's probably the only one who knew about the uneven ground here. There was clearly no love lost between him and Birna, so he wouldn't have told her about it even if she'd asked.'

'But someone's been here looking for something. If they were trying to find the foundations, they can't have been very observant. None of the holes were anywhere near the raised area.'

'You can hardly call them holes,' Matthew reminded her. 'But I agree that if our mysterious digger was looking for the house that burned down, he wasn't much of a detective.'

'I almost want to go back down into the basement to check the boxes thoroughly,' Thóra said, her mind racing. 'Maybe something in them would show us what was here. A photo perhaps.'

Matthew looked at his watch. 'I don't know if that's a good idea. Don't you have to go to fetch your kids and the caravan?'

'That can wait until tonight,' she replied. 'I phoned Gylfi just now and they're happy enough for the moment. They're going to walk over to a shop not far from where they parked.' She crossed her fingers. 'I just hope his girl-friend's let her parents know they're OK. I'm not phoning them, that's for certain. They never shut up about the trouble Gylfi's got their little baby girl into. They think it's all my fault.'

'What about your ex?' asked Matthew. 'Do you think Gylfi will tell him?'

'I hope not,' Thóra said. 'Hannes can worry himself sick for all I care. It's his fault they did a runner in the first place.' She patted the pocket with her mobile in. 'I've got hundreds of unread messages from him. I'll check them when I have time, or—' Her mobile rang and she fished it out of her pocket. It was Bella.

'Hello,' said Thóra. 'How did it go?' While she was talking to her secretary, she rummaged in her pocket for a pen and paper. 'No Kristín, you say?' She scribbled down what Bella was saying. Then she rang off and turned back to Matthew. 'He's buried there alone. No Kristín in any of the nearby graves.' She sighed, disappointed. 'His gravestone is inscribed with his name, dates of birth and death, and a short verse.'

'What fun,' Matthew said. 'More poetry. Go ahead.'

Thóra read Bella's message from the piece of paper:

> *A farm is better*
> *though it be small,*
> *every man loves his home.*
> *Bloody is the heart*
> *of he who needs*
> *to beg for every meal.*

She looked up at Matthew. 'Actually this one rings a bell, unlike the other verse, which I've never heard before. I might be able to find it on the Internet. I wouldn't be surprised if it's from *The Sayings of the High One*.'

Matthew tapped her on the shoulder. 'The police seem to have called out reinforcements,' he said, pointing to the patrol car pulling up at the hotel. 'I don't think you'll be going down to the basement just yet.'

* * *

'Why don't you want to come outside?' asked Berta, opening the curtains. The dim room brightened up at once. 'It's gorgeous weather outside.' She stood looking out for a while, then turned away from the window. 'Come on, it'll do you good.'

'You go,' Steini said curtly, picking at a little loose flap of rubber on one wheel of his chair with his good hand. 'I don't want to.'

'Don't be like that,' said Berta. She walked over and crouched so their faces were at the same level. Often she found he responded better if she made eye contact. 'I promise you'll feel better if you get some fresh air. Something's clearly bothering you, and who knows, it might help to have something else to occupy you.'

'It won't help,' answered Steini, still scowling.

Berta had got used to his monosyllabic replies. His speech was impaired by the burns on one side of his mouth, where the skin of his lips had somehow fused together. Berta had always been astonished that the doctors hadn't done a better job, and she had a suspicion that Steini had refused to undergo further surgery; he refused to discuss it whenever she asked. He couldn't still be on the waiting list, as he had told her once. A much more plausible explanation was that he hadn't recovered from the pain and discomfort of his first operations and couldn't face any more. The week before, she had heard a message from Steini's physiotherapist on his answering machine, asking him to call back to discuss resuming his treatment. Steini had clammed up completely when Berta asked him to return the man's call. He obviously needed more time to recover, mentally as well as physically.

'We can go for a drive if you'd rather,' she suggested

gently. 'I'm up for anything, but I do think we should go somewhere.'

'Anything?' echoed Steini, looking her right in the eye without blinking.

'Almost anything,' Berta replied, feigning cheerfulness as she stood up. She wasn't sure what he was trying to say, but she didn't feel confident about going there. Not now, and preferably not ever. 'You know what I mean.' She put a hand on his knee. 'Come on. Please?'

Steini yanked the little tag of rubber off his tyre. 'Don't you ever get scared?' he asked.

'Scared?' said Berta, taken aback. 'What have I got to be scared of?' She smiled. 'Summer's coming.'

He looked at her in silence for a while. Then he stared down at his lap. 'I feel bad.'

A pang shot through Berta's stomach. She could not bear to see him in this state. Things were bad enough for him already. It was so unfair. Why did he have to come away from the accident so damaged? Plenty of people walked away from accidents without a scratch on them. If only she hadn't telephoned him . . .

She forced herself to keep smiling. 'I know,' she said cheerfully, 'let's go over to Kreppa. I'm way behind with the packing, and we might find something interesting too. You remember how much fun we had last time.'

Steini laughed coldly. 'Fun, you say?' He sighed. 'Oh, I don't care. Let's just go.'

'Great,' she said. 'I promise you won't regret it.' She was relieved. As soon as they set off he would cheer up – he always did. Suddenly his hand darted out and clutched her wrist, startling her.

'Can you forgive me?' he asked weakly.

'Forgive you?' she said. 'Forgive you for what?'

'If the worst happens, can you forgive me?'

Berta shook her head, perplexed. This was the longest sentence she'd heard from him in months. 'What are you talking about?' She gently loosened his grip on her wrist and moved behind the wheelchair. 'The things you say. *Me* forgiving *you?*' she said, starting to push. 'Silly boy, what have you ever done to me?'

'Hopefully nothing,' Steini said, pulling up his hood as Berta wheeled him outside.

Thórólfur frowned and leaned against the door to the makeshift office at the hotel. 'We've made considerable progress. That's all I can say for now.'

Thóra stood in the corridor facing him, her arms folded. She whispered to avoid being overheard by Jónas, who was waiting for them inside. He had asked Thóra to be present when Thórólfur called him in, but no sooner had they sat down than Thórólfur read him his rights, adding that as a suspect he did not have to answer the accusations against him. Now she was arguing with the officer in the corridor.

'You haven't answered my question. Why is Jónas suddenly being treated as a suspect?' she asked. 'What's changed?'

Mirroring her stance, Thórólfur folded his arms, his face stern. 'We have spoken to several witnesses, both yesterday and today. The picture they have painted doesn't look good for your client.'

Thóra inhaled sharply. 'Meaning what? Are you going to arrest him?'

'That depends on what he says during questioning.' Thórólfur shrugged. 'Who knows, perhaps he can explain a few things.'

'A few things?' said Thóra. 'Like what? He's told you everything you need to know so far.'

'As I said, there were various developments yesterday and today, things we didn't know last time we talked to him. And anyway, I haven't found his explanations thus far at all satisfactory,' Thórólfur replied. 'Shouldn't we just get on with it? Then you'll know what it is we want to ask him.'

'Give me two minutes alone with him,' she said. 'I need to explain this change in his status to him.'

He didn't like it, but he had to capitulate. Now that Jónas was a suspect, she had the right as his attorney to provide private counsel prior to an interrogation. The detective called his assistant out of the office, and Thóra went inside. She hurriedly sat down beside Jónas, who looked at her in confusion.

'What's going on?' he asked anxiously. 'Why did you leave?'

Thóra put her hand on his knee. 'Jónas, things have changed,' she said. 'Until now you've been questioned as a witness and been informed of your rights accordingly at the beginning of questioning. Now you're a suspect.'

'What?' exclaimed Jónas, his voice cracking. '*Me?*'

'Yes, you,' she replied. 'We don't have much time, so let's not waste it. Listen to me.' She looked him in the eye. 'Thórólfur told me that various developments have occurred during questioning of witnesses, the outcome of which is that you've become a suspect.'

'What? I didn't do anything, I told them that,' said Jónas, almost shouting. 'They must be lying.' Thóra could feel his leg trembling.

'It's possible the witnesses aren't telling the truth, Jónas,' she said, tightening her grip on his knee in an attempt to steady him. 'Now it's vital that you explain your whereabouts and give convincing answers to Thórólfur's questions. If he's dissatisfied or unhappy with them in any way, you risk being arrested.'

Jónas's leg stopped moving. He turned pale. 'Arrested? What do you mean?'

'Arrested by the police, Jónas,' said Thóra. 'You'll be driven to the station in a police car, then appear before a judge tomorrow morning with the recommendation that you be detained in custody.' Thóra had only handled three cases involving short terms of custody, so she was not overly familiar with the process. Those cases had been quite trivial, but Thóra decided this was not the time to make Jónas aware of her inexperience.

'I can't go to prison,' Jónas said, shuddering so expressively that Thóra didn't doubt he meant it. 'I just can't. It's Monday.'

Thóra raised her eyebrows. 'Monday? Is that any worse than any other day?'

'No, no,' he said distractedly. 'I just don't want to get caught up in all this today. Monday is my unlucky day.'

Thóra interrupted him before he could begin rambling about stars and auras. 'Listen carefully. We'll let the police back in, and they'll question you. Hopefully you have an explanation for everything they think proves your guilt, and if so, I promise that you'll walk out of here with me.'

'What if I can't?' Jónas asked, grabbing her hand. 'What then?'

'Then we'll just have to take things as they come,' she said, patting him on the shoulder. 'Chin up, and try to act as normal as possible under the circumstances.' She stood up and walked over to the door. 'Ready?' she asked, one hand on the doorknob. Jónas nodded, but he didn't look ready.

'Um, I don't know,' Jónas said, glancing nervously at Thóra, who was sitting beside him.

Thórólfur affected a look of exaggerated surprise. 'Really? If you asked me whether I'd had sex with a beautiful young woman last Thursday, I wouldn't have any trouble remembering. Maybe it's a regular occurrence for you?'

Thóra groaned inwardly. 'My client chooses not to answer that question,' she said impassively.

'All right,' said the detective. 'We'll be demanding a DNA sample, so the answer is immaterial.'

No DNA test was required to answer the question. Jónas sat rigidly by Thóra's side, guilt radiating from every pore. It was obvious to everyone that Jónas had had sex with the architect that day, which unfortunately was also the day she met her grisly end.

'Was semen found in Birna's vagina?' asked Thóra. 'I remind you that I must be presented with all the documentation if my client is taken into custody, because we would certainly appeal to the Supreme Court against any such order.' She heard Jónas let out a faint moan.

Thórólfur was holding a pencil, and he chewed on it

while he thought it over. 'I see no legal impediment to confirming that semen was found in the deceased's vagina,' he said eventually.

'May I ask whether your investigation uncovered Birna's relationship with a local farmer?' Thóra asked, hoping the police were unaware of it. 'This semen could be his.'

'We know all about him,' Thórólfur said, and a peculiar look crossed his face.

'Really?' she said. 'Shouldn't you be questioning him rather than Jónas?'

'Oh, we are,' Thórólfur said, skilfully twirling the pencil between his fingers. 'Irrespective of the outcome of his DNA test, we will need a sample from your client.'

'Why's that?' Thóra asked. 'If the semen turns out to be the farmer's, it can hardly be Jónas's.' Thórólfur smiled cruelly and the truth dawned on Thóra. 'Was the semen from two different men?'

Thórólfur suddenly stopped playing with the pencil. 'Perhaps,' he replied, after a short pause.

That was all Thóra needed to hear. Birna had had sex with two men on the day of her murder. Jónas was definitely one of them, and the other was either Bergur or the murderer, unless they were one and the same person. She could feel Jónas freezing up beside her, and knew enough about men to realise what was worrying him. She leaned over to him to murmur in his ear without the police hearing: 'I'm sure you were first.' She had to stop Jónas getting any more nervous. She felt him relax a little. 'Having sex with someone is not the same as killing them, is it?' she remarked to Thórólfur, adding, 'Which is not to say that Jónas is admitting to anything of that sort at this stage in the proceedings.'

'No, not necessarily,' he replied. 'But when the murder victim sustains external and internal genital trauma consistent with rape, it starts to look a little different, doesn't it?'

Thóra chose not to respond. 'Is there anything else you would like Jónas to clarify, or is it just the semen?'

'There's more,' Thórólfur said. 'Let's go back to the text message sent from your mobile, Jónas. Can you explain it any better now than you could last time? For instance, by telling us where you were between nine and ten o'clock on the evening in question?'

Dismayed, Jónas turned to Thóra. She nodded quickly and blinked at him. 'I still can't explain the message. I didn't send it, so someone must have taken my phone. I went for a walk around seven and left my mobile behind. Someone must have stolen it while I was out.'

'Stolen, you say,' drawled Thórólfur sarcastically. 'Someone "stole" it and returned it afterwards, then?'

'Well, yes,' replied Jónas hesitantly. 'I don't always carry it; I leave it lying around, so it wouldn't be that difficult.' He rubbed his temple, his nerves frayed. 'The hotel was packed. There was a seance. Anyone could have done it.'

'Strange that you mention that,' the detective mused. 'That's precisely the detail we were having difficulty with. As you say, the hotel was packed, yet no one recalls having seen you that evening. Where did your walk take you? Down to the beach?'

'No!' barked the hotelier, thumping the desk. 'I went for a stroll, but first I walked down the drive to see if the contractor who was mending the drain had made any progress. Then I walked for maybe an hour afterwards. When I got back, I dropped into my office and then went to my room. Someone must have seen me at the hotel. I wasn't keeping a low profile. I got back just before ten, and the seance was still going on, if I remember correctly.'

'Nevertheless, no one admits to seeing you, either indoors or outside, at around that time. There was an interval between half past nine and ten. The seance guests were all over the hotel – some went out for a smoke; others bought coffee – but none of them saw you. Yet you say you came back around that time,' said Thórólfur. 'But let's change the subject. Last night another body was found in a stables nearby. Can you tell me where you were around dinnertime last night, Sunday?'

'Me? I was in Reykjavík,' said Jónas.

'When did you leave here?'

'I set off about two.' His voice was trembling slightly.

'And presumably you went via the tunnel?'

'Yes,' replied Jónas, before Thóra could stop him. There was something behind this line of questioning, and it disturbed her.

'Presumably in your own car?' Thórólfur persisted. He was smiling like the cat that got the cream.

'My client chooses not to answer the question,' Thóra quickly interjected. She put her hand on Jónas's leg and squeezed it tight.

'All right,' said the detective, smiling wryly. 'But we have established that you went to Reykjavík via the tunnel. Since it's strictly forbidden to go through it on horseback, on foot or on a bicycle, we have to infer that you were driving a motor vehicle of some description.'

'Yes, I went in my own car,' said Jónas foolishly, in spite of the pressure that Thóra was applying to his thigh. She couldn't resist the temptation to dig her nails in to punish his stupidity. Jónas winced and gave Thóra a reproachful look, but she ignored him.

Thórólfur smiled even more widely. Then his face filled with scorn. He picked up some papers that were stapled together and slammed them down in front of the hotelier. 'Here is a list of all the cars that drove through the Hvalfjördur Tunnel yesterday. Your car registration number isn't among them.' He glared at Jónas. 'How do you explain that?'

At last, Jónas had the presence of mind not to say anything. 'My client chooses not to answer the question,' said Thóra. 'I should make it clear that Jónas is very distraught at present, and what he said just now may have been a lapse of memory.'

'It was *yesterday!*' replied Thórólfur. When neither Thóra nor Jónas responded, he shrugged. 'Be that as it may, let's turn to another matter.'

Another? Thóra tried not to show the anguish she felt on Jónas's behalf. Whatever else could they have against him?

'Then Jónas argued with Eiríkur, the one they found dead in the stables,' Thóra told Matthew. 'Just before Eiríkur left the hotel. And what's more, his bloodstream was full of sedatives. The same type that Jónas keeps on his bedside table.' She sighed. 'The bastards had a search warrant.'

Matthew whistled. 'So surely that means he's guilty?'

'Damned if I know,' replied Thóra. 'His fingerprints

were found on Birna's belt, and he definitely had sex with her the day she was murdered, although he refuses to admit it. Then he lied about going to Reykjavík yesterday.' She showed Matthew the list of car registrations. 'They wrote down the number of every car that went through the tunnel. Some poor bugger spent the whole night watching the tape from the security camera. They left this list behind, so I took it.'

'Then what?' asked Matthew. 'Where did they take him?'

'To Borgarnes,' Thóra replied. 'He appears in the West Iceland District Court tomorrow morning. They'll demand a custody order.' She ran her fingers through her hair. 'And they'll get one, unless the judge is drunk.'

'Is he likely to be?' Matthew asked, shocked.

'No, it's just a figure of speech,' said Thóra, sitting up in the armchair. 'We can but hope, though.'

'Oh, I forgot to tell you what happened while you were gone,' Matthew suddenly announced. 'I had a coffee at the bar, and when I was going through my pockets for some money, I found the medal I bought for you in Stykkishólmur. When I put it on the counter with the change, the man sitting next to me went berserk. It was the old guy, Magnús Baldvinsson.'

'Really?' Thóra was amazed. 'What did he say?'

'No idea,' Matthew said. 'It was in Icelandic, but he didn't sound happy. In the end he picked up the medal and threw it down behind the bar. Then he stood up and walked away. The barman was speechless. He said Magnús was ranting about me provoking him. Then he gave me back the medal. He was as astonished as I was.'

'I bet he was,' said Thóra, who could hardly believe her

ears. 'Magnús also reacted very oddly when I asked him about the Nazis, didn't he? It wasn't the kind of reaction you'd expect in Iceland,' she explained. 'Icelandic Nazism had hardly any following or impact, so even though everyone finds their politics repulsive, people don't generally attack total strangers at the sight of Nazi memorabilia. Maybe we should talk to him again.' She reached for her mobile. 'But not yet – right now, my number-one priority is getting my kids back safely. It doesn't look like I'll be heading home myself any time soon.' She dialled her son's number.

'Hello, Gylfi. It's Mum. Having fun in Selfoss?'

25

'You go first,' said Thóra, giving Matthew a gentle shove. 'You can pretend to be a horse lover. They'll believe that, what with you being German.' They were standing in the yard at Tunga hoping to meet Bergur, the farmer. To Thóra's mind, he had to be the prime suspect in the murder of which Jónas was now accused. They had walked right up to the farmhouse, which seemed to have been built on the cheap. It looked like any other small detached house from the early 1970s, but in even worse repair. Large blotches showed on the corrugated-iron roof where the paint had flaked off, and there were rusty streaks down the dirty yellow walls wherever the steel reinforcing rods were exposed. 'Go on, don't be shy,' urged Thóra.

'You know it's not that, darling,' replied Matthew, wrinkling his nose. 'What's that disgusting smell?' He looked around the yard.

'Isn't it just a good old country smell?' Thóra inhaled deeply. 'Unless that beached whale is upwind of us. Come on,' she said. 'On second thoughts, I'll do the talking. It's probably best just to be honest about it.' She knocked on the weathered front door. On it was a wooden sign with the names of the occupants painted in flamboyant script: 'Bergur and Rósa'. Thóra hoped that the lady of the house wouldn't answer. Their business was with Bergur, and

Thóra didn't even know if his wife was aware of his relationship with Birna. She didn't want to be the bearer of news like that, and there would be no way to talk to Bergur without the subject cropping up. She crossed her fingers.

The door opened and a man in his thirties peered out. He was lean but well built, with broad shoulders and powerful biceps. Thóra could easily understand what Birna had seen in him – there was something very appealing about his strong features and dark curly hair.

'Hello,' she said. 'Are you Bergur?'

'Yes,' the man replied warily.

Thóra smiled. 'My name's Thóra, and I'm a lawyer working for Jónas from the hotel. This is Matthew from Germany. He's backing me up, so to speak.' Matthew nodded politely. 'We wanted to have a quick word with you.' She looked him in the eye. 'About Birna's murder, and the other body that's been found.'

Bergur glared at them. As Thóra had anticipated, he was far from happy to see them. 'I'm not sure I have anything to say to you,' he said wearily. 'I've been grilled endlessly by the police and I'm simply exhausted. Can't you just read the witnesses' statements? I've got nothing more to say.'

Thóra's face fell. 'Actually, I prefer to talk to people in person instead of reading their accounts. And the questions I need answered aren't always asked.' She sighed lightly. 'But if you don't want to talk to us, maybe we'll just contact your wife tomorrow. I presume she won't be as tired as you are.'

Bergur hesitated. 'She won't want to talk to you any more than I do.'

'We'll just have to find out, won't we?' replied Thóra. 'I'll call her to explain my business. I'm sure she'll want to see me.' That should do it, she thought, putting on her best poker face.

Bergur glanced back inside the house, then glowered at Thóra. He pretended not to notice Matthew. 'All right,' he said grumpily. 'I'll talk to you, but not here. There's a little coffee room in the stables where we can sit.' He reached behind the door, put on some shoes and called loudly, 'Rósa! I'm going out.' Then he shut the door behind him without another word, even though his wife had shouted back something unintelligible. He set off in silence.

'These stables,' Thóra called after him as he strode ahead towards a fairly new, corrugated-iron-clad building, 'are they where Eiríkur's body was found?' When Bergur didn't answer, Thóra rolled her eyes at Matthew – they weren't making much progress. Then she pointed to her mouth to indicate that he should join in the conversation. He just smiled and shook his head.

They followed Bergur to a large door, which he threw open. 'Come inside,' he said.

'Thanks,' Thóra said, amused by Matthew's expression when the smell of horse dung hit them like a slap in the face. 'That's a nice horsey smell,' she said, out of earshot of Bergur, and winked at Matthew. He had clamped his mouth shut so tightly that it was impossible for him to smile, but his face relaxed a little when they reached the coffee room.

'You can sit here,' said Bergur, pointing to three hard chairs round an old kitchen table. He leaned against a little sink unit on which stood a dirty coffee cup and box that had contained rifle ammunition.

'Thank you,' Thóra said as she sat down. She could see Bergur's lip curl as he watched Matthew dust off his chair before sitting. 'I don't know if you heard me ask just now,' she said, 'but are these the stables where Eiríkur's body was found?'

Bergur nodded. 'Yes,' he said reluctantly.

'And it was you who discovered him, wasn't it?' Thóra continued. When he nodded silently, she went on. 'And you stumbled upon Birna's body too. Isn't that weird?' she said disingenuously.

Instead of answering, Bergur stared fixedly at her from beneath his heavy brow, until Thóra was forced to blink. Only then did he speak. 'Are you trying to insinuate something?' he snapped. 'If so, I'll say the same to you as I said to the police – I had nothing to do with either of those deaths.'

'Murders,' she corrected him. 'They were both murdered. Be that as it may, we know you were having an affair with Birna. So was everything going well?'

Bergur flushed, and Thóra was unsure if it was from anger or shame at discussing his infidelity with a stranger. When he spoke, his voice suggested the latter. 'Things were just fine,' he said, thin-lipped.

'And did your wife know about it? What's her name again?' said Thóra. 'Rósa, that's it. Did Rósa know?'

His blush deepened. 'No,' he said. 'She didn't know, and I don't think she's heard about it yet. Not from me, anyway.'

'So it was just a fling?' asked Thóra. 'I only ask because you kept it hidden from your wife.'

'It had become more than that,' Bergur replied, stung. 'I was going to divorce Rósa. The time just wasn't right.'

'I understand,' she said. 'So there's probably no point telling her now, given what's happened?'

'That's none of your business,' he cried, his face blazing now.

'No, you're right,' agreed Thóra. Her chair creaked as she tried to make herself more comfortable. 'I heard one thing about Birna today that strikes me as odd in light of what you've just said.' She fell silent, as if wondering whether to let Bergur in on the secret.

'What was it?' His curiosity was aroused.

'No, I'm sure it wasn't true,' said Thóra, and started examining her fingernails. Then she looked up. 'OK. The day Birna was murdered, she had sex with two men. You, I presume, and someone else – perhaps the murderer, perhaps not. Is it possible your relationship was just a bit of fun for her?'

Bergur drew himself up to his full height and took a deep breath. 'I don't know where you got your information from, but I was told that she'd been raped. You don't have to be a genius to conclude that the second time was against her will,' he yelled.

'So you're saying you were one of the two?' asked Thóra.

Bergur sagged back against the sink. 'Yes,' he said. 'It was fully consensual and hours before she died. We were together in the afternoon, and she was murdered that evening.'

Thóra paused, thinking. 'Who do *you* think murdered Birna?' she asked. 'You were close; you must have wondered.'

'Jónas,' he snarled. 'Who else?'

Thóra shrugged. 'He says he's innocent. Just like you,' she said. 'And why would he want her dead? She was working on a project that meant a lot to him. Without her it'll all fall apart, or at least be seriously delayed. I understand that he'd come to terms with breaking up with her, so he could hardly have been jealous, could he?'

'They were never really together,' said Bergur angrily. 'They were having sex, but it was never a relationship.' He paused to catch his breath. 'But he missed her terribly, and it's not true that he'd recovered from the rejection.'

'How do you know?' she asked.

'Birna told me,' said Bergur petulantly. 'He was still chasing after her. That's why she stopped using her hotel room as a studio. He wouldn't leave her alone.'

Thóra was agog. 'So where *did* she work?' she asked. 'Presumably somewhere close by.'

Bergur could obviously tell that Thóra's interest was aroused and he took pleasure in drawing out his reply. 'She moved over to Kreppa,' he said eventually. 'The farm belongs to the hotel, but it's deserted. She moved her stuff in there.'

'I know the farm,' Thóra replied. 'I've even been inside, but I saw no evidence that anyone had worked there recently,' she said dubiously. 'Do you know which room she used?'

'It was one of the upstairs rooms,' he said, without elaborating.

'I see,' she said, determined to revisit the farm at the first opportunity. Some of Birna's belongings must still be there, hopefully something that can shed light on her death, although that might be wishful thinking. 'Tell me something,' she said. 'Do you know the history of the two farms, Kreppa and Kirkjustétt?'

Bergur shook his head. 'No,' he said. 'I'm from the West Fjords. I didn't move here until I was about twenty.'

'You never heard mention of a fire at Kirkjustétt?' she asked hopefully, although she knew it was unlikely.

'No, never,' said Bergur. 'Apparently the farms are still in their original condition, so there could only have been a fire there if it happened just after they were built and the damage was repaired immediately. I doubt that, though, because Birna was fascinated by those two farms and she never mentioned it to me.'

'Did she discuss their history with you?' asked Thóra. 'And did she ever mention Nazis in connection with them?'

Bergur looked startled. 'Actually, she did,' he said. 'We didn't talk about it much, but she once asked me if I knew anything about Nazis in the area sometime in the past. Of course I knew nothing, but when I asked her what she meant, she changed the subject and said it didn't matter. Odd that you should mention it too. I'd forgotten all about it.'

'What about Kristín?' she asked. 'Did she ever mention the name Kristín?'

Bergur gave a hollow laugh. 'Show me the Icelander who's never spoken the name Kristín at some time in his life.' He stopped smiling. 'But no, I have no particular recollection of her mentioning that name.'

'All right,' Thóra said. 'If you don't mind, I'd like to ask you about Eiríkur, the aura reader.' Not waiting for his response, she went on, 'Did you know each other?'

'No,' Bergur replied. 'I knew who he was. That was all. I never spoke to him.'

'Can you tell me how you found his body?'

'Don't you want to see for yourselves?'

Thóra and Matthew stood up and followed him back into the main part of the stables. Accustomed to the smell, Thóra put on a brave face, but Matthew grimaced at her as they left the coffee room. They went up to one of the stalls, which had higher partitions than the others.

'He was in here,' Bergur said, his face pale now. 'The stallion was in the stall too, and it had trampled him to death. That's how it looked to me at least.' He opened the gate to the stall. 'The horse isn't in there now.'

Thóra peered in. There was not much to see now that the floor had been cleared. 'Presumably the police have investigated the scene thoroughly?' she asked.

'Yes, they spent the whole night here,' he replied. 'It wasn't a pretty sight.'

'I bet it wasn't,' Thóra said. 'What were you coming in here for?'

'I have to feed them,' he answered brusquely. 'Unfortunately.'

'Unfortunately?' she repeated. 'What do you mean?'

'I wish I'd never seen it. It was horrible,' the farmer said frankly. 'It was an awful sight. The fox, the needles, the blood . . . and that poor man.'

'The fox?' Thóra asked. 'There was a fox in here?'

'Yes,' he replied. 'Tied to the man's chest. At first I thought it was a wig; then I realised. I stood here unable to move for ages. I just couldn't stop staring.' He closed the gate to the stall.

'Why would anyone tie a fox to their chest, or to someone else's?' Thóra speculated. 'Do foxes have any special significance in this part of the country?'

'Not that I know of,' Bergur replied. 'I have no idea what it was supposed to mean. Perhaps it was just to make it worse for the poor guy. The smell of the fox was disgusting. It had been dead much longer than he had.'

Thóra nodded, deep in thought. She couldn't think of a logical explanation. 'But what was that about needles? Had the man been injecting himself?' This might explain Thórólfur's bizarre questions about acupuncture and sewing sets.

Bergur frowned, clearly not enjoying the recollection. He swallowed loudly before speaking. 'Pins had been stuck into the soles of his feet.' He hesitated before adding, 'The same had been done to Birna.' He shuddered, then continued, 'Whoever did that was some kind of monster.'

'Pins?' Thóra asked in astonishment. 'Sewing pins?'

'Yes.' Bergur bit his lip. 'I'd prefer not to discuss it. I don't like to think about it too much.'

Thóra let the matter rest, so astounded that she had no idea what to ask next. Why would anyone stick pins into someone's feet before murdering them? Could Birna and Eiríkur have been tortured to extract information? Thóra abandoned her speculations and changed the subject. 'May I ask if you can account for your whereabouts at the time the police think Birna and Eiríkur were murdered?'

'Yes and no,' Bergur said. 'I can account for my whereabouts, but I generally go off by myself, so no one can back me up except my wife.' He looked defiantly at Thóra, as if daring her to contradict him. She couldn't, and thought him much smarter than Jónas, who had fabricated an alibi that was easy to disprove. 'She'd never lie to the police,' he added dryly, as if that were a great failing.

'One more thing,' Thóra said quickly. 'What does "RER" mean?'

Bergur opened the gate to the stall. 'I don't have a clue what it stands for.' He pointed to the wall. 'Eiríkur scratched it on the panelling before he died.'

Thóra went back inside with Matthew in pursuit. After she'd explained what Bergur had been saying, they bent down for a closer look at the scrawling. Matthew took out his mobile to photograph it.

'RER,' Thóra said, following him back out. 'Reb?' she said, '"Rebbi" is a nickname for a fox. Could he have tried to write "Rebbi"? That "R" could just as easily be a "B".'

Bergur shrugged. 'I told you – I have no idea.' He closed the stall. 'I've got to get back indoors. Are we done?'

There was a creak as the stable door opened. A woman of about Bergur's age came in tentatively. Thóra was struck by her appearance. She wasn't ugly, but there was something about her posture and clothing that made her look very unattractive. Her hair was lank and colourless, tied back with a band that had seen better days. There was not a speck of mascara on her stubby eyelashes. She was the kind of woman you'd have trouble describing five minutes after she'd left the room, and she looked like she knew it. From her expression, she wanted the earth to swallow her. Thóra tried to send her a smile of encouragement as she hesitated at the open door.

The woman cleared her throat, then said softly, 'Are you

coming?' She directed her words at Bergur, as if she hadn't even noticed Thóra and Matthew.

'Yes,' said Bergur, without a hint of warmth in his voice. 'You go in. I'm coming.'

'Well, then,' Thóra said breezily. 'We should be leaving.' She turned to Bergur. 'Thank you. It was good to have the opportunity to see the murder scene.' She turned to the woman she assumed was Rósa. 'Your husband was good enough to show us the stall where the body was found. I'm a lawyer, involved in the case on behalf of a client.'

Rósa nodded, without interest. 'Hello, I'm Rósa.' She did not offer her hand to shake. Her eyes lingered on Thóra for only a fraction of a second before she turned back to her husband. 'Are you coming?' she repeated. Bergur said nothing.

Thóra tried to defuse the tension with a final question, one she was glad Matthew couldn't understand. 'Last question, I promise,' she said. 'I saw a young man in a wheelchair outside the hotel. I think he's local. Do you happen to know how he was injured?' Bergur and Rósa stared at her, frozen to the spot. 'You know, the one who's badly burned?' she clarified. She didn't need to say anything else, because the stream of curses Rósa suddenly unleashed left no doubt that she knew who Thóra meant. Thóra looked on, speechless, as Bergur grabbed his wife by the arm and led her away.

Matthew put his hand on her shoulder. 'I can't tell you how badly I want to get out of this foul-smelling place, but I'm not leaving until you tell me what the hell you said to that poor woman.'

* * *

Magnús Baldvinsson smiled to himself. Old and tired though he was, he still had moments when he felt young again. This was one of those moments. He dialled the number and waited cheerfully for his wife to answer, took a good sip of the cognac he had bought at the bar and relished the warmth of the golden liquid before swallowing. 'Hello, Frída,' he said. 'It's over.'

'What?' she said. 'Are you coming home? What's happened?'

'The police have arrested a man for Birna's murder,' Magnús answered, lifting his glass and swirling the brandy in front of his eyes. 'You can tell Baldvin to come and fetch me whenever is convenient.'

'He's out east preparing for the party conference. I don't think he's expected home until late tonight,' said his wife, her voice tinged with fear. 'Do you want me to ask someone else to drive over and get you?'

'No, don't worry,' said Magnús jovially. The familiar glow of pride in his grandson added to his joy that the tension and fear of the past few days was finally over. 'I enjoy driving with him, so I can wait. Also, I want to hear all about the conference.'

'He's been asking after you constantly since he drove you out there,' she said. 'He'll be glad to have you back home.' There was a short silence before she added, with a mixture of suspicion and apprehension, 'Are you two up to something?'

'No, of course not,' said Magnús firmly. 'Well, I'd better go. Tell Baldvin to come when it suits him. I'll be here.'

They exchanged farewells and Magnús hung up. He let his hand rest on the receiver for a while. He didn't know whether it was the alcohol or the sight of his wrinkled, claw-like hand, but something had dragged him back into the real world, and he felt like an old man again. To his astonishment, he felt a tear run down his lined face, and he watched it drop on to his trouser leg. Staring at the stain, he was overcome with guilt and misery.

Oh, Kristín.

Thóra rubbed her eyes. 'I don't know how much this helps, but I was right – the verse on Grímur Thórólfsson's gravestone is from *The Sayings of the High One*,' she said as she leaned back in her chair from the computer. She beamed proudly at Matthew until she realised that he had no idea what she was talking about. '*The Sayings of the High One* are proverbs of wisdom, attributed to the god Odin. A lot of their advice is still very relevant.' Thóra recognised the lack of interest on Matthew's face from her own schooldays, the first time she learned about *The Sayings*. 'Anyway,' she went on. 'It says here that the verse describes how bad people feel when they are dependent on others.'

'Which doesn't really tell us anything,' said Matthew. 'Everyone knows that.'

'Actually, I think it tells us a lot,' she argued. 'For example, it was obviously carved on to Grímur's gravestone for a good reason. It wasn't chosen at random.'

She turned back to the screen and searched for the verse they'd found on the rock behind the hotel. The results were less productive; all she found was a reference to Jón Árnason's nineteenth-century folktale collection on a page about the practice of abandoning children outside, and although she tried several times, she couldn't locate the poem itself.

'That verse is connected with the abandoning of infants,' she told Matthew. 'It says here that the cries of unbaptised babies who were left out to die can be heard when the wind blows in the place where they died. Also that the ghosts of these babies can move around by lifting themselves on to one knee and dragging themselves along by one hand.' She looked up at Matthew. 'Was that what you saw out of the window?' He shot her an evil look, and Thóra turned back to the computer, grinning. 'The next time you see one, make sure it doesn't manage to crawl three circles round you, because you'll go mad. You should try to chase it away. Then it'll go off and eventually find its mother.' She looked back at Matthew, smiling innocently.

'Very funny,' he said grumpily. 'I wasn't joking – I definitely heard it.'

'I need to get hold of a copy of those folktales and look through them.' Thóra yawned. 'But that can wait.'

'No, there's no rush,' said Matthew. 'I have a feeling it won't get you any closer to catching the murderer.'

'You never know,' she said, entering the details for her final search – for information on the tuberculosis epidemic in Iceland. Very few pages came up, and she browsed through them. 'What rotten luck,' she said. 'TB drugs came on the market in 1946. A year after Gudný died.' After reading a little more, she logged out and stood up. 'I can understand why neither Gudný nor her father wanted to go to a sanatorium. According to what I just read, the attempts to treat or cure TB were very unappealing.

Collapsing one lung, removing several ribs, stuff that did no good and in many cases left the patients severely disabled.'

Matthew tapped on her shoulder. 'This is all fascinating, but I think you ought to look round and see who just walked in.'

Thóra looked over towards the lobby, but averted her gaze immediately. 'What does *she* want? Do you think she saw me?'

'Maybe she's come to beat you up,' he whispered in her ear. 'But if it's any consolation, my money's on you.'

Without answering, Thóra stole another glance. She watched Jökull, the waiter and groundsman, walk over to where Bergur's wife was hesitating at the reception desk. He was wearing an anorak and outdoor shoes, and hugged Rósa fondly before they left the building together. Neither seemed to notice Thóra or Matthew.

Thóra turned to him. 'How on earth do they know each other?'

26

'I know it's almost time for you to leave the office, Bella,' Thóra said wearily. 'I'm not asking you to do it tonight. You can check it out in the morning.' She shook her head at Matthew as her secretary complained at the other end of the line. 'Bella, I just thought it was an ideal job for you since you're so fond of horses.' As ever, Thóra wondered how the gargantuan Bella would ever manage to mount a horse. 'All you have to do is to find out whether there is any connection between horses and foxes, or between foxes and death.' She sighed and closed her eyes when Bella interrupted with another question. 'Bella, I don't know what you're supposed to look for. Just try and find out whether foxes and horses, especially stallions, have anything in common.' Thóra realised she'd have to explain herself better. 'The point is that a man was found in the stables, trampled to death by a stallion. A dead fox was tied to the body. There must be a reason.'

Matthew winked and smiled at Thóra. He was well aware of the friction between her and her secretary, and enjoyed listening in even when he didn't understand a word. 'Say hello from me,' he whispered.

Thóra pulled a face at him. 'Yes, yes, Bella. You'll find something. You did a great job in the cemetery and I'm sure you will now. And Matthew sends his regards.' She

smiled sweetly at him as she spoke. 'He really wants to go
to the stables with you when we get back. We went to one
earlier today and he was absolutely enchanted. Now he
can't wait to try mucking out and feeding the horses. The
Germans love Icelandic horses.' She said goodbye and
turned to Matthew. 'Bella has invited you to go with her
to the stables when we get back to town,' she said. 'She
sends her love.'

'Ha, ha,' Matthew said. 'Hilarious. I hope you told her
about the great welcome *you* received when we visited the
stables. You managed to say – what? – three whole words
before Rósa went berserk.'

'You must admit that she reacted very oddly,' said Thóra,
'no matter how inappropriate the question. I have to find
out what her relationship is with Jökull.'

'She did overreact a little bit,' he admitted, 'but I did
warn you not to go poking your nose in.'

'The funny thing is that I was trying to be polite because
I thought Bergur was so nasty to her,' said Thóra. 'Asking
about the boy in the wheelchair was all I could think of.'

'More's the pity,' said Matthew. 'Can't you find anything
about it on the Internet? His injuries clearly aren't congen-
ital; they look like they were sustained in a fire – and fires
are generally newsworthy. Especially if someone gets hurt.
You must be able to access old stories on newspaper
websites.'

'Yes, I'm sure I could try,' Thóra said. 'It would just be
so much easier if I found someone from here who could
tell me. I don't know what I'm looking for; I don't even
know whether it happened a decade or a month ago. The
papers seldom report injuries – they tend to say the victim

is in critical condition, badly injured, doing as well as can be expected, et cetera. Besides, I don't even know if it was a house fire or if the lad simply fell into a hot spring.' She sighed. 'And I really ought to concentrate on trying to help poor Jónas.'

Matthew grunted. 'If you can,' he said. 'You have to admit he might be guilty.'

'Yes, unfortunately I do,' she conceded. 'But I'm fairly sure that he didn't commit those murders.'

'Who did, then?' asked Matthew. 'Things would look a lot better if there was another suspect.'

Thóra thought about it. 'Bergur would be the obvious candidate, but I have no idea why he'd kill Eiríkur.' She bit her lip. They were leaning against Matthew's rental car in the hotel car park, where Thóra had gone to call Bella. 'We can rule out everyone who was at the seance, surely?' mused Thóra. 'It was going on at the time Birna was murdered, according to the police.'

'Do we know the exact time of death yet?' asked Matthew.

'Thórólfur said it was between nine and ten last Thursday,' she replied. 'He must have based that on the autopsy. That also fits with the text message asking her to turn up at nine.' She sighed. 'The seance began at eight o'clock. It took us about half an hour from the beach, so if the murderer left the seance on foot, he would never have got back before the interval at half past nine. The drive to the hotel had been dug up, so no one could have got there by car, and it would have taken too long to walk up to the main road.'

'Do you know who was at the seance?' said Matthew.

'There's not much point trying to rule out a whole group of people if you don't know their names.'

'No, but I'm sure Vigdís knows who was due to attend. She was in charge of selling tickets,' said Thóra. 'And a lot of people would have paid by credit card, so we could find out some of the names.'

'Shouldn't you be concentrating on the people who might be suspects rather than those who definitely aren't?' he suggested.

'Yes, but this way I can eliminate a lot of people. Also, it would give me a list of people who may have seen Jónas hanging around in the interval and could give him an alibi,' Thóra said. She watched as a seagull flew above them. 'Unless the murderer flew,' she said idly, then suddenly straightened up. 'What about by sea?' she said. 'Could he have had a motorboat and sailed into the bay?'

Matthew was unconvinced. 'Isn't that a bit tenuous?' he said. 'I've been to the bay and I don't much fancy trying to land on the beach. It would take the bottom of the boat out.' But then a thought occurred to him, and he added thoughtfully, 'Actually, there was a concrete jetty not far from there. That might be a possibility.' He paused, still thinking. 'In that case, the boat would have been tied up at the hotel jetty before the seance and someone might remember it. Let's go and check it out.'

They walked down past the hotel to the jetty, which lay in a small cove east of the main hotel building. When they reached the end of it, Matthew turned round and looked back at the hotel. 'We're not very visible here,' he said, pointing. They could see the roof of the hotel from where they stood, but no windows or doors. 'You could do pretty much anything here without being disturbed.' He looked around. 'But I don't see much evidence that the jetty gets a lot of use. There aren't even any ropes or mooring posts.'

Thóra leaned over the side of the jetty but saw no rubber tyres padding the edge, or any other sign that the jetty was in regular use. 'I agree,' she said, 'but I'm still going to ask Vigdís if she remembers seeing a boat that evening.' The wind changed, and the stench from the beached whale engulfed them. 'Jesus!' exclaimed Thóra, staring along the beach. 'There's the whale's carcass, look!' She pointed at a huge black mound, some distance away.

Matthew put his hand over his nose and mouth, but squinted in the direction Thóra had pointed. 'What on earth is that? This must be the worst smell in the world.'

'Should we take a look?' Thóra said. 'If we just follow this cove round, it won't take us a minute.'

Matthew looked at Thóra in disbelief. 'Honestly? You're serious. You want to go and look at a disgusting pile of rotting blubber.'

'Yes, of course I do. It's right there,' said Thóra, but then her mobile phone rang. She groaned when she saw the number. 'Hello,' she said.

'Were you planning to answer my texts, or were you just going to ignore them?' said her ex-husband angrily. 'I don't know where the hell you are, but I'm a little tired of playing hide and seek with you. I wasn't born yesterday; I know you've turned your phone off because you're off some-where with some man you only just met.'

Thóra didn't dignify that with a response, but she had to say something after a speech like that. 'If you'll shut up for one minute, Hannes,' she said, 'I'll be able to tell you that I'm out here working, and if you had ever ventured outside the big city you would know that not everywhere has good mobile reception.' She had no qualms about saying this, although she'd only known it herself for a few days. 'All I have to say is that Gylfi and Sóley are just outside Selfoss and they need to be collected. Sigga is with them.'

'What am I supposed to do about it?' yelled Hannes. 'I work too. I can't just come and go at your beck and call.'

'Can you fetch them or not?' Thóra asked. 'If not, I'll phone my parents and ask them to do it. But I'd like to remind you that technically this is your fault. If you hadn't sung "Eye of the Tiger" over and over again, they wouldn't have left.' Thóra realised she could hear music in the background. 'I can hear "The Final Countdown",' she said, shocked. 'Are you still playing *SingStar*?'

In the end Hannes agreed to collect the kids and Thóra hung up, annoyed at herself for being annoyed at him. She called Gylfi to tell him that his father would collect them. Then she shook herself. 'Just a family drama,' she said to Matthew, who was looking at her inquisitively. 'Let's go over to Kreppa and try to find Birna's office.'

'By all means,' he replied. 'I'd do anything except look at a dead whale. And who knows? Maybe we'll find more names of murdered people carved into the house somewhere.'

They were walking back towards the hotel when Thóra saw a man waving at them. It was the travel photographer, Robin Kohman. Thóra waved back and he came over.

'Hi,' he called as they drew close. 'I've been looking for you.'

'Really?' she called back, quickening her pace. 'We've been rushing around a bit.'

'I'm leaving tonight,' the photographer said when they had exchanged greetings, 'and wanted to give you Birna's photographs.' Then he added gloomily, 'I've heard what happened, and I really want to hand this over to someone who knew her.' He shook his head mournfully. 'This is all so tragic, and so unexpected in a country like Iceland.'

'Yes, it's awful,' said Thóra. 'We just have to hope that they catch whoever did it.'

'Have the police talked to you?' asked Matthew. 'No doubt they'll want to talk to all the hotel guests before they leave.'

Robin nodded. 'Yes, I spoke to them this morning, but I couldn't tell them anything.'

'So you didn't want to give the photographs to them?' Thóra asked. 'Not that we don't want them, of course.'

'No, I didn't think they were relevant,' Robin said. 'It's out of the question that they could be connected with Birna's murder in any way. They're just normal, innocent photographs.' He smiled. 'Although there is a slightly weird one of a dead fox.'

Matthew put down the photo. They were sitting at the bar with Robin and on the table in front of them lay a pile of pictures that Robin had taken from a large envelope marked with Birna's name.

'Where was this taken?' Matthew asked, pointing at the dead fox in the middle of the picture. The scrawny creature lay on its side in the grass. Its tongue was hanging out of one side of its mouth and its rich brown pelt was tattered and bloody.

'It was lying beside the path, down towards that old farm near here,' Robin replied. 'Birna asked me to go with her to take some photos and we came across this poor thing. Birna asked me to take a shot of it; she thought it was rather sad. You can't tell from the photograph, but the signs all around suggested that the fox had dragged itself there after being badly injured.' Robin pointed to a wound on the animal's side. 'It must have got away from the hunter, but the shot turned out to be fatal.'

'Did you take the fox with you?' Thóra asked.

'No, are you crazy?' Robin said. 'We didn't touch it. It was giving off a dreadful smell.'

'Do you think anyone else could have come along after you and taken it?' Thóra asked.

Robin looked from her to Matthew, startled. 'I don't quite understand your interest, but of course it's possible. The fox could be seen by anyone who walked past.' He grimaced. 'But I just can't imagine anyone being interested in taking a dead animal. Unless the skin is valuable.' He turned to Thóra. 'Are Icelanders particularly fond of foxes?'

She smiled. 'No, not to the extent of taking home dead ones. We're interested in this for completely different reasons, which would take too long to explain.' She picked up the pile of photographs and started flicking through them. 'Did Birna tell you why she chose these specific subjects?' she asked him. 'I see that many of the photos are of the old farm and the area behind the hotel, but here's one of a steel trapdoor, and another of an inside wall, as far as I can tell. Did she explain this at all?' She handed the photographs she was talking about to Robin.

Robin examined the pictures and nodded. 'If I recall correctly, this trapdoor was in the meadow by the old farm, on the other side of the hill,' he said. 'The photo of the wall was taken in the basement here, in the old part of the hotel. She asked me to take it the day after we'd been shooting, but offered no further explanation, any more than she did about the trapdoor. I thought it was something to do with architecture, but I still couldn't quite work out why she wanted these photos.'

'And did she say anything about this rock?' asked Matthew, showing him three photographs of the engraved rock they had found behind the hotel.

Robin looked at the pictures. 'Yes, funnily enough. I asked her about this rock while we were shooting it from all angles. She translated the verse for me, and because I thought it was rather unusual, I asked her whether it was an Icelandic tradition to write verses on rocks.' He put the photographs down. 'She said it wasn't, and seemed quite surprised to find an inscription there.'

'She didn't offer any explanation for this, or say what she thought the rock was doing there?' asked Thóra hopefully.

'Not exactly,' Robin replied. 'She was wondering whether the verse could have been written by the occupants of the farm, or whether a poet had lived there. Then she speculated that it might have been a pet's grave, although she didn't think the verse was appropriate. She didn't reach any conclusion that I remember.'

Matthew tugged at Thóra's sleeve. 'Here's an interesting

317

one,' he said, handing her a picture of Birna talking to an old man in front of the hotel entrance. Thóra snatched it from him. 'Maybe they were talking about converting his chalet for year-round use,' Matthew said slyly.

Robin leaned over to see what had aroused their interest. 'Yes, this one,' he said. 'I just took it for fun. We were setting off from the old farm when this man came out from the hotel and started talking to Birna. I know he's a guest here because I've seen him in the dining room several times.'

Thóra nodded. 'Do you know what they were talking about?'

'No, I have no idea,' Robin said. 'They spoke in Icelandic, but actually I didn't need to understand in order to realise that it wasn't a friendly chat. I only took the one photograph because they soon started arguing and it didn't seem appropriate.'

'Did she tell you what they'd been arguing about?' asked Matthew.

'Well, she muttered something about people having to take responsibility for their actions,' Robin said. 'She was quite annoyed, so I didn't press her.' He thought a little longer. 'Then she said something about old sins bearing fruit, just like old debts. I couldn't figure that out, so I changed the subject.'

Thóra and Matthew exchanged a glance. Magnús Baldvinsson. *Old sins?*

The nurse walked over to the old woman's bed and gently nudged her shoulder to wake her. 'Malla, dear,' she said gently. 'Wake up. It's time to take your medication.'

The old woman opened her eyes without saying a word. She stared up at the ceiling above her, blinked a few times and coughed weakly. The nurse waited in silence. She knew that sometimes it could take the old lady a while to get her bearings. She stood calmly beside her, one hand resting on her skeletal shoulder and a little plastic cup in the other. It contained the white and red pills she was supposed to administer. 'Come on,' she said kindly. 'You can lie back down afterwards.'

'She came,' said the old woman suddenly. She was still staring up at the ceiling and had not yet looked at the woman who was patiently standing at her bedside.

'Who did?' the nurse answered vaguely. She was well accustomed to all kinds of nonsense from the old people, especially when they were only half awake. It was as if they travelled back to times long past, when they were younger, fitter and not completely helpless.

'She came,' the old woman repeated, smiling. 'She's forgiven me.' She looked up at the nurse for the first time, still beaming. 'She wasn't angry. Always so sweet.'

'That's nice,' soothed the nurse. 'It's not good to be angry.' She shook the cup of tablets. 'Well, let's sit you up and give you your medication.'

Instead of looking at the pills, the old woman continued to stare at the young nurse. 'I asked her if she was angry,' she said, 'and she just said, "Why should I be angry?"' With difficulty she lifted herself on to her elbows. 'Always so sweet.'

'Do you want me to hold the water, or can you do it yourself?' asked the nurse, reaching out for a beaker on the bedside table. She handed the water to her patient.

'Of course I told her why she ought to be angry,' the old lady said, completely ignoring both water and pills. 'And I thought she always knew I was there.' She shook her head in surprise, her white curls bouncing. 'Apparently she didn't,' she said, closing her eyes. 'But she forgave me all the same.'

'That's great,' the nurse said, putting down the container of pills and the beaker. 'Come on,' she said and gripped under the woman's arms, 'you need to sit up more.' She lifted her into a better position. Her back was crooked and she couldn't be expected to sit up straight, but this would do. 'Now, let's take some tablets.' She picked up the pills. 'There are more people waiting, so we have to be quick.' She held the glass to the woman's thin, pale lips.

The old lady opened her mouth and allowed the nurse to pour the pills into it. She knew the routine by now and didn't swallow until she had been given the water. The pills disappeared with loud gulps that seemed not to embarrass her.

When she was done, she wiped her mouth with the back of her hand and looked up at the nurse. 'She was so good, so sweet. Just imagine.'

'Imagine what, love?' the nurse asked politely, privately wondering if the old woman was in full possession of her faculties.

'She forgave me,' she said, sounding even more surprised than before. 'And I'd done nothing to help her.'

'Oh, are you quite sure about that?' The nurse smiled. 'I'm sure you did a lot for her. You just don't remember.'

The old woman glared. 'Of course I remember. She died. How could I forget that?'

The nurse gently stroked the woman's white hair. Just as she'd suspected, the poor old dear was rambling. A dead woman visiting her? Taking care not to smile, she laid her back down in a comfortable position. 'There, there, Malla. Just try to go back to sleep.'

The old woman closed her eyes the moment her head touched the pillow. 'Murdered. Evil is everywhere.' She smacked her lips, then muttered sleepily, 'My sweetheart. My sweet Kristín.'

27

'It must be the same fox that was tied to Eiríkur's body,' said Matthew. 'At least, I can't see it anywhere here.' He and Thóra had followed the path that Birna and Robin had taken to Kreppa and were at the spot where they'd apparently found the fox. It was nowhere to be seen.

'It could have been eaten by another animal, but I'm sure you're right,' said Thóra. 'The only animals I've seen around here are sheep, and I doubt they eat foxes.' She looked skywards. 'Birds, perhaps, but then the bones would still be here.'

'So the murderer would be someone who uses this path,' Matthew said, swiping at the tall grass beside the path with a branch he'd picked up while they were looking for the dead fox.

'Either that or he shot the fox and tracked it here after Birna and Robin had left,' Thóra said. 'What I'd give to know why he did it.'

'Who knows, Wonderwoman Bella might find that out for us,' said Matthew. 'Perhaps the fox was supposed to signify something.'

'Like a message?' said Thóra, unconvinced. 'From an animal rights group or something?'

'No, from the murderer,' he replied. 'It could be some psycho who's trying to communicate something. Have we established that nothing like this was attached to Birna's body?'

'Not as far as I know,' said Thóra. 'They both had pins pushed into the soles of their feet, but no one's said anything about a fox or any other animal in connection with her.'

They stopped on the gravel driveway in front of the farmhouse. 'Whose car is that?' Matthew asked, pointing to a newish Renault Mégane.

Thóra shrugged. 'No idea,' she said. 'No one's supposed to be here.' She noticed a light in one of the windows. 'Maybe Elín and her brother are clearing the place out. I hope so.' She got the key out and they went up to the door, which turned out to be unlocked. Thóra opened it and put her head inside. 'Hello,' she called. 'Anyone here?'

'Hello!' someone replied, and they heard approaching footsteps.

'Hi there,' said Thóra cheerfully when Elín's daughter Berta appeared. She had tied back her hair with a bandana and was holding a filthy duster.

'You scared me to death!' Berta said. 'Do come in. I'm packing away some old things for Mum and Uncle Börkur.' She brandished the cloth. 'Everything's really dusty, so I'm trying to clean every item before I pack it up, even though it's taking me ages.'

Matthew smiled at her, delighted that someone had remembered he was a foreigner and was bothering to speak English. 'Hello,' he said, offering her his hand to shake. 'Nice to see you again.'

'You too,' said Berta. 'I had the presence of mind to bring a Thermos flask full of fresh coffee. Your timing's perfect because Steini doesn't want coffee and I made far too much.'

They followed her into the kitchen, where the young man sat in his wheelchair. As before, he had pulled a hood over his head to cover his face, and when they walked in, he glanced at them from under it but said nothing.

'Visitors, Steini,' said Berta, and he mumbled something unintelligible in reply. 'Help yourselves,' she said, pointing to some china cups by the sink. 'Don't worry, I've washed them.' She grinned.

'Thank you,' said Thóra. 'I hadn't realised how much I needed a coffee.' She poured a cup for Matthew and one for herself. 'Isn't this an awful lot of work for you?' she asked, after taking a sip.

'Oh, yes,' Berta agreed vigorously. 'I don't know what I was thinking when I offered to do it.' Then she added, 'Actually, it's quite fun. It's weird handling all these objects that my great-grandparents cared about so much.'

'I can imagine,' said Thóra. 'We dropped in to take a look at the room Birna was working in. We understand she'd set up an office here, is that right?'

'Yes, upstairs,' Berta replied. 'Shall I show you? There's not much in there, only drawings and stuff – no computer. She used a laptop and never plugged it in here.' She gestured at the socket where the coffee-maker was connected. 'The plugs are so old that you need an adapter for them. Birna was afraid the electricity was unreliable and didn't want to risk damaging her computer. She always charged it at the hotel before she came.'

'That doesn't matter,' said Matthew. 'We're not necessarily

looking for her computer. We just want to see what she was up to.'

Berta narrowed her eyes sceptically. 'Do you think her murder was connected somehow with the building she was designing? Doesn't it seem obvious to you that the murderer was some psycho who raped her?'

'No, it's not at all obvious,' Thóra replied, deciding not to mention Jónas's arrest just yet. That might make Berta think Thóra and Matthew were working for the murderer, and she might refuse to assist anyone connected with her friend's death. 'But it seems unlikely that her architectural designs had anything to do with the murder. We just want to see whether there's something in there that could help explain it.'

'I see,' Berta said. 'I haven't been in there since the murder,' she added. 'I expected the police to search the room, so I didn't want to disturb anything. They haven't come, though, so perhaps it doesn't matter.' She looked at Thóra. 'You're a lawyer, aren't you? For Jónas and the hotel?' she asked.

'I am,' Thóra said, praying the girl wouldn't start asking about her client.

'Then I don't see why you can't go in there,' she said. 'You'd hardly compromise the investigation, would you?'

'God, no,' Thóra lied fervently. 'I'd never do that. We're not going to take anything, just have a look around.' She sipped her coffee. 'This is great coffee.' She smiled.

'Thanks,' said Berta. 'Some people think I make it too strong.' She tilted her chin towards Steini.

'It is too strong,' said a voice from beneath the hood. 'Much too strong.'

Matthew clearly didn't feel as awkward as Thóra, because he answered Steini at once: 'Put more milk in it. That's the trick,' he said in a perfectly normal voice. 'You ought to try it. Cream's even better.'

'Maybe,' said Steini. 'I prefer Coke.'

Berta smiled warmly at Matthew, and Thóra wished she could think of something to say to the young man. The girl's affection for him was rather touching.

'Shall I show you, then?' Berta said suddenly. 'Steini and I were about to call it a day anyway.' She went over to the hall door.

'Please do,' Thóra replied, putting down her cup. Matthew did the same. 'You can leave if you want,' she said as they followed Berta. 'We won't take anything or do any damage.'

'That's OK,' Berta said. 'I have a few bits to finish off.'

The three marched in single file up the stairs and to the door to Birna's room. It turned out to be the room that Thóra and Matthew hadn't been able to get into when they first visited the house.

'I locked it as soon as I heard about the murder,' said Berta, rattling the key in the stiff lock. With a deft twist she finally managed to turn it and she opened the door. There was a bottle of fizzy drink on the desk, an ashtray stood on the windowsill, and various other trappings of modern life were scattered around the room. As in Birna's hotel room, drawings were pinned to the wall, mostly sketches, but some printouts.

Thóra examined the drawings on the wall, showing the planned location of the annexe and several cross-sections. 'What's this?' she asked, pointing to a sketch of a building with pine trees behind it. Buses and pedestrians had been added to the picture. 'Surely this wasn't her idea for the annexe to Jónas's hotel?' The building was a mass of glass and she could hardly imagine hotel rooms with only windows for walls.

Berta walked over to the drawing as well. 'God, no,' she said. 'Birna showed me her plans for the building and they were nothing like this.' She stooped to examine one corner of the printout. 'It's dated a week ago,' she said, 'and it wasn't here last time Birna invited me in.'

'But it was here when you locked the room, wasn't it?' Matthew asked. 'It can't have been hung up after she died, surely?'

The girl wrinkled her brow as she tried to remember. 'I honestly don't know,' she said. 'I only put my head round the door before I locked the room and I simply can't remember if this drawing was on the wall or not.' She looked embarrassed, almost guilty, as if she had been somehow negligent. 'But no one's been in here since I locked up. I'm sure of it.'

'When exactly was that?' asked Thóra.

'On Saturday,' Berta replied. 'I don't remember the time, but it was in the afternoon. Does that matter?' she asked anxiously. 'Do you think the murderer came here?'

'No,' Thóra reassured her. 'I doubt it very much. Not many people seem to have known about this hideaway of hers.'

She went over to the desk. More drawings were spread all over it, along with a few credit-card receipts. They told her nothing, except that Birna was a customer of Esso and the Hvalfjördur Tunnel. The desk drawers were warped shut, and it took all her strength to open them. Two were completely empty, while one contained a pencil, a sharpener and a key on a metal fob stamped with a logo she didn't recognise. She picked up the key. It was too small to fit a door, a car or anything else Thóra could think of. 'Do you know what this is for?' she asked.

Berta shook her head. 'No idea,' she said, 'but it's certainly Birna's because it wasn't in the drawer when she moved in. I cleared the room out before that.'

Thóra put the key in her pocket. 'I'm just borrowing it,' she told the girl. 'Don't worry about the police. I'll hand it over if they want it.'

'I don't care,' Berta said. 'I just want the murderer to be found. I don't mind who does it.'

'Are we done here?' Matthew said when they had searched the whole room. 'Are there any more of her belongings in the house?'

'There could be a glass downstairs,' Berta said. 'Yes, and boots in the hallway. Do you want them?'

Thóra smiled. 'No, no. But tell me one thing,' she said. 'Birna was particularly interested in a hatch outside. Do you happen to know why?'

The girl shook her head slowly. 'No, but it was presumably when she was considering an extension to this building,' she said. 'That was almost two months before I first met her here.'

'No, this was after that, very recently,' Matthew said. 'Do you know the hatch we're talking about?'

'Yes,' she said. 'I think so. There's only one hatch outside. Do you want to take a look at it?'

Thóra looked at Matthew and gave a shrug. 'Why not,' she said.

They followed Berta out of the room and stood by her side as she conscientiously locked it behind them. On the way out, Thóra grabbed the chance to ask her whether she had come across any old Nazi memorabilia while packing, or whether Birna had mentioned it at all.

Berta spun round on the front steps and looked at Thóra, baffled. 'No, why do you ask?'

'I just wondered,' Thóra said. 'There's some in boxes in the hotel basement.'

'Really?' Berta said, not attempting to conceal her surprise. 'That does seem strange. Could it belong to someone outside my family?'

'Maybe,' said Thóra, although she knew better. 'And another thing,' she went on as they resumed walking, 'do you recognise the name Kristín?'

'Kristín Sveinsdóttir?' Berta said without turning round. Thóra's heart skipped a beat. 'We were in school together for years. I haven't seen her for ages, though.' Then she turned to Thóra. 'Do you know her?'

Thóra tried to hide her disappointment. 'No, I was thinking about another Kristín who might have lived here or locally a long time back.'

Berta shook her head. 'No, I don't recall anyone by that name. I'm not the right person to ask about the old folks. Mum might be able to help you on that.'

Fat chance, thought Thóra. 'Is this the hatch?' she asked, pointing to a steel plate with a welded handle where Berta had stopped. They were about twenty metres behind the house.

'Yes,' said Berta. 'There's nothing remarkable about it. Do you want to open it?' she asked, signalling that Matthew should do so if he wanted.

He bent down and struggled to lift the heavy cover. The hinges creaked when he tugged, but he couldn't get it open. 'What's down there?' he asked.

'Nothing,' Berta said. 'It was used for storage, as far as I remember. There's an entrance from the basement. I think coal used to be kept here for heating the house in those days. It hasn't been opened since God knows when. The house has had electric heating for as long as I can recall.'

'Could we have a look in the basement?' asked Matthew, wiping his dirty hands on the grass.

Berta nodded, but warned him that there was nothing down there. She accompanied them down the steps, and after walking through a little door at the far end of the basement and along a short, almost tunnel-like corridor, they reached a steel door, which she pushed open. Inside was nothing but darkness. In the tiny light from the basement they managed to see that the coal store was covered in black dust with occasional black lumps on the floor.

'It's gross, really,' Berta said as she closed the door again. 'Birna wouldn't have been interested in this. I don't remember her ever even coming into this basement.' She walked over to the stairs. 'Of course, she was usually here by herself, so she may well have taken a look, but I can't imagine why she would have.'

Back on the ground floor, Thóra and Matthew decided to call it a day. They said goodbye to Berta and thanked her for her help. Matthew sent his regards to Steini, while Thóra struggled once again to suppress the urge to ask what had happened to him. Suddenly the question slipped out. 'Berta, I hope you don't mind me asking, but what happened to your friend?' she said in a low enough voice to be inaudible in the kitchen.

Berta sighed heavily. 'He was in a car crash. A car hit his and it caught fire. He was smoking,' she said, her voice as low as Thóra's.

'Jesus,' said Thóra. 'That's awful. Is he paralysed?'

'No,' replied the girl. 'At least, there's no spinal damage. His legs are just in such a bad state that he can't walk properly. Some of the muscles were burned, and the skin transplant is still bothering him. Hopefully I'll be able to get him to start physiotherapy again soon. It just takes time.' She took a quick peek round the corner to make sure Steini was out of earshot. 'The worst part is that the man who drove into him was drunk. Steini was stone-cold sober.'

'And what happened to him?' Thóra asked. 'Was he punished?'

Berta smiled coldly. 'You could call it that. He died in the accident. His wife too.' She paused for a moment as if deciding whether to say more, then went ahead. 'They were from a farm around here, actually. Their daughter is Rósa, Bergur's wife.'

Well, I never, Thóra thought. All roads led to Bergur the farmer.

28

Thóra sat at the computer in Jónas's office, speaking to him on the phone. 'The police will present the judge with evidence of your alleged guilt, and I'll try to show that it's irrelevant or insufficient. Afterwards the judge will question you and you have the chance to answer the allegations. You aren't obliged to answer, but I don't recommend you refuse, except in absolutely exceptional circumstances.'

'Don't I get the opportunity to plead innocent?' asked Jónas, frightened. 'I can't believe the judge won't be able to see that I'm telling the truth. Judges have to be particularly insightful, don't they?'

Thóra could not prevent a laugh from escaping her and had to put her hand over the mouthpiece. 'Jónas,' she said, recovering herself, 'judges are just ordinary people and they can reach wrong conclusions like anybody else. Also, the judge has to take into account the evidence presented to him. If it clearly indicates that you're guilty or hiding something, he has to base his decision on that, no matter how convincingly you declare that you're innocent.'

'I'm scared shitless,' Jónas said feelingly. Thóra hoped he could reproduce this level of emotion when he pleaded innocent the next morning. You never knew with judges.

'Of course you are, Jónas,' she said, 'but don't let it

overwhelm you. Just remember that I'll be with you tomorrow, and hopefully it will all turn out fine.'

'What are you going to say?' he asked. 'Will you come up with something new?'

'Well, a lot of things would have to happen tonight. You're being brought before the judge at ten o'clock, and I doubt that I can find anything out by then.' There was no mistaking the desperation underlying the silence on the other end of the line. 'But I'll do everything in my power, I promise.'

'Anything!' said Jónas. 'If only you could find the murderer, or someone who'd pretend to be him!'

'I'd have to try pretty hard to find an actor who'd confess in court to a crime he didn't commit.' Thóra jiggled the mouse and the screen in front of her lit up. 'What's your password, Jónas? I've switched on your computer but I can't get in.'

'hashish,' Jónas said. 'All lowercase.'

Thóra groaned. 'Are you out of your mind?' she said. 'I'll change it. If the police were to confiscate your computer, that's not the sort of password we want them to see. I'll choose something more innocent.' Immediately after they rang off she changed the password. 'amnesty,' she said out loud. 'All lowercase.'

'Who are you talking to?' asked Matthew as he came in. 'The ghost?'

Thóra looked up, smiling. 'Yes, I thought it was worth a try. Maybe it can tell us the name of the murderer before ten tomorrow morning.'

Matthew flung himself theatrically into the chair facing Thóra. He tossed a thick bundle of papers on to the desk. 'I identified several of the cars,' he said.

Thóra picked up the papers. Matthew had taken the list out to the car park to check whether any vehicle belonging to the guests or staff had gone through the Hvalfjördur Tunnel the day Eiríkur was killed.

'How did you manage to go through so many registration numbers and names?' she asked. 'How many are there, anyway?'

'About five thousand, but the police were kind enough to go through the list and mark those that might be linked to the murder. They include the cars of some of the hotel staff,' Matthew said. 'The rental cars were the problem, because the company is registered as the owner, so those entries aren't much use on their own.'

'So you've compared the numbers with the plates in the car park?' Thóra asked.

'Yes. I found a few rental numbers outside that were on the list, and I enlisted the services of Vigdís,' Matthew said. 'She came into the car park with me and told me who owned what. It's uncanny how good her memory is.' He reached over to the pile of papers and flicked through it. 'Unfortunately that wasn't much help. The drivers of the rental cars are all foreigners, of course, and none of them looks like a suspect. I do know, however, that neither the Japanese father and son nor Robin the photographer took the tunnel that day.'

'Robin said he'd been in the West Fjords,' Thóra said. 'That fits in with not taking the tunnel. According to Vigdís, the Japanese never go anywhere, so I'm not surprised they weren't travelling. What about the others?'

'I don't know if this means anything, but out of the cars ticked by the police, Bergur went through the tunnel and back before noon, so he's still in the picture,' Matthew said without looking up. 'That stockbroker on crutches didn't go anywhere – at least, I couldn't find his name on the list. Actually, I doubt he drives much in his condition. Thröstur, the canoeist, left here in his car at around six. The murder was committed at dinnertime, so he seems above suspicion. He came back much later.'

'How much later, exactly?' asked Thóra. 'There is actually a longer route – you go round Hvalfjördur instead of taking the tunnel. He could have driven through the tunnel, then come back round Hvalfjördur, killed Eiríkur, then driven back again – the long way – to the other end of the tunnel and turned round to come back through it.' She grimaced. 'It sounds rather improbable, I suppose. If he went through the tunnel half an hour or an hour before the murder, it's very unlikely that he could get back here, drag Eiríkur out to the stables, kill him and drive the whole circuit to the tunnel and back in such a short time. I don't know the exact time range for his death, they just said dinnertime.'

Matthew compared the times at which Thröstur left and returned. 'He came back two and a half hours after he went through the tunnel.'

'It's out of the question, then,' Thóra said. 'It would have been pretty much impossible, but I still think we ought to sound him out. He may know something. What else have you got there?'

'The staff seem to have stayed here, by and large; at least, there are only a few cars on the list belonging to them. Of course, there's a chance that I've overlooked something, but as far as I can see, only two employees used the tunnel that day. Jökull drove through the tunnel and back two hours later, so he's still a candidate. The police have ticked another car that Vigdís says belongs to the masseuse. She left around noon and didn't come back. There was one more female employee flagged up by the police, according to Vigdís. Her name's Sóldís and she's a cleaner. She left just after the murder. Vigdís said she was taking her car to a garage in Reykjavík on the Sunday and got a lift back. I don't recognise the name, but she could have come back any time, because we don't know who drove her.'

'Sóldís is just a girl, really. She's very unlikely to be involved,' said Thóra. 'I spoke to her briefly before you arrived and she seemed a decent kid. I don't really think women are in the frame, anyway,' she added. 'Not if we assume the same person committed both murders. Remember Birna was raped.'

'Quite possibly, but the police have marked the names of women as well as men,' Matthew said. 'After all, we don't know that in each case the car's driver was its owner. The women might have lent their cars to someone; the murderer could have travelled in a car other than his own. The same goes for the men's cars, of course. We can't take for granted that they were driving just because they're the registered owners.'

'No, that's true,' said Thóra. 'So it's not much help, then, is it?'

'Well,' replied Matthew, 'I browsed through some other names on the list, because you never know what the police are looking for.' He thumbed through the pages. 'I saw that Börkur and Elín both drove through the tunnel in this direction sometime before the murder. They didn't go back. Then there's that Berta girl; she was on her way to Reykjavík an hour before the murder and didn't come back that day.'

'Do you suppose the brother and sister could be the murderers?' Thóra asked. She frowned. 'I hadn't even thought of that, but it's hard to imagine why they'd want to kill those two.'

'You never know,' said Matthew. 'Oh, yes, I also asked Vigdís about that old guy, Magnús Baldvinsson, and she said he didn't come in his own car – his grandson drove him here – so he couldn't have gone anywhere all day, even if we did think him capable of murder.'

'Then there's Bergur's wife,' mused Thóra. 'It just seems so unlikely that all this could happen on their doorstep without them being involved. He's Birna's lover and stumbles across her body; then Eiríkur is murdered in their stables. She had ample reason to want Birna dead, even though I can't figure out why she would have murdered Eiríkur.' Thóra looked at Matthew. 'Don't you think she must have killed Birna? She was in quite a state in the stables today. Could she have had an accomplice who carried out the rape?'

Matthew shrugged. 'Yes, she could, but who? Her friend Jökull, perhaps?'

Thóra groaned and turned to the computer. 'I'm famished,' she said, looking at the clock in the corner of the screen. 'Shouldn't we see if we can get something to eat? If we leave it much longer, I'm scared the kitchen will close. The computer will still be here afterwards.'

They left the office. Matthew left the list behind and

Thóra took care to lock the door so no one could come in and take it. She was by no means sure that the police would give her another copy if it went missing, since she probably wasn't supposed to have it in the first place. Even if they did, it was unlikely she'd get another copy that had been marked up so conveniently, so they'd be back to square one.

'I hope there's shellfish on the menu,' Thóra said, as her stomach rumbled, 'or maybe meatballs.'

'I fancy a thick sandwich and a beer,' Matthew said. 'Anything but whale meat, and don't feel you have to share your shellfish with me, either.' He stopped talking when Thóra tugged gently at his sleeve. She nodded in the direction of a slender girl who was walking up to the lobby with an elderly woman.

'That's Sóldís,' Thóra whispered, 'the one whose name you didn't recognise on the list.' As they approached her, Thóra waved. 'Hello, Sóldís,' she said.

Sóldís and the other woman stopped, and the girl forced out an approximation of a smile. 'Oh, hello.'

Thóra introduced herself to the elderly woman and shook her hand. 'I'm a lawyer,' she explained, 'working for the owner of this hotel. Sóldís has been very helpful with various matters.' The woman introduced herself as Lára. Thóra smiled at her young companion. 'I just wanted to ask you one more question, if you're not in a rush.'

'Not on my account,' the old woman said. 'I only came to pick her up, and we're in no hurry. You go ahead, Sóldís.'

'Sure. Whatever,' said Sóldís with impeccable teenage nonchalance. She was chewing a wad of bubble gum that was obviously too large, because she was slurring slightly. 'What do you want to know?'

'It's no big deal,' Thóra replied. 'We were looking at a list of cars that drove through the Hvalfjördur Tunnel on Sunday, and it seems that you took yours to Reykjavík to be repaired.'

'That's right,' replied the girl. She jerked her thumb at the elderly lady beside her. 'I don't get it back until Wednesday, so my grandma's picking me up.'

'OK,' said Thóra. 'My question is, who gave you a lift back from Reykjavík? We're trying to work out everyone's movements for that day.'

Judging from her expression, Sóldís thought it was an odd question. 'I came back with Thröstur,' she said.

'The canoeist?' said Thóra, taken aback.

'Yes, I heard him saying he was popping over to Reykjavík, and I was a bit stuck, so I asked if he'd give me a lift back. He said that was fine.'

She blew a large bubble and popped it. Then she sucked the strands of gum back into her mouth with great panache. 'Steini let me down, so I was lucky Thröstur could help me out.'

'Steini?' Thóra asked. 'Who's Steini?' Surely she didn't mean the young man in the wheelchair.

'My friend,' the girl answered. 'Sort of. He was going to fetch me, but he blew me out at the last minute. He's a bit weird. He never used to be, but then he had that accident and . . .' She twirled her index finger at her temple.

'You mean the lad in the wheelchair, with all the burns?' Thóra asked in astonishment. 'He can *drive*?'

'Oh, yes,' said Sóldís. 'It's only his right side that's burned, and the other hand is fine. Both his legs are messed up, but he has a device in his car to help him use the pedals and he drives an automatic.'

'That must make a big difference for him,' Thóra said, trying to conceal her surprise. It had never occurred to her that he would be able to drive. She'd assumed he was completely dependent on others because he was confined to a wheelchair. 'How do you know him?' she asked.

'We were in the same class from the age of six,' said Sóldís. 'There was only one class for each year group, you know, and we were born in the same year. He moved into a house near here after the accident and I started visiting him – at first because I felt sorry for him and then just to chat.'

'So he's a good friend of yours?' Thóra asked, still struggling to understand. By way of explanation she added, 'He seemed very . . . reserved on the two occasions I've met him.'

'Yeah, he's cool. He's not good with strangers, though,' said Sóldís, snapping her gum. 'I think he gets uncomfortable when people stare at him. There are really only two of us who hang out with him, me and his cousin Berta.'

'I've met her,' Thóra said. 'Are you friends too?'

'Sure, I guess,' Sóldís replied. 'I didn't know her before, because she's from Reykjavík. I've only met her at Steini's, you know. She's really nice to him; she seems pretty cool.'

'That was a terrible business,' Sóldís's grandmother Lára suddenly chipped in. 'Not many people live around here, so you remember an accident in which two people are killed and one is badly hurt.'

'I understand it was a middle-aged couple from a farm close by here,' said Thóra.

'Yes, it was awful,' the old woman replied. 'Probably the

worst thing about it was that Gudmundur was drunk. It wouldn't have happened if he hadn't been drink-driving. It's been a great strain on their daughter, Rósa. She's become rather isolated since then. She wasn't that sociable to start with, but she withdrew into her shell completely after it happened, which is ridiculous, because no one's blaming her for it.'

Thóra nodded. 'So you're a local?' she asked Lára.

'Yes, born and bred.' She smiled back. Thóra noticed how much Sóldís looked like her. Although there must have been sixty years between them, they had the same facial features. 'I moved to Reykjavík for a few years when I was young, but soon realised it suited me better here. There's nothing to be gained by living anywhere else. I believe that more and more.'

Thóra smiled. 'I've come across all manner of intriguing things since I've been here. I don't suppose you knew the people who lived on the two farms belonging to this estate?'

'Kreppa and Kirkjustétt? I most certainly did,' Lára said proudly. 'We were the best of friends, me and Gudný, the girl from Kirkjustétt. That's why I so enjoy coming over here, even if it is difficult to see where the past stops and the present begins.'

'So you remember those times well?' Thóra said as she tried to think what she most wanted to ask.

'I do. Of course, my memory's starting to go, like everything else, but the funny thing is that the oldest memories seem to last longest. Please don't hesitate to ask anything you want. Grímur and his brother, Bjarni, weren't quite like normal people, so you'd probably find your own questions stranger than I would! Life on the farm here was pretty peculiar, so you won't shock me.'

Thóra could have kissed her. 'Oh, I'm so relieved to hear that. I've had trouble getting people to discuss it; either they know nothing or they don't want to talk about it.' She took a breath and then fired away. 'Do you recall whether the farm had any connection with Nazism? I found a flag and other articles that seem completely out of context and I must say I'm surprised that they should be in the basement of a farm in rural Iceland. Do you know anything about that?'

Lára sighed heavily. 'Yes, I'm afraid I do. Bjarni became obsessed with it. You should realise that after his wife, Adalheidur, died, in about 1930, he was never the same. She meant everything to him, and you could say that when she died his mind went with her.' The old woman grinned impishly. 'Actually, it was a stroke of luck in some ways, because he literally made money from being weird. He invested in all manner of wild projects that you'd expect to have bankrupted him, but they ended up making him a fortune because of the times we were living in. The war broke out just as he started investing, and luck was on his side. It was pure coincidence that the economy was transformed practically overnight, what with the military occupation and population growth. But poor Grímur, the voice of reason, wasn't so lucky.'

'Did he go bankrupt?' asked Thóra.

'No, it wasn't quite that bad, but I think he came close. He was a doctor, but since there was already a doctor here, he didn't have enough to do, so he increasingly devoted himself to farming. In the end he gave up his medical practice and put everything into building up his farm, but he couldn't get anyone to work for him. Everyone had gone to Reykjavík, where the Allied forces were paying better wages. Ultimately Bjarni rescued his brother from bankruptcy. He bought all Grímur's property but still let him treat it as his own – even though the two of them were barely speaking, so it must have been difficult for Grímur to accept his help.

'To cap it all, Grímur's wife, Kristrún, died around then, leaving him alone to raise their little girl. Kristrún was mentally ill. I hardly knew her, and she didn't socialise much,' the old woman said. She paused, then continued, 'As for this business with the Nazis, Bjarni was visited by people from Reykjavík who wanted to make him into a kind of nationalist leader for western Iceland. He was supposed to enrol young men to create a political presence in this part of the country. There was one in the south and I think in the north too, although they never made much headway.'

'And did he?' asked Thóra. 'Did he join the party and enlist people?'

'He started to, and he even made some progress.' Lára smiled again. 'But it wasn't the manifesto, the party or the swastika that appealed to the young men who came here. It was Bjarni's daughter, Gudný.'

'And you say she was a friend of yours?' said Thóra.

'Yes, she was. Friendship was very different back then, of course. We didn't meet up as often as girls do these days. Even so, it was a genuine friendship; we couldn't have been closer.' The old woman stared into the air, dreamy-eyed. 'She was so beautiful – a beautiful little girl who turned into a beautiful young woman, just like her mother. As soon as she hit puberty, the local lads worshipped her, so they jumped at the chance to go round to her house, even if they had to pretend to be nationalists for the evening. I doubt they had a clue what Nazism was about. They just wanted to be near Gudný.'

'Was she at these meetings?'

'Oh, no, dear, but she did make the coffee and serve the refreshments. I used to help her sometimes. We'd make eyes at the boys and fall about laughing.' Lára's eyes clouded and she shook her head sadly. 'I don't know how it would all have turned out, but fate intervened and what happened happened.'

'Do you mean tuberculosis?' asked Thóra.

'Among other things, yes,' she said. 'Bjarni fell ill and locked himself away – and that meant Gudný did too.' She sighed. 'I moved to Reykjavík with my aunt around that time, so I lost contact with her, apart from the occasional letter. The Nazi business fizzled out.'

'What do you think about the rumours that Bjarni abused Gudný?'

Lára looked directly at her. She exhaled briefly, then closed her eyes. 'Goodness, that was a long time ago. Actually, I've been thinking about Gudný a lot recently.' She pointed at Sóldís, who was still beside her, rolling her gum around her mouth. 'When Sóldís started working here, it brought it all back to me.' She hesitated for a moment, then looked firmly at Thóra. 'I don't believe Bjarni ever laid a finger on his daughter, either in anger or any other sin. For all his strange ways he was a good man, and I could tell from her letters that she loved him very much, so I simply can't believe it.' She looked down. 'Something did happen, though. Gudný's letters became less frequent, but in her last one she confided in me that she'd had a baby. The letter was written just after her father had died, and the child was four years old. She said she hadn't had the courage to tell me before. In those days that sort of thing was a great scandal. She would only have been sixteen when the baby was born. She never said a word about the father, but said she'd tell me the whole story later. She never got the chance, though, because the next thing I heard was that she'd died.'

'Who could have been the father,' Thóra asked, 'if not her own father?'

'There weren't many other candidates, that's for sure,' Lára replied. 'People were worried about TB, because it was so infectious and there was no cure at the time. The two of them were completely isolated after her father decided to stay at home instead of going to Reykjavík. She didn't want to leave him, so that was that. The only person I know who called on them was Bjarni's brother, Grímur. I've always suspected him of abusing Gudný, although I shouldn't say such a thing when I have no real grounds except for the fact that he wasn't a good man.'

'What happened to the child?' said Thóra. 'Was it a boy or a girl?'

'A girl. I don't know what happened to her, because no one seemed to know anything about her when I came back out here. The vicar who must have baptised her had just died, and the people I asked hadn't noticed a little girl. A few of them had heard that Gudný ordered certain items that could only be explained by there being a baby at the farm. Rumour said the baby had died of exposure, or of TB like its mother. The incest story started circulating after Gudný and Bjarni were both dead. My efforts to locate the child might even have started the rumours.'

'Did you discuss this with Grímur?' asked Thóra.

'I tried, but he wouldn't talk about it. He moved to Reykjavík not long after I came back here. No one wanted to help me get to the bottom of the matter because incest was such a taboo – there was so much shame attached to it.'

'Do you know the child's name?'

'Kristín. She talked about little Kristín in her letter. I've searched everywhere for a gravestone with that name on it, but never found one, so I have no idea what became of her.'

'Kristín,' mused Thóra. 'So she did exist.'

'Did?' said Lára. 'I still cherish the hope that she's alive. I've always believed that Gudný found a good home for her but kept it secret. She wouldn't have wanted anyone to worry about catching TB from the child. That may have been what she had in mind from the time the child was born, and she could have asked Grímur not to send the birth certificate to the authorities, or to forge it somehow. I presume that Grímur delivered the baby, because it was born after everyone stopped calling on Gudný and her father.' Lára set her jaw. 'My friend Gudný was a God-fearing girl. She wouldn't have entertained the idea of the child not being buried in hallowed ground, if she had died. She would have been buried in the churchyard here, so I choose to believe that she lived.'

Thóra nodded. No mother in her right mind would bury a dead infant in the countryside when there was a cemetery nearby. Kristín must have survived her mother. Thóra did not want to tell Lára about the message that had been carved into the pillar, claiming that Kristín had been murdered. It was better for her to believe that she was still alive.

Thóra changed the subject. 'Do you know what building stood out here at the back? It must have burned down a long time ago.'

'A building?' exclaimed Lára. 'There was only one building there and it's still standing, although it's been incorporated into the hotel.' She wrinkled her brow in thought. 'Unless you mean the barn,' she said suddenly. 'Now that you mention it, I suppose it has gone.' She turned her head, looking for a window on to the land behind the hotel, but there wasn't one. 'On the other side of the farmhouse was a building that acted as a barn and a cattle shed. It might have burned down, but that would have happened before I came back, because I don't remember a fire. I can't say for sure if the building was still standing when I returned to the area.'

'I know this must sound odd, but do you remember anything special about the coal bunker at Kreppa?' Thóra asked. 'It's underground but can be reached both from inside the basement and through a hatch in the meadow.'

Lára screwed up her face as she considered it. 'Not that I recall. Is it important?'

'What are that lot playing at?' said Sóldís suddenly, before Thóra could reply. 'Don't they know camping's banned here? There's a big sign on the slip road. This is a protected nature reserve.'

'Oh, no,' sighed Thóra as she watched her SUV and caravan bunny-hopping into the hotel car park.

29

The caravan stuck out well beyond the parking space. Thóra watched as Gylfi got out of the SUV and opened the doors for his little sister and Sigga, who were both sitting in the back. He had obviously not wanted the airbag to injure his unborn child if they had an accident. Gylfi certainly had his priorities right, if you ignored the fact that he had no driving licence. Sigga arched her back as she got out, her swollen belly seeming more disproportionate than ever in contrast with her fragile frame. Thóra hoped for her sake that the child would not take after its father's side of the family when it came to birth weight, because both Gylfi and Sóley had had heads the size of pumpkins when they were born. As she wondered how she could get rid of them, she remembered that it was ten in the evening – too late to arrange for a driver to collect them.

'Why didn't you go with your dad?' she called out to Gylfi, striding across the car park to greet them. 'He was supposed to collect you in Selfoss.'

'We just didn't,' Gylfi said, conscientiously locking the SUV door. 'None of us wanted to go back with him, or to Sigga's parents, so we decided to keep on camping. I told Dad so he wouldn't have a wasted journey, if that's what you're worried about.'

That was the last thing on Thóra's mind. Hannes could

chase wild geese halfway round the world for all she cared, but she was concerned about how to handle Jónas, Matthew and her two children, not to mention her pregnant prospective daughter-in-law, without messing something up – or everything.

'How are you feeling, Sigga?' she asked the girl, hugging Sóley, who had wrapped herself around her mother ecstatically.

'Well,' said Sigga, 'my back hurts.'

Thóra gasped. 'Do you think the baby's on its way? If so, there's no way you can stay here.'

'No, Mum,' said Gylfi, shocked. 'It hasn't been nine months yet.' He had clearly never heard of premature birth.

'Come inside,' she said, ushering her visitors towards the hotel lobby. 'We need to talk about this little jaunt of yours, Gylfi, but it'll have to wait,' she whispered in her son's ear. 'I'm very disappointed in you.' Then she added in a louder voice, for everyone to hear, 'I'll see if I can get a room for you. You've had enough camping. That can wait until the baby's born.' Envisaging Gylfi trying to erect the caravan awning with a newborn baby in his arms, she quickly added, 'And has started school.'

Matthew was standing at the door, wreathed in smiles. Thóra pulled a face at him over their heads. 'Kids, you remember Matthew. He's helping me with a case concerning the hotel. You have to be on your best behaviour because I need to work. Don't go anywhere and don't break anything.' She almost added, 'And don't give birth to anything,' but decided against it. The first two commandments would be difficult enough for them to keep.

* * *

'Don't worry,' Matthew said when they had sat down again at the computer in Jónas's office. 'This is fine. I like your kids. Although this isn't exactly the holiday I had in mind, I think it could be interesting.' He tipped her a conspiratorial wink. 'Maybe you could arrange a babysitter and we can find a restaurant that serves only organically cultivated chickweed.'

Thóra didn't look up from the screen. 'Why isn't Jón Árnason's folktale collection on the Internet?' she muttered.

'Can I take that as a yes?' asked Matthew.

'What?' Thóra asked vacantly, scrolling down the page she was reading. 'Oh, yes,' she added, with no idea what she was agreeing to. 'No matter where I search I can't find the folktale itself, only the verse. I have to get to a library.'

Matthew looked at his watch. 'You're unlikely to find one open now,' he said. 'Do you really think the inscription is that important?'

Thóra looked up at him. 'No,' she admitted. 'I just have nothing else to do. I'm clutching at straws for tomorrow – I don't have much to go on.'

'If either Bergur or his wife is the murderer, as you seem inclined to believe, I don't think that rock can have anything to do with it,' said Matthew. 'It makes more sense for you to concentrate on something more recent.' He crossed to the window and watched as a car pulled up at the hotel. It parked in a space directly below the window. 'I recognise that number plate,' he said, releasing the curtain. 'Where's the list?'

Thóra gawped at him. 'Are you saying you can remember

350

a single number from the thousands you went through?' she asked, passing him the list.

'It's a personalised number plate,' he replied. 'There weren't that many, so it stood out.' He flicked through the list. 'Here it is. An hour before Eiríkur was killed, this car came through the tunnel from Reykjavík.' He handed the list back to Thóra and pointed to the entry. 'There. "VERITAS",' he said. 'I specifically remember this one because it made me wonder what the owner's job could be. I couldn't think of anything connected with "truth", unless he was a mathematics teacher. Then I saw who it belonged to.'

Thóra took the list from him and read the owner's name. 'Ah,' she said, putting it down again. 'Baldvin Baldvinsson, the grandson of old Magnús, who we talked to.' She stood up. 'What's he doing back here again?'

'Visiting his grandfather, perhaps?' suggested Matthew. 'Or maybe he's drumming up votes.'

'Let's ask him,' said Thóra. 'If his registration plate is accurate, at least he'll tell us the truth.'

Baldvin stood in the lobby, drumming his fingers on the reception desk while he waited. Vigdís had her back to him, working on the computer. Thóra hoped she was reasonably well paid, because she seemed to be on the reception desk round the clock.

'Don't you ever take a break?' she asked as she approached Baldvin with Matthew. Rather than confront him directly, Thóra had decided that talking to Vigdís would be a good start. Since he appeared to be waiting for something, he was unlikely to leave immediately.

Vigdís looked over her shoulder at Thóra. 'Oh! Yes, of course I do. Jónas was going to take this shift but . . .' She hesitated. 'You know. He was meant to hire someone for the other shift, but he never got round to it.' After tapping at the keyboard for a moment, she turned to Baldvin. 'You can have room fourteen. It's next door to your grand-father.' She handed him the key.

Thóra turned to Baldvin. 'Aren't you Magnús's grandson? The city councillor?'

Baldvin was startled. He looked tired, which only height-ened the striking resemblance to his grandfather. Remembe-ring the photographs of Magnús as a young man, Thóra wondered what it must feel like, knowing exactly how the years would treat you. 'Er, yes, I am,' he answered. 'Do I know you?'

Thóra proffered a handshake. 'No, but I've heard about your grandfather. I was a friend of Birna's.' Before releasing her firm grip on his hand, she asked bluntly, 'You knew her, didn't you?'

Baldvin looked as if he had swallowed a fly. He gulped convulsively, then was back to his normal self. 'A friend of Birna's, you say? Unfortunately I don't think I know anyone called Birna.'

'Really?' Thóra said, but decided not to push her luck. She still hadn't let go of his hand and his palm had gone clammy. 'Are you sure? Weren't you here on Sunday?'

Baldvin tensed up, but she didn't know if this was because of her tight grip on his hand or the question. 'Me? No, you must be mixing me up with someone else.' He flashed a smarmy smile.

'Am I?' Thóra feigned surprise. 'I thought I drove up

here through the tunnel directly behind you. Maybe I am getting mixed up.' She finally released her grip and Baldvin jerked his hand back as if she had leprosy.

'I think you must be. I was somewhere else then.' He turned to Vigdís. 'Thank you,' he said, then, 'Nice to meet you,' to Thóra, with another pearly grin. A true politician.

'You too.' Thóra beamed back. When he'd gone, she turned to Matthew and whispered urgently, 'He's lying through his teeth.' Then she asked Vigdís, 'Do you remember him being here on Sunday evening?'

Vigdís shook her head and yawned. 'No, I've only met him twice before,' she said. 'The day he dropped his grandfather off and the evening of the seance.'

Thóra clutched the edge of the reception desk. 'Was he here then?'

'Yes, I just told you,' said Vigdís indignantly. 'He had dinner with his grandfather. Then they went to the seance. I think they soon realised it wasn't their cup of tea, because they'd left by the interval.'

Thóra widened her eyes at Matthew. He gestured towards Vigdís, who was standing up to leave. Thóra realised at once what he meant. She was holding a key identical to the one they had found in the desk at Kreppa.

'Is something wrong?' she asked, surprised that they were still standing there. 'Was the kids' room all right?'

'Oh, yes,' Thóra replied, staring at the key. 'Would you mind letting me have a look at that key?' She produced hers. 'I came across one just the same and I was wondering what it fits.'

'This is the key to my staff locker,' she said, reluctantly

showing her. 'If you found one, it must belong to someone who works here. People do lose them.'

Thóra compared the keys. They were virtually indistinguishable. She handed back the other. 'I don't think it belongs to one of the staff,' she said. 'Do you know if Birna had a locker at her disposal?'

Vigdís pursed her lips, thinking it over. 'Not as far as I know, but she could have. The lockers were only installed recently. She chose them and ordered them. Maybe she kept one for herself.' Vigdís walked round the desk. 'Come with me,' she said, setting off. 'There aren't many lockers, so it won't take long to see if it fits.'

Thóra and Matthew followed Vigdís to the staffroom, where there was a row of steel lockers along one wall.

'Shall I just start?' asked Thóra, brandishing the key.

'Sure,' said Vigdís. 'You don't need to try number seven: that's mine.'

Thóra tried the locks. She didn't need much time, because the key fitted on her third attempt. It gave a little click as it turned. She carefully revolved the chrome handle and opened the locker. With a deep breath and a glance at Matthew, she peered inside. Almost at once she pulled her head out, disappointed. 'Empty. Damn.' She stood aside to let him take a look. When he put his head inside and didn't withdraw it immediately, she tapped his back impatiently. 'What? Can you see something?'

Matthew twisted to peer up at the roof of the locker. 'Something's been stuck up here,' his voice echoed from inside the hollow space. 'Do you have any tweezers?' he asked, straightening back up. 'We don't want to cover it with fingerprints if it's something important.'

Thóra looked over at Vigdís. 'Is there a first-aid kit here?' Sticking her head into the locker, she noticed a small white rectangle of paper Sellotaped to its top. The edges were slightly curled. 'What on earth is that?' she wondered aloud, as she took a pair of tweezers from Vigdís.

Matthew and Vigdís watched as she tried to remove the tape, although they could see little more than her back.

'Bingo!' she said, extricating herself with the white piece of card gripped in the tweezers. 'It's a photograph.' She turned it over. 'Oh!' She flipped it round to show the others.

'Good God!' exclaimed Vigdís. 'Baldvin Baldvinsson! I didn't know he was a neo-Nazi!'

'It's not Baldvin,' said Thóra, placing the photograph on the staffroom table. 'It's his grandfather, Magnús. It was taken years ago.'

'Jesus, they're dead ringers,' marvelled Vigdís. 'I'd have thrown that photo away if I were Magnús. Or Baldvin.'

'Perhaps they never got the chance,' said Thóra. She turned to Vigdís. 'Don't tell a soul about this,' she said.

'God, no,' replied Vigdís. 'Of course not.' She was already trying to remember if she had her friend Gulla's new phone number and calculating what time Kata would arrive at the beauty parlour the following morning. Of course, they could be trusted. Everyone knew that telling your best friends counts as *not telling a soul*.

She collected her handbag from her own locker and went back to reception. As she passed Matthew, she placed a hand on his shoulder and told him kindly that the people of Iceland were very enlightened and he need not worry about prejudice. Bewildered, Matthew watched her walk away.

'What did she mean by that?' he asked Thóra in astonishment.

It dawned on Thóra that the sex therapist's oath of confidentiality was not as sacrosanct as Stefanía had implied. Thóra shrugged. 'They're all a bunch of weirdos around here,' she said, feigning innocence. Then she gave a weak smile. 'I suppose I should go and put Sóley to bed. It'll be a while before I get to bed myself, the way things are turning out.'

Thóra was back at Jónas's computer again. 'It all fits,' she said as she scanned the Google results for 'Baldvin Baldvinsson'. She opened a few links that contained nothing of interest, but she kept idly clicking while they talked.

'How?' asked Matthew. 'I admit that a photograph like that, hidden in a place like that, suggests that Birna wanted to prevent it being found. The only person likely to want it is Magnús, but he's too old to kill anyone. Besides, I'm not exactly sure why he would want to murder Birna, even if he knew she had the photo.'

'I don't think he's the only one, actually,' Thóra said. 'His grandson, Baldvin, has much more to lose. It says here that he's entering the primaries for the parliamentary election next spring and a recent newspaper article pointed out just how much he resembles his grandfather in every way. A photo of his grandfather in Nazi uniform, which could just as easily be of him, could sink his campaign.' She looked up. 'This man drives around in a car with a registration plate that says, "VERITAS". It's obvious what impression he wants to give. Nazis aren't exactly part of his image. Part of the reason for his stellar political career is his grandfather. If the old man's reputation is tarnished, it will smear Baldvin, although he wasn't even a twinkle in his eye at the time.'

'So what was Birna's motive?' wondered Matthew. 'Why didn't she simply hand over the photograph? Was she trying to blackmail them? Neither of them looks seriously rich. That car with the VERITAS plates is just an old Jeep.'

'When she found the photograph, presumably in that old album in the basement that seemed to have one missing, she might have taken it out just to examine it more closely. Obviously she was shocked to see a well-known person in it. Then she must have realised that she could turn it to her advantage, and I suspect that she wanted something other than money from them,' Thóra said, clicking yet another link. She read briefly, then looked up again. 'This is quite interesting,' she said. 'Baldvin is on the council committee to select a design for a new bus station they're building in Reykjavík. You remember that drawing of the glass complex on the wall at Kreppa? There aren't many wooded areas in Iceland. The proposed site by the hill on Öskjuhlíd is one of them. There were buses on the drawing.' She stabbed her finger in the air triumphantly. 'She was clearly determined to win that commission. That could also explain why she phoned him.'

Matthew looked dubious. 'Are you saying she would black-mail Baldvin into swaying the committee, just to win this project?' He shook his head. 'I'm not sure I believe that.'

'For an architect in Iceland, that sort of project is like a lottery win,' she said. 'It's a large public building in a busy place, and the designer becomes a household name at once. People queue up with new projects for them. That's the way it works here, and surely in other countries too.'

'But how can one member of a committee sway its choice?' he asked. 'The others must have some say as well.'

'Of course,' said Thóra. 'But he has access to information that isn't available to the other architects competing for the project, so he can find out the other members' priorities and so forth. Although all design competitions usually have to stipulate the basic requirements, the winning proposal often deviates slightly from the original specifications. For instance, if an architect knows that the committee actually wants a larger building than they're asking for –' Thóra shrugged '– he or she has a definite advantage. And I'm positive that one person can swing the rest of a committee if he's a smooth-talker who knows what he wants. I saw on one website that when Baldvin was at school, he was the debating champion two years in a row. He must be a very persuasive speaker.'

'So what are you going to do?' asked Matthew. 'This isn't watertight, and it doesn't explain Eiríkur's murder either.'

'Do you remember Baldvin's email address in Birna's diary?' Thóra asked.

'Yes,' Matthew said. 'Are you going to mail him?'

'No,' replied Thóra. 'I'm considering taking a little chance.' She picked up the telephone. 'I'm going to ask the police to search her computer for emails to Baldvin. They must have it in their custody, and it's by no means certain that they would have been looking for emails to him.'

When the telephone was finally answered after a long wait, Thóra introduced herself and tried to sound as official as possible. 'Could you put me through to Thórólfur Kjartansson, please? This is in connection with the murders on Snaefellsnes. I need to pass on an urgent message, or preferably speak to him in person.'

She whistled along with the muzak on the line as she waited to be connected. After a while it stopped and a weary Thórólfur said, 'What?'

Thóra lay on the bed with her arms round her daughter. She had carried her – fast asleep – out of Gylfi and Sigga's room and into her own, more from fear that Sigga would give birth all over her daughter than anything else. Matthew had moved back to his room without protest, and she was extremely grateful because she had quite enough to occupy her mind. Mainly she was apprehensive about the following morning, afraid that Thórólfur would not take the bait, which would leave her little more to do for Jónas than put up a standard defence. That was an awful prospect.

More thoughts plagued her, though. If either Magnús or Baldvin had murdered Birna, there was no visible explanation for their wanting to kill Eiríkur, nor any link with them. Was he Birna's accomplice? What purpose did the fox serve, and what did 'RER' mean, if anything?

Kristín was bothering her most. Thóra had discovered that she was Gudný's daughter, but that seemed irrelevant to the case. More thoughts crowded her mind but she was too tired to focus on them and they soon merged into one amorphous mass: coal, walls, horses, deeds of sale, lapsed claims, a broken leg . . .

She woke with a start to the sound of a baby crying. In a daze, she freed her arm from beneath her sleeping daughter's head and sat up. The sound came again and she got out of bed and went to the window, but could see nothing in the half-light. Somewhere out there, the strange wailing resumed, then stopped as suddenly as it had started. Thóra shut the window and arranged the curtains securely to block the view outside. A newborn infant dragging itself along by one arm in bloodstained swaddling clothes suddenly did not seem as preposterous as it had when she was teasing Matthew. She jumped back into bed with her daughter, determined not to mention this to anyone. She must have imagined the whole business. Through the closed window, she vaguely heard the pitiful crying start up again.

Tuesday, 13 June 2006

30

Dressed in a black robe trimmed with dark blue satin, the judge glared at Thóra. He had cupped his hands over his chin, covering his mouth, and she felt he might just as easily be poking his tongue out at her behind them, or hiding a grimace of boredom. 'Would the defence counsel please continue,' he boomed. 'This is most interesting.'

Thóra smiled politely. 'As I have pointed out, I came across this piece of evidence by sheer coincidence and informed the police of its existence immediately. I reject the prosecution's argument that I should have contacted them before removing the photograph, because I couldn't tell what significance it would have for the investigation until I saw what it showed. To do so, I had to remove it. I took every precaution not to disturb anything and touched it only with tweezers.'

'*CSI Miami*?' asked the judge, and removed his hands from his mouth. He smiled at Thóra.

'Yes, you could say that,' said Thóra, smiling back.

The judge turned to the official from the district commissioner's office, which had requested that Jónas be detained in custody. 'It appears that the commissioner's office did not make a proper investigation. Instead of objecting to the defence counsel's arguments, you ought to thank her for her assistance, otherwise the photograph in question might never have come to the notice of the authorities.'

The official asked permission to respond and stood up. 'It's true that we welcome this piece of evidence, and of course we shall examine this new angle on the case. An officer was sent to the scene immediately, even though this happened late last night, and the photograph is being examined as we speak.' He cleared his throat. 'However, we see no reason to reject the request to remand the suspect on these grounds alone. His alibi is inadequate, and he is still the chief suspect in these heinous crimes. The photograph alone does not alter that fact.'

'How do you answer this, counsel?' the judge asked Thóra.

'The photograph is far from being the only evidence. Baldvin Baldvinsson's car went through the Hvalfjördur Tunnel on Sunday at 17.51. That would have taken him to Snaefellsnes in time to commit the second murder, even though he denied to me ever making that journey. The police presumably have a comparable list of traffic for the day that Birna was murdered, and I am informed that Baldvin Baldvinsson was also present at the hotel on that day. He attended a seance that was held in the evening but left before the interval, which means that he had every opportunity to kill Birna. The police are undoubtedly in possession of email communications between Baldvin and Birna, but I have not been given the chance to see them, or indeed any other evidence apart from the list of traffic through the tunnel on Sunday, which they were kind enough to pass to me.' Out of the corner of her eye, Thóra saw Thórólfur shift in his seat. He was clearly burning to correct this fabrication, but the only way to do so was to admit that he had accidentally left the list behind, so he had to restrain himself.

Thóra continued, 'I should also point out that Eiríkur may have intended to abbreviate the name of Reykjavík on the wall but did not manage to write the final letter correctly. The "K" may have come out as an "R". It should be remembered that throughout his efforts a crazed stallion was in the process of trampling him to death. "R-E-K" could refer to Baldvin's position as a Reykjavík city councillor.'

The judge nodded slowly. 'We should not jump to conclusions. Baldvin Baldvinsson is a city councillor and his grandfather Magnús a former cabinet minister, so we should be very wary of insinuating that they are guilty of a serious breach of the law. I need not elaborate on the consequences if such a notion became public without reason.'

'It would be just as serious for my client were he to end up in the same position,' said Thóra. 'He also cherishes his reputation.' She thanked her lucky stars that the password to Jónas's computer was not common knowledge. 'My client has admitted to having sex with the deceased on the Thursday in question, but long before the estimated time of the murder. That explains his fingerprints on her belt, because she didn't change her clothes that day – at least I am not aware of any evidence to suggest that she did. Furthermore, my client has explained his whereabouts on both days, although there has not been time to corroborate his account. In his statement to the police he suffered a lapse of memory about his trip to Reykjavík on Sunday, but that can be put down to simple human error.'

The judge indicated to the official from the commissioner's office that he could speak. 'All this discussion has demonstrated,' said the latter, 'is that the investigation of the crime scenes is a long way from completion, since evidence is still being gathered. Even less cause, therefore, to release the suspect at this stage. We do not know what further evidence he might remove. Interesting as the hypothesis about Baldvin Baldvinsson may be, it seems highly implausible and in no way reduces the suspicion cast upon the person present here. For example, no connection has been demonstrated between Baldvin and Eiríkur. We therefore reiterate our request for fourteen days' custody.'

'With reference to Paragraph 1, Article 103 of the Penal Code,' replied Thóra, 'we consider the allegations against my client to be in no way sufficiently supported, besides which the conditions for such a request as stated in the article are lacking. Given that we have raised the question of investigative negligence on the part of the police, I put it to you that it is absurd to presume the suspect would jeopardise the investigation by removing evidence, as described in Clause A of the aforementioned article. Had my client been aware of the photograph in question, he would have had ample opportunity to either destroy it or make it public. He is therefore demonstrably unlikely to tamper with any evidence, because he could already have done so over the past few days. This he has not done, as the photograph proves, so we request that the police demand be rejected, with a reserve appeal for the requested period of custody to be reduced. If this conclusion is reached, I also insist on immediate access to all police evidence regarding the case.'

'If I may, Your Honour,' the official said, 'it is clear that two people have died at the hands of a murderer and we have probable cause to suspect the accused. Such crimes are obviously against the public interest, since it is unclear whether the murderer chooses his victims on any basis other than impulse. Anyone could be next. If the conditions of Article 1 are not found to be fulfilled, we request that the suspect be committed into custody on the basis of Article 2 regarding the public interest.'

The judge brought the proceedings to an end and stood up. He said he would consider the matter until noon and then deliver his ruling, and told them not to leave the vicinity of the court. He left the courtroom, followed by the recorder.

Thóra turned to Jónas. 'We can only wait and hope, then,' she murmured.

'What do you think he'll say?' Jónas whispered back. 'I thought you did a brilliant job, and the configuration of the planets is very favourable, to say the least. I can't imagine they'll do anything except throw out that ridiculous custody request.' He looked proudly at her. 'It was awesome how you remembered all the numbers of those legal articles.'

Thóra smiled at him. At last, someone who appreciated her recitals. She had been waiting a long time for this moment. If only the man singing her praises wasn't a murder suspect who'd mentioned the configuration of the planets in the same breath. 'That was nothing,' she said. 'You ought to hear me when I get started on letter apertures.'

*   *   *

Thóra collapsed into one of the cane chairs outside the lobby of the hotel with a groan and put a heavy folder of case documents on the table. She had been presented with them at the district court, wrapped in a supermarket carrier bag. 'Unfortunately it didn't work,' she said to Matthew as he sat down beside her. 'He was remanded in custody for seven days.' She looked around. 'Where are the children?'

'They went to look at the beached whale,' Matthew said. 'I'm not sure they quite understood my description, so they might get a nasty surprise.'

Thóra thought he was probably right. 'No, they can't have understood you,' she said. She knew her children well enough to realise that neither of them would go out of their way to see any decaying animal, let alone a whale. She didn't know Sigga well enough to tell whether she'd be able to handle it.

She tapped the orange plastic bag. 'I did get the case documents, though,' she said. 'Thórólfur tried to delay handing them over by saying he'd get someone in Reykjavík to photocopy them as soon as possible, but the judge offered the assistance of his own secretary, took the folder from them and made a copy for me. The police attorney had his own copy in court, of course.' She smiled, remembering this small but sweet victory. 'I have to rush through all this in the hope of finding something we don't know.'

'I hope it's nothing bad for Jónas,' said Matthew. 'Could the police have more evidence against him than they've told him, or you?'

'I promise you, they threw everything at him during the

hearing,' she replied. 'It was a very close thing.' She didn't think she was exaggerating, but at least the judge had shortened the custody term to one week, so she had done some good. She had to let herself believe that. 'Poor Jónas didn't take the news too well,' she said.

'What did you expect?' said Matthew. 'Where is he now?'

'The police took him to the prison at Litla-Hraun. It's a real pain that they keep remand prisoners there. It takes such a long time to drive from Reykjavík,' she said, then added, 'Even longer from here.'

'Don't you need to get back to town soon?' he asked.

'I'm better off here, actually,' she replied. 'Thórólfur said they wouldn't interrogate Jónas for the next two days. They're going to focus their investigations here and finish questioning witnesses they've been unable to locate. He wasn't too pleased with the judge's remarks about the handling of the crime scene.'

'Is there anything more to see here?' Matthew asked. 'It was sheer chance that we found the key to the locker. We won't get that lucky again.'

'I'm not sure. Something's bothering me, and I mean something other than all the loose ends in this case.' She stood up and clutched the plastic bag to her chest. 'I'll take a quick look through this to check if anything in it turns the case round completely. I also went to the library to take out a copy of those folktales, on the off-chance that the story behind that verse could provide an explanation. I won't be long, but it would be nice if you could send my children off on another mission impossible, if and when they return.'

*   *   *

Two hours later, Thóra walked out of Jónas's office having made no real progress. She had read every word of the documents in the folder, which contained numerous witness statements, scene-of-crime investigation summaries, two autopsy reports and the results of tests on the deceaseds' corpses and bodily fluids. The outcome of the DNA tests on the semen found inside Birna's body was not in the folder, but the documents included a request to that effect. However, there were results on the blood group of the source of the sperm, which revealed that it came from two men. Thóra couldn't work out if that discovery was a coincidence or whether it had been suspected when the test was requested. She wondered how common it was for a woman to have sex with two different men the same day, except on a professional basis. One thing that puzzled her was a report stating that besides the semen, another organic substance had been found inside Birna's vagina, described as *A. barbadensis Mill, A. vulgaris Lam*. Thóra wrote down the name in the hope that Matthew would recognise it, but it seemed unlikely. Perhaps the substance had been inserted there by Birna herself, although Thóra couldn't imagine why.

She waved to Matthew and crossed to where he was having a beer at the bar. She put the folder down and sat beside him. 'Are there still three children?' she asked.

'It was a close call,' he said. 'Your son and daughter were a bit green around the gills when they got back from the beach. The pregnant girl was the only one who looked OK. I bought them each a Coke at the bar and they took them up to their room to watch a video.'

'I was more worried about whether a fourth had joined

them,' she said, beckoning to the waiter and ordering a glass of Coke herself.

'You're not a grandmother yet, so relax,' said Matthew, clinking his glass against hers and indicating the folder. 'Did you find anything interesting?' He sipped his drink.

'No, I can't say that I did. There was confirmation of various things we'd either heard or guessed. Needles or pins had been stuck into the soles of the feet of both victims, a fox had been tied to Eiríkur's body, and according to tests carried out on the animal, it had been dead for some time – shot with a rifle. Unfortunately there was no explanation as to why the fox might have been put there.'

'Haven't you heard from the lovely Bella?' asked Matthew. 'Wasn't she going to check that out for you?'

'Damn, I'd forgotten her,' said Thóra. She took out her mobile and quickly dialled the office.

'Hello,' said Bella flatly as she picked up. No 'Central Lawyers', no 'Can I help you?' – nothing to suggest that the caller had reached a respectable law firm rather than a private home.

'Hello, Bella. This is Thóra. Did you find out anything about the connection between foxes and horses?' Thóra couldn't be bothered to scold her yet again for her telephone manner.

'Eh?' replied the girl idiotically. 'Oh, that.' When she stopped talking, Thóra thought she could discern a sucking noise followed by a quick exhalation.

'Bella, are you smoking in the office?' she asked, irritated. 'You know that's not allowed.'

'Of course not,' replied Bella. 'Are you crazy?'

Thóra was sure she could hear the crackle of burning tobacco. Could the girl have taken up smoking a pipe?

Before she had time to ask, Bella went on, 'The horse-riding types I spoke to hadn't heard of any specific connection between the two, so I talked to a fox-hunter I know and I got a bit more out of him.'

Thóra completely forgot about the smoking. 'What did he say?' she asked eagerly. Would her secretary prove useful for once?

'Well,' said Bella, 'he told me horses can go mad with fear if they smell the scent of a dead fox, especially if it's started to rot.'

'Is that something only fox-hunters would know,' Thóra asked excitedly, 'or would all riders be aware of this? Do you think the ones you spoke to could have been particularly ill informed?'

'Ill informed about foxes?' Bella asked sarcastically. 'I don't have the faintest idea, but I'd say they don't know about it, as a rule. I mean, how often do you come across a fox?'

'Thanks, Bella,' said Thóra, meaning it for probably the first time ever. 'Why don't you take the rest of the day off?' Her offer wasn't that generous, since the secretary's absence would have no discernible effect on the company's operation. She hung up and recounted the conversation to Matthew.

'So the murderer tied a fox to Eiríkur to drive the horse wild – to make sure the poor man would be killed and not just badly injured.' Matthew raised an eyebrow. 'A pretty cold customer.'

'But as a rule riders don't know how horses react to a dead fox,' said Thóra pensively. 'It's mainly fox-hunters who do.' After reflecting for a moment she added, 'I wonder if Bergur hunts foxes. He has an eider colony on his land.' She looked up at Matthew. 'There was a box of rifle cartridges in the stables, in the coffee room.'

Matthew stared back at her. 'Could "RER" have been an attempt at "BER", for "Bergur", but Eiríkur couldn't write it properly?' He took out his mobile and called up the photograph he had taken of the scrawl on the wall. It took him a while to enlarge the image and centre it. 'I'll be damned,' he said after scrutinising the photograph. He handed the phone to Thóra. 'The lower diagonal on the first "R" isn't straight like on the second one.'

Thóra put down the telephone and turned to Matthew. 'I think Thórólfur took the news quite well,' she said. 'He played it cool, but I could tell he was delighted. I predict Bergur will have a visit from the police soon.'

'Or his wife will,' said Matthew. 'You never know.'

'Yes, you do,' she replied. 'Some things you just know. I read the autopsy report and it's obvious that Birna was the victim of a very brutal rape, so no women are in the frame, except perhaps as accomplices. If Rósa did play a part in the murder, it wasn't with her husband. I doubt they could agree on the time of day, let alone something on this scale.'

Just then, Sóldís walked over to them. 'Granny wants a word with you,' she said awkwardly. 'She asked me to ask you to phone her. It's something to do with what you were talking about yesterday.' She looked down at her feet. 'You don't have to if you don't want to, you know, but here's her number.' She handed Thóra a Post-it.

Thóra thanked her kindly and took out her mobile immediately, while Sóldís turned round and quickly left the bar.
The telephone was answered after a single ring.

'Hello, Lára. This is Thóra, the lawyer from the hotel.
Sóldís told me you wanted a word.'

'Yes, hello. I'm so glad you called. I haven't been able
to think about anything but Gudný since we talked
yesterday. I believe that you'll lead to the child's fate being
discovered at long last.' Thóra had the feeling that Lára
was in a very emotional state, although her voice didn't
betray it. 'I'm holding the letter from her, the one I told
you about yesterday,' said the old woman, sniffing almost
inaudibly. 'I searched everywhere and eventually found it
stored away with a couple of other things that I still keep
from that time. I've read it over and again, and I think I've
found something by reading between the lines.'

'What do you mean?' asked Thóra.

'In one place she says the baby takes after its father and
I'll see the resemblance at once,' said Lára. 'At the time,
when all that talk about incest started up, I half believed
she was referring to her father or uncle. Now that I'm
older, I realise that no woman would say that about a child
born under such circumstances. She also asks whether I
know the whereabouts of a young man she was keen on
before I moved away. She wanted to drop him a line.' Lára
stopped to take a deep breath. 'I think that young man
must have been the child's father. He moved to Reykjavík
soon after me, and I remember how strangely he acted
when I bumped into him a year or so later. He refused to
talk to me. I didn't understand it then, and still don't,
really. The baby might explain his reaction. Perhaps he

thought I knew about the baby or Gudný's pregnancy and didn't want to discuss it. He had a young lady on his arm.'

'Who was it?' Thóra asked. 'Is he still alive?'

'Most definitely,' Lára replied. 'When he dies, it will be reported in all the newspapers. He used to be a cabinet minister.'

Thóra felt her grip tightening on the handset. 'Magnús Baldvinsson?' she asked, as calmly as she could.

'Yes, how did you guess?' exclaimed Lára, astounded. 'Do you know him?'

'He's staying at the hotel,' replied Thóra, 'but he may have left by now – his grandson came to fetch him yesterday evening.'

'How odd,' Lára said. 'He's only come back for a few flying visits since he moved to Reykjavík all those years ago.'

'Well, I never,' was all Thóra could think to say. 'Could he have been so unhappy about the baby that he . . .' she hesitated, searching for a suitable phrase. Adults were one thing, but babies quite another '. . . that he somehow had the child adopted after Gudný died, or simply . . . disposed of it?' She hoped her euphemism would be clear enough.

'I don't know,' said Lára. Her elderly voice faltered. 'Heavens, I can't believe anyone could do such a thing. Magnús was spineless, yes, but *evil*? I just don't know. I can't really imagine anyone behaving that way. They wouldn't be shown any mercy in our society. Not today, and not back then.' She stopped to blow her nose. 'Then there was your other question – about the coal bunker. I had a think about that and remembered that both farms switched to electric heating before I moved away, which everyone thought was very posh. Bjarni set up a small generator by one of the waterfalls on the mountainside, north of the main road. I don't know if it helps you at all, but both farms stopped having to bother with coal then and the coal bunkers were never used again.' Talking about something as down-to-earth as central heating seemed to restore the strength to Lára's voice, and she spoke now with no hint of sadness. 'In the box where I kept Gudný's letter I found an old photo of the two of us behind the farm, and when I looked at it more closely, all this came back to me. You can see the coal hatch and the memories just flooded back.'

Thóra interrupted her. 'When you say "behind the farm", which farm do you mean?'

'Kirkjustétt,' Lára said. 'We didn't go to Kreppa much in those days. Bjarni and Grímur were barely on speaking terms and I'm fairly sure that their only contact was over the generator, which supplied both farms.'

'So Kirkjustétt had the same type of coal bunker as Kreppa?' said Thóra. 'There are no signs of it behind the hotel. Could it have been covered over by the annexe?'

'No, it shouldn't have been,' replied Lára. 'If I recall correctly, it was a little way away from the farmhouse, not in the area where the annexe was built. The hatch ought to be in the lawn behind the hotel. Both farms had the same layout. It was considered awfully modern to have the coal bunker away from the house, because it was much more expensive than tipping the coal straight into the basement. The most impressive thing of all was to have an entrance to the bunker from the basement even if it was some distance away.'

Thóra looked at Matthew, her eyes wide. She ended her conversation with Lára, excited at the prospect of exploring the basement for a door to the bunker, but before she rang off, she promised to let Lára know if she found any clues about the fate of the mysterious child.

'I need to make a quick call,' she told Matthew as she dialled the number of the prison. 'I promise you I'll explain everything in a minute.' Thinking back to the photograph that Birna had asked Robin to take of the basement wall, Thóra didn't expect to find a door down there. When Jónas was brought to the telephone, she got straight to the point. 'Jónas, I might need to make a hole in the basement wall, under the old part of the hotel. I just wanted to let you know. Are you all right otherwise?'

Thóra, Matthew and Gylfi stood in the basement, in front of the wall they had agreed must be the one backing on to the lawn. It had taken them a long time to figure out where to begin, but by lifting Sóley so that she could see out through the dirty little windows, they could confirm that the wall from Birna's photograph was the right one. Matthew put down the photograph and picked up a sledge-hammer. Thóra moved back to where Sigga and Sóley were watching excitedly. Gylfi stood by Matthew, ready to take turns when the German wanted a break.

Her son had insisted on joining them when they took shovels out on to the lawn – to make sure that the hatch was there before they began modifying the interior of the hotel – and the girls insisted on coming too, delighted to have something different to do. They found the hatch some thirty centimetres down, just beyond the inscribed rock, but instead of arduously digging around it, they had gone to the basement to look for the door they knew was there somewhere – a hatch that had been buried for decades, said Matthew, would be no easier to open than the one they had struggled with behind Kreppa.

'What do you reckon you'll find back there?' asked Gylfi, not entirely convinced of the wisdom of breaking it down.

'Honestly? I have no idea,' replied Thóra, 'but it was obviously designed to keep people away. There's absolutely no reason to concrete over a basement door. It would only have been sealed this way if the point was to hide it.'

'And what if there's nothing there?' he said. 'What will the owner say?'

'Nothing,' she reassured him. 'I've informed him of our plans, and if the worst comes to the worst, he'll just extend his property by a couple of square metres.' Impatiently, she waved them on. 'Fire away!'

Not needing to be told twice, Gylfi and Matthew pounded at the wall. Thóra and the girls looked on expectantly, but soon realised that it would be a lengthy operation. It was more than half an hour, in which time Sóley had fallen asleep from boredom on top of a pile of boxes and Sigga was yawning almost constantly, before the gap in the plaster, timber and rock was big enough to climb through. Matthew and Gylfi stood back with their sleeves rolled up, dirty, sweaty and out of breath.

'I'm not going in first,' Thóra said as she withdrew her head from the hole. 'It's awfully stuffy in there. It smells like burning.'

'I'll go,' offered Gylfi, but Thóra knew him well enough to realise that he didn't mean it.

'Matthew, you go first,' she said, pushing him towards the hole. 'Where's the torch?'

After all three had squeezed through the hole, Thóra and Gylfi followed Matthew along the dim passage. The slender beam from the torch only helped Matthew in front, and the Icelanders bumped into him when he stopped at a door at the end of the passage. He turned round, shining the torch under his chin. Both Thóra and Gylfi recoiled in horror, much to his amusement. He took the torch away from his face and lit up the door. 'Shall I open it?'

They should have said no.

31

'So I imagine you found this by pure coincidence, like the photograph?' said Thórólfur. 'You just happened to be down in the basement armed with sledgehammers and thought it would improve the décor if you removed one of the walls?'

Thóra plucked a sliver of wood from her hair and was pleased to see that it was not a tooth, as she had feared. 'No,' she said. 'I thought I made myself clear. We wanted to be sure we weren't sending you on some fool's errand and wasting the taxpayers' money. There was no way to verify what was down there without checking it. I must admit I didn't expect this.' She shuddered as two detectives passed pushing a wheelbarrow full of bones. A stench of burning wafted past with them.

The hotel was teeming with police officers from neighbouring constabularies, as well as expert investigators from Reykjavík. Thóra suspected that few of them had any genuine reason to be there, but were driven by mere curiosity. She winced. 'As I said, I expected to find the skeleton of one child, not bones stacked up to the ceiling.'

'You didn't realise they were animal bones?' asked Thórólfur. 'Maybe it was hard to see properly in the dark down there?'

'The bones I saw first weren't from an animal,' Thóra

said firmly. 'Before the heap collapsed, the torchlight lit up a little woollen mitten. A bone was sticking out below the cuff, so I can only assume there's a dead child in there somewhere. There couldn't be anything except a hand inside the mitten. It was protruding from the stack before it collapsed, so it presumably won't be found until all the bones have been removed. In your shoes, I'd tell the men to proceed with caution because underneath there's a—' She couldn't finish the sentence.

'As you may have noticed, this is a slow job,' Thórólfur said, gesturing at the men and women working around him. 'We follow all the procedures governing the investigation of a crime scene, whether we find human bones or not. We need to establish what happened, because it's hardly normal to bury half-burned carcasses like this. So don't worry about us destroying any evidence. You'd do better to keep worrying about Jónas, because this has no bearing on the issue of his guilt.'

'Not even if I told you that under all this lies the skeleton of the illegitimate child of Magnús Baldvinsson, from the Second World War?'

'I don't see why that would make any difference,' said Thórólfur offhandedly, although his interest was clearly aroused. 'Or perhaps you mean that he murdered his own child, then slaughtered dozens of animals and threw their bones over the body?' He smirked. 'And then came back, sixty years later, to pick up where he left off?'

'It's up to you what you deduce from all this, but paternity will be provable because a DNA sample must be taken from the child's remains. Even though it won't prove who killed her, the paternity test is bound raise questions and

I don't think Magnús Baldvinsson will come out of it smelling of roses.'

'So you're sticking to your theory that Magnús or Baldvin killed both Birna and Eiríkur?' Thórólfur asked.

Thóra picked more debris from her hair. 'Actually, I was beginning to think that it could be either Bergur or his wife with a male accomplice,' she said, and proceeded to explain what she and Matthew had discussed earlier that day about the rifle, the foxes and Eiríkur's mysterious 'RER' graffiti. 'Matthew and I saw her leave the hotel with a waiter who works here. They seemed very close,' said Thóra. 'It occurred to us that Rósa might have seduced him and got him to kill Birna. She could have done that in revenge for the affair with her husband.'

Thórólfur's eyebrows rose so high they disappeared into his hair. 'You've met Bergur's wife,' he said. 'Does she seem a likely seductress?'

'No, actually, she doesn't,' admitted Thóra, 'but beauty is in the eye of the beholder, so you never know.'

Thórólfur grinned maliciously. 'Does this waiter's name happen to be Jökull Gudmundsson?' he asked.

'Yes,' Thóra said. 'I can't remember his second name, but his first name is certainly Jökull. Did you know they were an item?'

'They're brother and sister,' he said. 'That presumably explains how "close" they seemed when you saw them.'

Thóra said nothing. Now she understood Jökull's antipathy towards Birna; his brother-in-law had been having an affair with her. It also explained his reaction to her question about Steini. His father had caused the accident, so he was bound to be as touchy about discussing it as his sister was. 'Ah,' she said finally. 'That changes things slightly.'

'Yes, doesn't it?' replied Thórólfur. 'But there's no harm in telling you that we're still investigated Bergur's possible involvement,' he added mildly, giving her no hint as to whether he was a suspect along with Jónas. 'I can also tell you that his rifle is being cross-matched with the shell found in the fox's carcass. We don't have the facilities in Iceland, so it was sent abroad. Unfortunately it takes a few days to get the results from there, but in the meantime we've got a few things to look into.' The police inspector took his leave of her, and headed down to the basement to see what progress was being made.

Thóra went over to Matthew, who was reaching the end of his statement to the police. This had taken a considerable time because the officer insisted on using an interpreter.

'Do you reckon we're off to join Jónas in prison?' grinned Matthew as they walked away. 'The way I look right now I'd fit right in there,' he added. His clothes were covered in dust and earth, since he hadn't had time to change since the bones had fallen on them.

Thóra looked him up and down, amused. 'How long is it since you've got this dirty?' she asked, removing what turned out to be a fragment of bone from his sweater.

'Ages,' he replied. 'We don't break down many walls at the bank, and I've never encountered a heap of bones the size of that one downstairs.'

Thóra shuddered. She told him about the connection between Rósa and Jökull – hardly the Bonnie and Clyde they'd imagined. 'You know,' she said, 'I bet the person who put up that inscribed rock out here knew what was underneath it. It must have been intended as a kind of gravestone. A secret memorial.'

'Which presumably means the child didn't die a natural death. Otherwise why would it be disguised?' said Matthew, as they arrived at Thóra's room. 'Besides, no one in their right mind would put a dead child in a place like that unless they had something to hide.'

'I think Magnús laid that gravestone,' she replied, opening the door. She went straight over to the telephone on the bedside table. 'I'm going to call Elín and ask if she knows anything about it. Maybe she and her brother remember when it was put up, and by whom.'

'Do you think she'll want to talk to you?' he asked.

'I doubt she'll slam the phone down on me this time,' she said. 'Not when I tell her the skeleton of a child has been found on land where her grandfather and his brother lived, and which has been owned by the family for decades.' She looked up Elín's number. 'And I'll trick her by using the hotel telephone in case she happens to recognise my mobile number.' She turned back to the telephone. 'Hello, this is Thóra Gudmundsdóttir,' she said when it was answered.

'What do you want?' snapped Elín peevishly. Thóra could hear that she was in a car.

'Firstly, I wanted to let you know that a huge stack of bones has just been found at the farm.'

'And what business is that of mine?' cried Elín. 'It's the same old story. There seem to have been dozens of bodies found in the area since Jónas bought the land. I heard on the radio that he was taken into custody this morning.'

'Yes, that's right,' said Thóra, trying to conceal her annoyance that the media had got hold of Jónas's case. 'However, these bones have nothing to do with him, as they were probably there long before he acquired the property. If memory serves, your family built the current farm buildings, and have always owned them. Isn't that right? I'm afraid this could be far worse for you and your brother than for Jónas. Most of the bones are from animals, but in all probability a child's skeleton will also come to light.'

'What?' Elín exclaimed shrilly. 'A child's skeleton?' She seemed genuinely shocked and confused. 'What child?'

'We don't know yet,' said Thóra. 'The police will be speaking to you very soon, so it's probably best I don't tell you too much. I just wanted to ask you one thing.' She paused, but Elín said nothing, so she continued. 'Behind the house, on the eastern side, is a large rock carved with a verse that I think comes from a folktale. Someone must have put it there, because it's not a work of nature. Do you know anything about this rock, or do you know who put it there?'

'The rock?' said Elín, astonished. 'What's that got to do with anything?'

'Maybe nothing,' said Thóra untruthfully. 'I'd just like to find out what it is, in order to rule it out as evidence.' She crossed her fingers, hoping Elín would believe her.

'I can assure you it's nothing to do with this,' declared Elín. 'My mother put that rock up many years ago. It was an advance wedding present to herself, or so she said. Don't ask me why – she never explained it any further – but you can be quite sure it has nothing to do with any dead child.'

Thóra was surprised to hear that Málfríður, Grímur's

daughter, had placed the rock there, but she carried on. 'One last thing. What were you and your brother, Börkur, doing over this way on Sunday evening? I have a printout from the police showing the vehicles that passed through the tunnel that day and you were both there.'

'We came to meet you,' answered Elín irritably. 'Don't you remember? You came to see us on the Monday. We'd decided to beat the morning traffic and go up to Stykkishólmur the previous evening. Surely you don't imagine Börkur and I are involved in this murder case?'

Thóra demurred awkwardly. 'It's just one of a number of points I want to be able to tick off,' she explained.

'Well, you can tick this off too: Börkur didn't go west to kill anyone on Thursday either,' snapped Elín.

Thóra said nothing, not wanting to reveal that she'd had no idea Börkur had been on the move that day. Elín obviously thought Thóra had a list of cars for each day. 'So why did he come?' she enquired cautiously.

'He won't be pleased that I've told you,' replied the other woman. 'I had a hard enough time getting it out of him.' The loud screech of a horn cut her off, and when she came back on the line, she was swearing. 'Stupid old bastard! Why don't they take their driving licences away before they go senile at the wheel?' she said crossly, before continuing, 'The only reason I'm telling you what he was up to is to get rid of you, and prevent any more unfounded allegations against us.'

'I really don't mind *why* you're telling me,' retorted Thóra. 'So what was he doing?'

'He went to see an estate agent who was very keen to see the remaining farming properties, with a view to selling them,' said Elín. 'He knows I want to wait, and he did it against my wishes. The estate agent can confirm it, if you want to check.'

Thóra said goodbye and hung up. 'Börkur and Elín's mother had the rock placed there,' she told Matthew. 'They're very odd people, which is hardly surprising in view of their family medical history – both of their mother's parents had mental problems – but they're probably innocent of both murders. She gave me reasonable explanations for being here, at any rate.'

Thóra stood up and picked up the bags containing Jón Árnason's folktale collection. 'If I can find the verse, there may be some further explanation of it in the accompanying text. That might tell us why their mother had the verse carved into the rock, and had it put there.' She put the bags on the desk. 'I must remember to return the books on our way back to Reykjavík,' she said. 'My fines are already enough to pay for a whole annexe to the library at home. I don't want to do the same all over the country.'

'You're not going to read all those, are you?' asked Matthew as he watched Thóra extract one weighty volume after another. 'Maybe I'll have a shower in the meantime.'

'It won't take long to look it up,' said Thóra. She turned to the contents page in Volume I and found the entry for 'abandoned children'. 'Here it is,' she exclaimed eagerly and looked up from the book. 'Here's a story with the title "I Should Have Been Wed". That must be it.' Thóra rapidly scanned the brief story, then placed the open book in her lap.

'What is it?' asked Matthew. 'I can't tell if that expression means good news or bad.'

'Nor can I,' said Thóra. 'It's the story of a mother who left her infant outside to die. Some years later she had another daughter, whom she raised. When the girl reached marriageable age, a young man asked for her hand and they were betrothed. At the height of the wedding ceremony, there was a banging at the window, and the guests heard this verse chanted: "Kerns I should have cast, a farm was meant for me, I should have been wed, just like thee."' She looked at Matthew. 'It was the ghost of the dead child, speaking to her sister.'

'So the verse is a reference to the fact that the sister is enjoying what should have been the lot of the child left to die?' asked Matthew.

'Yes, that's the obvious meaning,' said Thóra. 'Could Gudný have had another child?' She was shaking her head even as she said it. 'No, I don't think so.'

'But who got what should have belonged to the child?' asked Matthew. 'Presumably the child was her mother's heir?'

Thóra puffed out her cheeks, then slowly let the air escape. 'It depends when Gudný died of TB. If the child predeceased her, of course the child couldn't inherit anything from her mother. If the child died after Gudný's death, that changes things. Gudný's father died first. Since he was a widower, and she was his only child, Gudný would have been his sole heir, so the child would have inherited all her mother's assets on *her* death.'

'And if that's the case, someone would have profited from the child's death,' said Matthew, 'inheriting all Gudný's assets, which would have gone to the child. Who would it be, in this case?'

'The mother's closest relative,' said Thóra. 'Grímur, Gudný's uncle and the child's great-uncle.' She closed the book. 'Lára, Sóldís's grandmother, said he had money troubles, so he could have killed her to prevent her reaching adulthood. As soon as the girl married or had a child of her own, Grímur would lose his claim to the inheritance.'

'That's incredibly callous,' said Matthew. 'But he wasn't the one who put the rock there. His daughter, Málfrídur, Elín and Börkur's mother, must have known of the body under there. It's no coincidence that she placed a stone with that inscription in that very location.'

'Málfrídur,' said Thóra thoughtfully. 'Málfrídur inherited what should have belonged to the child when her own father died years later in Reykjavík. If there is indeed a child, and if it's Gudný's.'

'There are a lot of "if"s in this story,' commented Matthew, 'but I have to admit it sounds plausible. Could she be the murderer, rather than her father, Grímur?'

'Hardly. She was just a little girl during the war. When Lára came back here after the war, Gudný's child had vanished from the face of the earth. It's a reasonable assumption that Gudný's daughter, Kristín, is the Kristín mentioned in the message scratched into the post upstairs. If so, it's more than likely that it was Málfrídur who carved "dad killed kristín. i hate dad" in the attic. It was in their house, after all. Perhaps she found out about it, or witnessed the murder, or maybe he even told her.'

'You're probably getting close to solving this old case,' said Matthew, going into the bathroom to wash the dirt from his hands. He called over the noise of the running water, 'It's a pity it doesn't help Jónas. I don't suppose this is why Birna and Eiríkur were killed?'

'Well, I don't know,' Thóra called back. 'Maybe Birna found out about it and that led to someone wanting her dead – someone who didn't want the truth to come out. She was going through that old stuff, as we know from the photo of Magnús. Maybe she'd found something that gave her a clue.'

Matthew appeared in the doorway with a towel and dried his hands. 'But who would want her dead because of it? Elín and Börkur?'

'Unlikely,' said Thóra. 'They would scarcely have sold the property if they'd been desperate to keep the secret.'

'Maybe they knew nothing about it,' said Matthew, putting the towel back in the bathroom. 'Birna may have told them about it and tried to blackmail them. She seems to have already tried to blackmail Magnús and Baldvin, so we know she was capable of it.'

'Maybe,' said Thóra, 'but I have a feeling she didn't know. From her diary I'd say she suspected something odd had been going on in the house, but there's no indication she was on the right track.' She fetched the journal and slowly turned the pages. 'Do you remember where the annexe was located in the plans on the walls at Kreppa?' she asked. 'Did it include the area of the rock and the hatch?'

Matthew tried to visualise the sketch. 'I think it did,' he said. 'Why do you ask?'

'Could Birna have been killed to stop the building project?' Thóra speculated. 'As soon as construction work began, the hidden part of the basement would have been excavated. Perhaps it was preventative action. Someone had been digging here and there in the field, remember. Maybe they were trying to find the hatch, and the child's remains, before construction began, but they couldn't find them and resorted to the desperate measure of killing Birna.'

'Which brings us back to the question of who would want to keep it a secret,' said Matthew. 'The last thing Elín and Börkur would want was for the truth to come out. Nobody wants unnecessary attention drawn to the fact that their grandfather was a child-killer, but it'd hardly be normal to commit murder to conceal it.'

'If they'd wanted to keep it secret, though, they'd never have sold the land,' Thóra reminded him. 'And I quite agree: it's a bit extreme to kill someone just to avoid a scandal.' She closed her eyes. 'I'm missing something. It's something really obvious, but I can't put my finger on it.' She reached for the police file and flicked through it. 'I don't even know what I'm looking for,' she sighed.

Matthew came up to the bedside table and picked up the list of cars that had driven through the Hvalfjördur Tunnel. 'What if the killer isn't directly involved? What if it's someone who wants to protect the family?'

Thóra looked up from the file and tilted her head curiously. 'Who do you mean?'

Matthew handed her the list and pointed out one of the registration numbers. 'While you were out this morning, I asked Sóldís for Steini's full name. Since he can drive, it occurred to me to check whether he was on the list, and he was.' He pointed out the entry that a car had been driven through the tunnel from the Reykjavík direction: owner Thorsteinn Kjartansson. 'You remember he said he couldn't give Sóldís a lift because he wasn't going to Reykjavík,' Matthew added, 'but he did go, and he appears to have driven back here via the tunnel about an hour before Birna was murdered.'

'What, you think he killed her so that Berta wouldn't be traumatised by the scandal?' asked Thóra. 'That's ridiculous. And he's disabled. Would he have been capable of that?'

'I feel like we keep on hearing things that prove he's less handicapped than we thought,' said Matthew. 'If you look at the other list, the vehicles driving through the tunnel from here towards Reykjavík, you'll see that Berta's car left here at about the same time. Maybe Steini wanted to ensure she wouldn't be a suspect, which is why he carried out the murder in her absence. There wouldn't be much point in killing Birna and Eiríkur, and getting Berta into even more trouble than he was trying to prevent.'

Thóra frowned. 'Even if he's less disabled than we realised, I somehow can't see him manhandling someone into a stall with a wild horse.'

'What if Eiríkur wasn't quite unconscious?' said Matthew. 'Maybe the drugs just made him confused – confused enough to do as Steini said. Perhaps Steini planted Eiríkur in Bergur and Rósa's stables as revenge for her father causing the accident. He may have assumed Bergur or his wife would be suspects. He needn't have been motivated only by wanting to protect Berta.'

Thóra nodded, deep in thought. 'But what about the

rape?' she asked. 'Steini would also have had to rape
Birna, and she wasn't drugged.' She looked up the
autopsy report. 'The theory is that she was attacked
from behind and hit on the head with a rock.' She read
a little further. 'You don't happen to know what
A. barbadensis Mill, A. vulgaris Lam is?' she asked when
she came across the reference to the substance found in
Birna's vagina.

'I can't say I do,' smiled Matthew ruefully. 'I think
"vulgaris" means "common", but that's not much help.
Can't you find it on the Internet?'

'Yes, I'm sure I can,' said Thóra. 'I just haven't had
time. Perhaps I'll ask Gylfi to look it up for me. It'll do
him good to think about something else, after the shock
of finding the bones.' She phoned Gylfi's room and
asked him to look it up on the guests' computer in reception. 'He says he'll do it in a minute,' said Thóra,
hanging up. She looked over at Matthew and smiled.
'When children reach the age of twelve, they stop being
able to do things when they're asked. It always has to
be in a minute. My dad says I was just the same, and
that Grandpa said the same about him. Maybe it's
genetic.'

'Shall we try to get hold of Steini, or even Berta?' asked
Matthew. 'She might be able to tell us something to corroborate my theory. Although she's his friend, I'm not sure
she'd cover for him under these circumstances.'

'You may be right,' said Thóra, and went to stand up.
'Let's do it. You broke down a wall for me. The least I can
do is repay you by investigating your crazy theory as well
as mine.'

'You could always find another way to repay me,' said Matthew with a smile.

Thóra didn't answer. She stood with the book of folk-tales open in her hands. 'Hang on,' she said excitedly. 'What's this?'

32

Thóra stabbed her finger at the page. Matthew looked at it, understanding nothing. 'Right here, on the page before the story of the abandoned infant at the wedding, it says that if you want to stop someone's spirit walking, you must drive needles into the soles of his feet.' She slammed the book shut. 'The murderer must have wanted to ensure that his victims' ghosts wouldn't go wandering.'

Matthew looked sceptical. 'What on earth for?'

'We might not get it, but presumably he believes in ghosts,' said Thóra, blushing slightly as she recalled the wailing she had heard, like an infant left to die. She had stuck to her resolution not to mention it to anyone, least of all Matthew.

'Why are you blushing?' he asked. 'Starting to believe in ghosts in your old age?' He prodded her arm. 'Did you hear it too?'

Thóra was no good at lying to people she cared about, so she decided to confess. 'Yes, I heard something,' she conceded. 'Of course, it wasn't the ghost of an abandoned infant, but I did hear crying and it sounded like a baby.'

'That's great!' said Matthew, pleased. 'Now, you have been careful about letting the baby go round you three times, haven't you? You don't seem any more insane than usual, anyway.'

Thóra stuck her tongue out at him. 'Come on,' she said, 'we've got more important things to do than talk about ghosts. Let's go and find Berta or Steini.'

'You must try to send the ghost baby back to its mother,' Matthew persisted. 'That's what you're meant to do . . .'

Thóra couldn't wait to get out of the reception area. A scorched smell hung about the place from the charred carcasses that had been carried through the building. She would have liked to pinch her nose as she went past Vigdís, but decided to just hold her breath and keep walking. As she hurried past, she bumped into Thröstur Laufeyjarson.

'Oh, sorry,' she said, trying to regain her balance. 'I didn't see you.'

'That's all right,' said the canoeist grumpily. He was wearing a dry-suit, his hair wet. 'No harm done – shame I can't say the same for my canoe,' he added.

'Oh?' asked Thóra. 'Has it been damaged?' When she saw Thröstur's fierce expression, she involuntarily blurted, 'I haven't touched it.'

'No, I know,' said Thröstur, continuing on his way.

'Hang on, I wanted to ask you something,' said Thóra, grabbing his arm. She was startled to realise how muscular he was. 'I've been trying to find you, but you're hard to get hold of.'

'What do you want to ask?' he said. She let go of his arm, not wanting to push her luck. 'Whether I've ever got stuck with my head under water when I've been out in the canoe?'

'Er, no,' replied Thóra, baffled. 'That had never occurred

to me. No, my question is about the two murders that have been committed here. You must have heard about them.'

Thröstur's expression was a strange mixture of irritation and apprehension. The hotel doors opened and he caught sight of the pile of bones that was being carried past. 'What's going on there?'

'Quite a lot,' said Thóra. 'None of it good. Have you got time to talk? It could be important.' She hoped the sight of the bones would sway him.

'Yes, all right,' he replied abruptly. 'I was on my way to talk to the police, anyway. Since my canoe's damaged, there's no reason to keep quiet any more.'

'About what?' asked Thóra, directing him to a table outside. They sat down, and Thóra introduced Matthew. 'What were you going to tell the police?'

Thröstur looked grave. 'On Friday morning, I went out to train and found my canoe all covered in blood.' He checked himself. 'Well, not exactly *covered*. There was blood on the paddle and the seat, and splashes here and there. It wasn't my blood, and I assumed it must have something to do with the murder committed on Thursday evening.'

Thóra stared at him. 'It's Tuesday today,' she said. 'Why on earth haven't you said anything before?'

'I didn't know anything about the murder until Saturday, when some woman in reception told me, and I'd cleaned most of it off by then,' said Thröstur impatiently.

'So there's still some blood left?' asked Thóra hopefully. Perhaps the murderer's fingerprints could be preserved.

'Er, no, there isn't,' muttered Thröstur sheepishly, adding by way of mitigation, 'I'm due to compete in the world championships in two weeks' time. I couldn't have my canoe being taken off to some lab, so I cleaned the rest off and decided to keep my mouth shut. The damage had been done, because I'd already removed most of the blood.'

Thóra didn't envy him; he'd have to confess all to Thórólfur. 'But what made you change your mind?' she asked.

'Whatever idiot did it must have run the canoe up on to some rocks and damaged the bottom. I couldn't understand why my times were so bad, but I only just noticed the damage. The bottom was fine when I checked it last week, so it's that bloody killer who's caused me all this trouble.' He leaned back and crossed his arms. 'The police may as well take the canoe. I won't be able to compete now.'

Clearly what upset Thröstur most about the case was that the murderer had damaged his canoe.

'I'm not sure you understand,' said Thóra, 'that if you'd come forward with the information about the canoe at once, on Saturday, it might have been possible to prevent the murder that took place on Sunday evening.'

'Hardly!' Thröstur argued. 'There wasn't much blood left – I told you.' He looked to Matthew for support, then tried to change the subject. 'I'm definitely going to sue the murderer when he's discovered and get compensation for the damage. I was on course for a medal.'

'It's a tragedy,' said Thóra, striving unsuccessfully to keep the sarcasm out of her voice. 'One more question.

You drove through the Hvalfjördur Tunnel on Sunday evening, didn't you?'

'Yes,' snapped Thröstur. 'I ran out of my protein supplement and I had to get to a decent pharmacy.' He glared defiantly at Thóra. 'Don't you believe me? I've got the receipt, from a pharmacy in the city.'

'What? Oh, yes,' said Thóra absently. She was thinking of something else: the fact that they could no longer rule out the people who had been at the seance, or any hotel staff who had been in the vicinity. 'How long does it take to paddle from here out to the inlet where the architect was killed?' she asked.

'No time at all,' he replied. 'It's a very short distance by sea. You don't have to follow all the twists and turns of the overland route. It would take me about five minutes if the sea was calm. Someone not used to a canoe might take ten minutes.'

'Can a first-timer paddle one fairly easily?' asked Matthew, who until then had just been listening.

'Yes, unless they're really inept,' said Thröstur. 'You need practice to paddle a canoe well, but to go from A to B in calm water you don't need any expertise, just strength.' He stood up. 'I'd better take a shower before I go and see the police. I want my case taken seriously because I'm not kidding about this.' He pushed the heavy wooden chair up to the table and turned away. Then he suddenly recalled something and turned back. 'Also, that lad in the car is sure to remember me,' he said. 'He should be easy enough to trace.'

'What lad? Who do you mean?' asked Thóra.

'When I drove out of the tunnel, I saw a car stopped at

the side of the road. I thought it had broken down. I pulled over to offer the driver a lift, but it was a terribly disfigured boy, who said he wasn't going anywhere, that he was just going to sit in the car for a bit and everything was fine. Then he wound up his window and refused to speak to me.'

'What time was this?' asked Matthew.

'About six, I think,' replied Thröstur. 'He was gone when I got back later that evening. He probably got fed up with reassuring people that he was OK. I can't have been the only one who thought he'd broken down. Another car was pulling up as I left,' he added, then turned and went into the hotel.

Matthew nudged Thóra's leg under the table. 'I think Steini followed Berta through the tunnel to make sure she was definitely gone, then pulled over and watched her drive away before turning back to finish off Eiríkur. Thröstur must have turned up while he was waiting. It all fits.'

'It's a bit tenuous,' said Thóra. 'If he was at the tunnel at six, he still had to drive all the way up here, which is a fair distance.'

'We don't know Eiríkur's time of death with any accuracy,' said Matthew. 'They said "dinnertime". People eat their dinners at all sorts of times.' He stood up. 'I'm just going to get the list. I want to see when he drove south. I wasn't looking for that when I found his name.'

Thóra couldn't bear the idea of going through the reeking lobby again, so she decided to wait outside. Matthew soon came hurrying back with the sheaf of papers. 'He went through the tunnel towards Reykjavík five cars after Berta. It all fits my theory. He must have wanted to be sure she was gone.' He slapped the papers down on the table in front of Thóra. 'I think we have to speak to her, in case she knows something that may complete the jigsaw.'

'Even if she knows something, we have to hope she's willing to share it with us,' said Thóra, standing up. 'We can't be sure she'll give him up, even when she realises what he's done. Let's not expect her to jump for joy when we tell her that her friend and relative may be a murderer. It may take longer for her to realise fully what a terrible thing he did.' She frowned. 'If he *did* do anything. I'm far from sure.'

Thóra clapped her hand to her forehead. 'Now I know what it is that's been bothering me,' she said. 'It's the order of inheritance. If the child outlived her mother and grandfather, all the assets are in completely the wrong hands. Of course Grímur wouldn't have been the child's heir.' They were sitting in the car in the drive outside Kreppa, where they had hoped to find Berta. There was no sign of her car, and the house was deserted.

'What do you mean?' asked Matthew. 'Wasn't he next of kin, once the mother and grandfather were dead?'

Thóra shook her head. 'It was the father, of course. The child's father would have inherited everything upon her death.'

'And that's probably Magnús,' he said. 'I hadn't thought of that. Grímur should never have inherited anything, of course. That's why he hid the girl and tried to destroy any information about her life, what there was of it.'

Thóra gasped. 'What's more, if his daughter Málfrídur knew about the murder, her inheritance was unlawful too.'

'Doesn't that go without saying?' asked Matthew. 'If her father got the inheritance fraudulently, he isn't entitled to it, so neither is she.'

'I'm not absolutely sure, but I think the case is different if she knew nothing about the crime. If my theory's right, she did know, and what's more, she's still alive. Her children had power of attorney to sign on her behalf when the land was sold to Jónas. They haven't formally inherited anything, so whether they knew is irrelevant. The power of attorney stated that their mother was in charge of the parental estate, which hasn't been through probate, so the question of complicity wouldn't apply to them.'

'They've got a lot to lose,' said Matthew, 'and there's a lot to gain for the child's father, Magnús.'

'Yes, it's pretty clear that he wouldn't have gained much by killing Birna to prevent the child being discovered. Quite the contrary.' Thóra gazed at the old farmhouse through the windscreen. 'But it's a different story for Elín and her family. Berta, for instance, wouldn't have a place to stay here in the west. The house in Stykkishólmur belonged to Bjarni after Grímur got into financial difficulties, and his farm too. If Berta had no home here, Steini would have a pretty lonely life.' She looked at Matthew. 'Shouldn't we speak to Steini in person?' she said. 'We've no idea when and where we'll catch up with Berta. Sóldís must know where he lives, so that shouldn't be a problem.'

'But what about Thórólfur?' asked Matthew. 'Shouldn't we let him know, or even get him to go instead?'

Thóra thought for a moment. 'No, no. It's like with the wall. We have to be sure we're right before we inconvenience the police, and they've got their hands full at the moment.'

Matthew and Thóra stood waiting at Steini's. He'd called out that he was just coming, but they had been waiting a while.

'He's not very fit – it's taking him ages,' said Matthew, pulling his jacket closer around him. The temperature had dropped suddenly, and the air was damp, so they were chilled to the bone. 'Brr. Are you sure it's June?'

Before Thóra could answer, the door was opened, but only halfway. 'What?' they heard, from beneath the familiar hoodie.

'Hello,' said Thóra as warmly as she could manage. 'Do you remember us? We came out to Kreppa yesterday and met you with Berta, and we met down at the inlet too.'

'Yeah, so, what do you want?' Steini's voice was so muffled that he sounded like he was talking with his mouth full. Thóra suspected this was because he found it hard to open his mouth. She hoped it wasn't painful for him to speak. Whatever he had or hadn't done, she felt truly sorry for him.

'We wanted to speak to you,' said Thóra, hoping he would agree to let them in. 'It's about Sunday evening.'

The wheelchair backed away and the door opened wider. 'Come in,' he mumbled. Because of his impediment, it was impossible to tell whether he was worried at the prospect of speaking to them. Thóra and Matthew exchanged discreet glances as they entered, but said nothing.

'Have you lived here long?' she enquired companionably as they sat down in the modest living room. At first glance,

Steini's home seemed rather depressing. Everything was neat and tidy, but there was no sign that anyone lived there: no pictures on the walls, no personal effects, only his crutches propped up in the doorway to the living room, which was more welcoming than the hall. There was a vase filled with wild flowers. Thóra supposed Berta had brought them, since it seemed inconceivable that the young man in the wheelchair would have picked and arranged them.

'Yes,' answered Steini, without elaborating.

'I see,' said Thóra. 'I'd better get to the point. We were wondering whether you drove through the tunnel on Sunday evening. A car registered in your name went through at about dinnertime.'

Steini said nothing. His head drooped even more. Then he spoke. 'Yes, it was me,' he said. As before, it was impossible to tell from his tone what he was feeling.

'May I ask what you were doing in Reykjavík?' she said.

'No,' replied Steini. He glanced up suddenly from beneath the hood, and Thóra had to steel herself to show no reaction. 'Do you think I killed that man?' he asked. Now his feelings were clear enough. He was obviously furious. 'Is that what you think?' He pushed himself up out of the wheelchair. He managed to keep his balance by grasping the armrests. One of his legs looked twisted and shrunken. There was no way a healthy limb could stay at that angle.

'No,' she replied hurriedly. 'That's not what we think at all.' She added a white lie to cover her embarrassment. 'We thought you might have lent someone your car. We're trying to work out who was where when Eiríkur was murdered.'

'I was nowhere near there, and not when Birna was murdered either,' said Steini, collapsing back into the wheelchair.

Thóra had grown accustomed to his strange voice, and now she could distinguish almost every word. He still looked very angry, and his breathing was shallow and uneven. Thóra hoped he wasn't having a fit of some kind.

'An old grave has been discovered at the farmhouse by the hotel,' she said, hoping to take him by surprise and defuse his temper.

'Get out,' he said unexpectedly. 'I don't want you here.' He rolled the wheelchair towards Thóra.

Matthew, while not understanding the conversation, could see that the interview was over, and that the exchange between Thóra and Steini had taken an unfortunate direction. 'Well,' he said, 'let's be going.' He took her hand and pulled her to her feet. He then turned to Steini to thank him before walking out of the room, making sure that Thóra went first.

'He's not all there, but he's hardly capable of murder,' he said when they'd shut the door behind them. Steini hadn't seen them out.

'But there's something strange about it,' said Thóra. 'His reaction to the news about the grave wasn't quite natural. Or what he said about the tunnel, for that matter. Could he be covering up for the murderer?'

'I doubt it,' said Matthew, holding the car door for her. 'If he's not the killer, then it must be either Bergur or Baldvin. According to your theory, Steini has a grudge against Bergur because he's related to the person who caused his accident, and as far as we know, he has no connection to Baldvin, so he could hardly be covering for either of them.'

'Damn,' said Thóra. 'It was such a good theory.' She got into the car and waited for Matthew to get behind the wheel. 'But I quite agree that he couldn't have done it. He hasn't the physical strength. I also have my doubts about Bergur. He could have walked over to the hotel, taken the canoe and paddled across to the inlet to kill Birna, but it's so illogical. Why wouldn't he simply drive over there? He wouldn't have had to pass over the hole in the road, as he wasn't coming from there. And when is he supposed to have stolen Jónas's phone and sent the text message to Birna?' She shook her head. 'I don't think he's in the frame. Baldvin, however, *was* at the hotel, and he could easily have taken the phone. He was at the seance, but he left before the interval, so he could have hurried down to the jetty, stolen the canoe, gone over to the inlet and attacked Birna. He had plenty of motive.' Thóra's phone rang.

'Hi. I've found it for you,' said Gylfi. 'It's the Latin name for aloe vera.'

Thóra thanked him and hung up. She looked at Matthew, who was fastening his seatbelt. 'What?' he asked when he realised she was staring at him.

'Why would a woman put aloe vera in her vagina? Is it used as a lubricant?' she asked.

Matthew laughed. 'Why are you asking me? Do I look that worldly? Talk to your friend the sex therapist, not me.' He backed out of the parking space. 'Baldvin's VERITAS car was still outside the hotel when we left,' he said. 'Shall we go and have a word?'

'Good idea,' grinned Thóra. 'He's bound to tell the truth, right?'

Matthew turned the wheel and skidded off down the gravel road. 'Absolutely. He's a politician.'

33

Matthew knocked loudly on the door of Magnús's hotel room. There had been no answer from Baldvin's, so Matthew and Thóra were hoping he was with his grandfather. VERITAS was in its usual place outside, so they must still be around somewhere. Thóra rubbed her hands together as they heard a noise from inside. The door opened and Magnús stood before them. When he saw who his guests were, he scowled, but he looked too exhausted to be intimidating. 'What do you want?' he snarled.

'We're actually looking for Baldvin,' said Thóra politely. 'Is he here?'

'Who's asking?' called another voice from inside the room.

'It's the lawyer and the German,' Magnús replied, his frail hand still on the doorknob.

'Let them in,' said Baldvin. 'We've got nothing to hide.' Magnús opened the door fully.

'Have a seat,' said Baldvin, indicating two chairs. He sat in a third, while his grandfather made do with sitting on the bed. 'What can we do for you?' he asked, resting his forearms on the table in front of him. Thóra was transfixed by his large, strong hands, recalling Thröstur's remark that physical strength was needed to paddle a canoe. Baldvin would have no trouble, even in rough seas.

'I just wanted answers to a few questions,' said Thóra, shifting in her seat. 'As I expect you know, I represent Jónas, the hotel owner. He is in police custody, in my view unjustly, for the murders that have been committed here.'

'We know all about that,' snapped Magnús. 'If you're here to try to fit one of us up for the murders, it won't work. Neither Baldvin nor I had anything to do with them. In general the police arrest the right person, my dear. Maybe you should accept that fact, instead of pestering us.'

'Now, now,' said Baldvin to his grandfather, darting an apologetic smile at Thóra. 'We're both a little bit annoyed because we can't go home. The police asked us to stay here, as they want to talk to both of us. I'm not qualified to judge this Jónas's guilt or innocence, but I can declare in good conscience, like my grandfather, that we had nothing to do with it. Just ask your questions and maybe we can convince you.'

'What brought you here on Sunday evening?' Thóra asked bluntly. 'Your car was driven though the Hvalfjördur Tunnel.'

Baldvin leaned back in his chair and took his hands off the table. 'You don't mince your words,' he said. 'I didn't come here to kill that poor man, if that's what you mean.'

'So what did you come for?' demanded Thóra. 'Surely you didn't drive all this way just to see your granddad?'

'No,' said Baldvin. 'I can tell you everything – I've decided to come clean. Although I'm not proud of what brought me here, I won't try to conceal it.' He sat up straight. 'I gather you found the photo, and I understand from the police that you're aware of Birna's attempt to blackmail me into ensuring she would win the competition for the new bus-station project.' Thóra nodded. 'That woman was extraordinarily greedy,' he said, adding hurriedly, 'I'm not saying that justified someone killing her. Not at all. She phoned me; she emailed me; she hounded me, basically. She did the same to Granddad, who ended up discharging himself from a rehabilitation programme to come up here and try to talk her round. He was devastated that his past had come to be a threat to me.'

'That's very sad,' remarked Thóra sarcastically, 'but you still haven't told me what you were doing here on Sunday.'

'I came to break into Birna's room,' Baldvin said candidly. 'I'd heard the police hadn't finished searching the room properly and I was hoping to find the photo. It wasn't there.'

'And on Thursday?' asked Thóra. 'The two of you left the seance just after it started and didn't go back. What happened?'

Baldvin smiled and gestured towards his grandfather. 'Granddad felt faint. He wasn't well, so we left the seance. We weren't really interested in it, anyway. We only went because we were hoping to see Birna.'

'Can anyone corroborate this?' Thóra asked.

'Yes, absolutely,' answered Baldvin cheerfully. 'I took Granddad up to his room and called a doctor. I got the phone number of a colleague of his who was on duty locally and he came here. I should think he arrived about nine and left around ten.'

Thóra realised at once that this excluded both of them as suspects – in Birna's murder, anyway. She didn't need to ask for the doctor's name; she would leave it to Thórólfur to corroborate the story. 'I see,' she said, glancing at Matthew. 'Well, I don't think there's anything else.' She stood up. 'Actually, there is one more thing. I probably ought to tell you, Magnús,' she said, 'that the skeleton of a child will be found here shortly. I believe the child was your daughter by Gudný Bjarnadóttir, little Kristín.'

'What?' croaked the old man. 'My daughter?'

'Yes, the one Gudný wrote to you about,' said Thóra, taking a chance. 'I think Grímur, Bjarni's brother, who lived on the next farm, killed the child to ensure that he, and not you, would inherit his brother's assets.'

'Me? Inherit?' echoed Magnús, grey-faced. Thóra noticed that he did not deny having received a letter.

'Actually,' she interjected, 'I believe you've forfeited your right to the inheritance by your failure to pursue the matter. You knew about the child, and you should have put in your claim for inheritance at that point. In fact, there's plenty more you should have done. For instance, you could have asked what had happened to the child, or acknowledged paternity at the time.' She went to the door, followed by Matthew. 'Perhaps if you'd done the right thing, there'd be no skeleton in the basement.'

'But . . .' said the old man, his words trailing off. Baldvin said nothing, merely regarded his grandfather inscrutably. 'How can you say that?' Magnús managed to say.

Thóra turned in the doorway. 'Because if Grímur had realised that Kristín had a father who knew of her existence, he wouldn't have been able to make her disappear.' She smiled at the two men. 'Goodbye. Nice to have made your acquaintance.' They left their hosts sitting as if turned to stone.

'That only leaves Bergur,' sighed Thóra, once they were

outside. 'He's the least likely of all, really. I can't see him getting in a canoe unless he had to, let alone sticking pins into someone.'

'Life is full of surprises, though,' said Matthew, putting his hand on her shoulder. 'Who would have thought, for instance, that I would fall for a woman wearing dirty trainers?'

Thóra looked down at her feet and grinned. Her trainers were rather shabby in comparison with Matthew's freshly buffed shoes. 'Maybe the same person who could imagine I would fall for a man with a shoe-shine fetish.'

Thóra paced back and forth, trying to jump-start her thought process, with little success. She and Matthew had returned to her room, where she hoped to find inspiration. She marched up and down past the bed, while Matthew sat serenely in the armchair by the window, sipping a beer. 'It must be Bergur. There's no one else left,' he said, setting his glass down. 'Unless it's Jónas.'

Thóra sighed. 'We're screwed if that's the answer.' She clutched at her hair, and continued pacing. 'Is there really no other possibility?'

'I really don't think so – we've run out of men. Bergur and Jónas are the only two left.'

'Pity the killer can't be a woman,' said Thóra. 'I liked Rósa and Jökull as Bonnie and Clyde types. That rather lost its appeal when they turned out to be siblings.' She stopped in her tracks and looked at Matthew. 'Have you ever heard of a criminal brother and sister?'

He shook his head. 'No, never. Only brothers. The Kray twins, for instance. Never brother and sister.'

'Is it completely out of the question that Rósa could have come across Birna after the rape and killed her?' wondered Thóra aloud. 'No, that doesn't make sense,' she continued.

Someone knocked at the door. Expecting it to be one of the children, Thóra was a little surprised to open the door to Stefanía.

'Hello,' said the sex therapist, smiling nervously. 'I just wanted to bring you something. I was actually hoping you'd come to me of your own accord, but apparently that's not going to happen.' She shifted from one foot to the other, her hands behind her back, and Thóra wondered what she was hiding there. 'I can help you,' Stefanía added, still smiling.

Thóra felt a knot form in her stomach. Surely the woman wasn't here to give her and Matthew advice on safe sex? She swallowed the saliva that suddenly flooded her mouth. It would be hard to blame language problems, or claim this was a misunderstanding. 'That's very kind of you,' was all she could say. She didn't step back from the door, fearing that Stefanía would come in and start talking to Matthew about AIDS.

'Anyway,' said Stefanía. 'I can see you're busy, so I'll just leave this with you.' She handed Thóra a small box and went on, 'You can call me anytime. I've put my business card in the box. The appliance is self-explanatory – it's a dildo, but a completely new kind. After repeated motion, gel squirts from the end. It makes it all far more . . . realistic. It's new on the market.' She beamed proudly.

Thóra stood gazing at the box. 'Oh. Gel. I see,' she said, embarrassed. Suddenly she had a flash of inspiration. She shoved the box at Stefanía and hurried back into the room. 'Hang on,' she said to the sex therapist, who was staring at her open-mouthed. She returned with the box she'd borrowed from reception when collecting things from the basement. 'Is this the same thing?' she asked, pointing out the words 'Aloe Vera Action'.

Stefanía gaped at Thóra, clearly doubting her sanity. 'Um, no,' she said, watching as Thóra's enthusiasm gave way to disappointment. 'This is the older model. Yours is newer.' She regarded Thóra suspiciously. 'Those sold out recently. They were hugely popular. Actually, the last one was stolen,' she added. 'Only last week there was a break-in, and I've just done my stocktake and found out what's missing. I was intending to give you the last one.' She looked at Thóra, still a little confused. 'The model I gave you is just as good. The only difference is that the lubricant gel isn't made with aloe vera.'

'A break-in?' exclaimed Thóra. 'When did this happen?'

'Last week,' said Stefanía. 'Let me see, I left on holiday on Tuesday and everything was in its usual place, but when I got back on Friday, I saw that the lock had been forced. Birna's murder was more important, of course, and in any case I thought at first that nothing was missing. Not until just now, when I was looking out the toy for you.'

Thóra turned back into the room, still holding the box. 'Guess what?' she said. 'Rósa's back on the list. Right at the top of it, in fact.'

Matthew gazed at her, bemused by her agitated state. 'How did that happen?' he enquired.

'Birna wasn't killed by a man; it was a woman. The rape was staged to mislead the police.' Thóra placed the box on the floor. 'Who would do such a thing?' She answered her own question. 'A woman, of course. A woman who didn't know about the aloe-vera gel.'

Matthew was still regarding Thóra quizzically. 'I think you may need to explain this to me a little more clearly,' he suggested, taking another sip of beer.

Thóra took the file of police documents, flipped through it and passed it to Matthew. She pointed out a photocopied picture of a dildo lying in a steel tray. 'It was found on the beach, with a load of other stuff, so the police may not have picked up on it.' Thóra waved a hand towards the box she had borrowed. 'It's the same model as was in there, if you're wondering how I happen to suddenly be an expert on sex toys.'

Matthew looked at the box, grinning. 'I see,' he said, looking back at her. 'But I still don't quite get how it fits together.'

'According to the description on the box, the thing squirts aloe-vera gel,' she said, her cheeks flushing pink. 'Don't ask me why.' She pointed to the picture again. 'It's quite possible that two men's semen was found in Birna's vagina, but neither came from a rape.'

'But how can you know that?' asked Matthew. 'Although two men have admitted having sex with her, it may not have been consensual.'

'I think the murderer tried to make it look like rape,' she replied, 'using the sex toy. It's the only plausible explanation for the presence of aloe vera. A woman who's just had sex with two men in one day is hardly going to wander down to the beach with a gadget like this.' She pointed to the picture again. 'And why would anyone want to make it look like rape? To deceive the police. It can only mean that the murderer was a woman. Women don't rape other women, so by making it look like a rape, the murderer would have diverted suspicion away from herself.'

'Well,' said Matthew, 'you have a point, but there are plenty of other women who could have killed her. It needn't necessarily be Rósa.'

'True,' said Thóra, 'but it has to be a woman with a good motive, and Rósa certainly had that.'

'Quite,' said Matthew, then fell silent. He watched in surprise as Stefanía came in.

She smiled at both of them, still carrying the small box, which she handed to Matthew. In her excitement, Thóra had completely forgotten the sex therapist.

'Here, this for you. You may have. Believe me, it have help many men like you,' she said to Matthew in broken English, then turned and left.

Matthew sat rooted to the spot. In one hand he held his beer glass, in the other the sex toy. He stared at it, lost for words, but as soon as the door closed behind Stefanía, he looked at Thóra. 'Surely you didn't tell that woman I was gay?'

'No, are you crazy?' answered Thóra innocently. 'I would never do that. Come on, let's go and find Thórólfur. He may not have figured it out yet.'

'Unless that weird woman is distributing her kinky toys to all and sundry,' said Matthew. He put the box down and stood up.

In reception, Vigdís told them that Thórólfur and another police officer had gone out with Thröstur to find and remove the canoe. Thóra assumed they would send it for tests, in case Thröstur had not succeeded in obliterating all the evidence, but she didn't hold out much hope, based on what Thröstur had said.

While she and Matthew stood with Vigdís, deciding whether to wait for Thórólfur or try to contact another police officer, she noticed the injured stockbroker limping towards reception. He was pulling a suitcase behind him with some difficulty. 'I'm going to give him a hand,' she said to Matthew, and hurried over to Teitur. 'Hey, I'll do that,' she called, and was rewarded with a smile.

'Thank you,' he said with relief, allowing Thóra to take the case. 'I'm still not a hundred per cent better, but I've got to get home.'

'Is someone picking you up?' she asked. She didn't think he should be driving in his condition.

'Yes, my brother,' puffed Teitur. 'I'll have someone collect my car later. You don't need a car to get to town, do you?'

Thóra laughed. 'No, actually,' she replied, thinking of the SUV and how she would get it back to the city. Gylfi wouldn't be driving it, that was for sure.

Teitur stumbled and winced. 'That bloody mare,' he said. 'I don't think anyone will ever get me on horseback again.'

'You're lucky it wasn't worse,' said Thóra. 'I don't understand why the place you rented it from didn't give you a safer horse. Which riding stables did you go to?'

'Oh, it was the farm just up above here – Tunga, I think – but it wasn't their fault,' said Teitur. 'The woman was terribly upset. Not a good start to a new business.'

'Tunga?' asked Thóra. 'You hired a horse from there? Was it a wild stallion, by any chance?'

Teitur laughed. 'No, I'm not that daft. It was just an ordinary horse. I was incredibly unlucky, though. I mean, what are the chances of coming across a dead fox? The horse was still panicking long after I had fallen off.'

Thóra stopped in her tracks. 'Was it near here? Was the dead fox near the path to the old farmhouse?'

Teitur nodded. 'Yup. I had no idea horses hated them so much.'

'Did you tell the horse-rental people about this?' Thóra was struggling to stay calm.

'Yes, of course,' said Teitur, surprised that Thóra was so interested. 'I had to go back and let them know their horse had run off into the wild blue yonder.'

'And you told them what happened and where?' asked Thóra. 'You told them about the fox and how the horse reacted?'

'Yes,' said Teitur. 'The woman was in shock, of course, because the horse was gone, and also because I was injured.'

'This woman,' said Thóra. 'Was her name Rósa?' Teitur nodded. 'Was there anyone with her who could have heard the story about the fox?' she asked. 'Her husband, maybe?'

'No,' answered Teitur. 'She was home alone. I wouldn't know if she told him, but I'd imagine she probably did.' He looked searchingly at her. 'Why do you ask?'

'No special reason,' said Thóra vaguely. 'Well, I hope you get home safely and make a swift recovery,' she added, and set the case down by the reception desk.

'I will,' said Teitur. He reached into his jacket pocket for his wallet. For a moment Thóra thought he was going to tip her for her assistance, but he handed her a business card. 'Do get in touch if you're ever wondering what to do with your money,' he said with a smile. 'I get good returns on my clients' investments.'

Thóra took the card, politely read it and put it in her pocket. Something major would have to happen in her life for her to ever scrape together enough money to make an investment. 'Thank you,' she said. 'You never know.'

'There's one thing that doesn't make sense,' said Matthew. 'We don't know if Rósa came here the evening of the seance. And how does this fit in with Jónas's phone and the canoe?'

Thóra watched the front door open, hoping it would be Thórólfur at last. It was not. A young couple entered pulling a suitcase behind them: new guests, heading for reception. She turned to Matthew. 'Maybe Jökull pinched the phone for her and sent the text message.'

'That doesn't explain the canoe,' said Matthew. 'She must have come here, otherwise using the canoe makes no sense.'

'Maybe she *was* here,' said Thóra. 'She needn't have been at the seance.'

Matthew looked dubious. 'It seems to me that the only reason for using the canoe was to be able to leave the seance unnoticed and return before the interval. Perhaps there's another explanation, but I can't see it.'

Thóra stood up. 'I'm going to have a word with Vigdís.' She went over to the desk and waited while the receptionist dealt with the young couple, who finally left happily with their key.

'Vigdís,' said Thóra, 'do you know Jökull's sister by sight?'

Vigdís removed a sheet of paper from the printer on the desk in front of her and reached for a hole-punch. 'Rosie, or whatever her name is? Yes, I do,' she answered, punching holes in the paper. 'Why? Are you looking for her?'

'Her name's Rósa, actually,' Thóra corrected her. 'No, I'm not looking for her. I was just wondering if you remember whether she came to the seance last Thursday?'

'No,' said Vigdís firmly. 'She wasn't here.' She opened a binder and placed the sheet of paper in it. Then she stopped and looked up at Thóra. 'Oh, wait, yes. She was here.'

'She was?' Thóra tried to conceal her excitement.

'Yes, I remember I felt kind of sorry for her. She had brought a bunch of flowers for that man who got hurt falling off her horse – Teitur, the one who just checked out.' Thóra nodded. 'She had to walk all the way down the drive because there was a gap in the road, and the flowers were a bit wind-blown.'

'Are you sure this was on Thursday evening?' persisted Thóra.

'Absolutely,' replied Vigdís. 'I remember I had no time to talk to her because I was so busy dealing with people who were arriving for the seance. I took the flowers and said I'd deliver them. She thanked me and asked if she could pop into the kitchen to see her brother.'

'Did you see her leave?' asked Thóra.

'No, I don't think so,' answered Vigdís. 'I wanted to go the seance myself, so I left a note on reception asking people to come inside if they needed anything. I had the cordless phone, in case there were any calls.'

'Do you know if she had anything to do with Eiríkur, the aura reader?' Thóra said.

Vigdís slowly shook her head. 'No,' she replied. 'I don't think so. Actually, Eiríkur came to see me before he went to meet Jónas to ask for a pay rise. He wanted information about the local landowners. He needed the phone number of that brother and sister, Elín and what's-his-name . . .'

'Börkur,' said Thóra. 'Why did he want to contact them?'

'I don't know. I thought it had something to do with the haunting. He'd been fascinated by all the commotion. I didn't have their phone numbers, of course, but I did have a number for Berta, the girl who's clearing out the old farmhouse, so I suggested he ring her to get their numbers.' She shut the file and put it back in its place. 'Eiríkur tried to call her from the phone here in reception, but there was no answer, so I gave him the number of another local landowner, the only one I had apart from Berta's.'

'Whose number was that?' asked Thóra.

'It was Rósa's,' answered Vigdís. She took a sheet of A4 paper from a pile on the desk and handed it to Thóra. 'It's an ad for the riding stables that Jökull asked me to hang up. It has her name and phone number.' She took the sheet back. 'I took it down after that guy got hurt. I didn't want any more guests getting crippled.' Vigdís seemed to suddenly notice that she had Thóra's rapt attention. 'I told the police about it because it was just before Eiríkur was killed in the stables.'

'So do you know if Eiríkur rang Rósa?' asked Thóra impatiently.

'No idea,' said Vigdís. 'I wrote down both numbers and gave them to him.' She leaned over the desk and pointed. 'He went and made a call from that phone over there. I think it's the one and only time it's been used, as it's in such a silly place.' She straightened up. 'I heard him talking for quite a while, so he must have got through.' She scribbled on a Post-it and handed it to Thóra. 'Here are the numbers, if you want to ask Rósa and Berta about it.'

The phone was pushed back on top of a cabinet, under a gigantic stuffed elk's head hung far too low on the wall. Thóra picked up the phone, taking care not to poke her eye out with a prong of its antlers. She pressed the 'last number recall' button. The first number was neither of those on the Post-it, but the next was Rósa's home number, followed by Berta's mobile number. Thóra had to assume the first number was the most recently called, and irrelevant to Eiríkur. He had tried to call Berta and received no reply, and then he had contacted Rósa.

It was all coming together.

Thóra sank back in her chair. 'You see, it all fits,' she said triumphantly.

'Isn't it time we found Thórólfur?' suggested Matthew. He glanced at his watch. 'I'm beginning to think he must have left. It's been an awfully long time.'

'The fog will probably delay him,' said Thóra, looking out of the glass doors. Visibility outside was very poor. She jumped as the basement door was suddenly flung open. 'What now?' she said. 'Are they still down there?' Something significant was clearly happening in the basement. The last of the animal bones must have been removed, as the men who emerged were empty-handed. They hurried past Thóra and Matthew without looking at them, then quickly returned loaded with equipment: cameras, vacuum cleaners and spades.

'I think the child's skeleton has been uncovered,' said Matthew. 'They're making more fuss than they did about the animal bones.'

'Ugh,' said Thóra with a shudder. 'I just can't understand how anyone could do that to a little child. To shut her up in a coal bunker just because of an inheritance and leave her to die.'

'Grímur wasn't all there, so there's no way to comprehend what he did,' said Matthew, watching a man with a large arc light descend into the basement.

Thórólfur sat down heavily in the chair opposite them. He had approached astonishingly quietly for such a large man. 'Now, then,' he said, 'I gather you want to talk to me.' He jerked his thumb at the basement. 'I haven't got much time – I really have to get down there. What's up?'

Thóra passed him the binder containing the investigation documents. 'I think I know who killed both Birna and Eiríkur,' she said. 'We need more than a few minutes to explain it, but I don't think you'll find it a waste of time.'

Thórólfur harrumphed. 'Don't be too sure,' he said, leaning back in his chair. 'Go ahead. No fancy talk, just the bullet points, please.'

When Thóra had finished telling Thórólfur about Rósa, the fox, the aloe-vera gel, Eiríkur's phone call and everything else she'd learned, she looked anxiously at him. 'Rósa is definitely the killer, and her brother may be an accomplice at least. You can investigate fully, but I can't.'

Thórólfur gazed thoughtfully at her. He had listened patiently and asked no questions. 'I have spoken to her, in fact, about Eiríkur's phone call,' he said. 'She said he called to ask about hiring a horse, whether it was based at the farm or elsewhere.'

Thóra frowned. 'What for?'

He shrugged. 'I don't know. I thought it was all a bit odd, but your story about the flowers and the gadget with the gel is most interesting.' He stood up and yawned. 'I was hoping I could call it a day. I'd better look in on those two.' He glanced towards the basement door. 'The discovery downstairs has been waiting for decades. It will hardly matter if it waits another half-hour.'

Thóra could not conceal her pleasure. Thórólfur seemed to be taking her story seriously, whatever else happened. 'Thank you, Thórólfur. Perhaps you'll keep me informed?' She stood up.

Thórólfur beckoned to a police officer to accompany him out of the building. He looked at Thóra. 'I didn't say that.' He left without saying goodbye.

Thóra finished mashing potatoes and fish together for her daughter, who was carefully observing that the butter was evenly distributed throughout the mash. The chef certainly wouldn't have imagined that his beautifully presented meal would end up like this. There were few diners in the dining room and the service was quick and efficient.

'I don't know if I should eat this,' said Sigga, gazing at a pile of shellfish. 'I thought I was ordering pasta.' Gylfi, who did have pasta, looked at her plate, clearly debating with himself whether he should offer to swap with the mother of his unborn child. In the end he said he would share his meal with her and the shellfish went to Matthew as an extra main course, along with the big steak he had already started on.

Thóra placed the pile of fishy mash in front of her daughter, who dug in. She reached hungrily for her own plate. She'd had enough of wondering who'd done what and why. She thanked her lucky stars she'd met the stockbroker before he left. He had contributed more to the search for the murderer than anything they'd done over the past few days.

She put down her knife and fork. 'How did he get back to the horse rental when he fell off?' she said, puzzled.

'Who?' asked Matthew, putting down an empty shell.

'Teitur. He was injured and couldn't drive, and he can hardly have walked,' she said. 'Someone must have given him a lift.'

'Yes,' said Matthew. 'So?'

Sigga and Gylfi listened, comprehending nothing. Sóley, on the other hand, was not interested; she was comparing the levels of Coke in her glass and Gylfi's.

'If someone gave him a lift, or helped him out, that person also knew about the horse's reaction to the dead fox, and knew where the fox was.' She reached for her phone and took Teitur's business card out of her pocket.

'Hello. This is Thóra, the lawyer at the hotel. Sorry to bother you, but I was wondering who drove you back to the stables from the place where you fell off.'

'Oh, hello,' replied Teitur. 'I was hoping you'd decided to invest. The market's looking good right now.'

'No, not at the moment, thanks,' said Thóra. 'For the moment I'd like to focus on your accident.'

'OK,' said Teitur, sounding slightly disappointed. 'It was the girl. I thought I told you when you first asked me about the accident. She saved my bacon, pulled me away before the horse finished me off. It was crazy.'

'What girl was that?' asked Thóra evenly. 'Did you get her name?'

'Yes,' he said, 'but I don't remember it. She just happened to be there. She was carrying some boxes into the old house at the end of the path. I've often wondered what might have happened if the dead fox had been a bit farther away, out of her view. She was kind enough to drive me to the stables and then back to the hotel.'

'Was her name Berta?' asked Thóra, her voice still calm although her insides were in turmoil.

'Yes,' said Teitur cheerfully. 'That's it. Berta.'

34

RER. BER. Thóra set her phone down on the table and stared into space. Matthew, Gylfi and Sigga waited silently with their cutlery in their hands, keen to hear what she'd found out.

'It might not be Rósa after all,' said Thóra into the silence. 'Berta knew about the fox.'

'Remember she isn't necessarily guilty, even if she knew about it,' said Matthew.

Gylfi and Sigga listened closely, understanding nothing.

'That's not all,' said Thóra. 'Firstly, she's got the most to lose, apart from her mother, Elín, and her Uncle Börkur. She was here, at the seance, and she believes in ghosts, so she could conceivably have pushed pins into the soles of the victims' feet to stop their spirits walking.'

'But aren't you forgetting that Berta wasn't here when Eiríkur was killed?' asked Matthew. 'She'd gone to Reykjavík. The records from the tunnel prove it. Do you think there are two different killers?'

'Not at all,' replied Thóra. 'If you think about it, she probably never even went to Reykjavík.'

Matthew raised his eyebrows. 'Do you think she lent someone her car?'

'No, I think she swapped cars with Steini,' said Thóra. 'It's far too much of a coincidence that the two of them should have been driving through in opposite directions. He wasn't watching her drive away as we thought. He must have gone through, waited for Berta and switched cars at the other end of the tunnel. Then she drove back here to kill Eiríkur. He must have been waiting at the side of the road for her to turn round and come back, when Thröstur, the canoeist, came along. It was probably her car Thröstur saw pull up as he was driving away. It gives her an alibi.'

'What about him?' asked Matthew. 'That would put him in the line of fire instead.'

Thóra shook her head. 'Who'd ever believe he could manhandle Eiríkur into the stall with the stallion? You saw him. He couldn't do it. She's as strong as an ox, however – she's been pushing him all over the place in his wheel-chair.' Thóra clasped her forehead. 'Do you remember the picture of her dead relative, Gudný, in the frame on my bedside table?' Matthew nodded. 'When you think about it, Berta looks a lot like Gudný, especially if you imagine her with a different hairstyle.'

Matthew smiled. 'I don't remember Gudný's face clearly, let alone her hair. Does it matter?'

'That was the photo that upset Jónas,' said Thóra. 'He said he'd seen a ghost that was just like the girl in the photo. He had last seen the ghost in his own apartment.' She closed her eyes and recalled the photo of Gudný's pretty face. 'I bet it was Berta, and I bet she stole the sleeping pills too. I don't know what she was doing there. Maybe she was trying to find out Jónas's plans for the annexe. He must have come back unexpectedly. He was prob-ably high as a kite and couldn't tell whether he was seeing a real person or a ghost. Maybe she was planning to use the sleeping pills for Birna, then changed her mind after Jónas spotted her. When she came to kill Eiríkur, she may have thought it was safe, or simply had no choice, if the sleeping pills were the only sedative she had available. She's probably also the ghost they saw out in the fog behind the hotel. I bet she was out there with a shovel, searching for the hatch. Maybe she hoped to remove the bones before Kristín could be found.'

'What are you going to do about it?' asked Matthew. 'I'm pretty sure that speculation alone isn't enough. Why would she kill Eiríkur, for instance?'

Thóra puffed out her cheeks. 'I don't know. Maybe he was involved, or perhaps he saw her. She's probably the only person who knows why she did it.'

'Shouldn't we go to the police with this?' he said. 'Thórólfur seems all right really, and he won't be too offended if you send him off in a different direction, as long as the information is good. Remember, he's talking to Rósa, who you were sure was guilty an hour ago.'

Thóra sighed and stood up. 'I have to go there and tell him. The sooner the better.'

'Cat!' yelled the only person not captivated by the progress of the case. Sóley beamed at Matthew and then turned to her mother. 'Tell him I speak English,' she said contentedly.

'That's wonderful, sweetheart,' said Thóra, stroking her little fair head. 'You can practise some more while I pop out. Matthew will stay with you.'

'Dog!' she heard Sóley proudly pronounce, as she headed out of the restaurant to her car.

* * *

Lára made herself more comfortable on the hard chair, taking care not to crease the coat she held on her lap. The flowers she'd brought with her did not appear to have perked up when put in water and hung limply in a steel vase on the bedside table. In the bed lay Málfrídur Grímsdóttir.

Lára cleared her throat and took the old lady's dry hand. 'I haven't been able to think of anything else lately. The memories have come flooding back since my grand-daughter, Sóldís, started working at the hotel back west. You know the truth, and I'm hoping you'll tell me everything now, before it's too late.' She looked at the drawn features of the woman in the bed. Strange how people aged differently. Málfrídur was much younger than she was, yet here she lay, seemingly incapable of even holding her head up, while Lára sat straight-backed at her bedside. She hoped she would go quickly when her time came. She didn't want to fade away like this.

A tear formed in the corner of the old woman's eye. As she was lying down, it didn't run down her cheek, but pooled by her eye. 'I hope God will forgive me,' she said, and closed her eyes, sending the tear trickling down on to the pillow. 'I was so young. I didn't dare go against Dad, and then he got ill and I had other things on my mind.'

'I'm not accusing you of anything, Málfrídur my dear,' said Lára affectionately, and grasped the woman's hand tighter. 'I quite understand that you couldn't talk to me about it back then, but now we're running out of time, both of us, and I can't bear to think of leaving this world without knowing where the child is. I owe that to Gudný.'

Tears now poured down Málfrídur's cheeks as she lay

with her eyes squeezed shut. 'She's dead,' she said in her cracked voice. 'Dad made sure of that.' She started to sob and Lára patiently waited for her to calm down. 'He shut her up in the coal bunker, and she died there during the night. I'd gone over to Kirkjustétt to fetch a doll of hers that she was missing, and I saw him out of the window. Oh, God,' said Málfríður, struck dumb by the memory. She rallied and went on. 'After he burned down the outhouses, because of the stench, he flung the remains of the animals down into the coal bunker and turfed over the hatch the following spring. He had closed off the entrance to the bunker from the basement, and later he walled it up so no one could even tell there was a door there.'

'Why?' asked Lára, close to tears.

'The livestock died because Gudný couldn't care for them after her father died. She was mortally ill herself. When Dad finally got in touch with her, the animals were beyond saving. The smell was horrible. He set the outhouses on fire, and buried the animals, to conceal the fact that he hadn't helped his brother and niece. Of course, he should have looked after the animals for Gudný, after she became bedridden.' The old woman blinked hard. 'He didn't even check whether all the animals were dead. At least one of the cows was still alive. I saw her at the window, maddened with fear. I still see her today, when I close my eyes.'

'I'm not talking about the cattle,' said Lára. 'Why did he do that to Gudný's daughter? I'm trying to understand.' She felt tears running down her own cheeks now.

'Kristín,' said Málfríður. She opened her eyes and gazed up at the white ceiling. 'Dad hated her. I didn't understand at first. She was so sweet and gentle, so quiet, but such a lovely girl. She was a couple of years younger than me, and for the few days she was with us, after Dad brought her and Gudný to our house, she was mostly busy taking care of her mother. Dad didn't want to go into the room because he was afraid of infection, but the little girl sat with her, fed her and tried to make her as comfortable as possible, until her mum died one night.

'Kristín was special, but Dad couldn't see it. I was so happy to have her with us, and I assumed naïvely that she would stay on with us after her mother died. That didn't happen.' Málfrídur paused. 'Instead of allowing her to live with us, he decided to kill her and obliterate any sign that she had ever existed. When Kristín was born, he hoped she would catch tuberculosis from her grandfather and die before she came of age, so he never filled out a birth certificate for her, because he saw a bastard child as a blot on the family. That turned out well for him later.'

'Why did he do it?' asked Lára. 'I'd happily have taken in Gudný's child and loved her like one of my own. She would have been no trouble to him.'

Málfrídur turned to face her. 'He was eaten up with rage at being dependent on her. Dad had lost everything. His brother, Bjarni, had helped him out by buying the farm and guaranteeing all the debts, but instead of making Dad happy, it sowed the seed that destroyed him in the end. He committed suicide, mad with self-hatred and shame over what he had done for money. He told me everything before he killed himself. I think he wanted absolution, but I couldn't give it to him. I was appalled by his cruelty. Although I saw what happened, and I knew the facts, more or less, I was horrified when he confirmed what I'd suspected.' Málfrídur gazed up at the ceiling again. 'I had the inscription on his gravestone cut in keeping with the way he lived his life: "Bloody is the heart".' She fell silent again, then coughed feebly. 'It has affected me all my life. I let her down, and I've lived in constant fear that she would come back to haunt me. And she has, in a way. Until now it has only been in the form of a bad conscience, but now she has visited me in a dream.'

'I shall have her dug up,' said Lára, who wanted to leave. She had had enough. 'And have her buried next to her mother. I can't keep quiet over this.'

Málfrídur raised herself up from the bed a little, for the first time since Lára's arrival. 'There's no need. I've made sure that it happens.'

Lára looked at her without comprehension. 'The child hasn't been found yet,' she said.

'Then something's gone wrong,' said the old woman. 'I told my granddaughter, Berta, Elín's girl, about it, and she said everything would be all right. She promised to take care of it.' She smiled feebly at Lára. 'It's strange – I couldn't tell my children about it, but then Berta came to see me. There's something about the lass that reminded me of Gudný and the little girl. She's a good soul, Berta. She'll do the right thing.'

Lára stood up. Rage suddenly flared in her. 'I wouldn't be surprised if she turned out to have more in common with your father than with Gudný and her daughter.'

'We'll simply have to hope that Málfrídur's remorse can withstand the challenge. She may not be so truthful when

433

she realises what's in store for her own grandchild,' said Thóra. She said goodbye and hung up. No more evidence was needed: Lára's telephone call confirmed that Berta was the killer. Thóra had pulled over when Lára phoned, and now she drove on at a snail's pace through the thick fog towards Tunga. Here and there the fog lifted slightly, and bizarre shapes appeared in the mossy lava field. She felt a shiver down her spine as the fog thickened once more, swallowing the weird forms. Thóra hoped she was on the right road. It was only a stone's throw, but due to the poor visibility, she drove slowly and she'd lost her bearings.

Suddenly an outstretched arm seemed to appear out of the fog; it was the sign for the Tunga farm. She turned down the drive and speeded up slightly. A little farther on she saw the farmhouse looming in the fog, with Thórólfur's car outside. She parked next to it and saw it was empty. She went over to the entrance, but after a few steps she froze. From the fog she could hear a baby's low wailing. She turned, trying to determine where the sound was coming from, but without success. The crying stopped as suddenly as it had begun, and Thóra rubbed her arms to calm the shudder that had run through her. What the hell was that? Could a woman be wandering around with a baby in the fog? Thóra squinted, attempting to see better. She jumped when she saw a movement where she thought the stables ought to be. Propelled by curiosity, she went in that direction, taking care to tread softly on the gravel.

She had reached the stables when the crying started again. She looked back, but saw nothing, then jumped when she heard a loud crash behind her. The stable door was unfastened, and it was banging against the wall.

Someone had clearly left it open. Thóra hurried out of sight when she heard movement inside the stables. She pressed against the wall, hoping she couldn't be seen in the fog. She caught a glimpse of a human figure in the doorway, and watched someone emerge from the stables and close the door. Thóra quickly realised she couldn't hide any longer.

'Hello, Berta,' she said. 'What are you doing here?'

The girl was taken aback. She turned and looked at Thóra, wide-eyed. 'Me?' she said. 'Nothing.'

'I saw you come out of the stables,' said Thóra. 'Do you know the people here?'

The cries started up again and Berta peered out into the fog. 'I heard the crying and I came out to check,' she said, shuffling her feet.

'Inside the stables?' asked Thóra. 'That noise is clearly coming from outside.' She looked at the girl, who was chewing her lower lip. 'Berta, you must realise it's over,' she said calmly. 'Kristín's body has been found. There's no point in trying to put off the inevitable. Why don't you come with me and talk to Thórólfur? He's from the police and he's here at the farm.' Thóra pointed in what she thought was the direction of the farmhouse. She could now hardly see anything in the fog.

'What do you mean?' asked Berta. Her attempt at nonchalance was belied by the tremor in her voice. 'What's that?' she asked, as the wailing grew louder and more insistent.

'It's probably the ghost of a baby left out to die,' said Thóra calmly. 'Or your relative, little Kristín. I gather your grandmother's already seen her.' Thóra was relying on

Lára's hazy account of Málfrídur's dream, in which Kristín had supposedly appeared. 'Come on,' she said, 'we're better off going indoors than standing out here, waiting for the ghost to circle us three times. I think it may already have gone round once.'

Berta looked at Thóra feverishly. She was deathly pale, her eyes bloodshot. 'How did they find Kristín?' she mumbled.

'That's not important,' said Thóra. 'It had to happen, and it's just as well it has. Now you have to face the music.'

'Mum and I will lose everything,' said Berta suddenly. Thóra was not sure whether she was talking to her or to herself. 'And Steini. We own the house he lives in. His parents sold up and moved to Reykjavík. He'll have to move in with them.' She looked out into the fog and took a deep breath.

Thóra saw tiny beads of perspiration on her forehead and temples. The wailing grew quieter and then faded away. Berta seemed to calm down a little.

'There are worse things than losing your property,' said Thóra. She couldn't help adding, 'Like losing your life.'

Now Berta looked at her. 'Birna didn't deserve to live, and neither did Eiríkur. They weren't nice people. She blackmailed the old man, and Eiríkur tried to get money out of me. He rang me and said he'd seen me leave the seance. He said he'd tell Mum and get her to pay him to keep his mouth shut. He thought we were filthy rich because of all the properties we own here. I told him to meet me at the riding stables, and then . . . you know.'

'Yes, unfortunately I do,' said Thóra. She wondered how the girl could give the impression of being so sane and normal when she was clearly deranged. 'I read Birna's autopsy report. It said she was struck repeatedly in the face with a rock. Were you hoping she wouldn't be identified?' asked Thóra.

'No,' gasped Berta. 'I was going to hit her in the back of the head, but she turned round too quickly and I hit her in the face. She must have heard me coming. I was going to make it look as if her head had knocked against the rocks on the shore when she was being raped, but hitting her in the face made that impossible. I'd planned it so carefully. I picked the day of the seance and made sure people noticed me there. I sat at the back and sneaked out once the medium had the audience's attention, and then I used the canoe to get there quickly. I heard about the boat from Sóldís, and I knew the owner wasn't staying much longer, so I had to do it then.' She gritted her teeth. 'Sóldís talks a lot. I heard about Jónas's medication from her, and also that he was in the habit of leaving his mobile phone lying around. She also told me what the sex therapist sold, and other things that came in useful.' Berta sighed, and her eyes filled with tears. 'It was all supposed to go perfectly, but it still went wrong. Birna didn't die from the first blow, so I had to hit her again and again. And again.' She looked down at her feet. 'I thought I'd throw up when the gulls flew down.'

Thóra was close to vomiting herself, but she steeled herself and kept talking. This was clearly her one chance to talk to the girl. 'Why did you stick pins in the soles of their feet?'

'I wanted to make sure their spirits wouldn't walk. That

does no one any good, neither the departed nor those of us who live on,' said Berta, who looked like she was about to faint.

'Are you all right?' Thóra asked anxiously. 'What were you doing in there?' Thóra wondered if she had taken something. Then she realised that it was because the girl's life was collapsing around her.

'I was planting the drugs,' said Berta tonelessly. 'I hoped it would cast suspicion on Bergur and Rósa if Jónas was released. I was worried the police might find out that Jónas didn't send Birna the text message.' She sighed and looked up at Thóra. 'I took his phone. It was all so easy, once I'd decided how to do it. Birna had to be stopped. She wouldn't listen to me when I told her it was the wrong place to build. If she'd only done as I said, it would all have been all right.' Berta hesitated, then said, 'I did it for Steini.' Thóra couldn't be sure if the girl was justifying herself to her or to herself. 'It was the least I could do. What happened to him was my fault – I'd called to ask him to pick me up on the night of the accident. Now he feels bad because he thinks it's his fault I did it, and he keeps asking me to forgive him. But it was my decision to do it for him, so there's nothing to forgive. I only did it for Steini.' She collapsed.

'Do you think so?' said Thóra, as she helped the girl to her feet. 'I really doubt it.' They walked towards the farmhouse, Thóra supporting Berta so she wouldn't fall again.

They heard the wailing once more, then just as suddenly it stopped. Thóra was feeling quite unsettled by the time they reached the farmhouse steps, and the girl was shaking like a leaf. Thóra glanced over her shoulder as she rang the doorbell, hoping someone would come quickly. The door opened, revealing Rósa. She said nothing, but gazed past them. Thóra turned, half expecting to see a spectral child pulling itself laboriously up the steps with one arm.

'Gulli!' called Rósa. 'There you are, you naughty cat. Where have you been?' The crying had resumed as she opened the door, and now it stopped as she finished speaking. 'Puss!' she called in a soothing falsetto. 'Come here, you silly mog!' A marmalade tomcat casually strolled up the steps.

Sunday, 18 June 2006

35

The lemonade from the minibar was expensive, but to Thóra it was worth every penny. She put down the can and wrapped the thick white dressing gown more closely around her. She went to the window of her room, opened the curtains a crack and looked out over Austurvöllur Square. Not many people were around, and the few who were up and about seemed to be the last few stragglers from the previous night's revelry. Thóra smiled. She let go of the curtain and walked back over to the bed, where Matthew lay asleep. Now that she had finally met someone who was neither divorced nor alcoholic, megalomaniac nor sports fanatic, just her luck that he had to be a foreigner who was hardly likely to want to move to Iceland.

Perhaps that was exactly why she liked him.

She heard a faint ringing somewhere in the room and listened carefully to identify where her phone was. Finally she located it in her bag. She answered quickly. 'Hello,' she whispered, taking the phone into the bathroom so as not to wake Matthew.

'Mum,' shouted Gylfi, 'Sigga's dying!'

Thóra shut her eyes and put her head in one hand. She had left Sóley with Gylfi and Sigga – mainly so that she could be with Matthew for his last night in Iceland. They would soon be taking care of a baby, so they ought to be able to babysit a six-year-old for one night, and Sigga had hitherto shown no signs of going into labour.

'Gylfi, sweetheart,' she said, 'she's not dying. The baby's coming.' She heard Sigga moaning in the background. 'Is she in a lot of pain?'

'She's dying, Mum,' said her son. 'Really. Listen.' The moans grew louder, then suddenly stopped. 'It comes and goes,' he added.

'She's in labour, darling,' said Thóra, more calmly than she felt. 'I'm on my way. Get yourself and your sister dressed. If Sigga feels able to get dressed, that would be good, but otherwise she can go as she is.' Thóra opened the bathroom door and went back into the bedroom. 'Has Sigga called her mum? Is she on her way?' she asked as she pulled her clothes on.

'No,' said Gylfi firmly. 'Sigga wants me to call, but I won't. She's horrible.'

Thóra couldn't disagree, but she urged him to ring all the same, as Sigga's parents would certainly want to be there for their daughter. It would be the last straw for Sigga's mum and dad if Gylfi failed to let them know.

'I'm coming, anyway,' she said. 'You make sure you're ready. If they want to pick Sigga up, they can. It's up to you whether you go with them or come with me and Sóley.' She hung up and zipped up her skirt. Uncharacteristically, she had dressed up for the occasion – high heels and everything. She'd wanted to celebrate the end of the case and enjoy her time with Matthew before he left. She looked at her tights, draped over the TV. She grimaced, but decided she would rather put them back on than expose her pasty white legs.

'Matthew,' said Thóra, nudging him gently, 'I've got to go. Sigga's in labour.'

Matthew, who lay face down, lifted his head from the pillow and blinked groggily at her. 'What?'

'I've got to go to the hospital,' she repeated, 'Sigga's screaming blue murder, so it shouldn't be long. I'll ring and let you know.'

Thóra drove home faster than usual. She smiled to herself as she turned into her road, remembering how Gylfi and Sigga had betrayed their ignorance when they had talked about the birth. Sigga had at various times expressed a desire to give birth underwater, or standing up outside surrounded by nature, or silently, like Tom Cruise's wife, all depending on what she had been reading on the Internet that day. All these idyllic births took place without any pain medication, but Thóra suspected that would change when the girl was faced with reality. After the first session of a course for expectant parents, both had refused to return. Sigga had scandalised the midwife by asking whether there was MTV in the delivery room.

'I'm here,' called Thóra as she entered, but she could not be heard over Sigga's howling. She wouldn't be welcome in a Scientologist delivery room.

'There's something wrong,' shouted Gylfi when he spotted his mother. 'I think the baby's trying to come out sideways.'

'No, it isn't,' said Thóra. 'Unfortunately this is just what it's like.' She went over to Sigga, who was sitting in the dining room with her head in her hands.

'It's because she's got such narrow hips,' said Gylfi anxiously. 'Everybody says that makes it really hard to give birth.'

445

'It's not the hips that are the bottleneck in this process, sweetheart. That comes a bit further down.' She leaned over Sigga. 'Just breathe deeply, Sigga,' she said. 'OK, let's go out to the car. Have your waters broken?'

Sigga looked at Thóra blankly. 'Waters?'

'Come on,' said Thóra, clapping her hands briskly, 'you'll find out soon enough.' She helped Sigga out of the house, while Gylfi hurried ahead to open the car door. Sóley followed sleepily, unclear what was happening. 'Just say yes, Sigga, if they offer you an epidural. It's the fashion,' said Thóra, helping Sigga lie down in the rear seat of the SUV. She had decided to sell it, and the caravan, in order to clear her debts, but the SUV was bigger than her old banger and had room for all of them.

Thóra sat in the driving seat and started the engine. Just as she backed out of the drive, Sigga shouted out and she slammed on the brakes. Gylfi and Thóra looked into the back. She sighed. She would have to knock something off the price of the SUV, now that the rear seat was awash with amniotic fluid.

Sóley sat swinging her legs. She had nothing else to do in the waiting area. Thóra was impressed by how good she was being, especially since they'd been waiting in the little room for nearly three hours. Their time there wasn't made any more enjoyable by the presence of Sigga's father, who barely spoke, just sent Thóra an impressive range of contemptuous looks, so Thóra was relieved when her phone rang, breaking the oppressive silence. She answered and took the call in the corridor.

'Hello, Thóra, this is Lára on Snaefellsnes, Sóldís's

grandmother,' said the old lady's pleasantly modulated voice. 'I hope I haven't rung at a bad time.'

'No, not at all,' replied Thóra. 'I'm so pleased to hear from you. I was going to call you myself, as I didn't manage to see you before I left.' Five days had passed since Berta and Steini had been arrested, and Thóra had been busy tying up the case and working off the backlog that had accumulated at the office. Jónas had fortunately decided not to take legal action against Elín and Börkur, after it transpired that the 'ghost' had been Berta all along. 'You know they found Kristín, of course.'

'Yes, that's why I'm ringing,' said Lára. 'There are actually two things I wanted to mention. I'm arranging to have her buried next to her mother, and I was hoping you'd come to the service. It was thanks to you that she was found. I don't suppose her relatives will be attending en masse, and I feel it's important that it shouldn't just be me and the priest.'

'I'd be honoured,' said Thóra warmly.

'Good,' said Lára. 'I'll let you know as soon as the date is fixed.' She cleared her throat delicately. 'Then there's the other matter. The policeman who handled the case came to see me earlier.'

'Thórólfur?' said Thóra, surprised. 'What did he want?'

'He brought me a letter, or to be more precise a copy of a letter,' replied Lára. 'A letter that's taken sixty years to reach me. It's from Gudný.'

'Where was it found?' asked Thóra. She was astonished. 'Was it in the coal bunker?'

'It was in Kristín's coat pocket,' said Lára. It seemed to Thóra that her voice might break, but when she spoke again, she sounded strong and steady. 'Most of what's in the letter is my private business, but I wanted to share one thing with you.'

'Of course,' said Thóra. 'I think it must explain quite a lot.'

'When Gudný wrote the letter, she knew she was dying. She realised it was her last chance to tell her story. She starts by apologising for not telling me the truth in her previous letters. She says she didn't feel able to as she was afraid I would come to visit her, and she or her father would infect me. I'd started a new life in Reykjavík and she didn't want to unsettle me by complaining about her own problems.'

'Presumably she meant the tuberculosis,' said Thóra. 'It can't have been the child that she saw as a problem.'

'No,' Lára replied. 'She loved her daughter more than life itself. She calls her "a light in the darkness". She says she's such a good little girl, sweet-natured in spite of her unusual upbringing, cut off from everyone except her mother and grandfather. I can't deny that Gudný seemed terribly ashamed of having had an illegitimate child, but it didn't affect her love for Kristín.'

'Children are incredibly adaptable,' said Thóra, thinking of her own little grandchild starting his or her life, possibly by coming out sideways.

'Absolutely,' said Lára. 'Kristín was lucky to have such a loving mother, and she didn't need anyone else.' Lára hesitated, presumably scanning the letter for something specific. 'Gudný states quite clearly that Magnús Baldvinsson is the father,' she said eventually. 'They were intimate only once, when he came to meet her father on

Nationalist Party business and she became pregnant. She says she has never slept with any other man, neither before nor since, and jokes that there are unlikely to be any more men in her life now.'

'Does she says whether he knew about the child?' asked Thóra. Even if he did, he could hardly lay claim to inherit from her.

'She says he went to Reykjavík to study before she was aware of her condition, but she wrote him a letter after Kristín was born. He never replied.' Lára sighed. 'It's clear from her letter that she was very hurt, particularly on her daughter's behalf. If she had ever loved him, that put an end to it, understandably.'

'Yes, there are things you can never put right in relationships,' agreed Thóra, 'and refusing to acknowledge your own child is one of the worst.'

'Gudný wrote me the letter to ask me to take her daughter in,' said Lára. 'Her father was already dead, and she and her daughter were living with her Uncle Grímur. Gudný says she doesn't trust him, that he's deranged. She says he looks at her and her daughter with such hatred that she finds it quite frightening, and that she definitely doesn't want to leave her daughter in his care. She even asks me to find out whether anything can be done for his daughter, Málfrídur, as she's also concerned about her, although she's older and more capable of looking after herself.'

'Well, well,' said Thóra. 'Do you suppose he knew Gudný wanted you to be Kristín's guardian?' asked Thóra. 'If Kristín went, he'd lose all his property along with her.'

'I don't know,' said Lára. 'She doesn't say so, just that she doesn't know when the letter will reach me as she doesn't trust Grímur to post it. She says she's going to give it to her little girl in the hope that she can pass it to someone. She says she's talked to Kristín and told her about me, how kind I am, and that maybe she'll be able to see me soon. Then she adds that she can trust the child to take good care of the letter, although she's young. She's so conscientious and good.'

'She managed to keep the letter a secret, at any rate,' said Thóra.

'Yes,' said a faint voice at the other end of the line. The old lady was obviously weeping now. 'No doubt I'll speak to you about it again after the funeral,' said Lára through her tears. 'I think I should go now.'

'No problem,' said Thóra. 'I'll be there. You can rely on me.' She said goodbye and hung up.

She had been pacing up and down the short corridor as she spoke on the phone, without paying much attention to her surroundings. Suddenly she realised that behind most of the doors along the corridor women were busy bringing children into the world. The shouts from Delivery Room C sounded familiar, and she listened, hoping to hear a baby cry. She couldn't make anything out, and anyway it was unlikely that its little lungs would be any match for the noise coming from its mother. Thóra distinguished a sentence between the howls: 'It wasn't meant to hurt this much!' Mentally agreeing with Sigga, Thóra smiled to herself. The baby was clearly about to arrive.

She listened at the door, and after a few more groans and shouts the forlorn crying of a baby was heard. Her eyes filled with tears, and she moved away from the door. She hoped that the fact that she hadn't heard Gylfi's voice didn't mean he'd fainted, but then she heard him say, 'Ugh, take that horrible thing away!'

Thóra was taken aback, but Sigga's mother snapped, 'Don't be silly, boy! She's only showing you the placenta and caul. Some people dry them to make lampshades.' Thóra could only hope that there wouldn't be a nasty surprise among her Christmas presents this year.

The door opened and Gylfi emerged. He hugged his mother, his face glowing. 'It was pretty disgusting, but I'm a dad! It's a boy.'

Thóra kissed him over and over again on both cheeks. 'Oh, Gylfi!' she said between kisses. 'Congratulations, my darling boy. Is he adorable?'

'He's all, like, covered in white stuff,' answered Gylfi with a little shudder. 'And the umbilical cord's a bit . . .' Instead of finishing the sentence, he opened the delivery-room door. 'See for yourself,' he said, going in.

Thóra didn't want to intrude, so contented herself with peeking round the door. She had a vague impression of Sigga's mother and the midwife at the other end of the delivery table, but the baby in the arms of the new mother captured all her attention.

She entered the room in a trance. She was a grandmother. She was surprised to realise that once she had seen her grandson, she longed above all else to hurry back to Matthew.

Saturday, 24 June 2006

Epilogue

It was Thóra's turn. She stepped up to the open grave. 'Ashes to ashes, dust to dust,' she murmured, sprinkling earth over the little coffin. She made the sign of the cross and turned away.

Only a few people had come to the tiny church and silently followed the coffin out into the churchyard, and now they stood in the drizzle. Thóra had taken Lára's hand for the short procession. She felt that the old lady appreciated the gesture, and she didn't let go until Lára walked sadly over to the coffin to pay her last respects to the dead child. Only she and an elderly man among the mourners appeared to be affected by the ceremony. He was a sad sight. It was Magnús Baldvinsson. He had arrived just as the service was beginning, and had quietly taken a seat at the back of the church. In the procession, too, he had stayed a few steps behind the others. His hat was clutched tightly in both hands, and whenever Thóra looked at him his eyes were fixed on the ground. She felt sorry for him. She wondered whether she should go over to him, but decided to stay with Lára. She needed her, but Thóra had no idea how Magnús would react if she approached him.

The pastor closed his eyes and began the prayer, and

Thóra followed suit. She had a feeling that Kristín would have approved of his choice:

> *Now I lay me down to sleep*
> *I pray the Lord my soul to keep,*
> *And if I die before I wake,*
> *I pray the Lord my soul to take.*

The mourners stumbled their way through 'Abide with Me' before leaving, one by one, with the pastor's blessing. Finally only three remained: Lára, Thóra and Magnús. He still stood apart, head bowed.

'Come with me,' said Lára quietly. 'I'll make you some coffee.' She put her arm through Thóra's. 'I want to show you the letter. Are you in a hurry?'

'No,' answered Thóra. They walked out of the churchyard, leaving Magnús Baldvinsson standing alone over the remains of his long-dead daughter.

Thóra smiled to herself as she heard a faint cry from the lava field beyond the churchyard. That damned cat, she thought, but then she remembered that she had spotted the ginger tom when she drove past Tunga on her way to the funeral. He could never have made it all this way in such a short time. The crying grew more piteous and Thóra grasped the old lady's thin, frail arm more firmly. 'Could we walk a little faster?' she asked, shivering. 'This place gives me the creeps.'